Stop at a Winner

a Winner

R. F. DELDERFIELD

SIMON AND SCHUSTER
NEW YORK

Copyright © 1961 by R. F. Delderfield
All rights reserved
including the right of reproduction
in whole or in part in any form
Published by Simon and Schuster
A Division of Gulf & Western Corporation
Simon & Schuster Building
Rockefeller Center
1230 Avenue of the Americas
New York, New York 10020
Designed by Edith Fowler
Manufactured in the United States of America

1   2   3   4   5   6   7   8   9   10

Library of Congress Cataloging in Publication Data

Delderfield, Ronald Frederick, 1912-1972.
   Stop at a winner.

   1. World War, 1939-1945—Fiction.   I. Title.
PZ3.D37618St   1978   [PR6007.E36]   823'.9'12
78-6931

ISBN 0-671-24229-6

Published in Great Britain by Hodder and Stoughton Ltd.

For all the Judies and Erks
who had difficulty in taking the R.A.F. seriously,
and particularly for Anne,
who seemed to find it all so uproariously funny!

R.F.D.

CHAPTER ONE

When Pedlar Pascoe—the youngest, heaviest, and by general reckoning the most stupid of the Pinehollow Pascoes—drifted into Exeter in his mother's 1924 bull-nosed Morris that cheerless January morning in 1941, he had no intention of remaining in the city longer than it would take him to dispose of the car, drink several pints of beer, and make his way back to the Pascoe shanties by the quickest and cheapest means available.

He certainly had no intention at all of enlisting in His Majesty's armed forces, or taking a voluntary part in the war against German Fascism; to understand why he did in fact commit such an outrageous folly, it is necessary to know something of Pedlar's domestic background.

The Pascoes of Pinehollow were not averse to fighting. Over the centuries they had fought lustily among themselves, using boots, bottles, knives and even firearms with a cheerful disregard for the niceties of codes laid down by the Hague Convention and the late Marquess of Queensbury. For a long time now, however, the vagrants had shown a disposition to avoid other people's quarrels as they might shun contact with the bubonic plague. They were ready, if necessary, to fight any number of personal battles and to dispute a variety of issues with members of the Westcountry constabularies, water-bailiffs, landowners, foresters, gamekeepers, and such smallholders who actively resented the levying by Pascoes of poultry, grazing rights, ponies, coils of wire, sawn timber and other necessities, but for hundreds of years now they had manfully resisted the appeals of successive sovereigns to step forward and participate in Continental affrays, or the defense of their homeland.

There had been no Pinehollow Pascoes at Crécy or Agincourt, and none at Trafalgar or Waterloo. When billmen and bowmen of feudal levies had contended within range of their camps during civil affrays they had moved away, returning to their familiar heaths and coppices when the tumult was over and there was discarded ironmongery to be recovered from the ferns and brambles. In a sense they were the vanguard of the pacifist movement in Britain. Neither Caesar, Alfred, Canute, or William the Norman had been able to locate them, and never once, in the violent history of these islands, had the claims of kings, liege lords or pretenders touched their hearts. Their amiable spirits had never once been inflamed by pamphleteers advocating this or that. In their time they had listened with apparent interest to strident appeals for liberty, universal suffrage, freedom of conscience, more popery, less popery, church services in Latin, church services in English, the repeal of ship money, the repeal of corn laws, and dozens of other admirable pleas, but when the drummer beat his tattoo for recruits they faded away and were not to be found. One moment they were there, their big, sunburned faces uplifted to the rostrum, and the next they had shredded away into the forest and no one had witnessed their going.

Now and again they made an eccentric patriotic gesture, as when they lit private beacons as the Armada sailed up the Channel, but it is fair to state that the flames of that particular beacon warmed stray partridges rather than Protestant hearts. Again, in Devon and adjoining counties, they shambled forward with selfless offers to mind the jackets of sweating fencibles who were drilling to resist Napoleon's landings, but when the heat had gone out of the sun, and the tired fencibles looked for their clothing, neither the coats nor the genial rustics who had stood guard over them were to be found. Once more they had drifted into the haze on the rim of the Common.

All in all the Pascoes preferred a civil war to a foreign war. They had good pickings from the Cavaliers and a somewhat more modest one from the Roundheads. There was an unexpected harvest from Monmouth's foray at Sedgemoor, where the Somerset branch of the family lived for almost a year on the proceeds of stray horses.

It was the iniquitous Derby Act of 1916 that put a term to their long spell of neutrality. Some years before the end of the Edwardian epoch they had settled, a whole tribe of them, in Pinehollow on the edge of Exmoor and here, who knows, they might in time have become as prosperous and permanent as their forerunners, the Doones, had not the Asquith Government (until then so benign toward vagrant Englishmen) suddenly turned sour and sent them a sheaf of printed enlistment forms.

Few of the Pascoes could read, so the forms excited little interest in the hollow, but in the wake of the printed forms came uniformed policemen, who carefully explained to the men of the clan that those of them within the required age-group were forthwith expected to exchange corduroys and moleskin leggins for khaki and puttees, and afterwards cross the sea in order to fight the German Emperor.

The Pascoes debated this monstrous decree over their camp fires that same night and unanimously decided that they had no quarrel whatsoever with the German Emperor. For their part he was welcome to come and reside in Buckingham Palace if that was what he wanted, for who were they to thwart ambition, who had always held freedom of movement the first among human liberties?

When the local constable cycled down into Pinehollow after breakfast the next morning there were no male Pascoes within miles, and although the police watched the shanties and caravans until hooters blared news of the Armistice, the male population of Pinehollow was limited, throughout 1916, '17 and '18, to a group of starveling boys and shambling old men.

The missing Pascoes returned in force early the following spring, presumably from the shambles of the Somme and Passchendaele, but it was remarked that their inherited skill in moving unseen at night must have stood them in good stead during spells of trench warfare, for not one had a scar to exhibit to the Board of Pensions.

The clan drifted about a good deal during the twenties and thirties but they always came back to Pinehollow. Sometimes, as busybodies on Councils fussed over Town Planning Acts and Rural Development schemes, there would be a mild, local outcry against them and they would disappear for months on end, but one morning Farmer Stogden, their nearest neighbor, would see blue smoke rising above the trees and would call to his men as they drove the red Devons in for milking:

"Harry! Ned! They bliddy wasters are yer again! Get out the chains 'n' padlocks, will 'ee?"

The long-suffering Stogdens had been intermittent neighbors of the Pascoes for three hundred years. They had learned to live with them.

The night after Hitler invaded Poland and touched off the Second World War was a memorable one for both Farmer Stogden and the Pascoes. The former owned a radio and thus heard all about the blackout regulations. The Pascoes, owning no radio, concluded that something must have gone wrong with the Stogden electricity plant, and descended on the holding in skirmishing order to discover what was afoot. Stogden's pullets were probably the first casualties suffered by the British in the Hitler war. They were dead and plucked hours before Mr. Chamberlain walked into Broadcasting House and urged the nation to oppose bad faith and evil things.

When it became clear that the outrageous demands of the Derby Act were liable to be exceeded in 1939, the Pascoes took countermeasures. All the men of military age drifted away once more and this time there was no need for a family conference round the fire. The Pascoes had inherited the memory of how to defeat authority, whether that authority stemmed from Westminster, the County Council, or the Rural

District Council of the area in which they were living at the time of crisis. Long before the first buff cards began to arrive at the encampment all the young men were gone and only old Fiddler Pascoe, the acknowledged leader of the brood, and his youngest son, Pedlar, remained behind, squiring nearly a score of womenfolk.

Throughout the autumn of 1939 these sturdy breeders of Pascoes did not miss their men as much as they might have done had they been accustomed to leading conventional lives, or had either Old Fiddler or Young Pedlar proved less virile or less accommodating. Men and women of the Pascoe clan had always subscribed to the ethics of frontier communities. To breed was to survive and both sexes bowed to the demands of the situation.

For a year or more all went well. Fiddler Pascoe had been a very irascible old man until the camp was swept clear of young males; with half a dozen wives at his disposal he mellowed and became almost patriarchal, so that the displays of violent temper that had once enlivened the hollow became the prerogative of Gipsy Pascoe, Fiddler's original wife, whose bellow could sometimes be heard as far away as Stogden's yard in the next fold of the moor.

Life was hard on Gipsy that winter, for Fiddler slept most of the day and the leadership of the clan devolved almost exclusively upon her. None of the Pascoes had ever actually worked in the accepted sense of the word, but then, no previous clan leader had ever lived through a period of total war in which rationing was enforced almost at once, and the fences surrounding local livestock and poultry soared with the inflated marketing price of stock. Petrol became very scarce and even firewood was hard to find. The blackout, which had promised so much, yielded little or nothing, blanketing the rural areas so effectively that a nocturnal reconnaissance became a dangerous undertaking.

Apart from this, people's tempers seemed soured and they were disposed to slam doors in the faces of Pascoe womenfolk when they called offering rush mats, osier baskets, and peeps into the somber future. Policemen visited the camp more frequently, and there was even talk of demolishing the shanties to make way for an extension of the local airfield.

Pedlar, as the sole active male about the place, bore the brunt of Ma Pascoe's bad temper. He was a very amiable soul, patient to the point of martyrdom, but as the second Christmas of the war approached his mother's nagging, coming on top of the steady demands of half a dozen younger members of the tribe, began to work upon the leaven of Pedlar's self-pity. He brooded as he drove out on his long, circular, reconnaissance trips and sometimes he almost wept for the timeless splendor of his adolescence, when he had fished, poached, and roamed abroad in the company of his chattering brothers and cousins, when kindly tourists had paid him in silver to extricate them from the tangle of high-banked lanes in the Exmoor Forest, when it had been absurdly simple to corner stray hens and ducks in overgrown streambeds and spinneys, and when an hour or so in the long grass with a snub-nosed cousin, or a complaisant village maid, had been a pleasure instead of a monotonous obligation.

Soon, spells of foraging by day and solacing by night made inroads into Pedlar's vast store of nervous energy, and when Gipsy took it out on him one morning for letting the fire go out he lost his temper for the only time in his life, lifting her up and sitting her in the rainwater tub.

This, in itself, was no mean feat, for Gipsy weighed over fifteen stone, but Pedlar accomplished it with ease. He would have been six feet four inches in his socks had he worn socks inside his size-twelve gumboots, and his forearm was as thick as the shaft of the cart that he balanced on his belly when he was inclined to show off.

The immersion was greeted with shrill delight by the women of the tribe but with shocked disapproval by Pa Pascoe, who emerged from the horse caravan in time to help a sulky Pedlar disengage his mother's vast buttocks from a chevaux-de-frise of shattered barrel staves.

For a week or two after this incident Pedlar was uncommunicative. He performed all his duties about the camp but said little or nothing to anyone. His moon face brightened a little when one of the aircraft from the High Moor field came skimming over the hollow, its wing-tips glinting in the wintry sun, its engine strokes reverberating among the rockstrewn hills of the valley, but he said nothing about the strange effect these engines produced upon him, a sudden quickening of the blood, a spasm of envy for the man who could soar through the clouds high above the bog and heather of the moor, the momentary release they gave him from the drudgery and ennui of a life that had suddenly become hateful in its loneliness and edginess.

It was as though, after almost twenty years of complete freedom from personal responsibility and social obligation, the shackles of civilization had been clamped on Pedlar's thick, hairy wrists, and had been chafing him for weeks leading up to the day that Gipsy abandoned her struggle of trying to get petrol without paying for it, and made up her mind to dispose of the runabout. Pedlar went off gratefully enough, glad of an excuse to spend an hour or so in a city populated by men as well as frustrated womenfolk.

2

Gipsy had told him that he should get about twenty pounds for the car.

She had purchased it for thirty-five pounds some fifteen years ago and reckoned deterioration at twenty shillings per annum. Isolated in Pinehollow, Gipsy had lost touch with the war and Pedlar, who had not been in a city for years, was scarcely more realistic. He asked eighteen pounds and waited for the garage man to open the bargaining. The man looked hard at the Morris, then at Pedlar, then at the Morris again and finally retired, murmuring "Jesus!"

At the next garage the man approached by Pedlar thought the joke good enough to pass on to a boy who was cleaning the windows, but apart from repeating Pedlar's offer in an astonished squeak he made no further comment. A third man was even less helpful. After a swift glance at the car he urged Pedlar, in deplorably coarse terms, to essay an acrobatic impossibility.

Pedlar was not so much dismayed as puzzled. He drank a glass of beer and got into conversation with the owner, an elderly man with the expression of a defeated clown. The man walked slowly round the car, giving it disparaging little kicks and hissing at it through broken front teeth. When he spoke he expressed himself in flat, staccato sentences.

"Get scrap price! Fiver! If you're lucky!" he said, and when Pedlar began to protest he waved his hand in the direction of a downsweep of terraced houses, below the tavern. "Car like this in every one o' them 'ouses!" he added. "Been there since war started! Be there till it finishes! Jacked up, most of 'em! Not gonner be no petrol, see? Pub trade's done too! Not like the last war!"

He gave the rear tire one last kick before directing Pedlar to a scrapyard near the center of the city. The car finally changed owners at four pounds fifteen.

It was not until he had laid out the money on a little table in the window of another tavern that Pedlar began to assess the situation as it had developed. He found it extremely difficult to think of more than one thing at a time and his powers of concentration had been fully engaged with the haggling. Now, as he looked down at four pound notes, a ten-shilling note, and two half-crowns, he was able to picture Gipsy's expression as he handed over the money. Although from her earliest infancy Gipsy Pascoe had led a hand-to-mouth existence that would have driven the average suburban housewife to suicide, her attitude toward money remained conventional inasmuch as she always wanted more and she hated to part with what she had. Pedlar realized that the explosion occasioned by his dismal transaction would rattle the roof of every shanty in the hollow and set dogs barking as far away as Stogden's yard. Without pondering the problem any further he realized that he would never accumulate sufficient courage to return to the hollow and hand over the money.

From this point it was a short step to a determination not

to return to the hollow at all, and the elation that succeeded this decision caused him a certain amount of surprise. He had never known another kind of home and had never made a friend outside his family circle. He had never thought about this before but now that he did it encouraged him to widen his field of contemplation. He asked himself why this should be so, and at once found the answer. The Pascoes, he suddenly realized, were outsiders looking in, without any kind of link binding them to people who lived in towns and villages, or even people on lonely farms, like the Stogdens. They were a community of outcasts, dodging about on the fringe of the real world, and without the slightest hope of edging themselves into its orbit. Pedlar remembered now the bleak looks that had greeted him whenever he knocked on cottage doors, or encountered anyone who wasn't Pascoe born in country lane or on moorland paths. It was always the same look and the memory of it punctured his new confidence. He got up, ordered another pint of beer and three large pasties, and returned to his window seat to pursue this disturbing line of thought.

Suddenly it occurred to him he was terribly lonely, not just temporarily so, but permanently and most desperately lonely. He had always been the butt of the tribe and had never minded the distinction while his brothers and male cousins were around. They had jeered at him, played painful practical jokes on him, made a drudge of him, but they had always accepted him and taken him along. Now, for months on end, he had been utterly alone. The women of the tribe had taken him and used him for an hour or so, but their brief intimacies had struck no roots of comradeship. Sometimes they had addressed remarks to one another while he was in bed with one or other of them, and quite suddenly the memory of this galled him like a thorn, penetrating layers of hide until it touched his heart and made his eyes smart. Suddenly, and without shame, he found himself weeping.

The release of tears acted upon him very strangely. As soon as he realized that he was alone in the bar, and that his face was turned away from the barmaid, he let the tears flow

17

and found that they soothed him like the song of a stream and the warmth of the sun. For a long time he sat quite still, reveling in a sensation of blissful repose, and presently his tongue peeped out and licked the salt from the corner of his wide, slack mouth.

When the flow had ceased Pedlar again addressed himself to the Pedlar of the immediate future. If not to Pinehollow and Gipsy's shrill scoldings, then where? He could get a job, he supposed, driving, or hedging and ditching.

He understood horses and had known men who earned good money looking after them. He was stronger, physically, than any two men he had ever met, and powerful men could earn money in a variety of ways; carrying stone, shifting furniture, building roads. He finished his beer with a triumphant flourish. There were dozens of things he could do, apart from drifting back to the camp and shambling about under the lash of Gipsy's tongue and the casual contempt of Fiddler and the girls.

That was settled then, but where would he live? In lodgings? How much did lodgings cost, and how did one go about getting them? What was the relationship between, say, the wage of a laborer, and the cost of his bed and board? There was so much that he did not know. Perhaps he need not take lodgings, perhaps he could make do with Gipsy's four pounds fifteen (it was already four pounds ten) and sleep out somewhere, in a shed or hayrick.

He thought about this for a long time before deliberately rejecting it.

He was accustomed to living rough but today the prospect did not suit his mood. He wanted to be finished with living rough, as well as with Gipsy's nagging and the girls' contemptuous demands on him. For the time being he wanted to be done with the whole of it, the smoking camp fires, the leaking, tin-roofed shanties, the interminable scrambles through barbed wire and wet hedges to get one's belly filled and, above all, the bleak looks at cottage doors and on humped-backed bridges in the lanes. In exchange he wanted warmth,

18

regular meals, a niche in life and, above all, a small but steady measure of jolly companionship.

Where could he find these things? Already they seemed to him very modest demands, the kind that might be made by any man in possession of his strength and faculties. The effort of sustained thought made him sweat but it was at that moment that Providence, until now as indifferent as everyone else toward Pedlar Pascoe, revealed to him the queue under the poster immediately across the narrow street.

It was a long queue and a big poster. The queue was composed exclusively of young men, and the poster occupied half the side of the drab-looking building outside which the queue had formed. It was a life-sized picture of a well-groomed young man, with finely chiseled features, a well-mannered smile, and a head of sleek, shining hair. In the foreground was a grounded airplane, the type of airplane whose blunt, rounded wings had reminded Pedlar of a buzzard when one exactly like the illustration had skimmed over the hollow. In large white letters, nearly two feet high, were the words *"Fly with the R.A.F."*

Pedlar studied the poster for more than a minute, spelling out the words, and wondering why the young man's hair glowed with such luster. Then he crammed the remains of the last pasty into his mouth, scooped up his money, and left the pub. The middle-aged barmaid looked after him wistfully. It was a long time since she had seen so much masculinity in one piece.

3

Sergeant Rawlins was not enjoying his temporary detachment from the neighboring Operational Training Unit. Someone had rung through from the recruiting post in the city and asked for the loan of a regular airman with some clerical experience, needed as a temporary replacement for the recruiting corporal now on leave. Rawlins had no clerical experience, but there was no orderly room staff available, so they had sent Rawlins as a stopgap. After all, Rawlins had been carefully trained as a fitter, and there were already more than two hundred at the airfield but so far no aircraft for them to fit.

Rawlins did not question the wisdom of this decision. He had served many years in the R.A.F., commencing with boys' service at Halton, and ending with a conversion course in the Isle of Man, and had thus learned enough about R.A.F. procedure to accept with a shrug the employment of a skilled mechanic in a job that almost any untrained recruit could have performed with superior skill.

Down at the fighter stations on the coast they were screaming for fitters but until posting notices arrived, and unemployed personnel had been cleared for laundry, barrack-room damages, overseas inoculations and equipment stores, no tradesman could leave the station to which he should never have been sent in the first place. Before the war Rawlins' professional pride would have resented his selection for the job, but lately the tide of lunatic disorganization had swept away any professional scruples he might have possessed. They said the R.A.F. was expanding. To Rawlins and the other regulars it was disintegrating in the process.

The sergeant collected his small kit and hopped a lorry into the city. Then, for two whole days, he sat at a trestle table behind a mountain of printed forms, telling the men who passed before him in an endless queue that there were no vacancies in the R.A.F., and that they had better try to join the Ordnance Corps, or the Royal Army Service Corps, at depots farther down the street.

When he had explained this to something over six hundred men, one of them, a typically knowing civilian, suggested that it might be an excellent idea if he erased the chalked notice outside the door. The notice read: *"Men Urgently Wanted in All Branches of the R.A.F. Apply Within."*

This gratuitous advice piqued Rawlins. The internal organization of the R.A.F. might be inferior to that of a Girl Guides' Rally on a wet August bank holiday, but it was not for civilians to imply as much when addressing a uniformed N.C.O. of the Junior Service. He sprang to his feet, tore six enlistment forms across the middle, and howled at the civilian like a pain-maddened gorilla. The knowing civilian ran for his life and the queue recoiled into the street, men cannoning into one another like a long row of shunting trucks. Spent eddies of the sergeant's outburst reached all the way down to High Street. It was some time before the queue re-formed and began to flow back into the dimly lit office.

Rawlins sat down again and lit a cigarette, feeling much better for the explosion, and mildly flattered by the sniggers of men now standing just outside the door. He did not realize that the men had forgotten his outburst and were now watching a bold spirit write *"Balls!"* across the chalked notice.

The queue moved forward very slowly. It took a long time to explain to each man individually that the notice outside did not mean what it appeared to mean, and that there were in fact no vacancies at all in any trade in the R.A.F. at that particular moment of history. The men were all from Civvy Street and it appeared that in civilian life a notice like this might well mean exactly what it said. Not one man who took his place in front of the table seemed to understand that the notice had only meant what it said when it was put there, and that was nearly a month ago, and that since then no one employed at the recruiting post had received orders to take it down, or change it in any way. They also failed to appreciate that until such orders were received the notice would stay there, even if every single male between the ages of eighteen and forty-five now living in Great Britain was already enlisted in the Air Force, and camps were as crowded as the Black Hole of Calcutta, with overflows sleeping in tightly packed rows along every flare-path in the country.

Civilians, Rawlins had noticed, were slow to appreciate these things. That was why they made such tiresome, obstinate recruits. They looked for all kinds of odd, romantic things in the Service, things like justice, logic, and a reason for going in a certain direction at an advertised time, and by the shortest available route. It comforted him to reflect that if any of them

21

ever succeeded in fighting their way into the R.A.F. they would have to set about remolding their entire cast of thought.

The light outside was fading when Pedlar shuffled in front of the table and Rawlins opened his mouth to reiterate the rejection speech that he had been reciting like an automaton since he had opened the recruiting office doors at 0800 hours that morning. Then Rawlins took a long, steady look at the volunteer and closed his mouth again. It was not the kind of scrutiny that Pedlar had anticipated. In place of bleakness there was incredulity and awe, and accepting this for a kind of welcome Pedlar grinned, his huge face splitting, his small blue eyes half-closing under brows so big and bushy that they might have passed for tufts of brown Exmoor heather.

"I want to go right off," he said.

The man immediately behind Pedlar blew his nose, cocking a wary eye over his crumpled handkerchief in order to know exactly when to jump and in which direction, but this time the sergeant did not leap from his chair and howl. He merely swallowed twice before asking:

"*Go?* Go *where,* Swede?"

Pedlar was nonplussed for a minute and shook himself like a mastiff.

"To the airport, I reckon," he said at length.

The man behind Pedlar relaxed and his titter was taken up by others nearer the door. The laughter recalled Sergeant Rawlins to his duty. He looked past Pedlar, straight at the man with the handkerchief.

"What's so bloody funny about that?" he bellowed, and before the man could compose his features he was on his feet again. "Clear out! The whole ruddy lot o' you! Clear out, d'you hear me? Sodding lot o' Swedebashers! *Out! Out! Out!*"

Rawlins was very gratified by the speed with which the room emptied. He was accustomed to being obeyed, but instant obedience like this never ceased to give him pleasure. Then he discovered that the office was not quite empty, for Pedlar had not fled with the others but had merely stepped smartly to one side to make room for the sergeant's charge.

22

Rawlins wheeled on him but suddenly checked himself and sat down.

There was something appealing and pathetic about the way this man stood, his huge hands resting on the edge of the table, his vast head slightly tilted. He looked, Rawlins thought, like a St. Bernard dog inviting a snowbound traveler to reach up and uncork his brandy bottle, and for some reason that he could not have explained, Rawlins was touched. His spurt of wrath had spent itself on the queue, leaving him tired and listless, yet vaguely emotional.

"It's no go, mate," he said finally, "we can't take no more! Come back another day and let me close up to get a pint!"

"I can't come back another day, sir," said Pedlar.

"Why not?" said Rawlins, "what's a day?"

"If I showed up wi' four pound ten she'd whale into me with the long-handled pan and I'd never get the chance to come again!"

The sergeant was interested in spite of himself.

"Who's she?" he asked.

"Me old woman—Gipsy!"

"Your wife?"

"No, no! *Gipsy!* Me mother!"

The sergeant rubbed his stubble. While on overseas tours he had done a good deal of boxing as a middleweight, and he was now assessing Pedlar's stripped weight. He put it at round about sixteen stone.

"She'd whale into *you!*" he exclaimed, his eyes traveling up to the summit of Pedlar's six foot four inches and down again. "You kiddin'?"

"Not just me," said Pedlar, reverently. "She'd whale into anyone with that pan. I've seen her knock a copper off a bicycle with it!"

Sergeant Rawlins relaxed. The huge idiot fascinated him, not only on account of his bulk and crass stupidity, but also by his childlike air of resolution. For two whole days Rawlins had been hectored, reasoned with, cajoled, bribed, insulted, plagued and persecuted by smartly dressed and plausible men, men falling over themselves to throw up good, civilian jobs and enlist in the R.A.F., but here was someone who simply stood still and talked about a mother called "Gipsy" who would hit him with a long-handled frying pan if he went home and gave her four pounds ten. Whichever way one looked at it it was interesting.

"Tell me about it!" he said simply, and listened in silence to the story of Pedlar's sale of the bull-nosed Morris. When it was finished he reached over and took one of the foolscap forms, folding it carefully and putting it in his tunic pocket.

"We'll go over and have a pint," he suggested. "She won't lam you any more for four pounds than she would for four ten, will she?"

"No," said Pedlar after a moment's thought, "I don't reckon she would, sir!"

They were soon drinking their way through the second of Gipsy's pound notes.

The bar had half-filled without their noticing as much. A man in a raincoat was sitting at the piano and playing a one-finger version of "There'll Always Be an England." Two other men were playing darts and their score cries rose above the murmur of another pair, discussing the invasion of Albania.

"Double nineteen, one-double-one to finish!" said a dart player.

"Musso's had it," said one of the strategists at the bar, "them mountains take some getting over, mark my words!"

Sergeant Rawlins was not listening to either group. He had even stopped listening to Pedlar. Adrift on a tide of beer, his mind was exploring unfamiliar backwaters. Although by no means a philosophical man he had been oddly stirred by this encounter and the impact of Pedlar's personality was having as much effect upon his mind as was Pedlar's hospitality. He saw the huge, lumbering waif as a kind of haphazard experiment on the part of an apprentice creator. It was as though a young demigod had been watching his master make ordinary men through a celestial century, and had suddenly decided, during his master's lunch break perhaps, to try his hand at something more original. Where the master had used handfuls, the apprentice gathered armfuls of clay, molding thighs twice as thick as everyday thighs, and shaping shoulders more than twice as broad. Then, when he had finished the neck, he had found himself short of material and had gathered up a sparse helping of barrel scrapings for the head, finishing it off with a thatch of old hay and not even bothering to match the two sides, so that his protégé had been launched with a slightly lopsided face and absurdly small eyes for so massive a body. Rawlins' mind was still toying with this strange fancy when something happened to switch it back to a more mundane aspect of the recruit.

The man who had been fingering the piano finished his beer and walked past Rawlins to the exit. The sergeant had slipped down in his chair and the man stumbled over his extended legs. Rawlins, jerked back to reality by a sudden pain in his shin, snarled an oath as the man recovered his balance. The next moment the stranger was flat on his back, hammered to the floor by Pedlar, who had apparently seen in the man's clumsiness a gross affront to his R.A.F. friend.

It all happened so swiftly that no one in the bar noticed the prelude. The barmaid looked over and saw the piano player rising shakily to his knees and Pedlar standing over him, apparently giving him a helping hand.

"Well, I don't know!" she said, giving the dazed man a swift, professional appraisal. "And him so quiet with it!" Then, more shrilly, "Get out of here, you! We don't want no trouble!"

The man rose, swaying, peering doubtfully at Rawlins' feet and then at Pedlar, who was smiling down at him.

He was a large, well-built man, whose hands and tieless collar gave Rawlins the impression that he had, in his time, handled a great deal of coal, but after another glance at Pedlar he stumbled past and into the street.

Pedlar sat down again, hands on knees, and Rawlins' fuddled mind at once wandered off into another backwater. Although a skilled tradesman he never thought of himself as a technician. If he thought of himself at all it was as a soldier, and therefore all un-uniformed men qualified as "a shower." Militarily, he had not advanced with the times. His requirements as a recruiting sergeant were much the same as those of an officer who had recruited for Marlborough or Wellington. To Rawlins a soldier was still a trained hulk, a thing of automatic reflexes, who jumped this way or that at the word of command. When the coalheaver had hurt his shin the sergeant's instinctive impulse had been to jump up and punch him hard on the ear, to hurt him as much or more, and then call it square. But long before he had been ready to do this the big Swedebasher had risen and floored the opposition. Built like an elephant he had moved and struck like a cobra! It was clear that, in addition to enormous strength, he possessed terrifying speed.

Surely, *surely* this was the kind of man the R.A.F. really needed! Surely an electrically charged pile driver like this would be far worthier of the King's shilling than all those know-alls from Civvy Street who had argued with him over the last two days. He felt in his tunic, took out the folded enlistment form, and spread it between them.

"Fill that in, chum!" he said briefly. "And this one's on me!"

When he came back from the bar with two more pints, Pedlar was spelling out the questions. The enormous concentration demanded by the small print was making him pant and sweat. Rawlins looked at him affectionately and took out his fountain pen.

"Most of it's sheer bumff," he said gently. "I'll do it and you can put your moniker at the bottom."

He did not consult Pedlar at all while making out the form, but relied on guesswork and on information passed to him over their earlier pints. He gave Pedlar the profession of lorry driver, his age as twenty-one, and his next of kin as "Mrs. G. Pascoe." He had started to write "Gipsy," but he crossed it through because it looked so silly.

Pedlar was immensely gratified.

"You been real nice to me, sir," he said, beaming.

"You *got* something," said Rawlins, by way of extenuation. "I don't know what it is but you *got* something! Sign here."

Pedlar took up the pen, licked his lips and drew rather than wrote a large, sprawling "P" in the blank space at the foot of the form.

"Was you christened 'Pedlar'?" yawned Rawlins, who suddenly felt very sleepy.

"No," admitted Pedlar, "but no one ever called me by me real name."

"What is it?"

"Abednego!" said Pedlar.

"*What?*"

"Abednego," repeated Pedlar. "Fiddler said we run out o' names time I come. We got 'em from the Bible you see . . . and I was the seventh boy!"

" 'Struth!" said Rawlins, impressed. "What was all the others called?"

"Matt, Mark, Lukey, John, Shad and Shak!"

Rawlins digested this. Then he said slowly:

"Those last two, what kind o' names are they?"

"It's in the Bible," insisted Pedlar, with what seemed to Rawlins unnecessary reverence. "Shadrach, Meshak and Abednego! They got roasted, remember?"

From somewhere far, far away, Sergeant Rawlins, Group I tradesman of the Royal Air Force, heard a lost echo of his Newcastle childhood, an improbable and bloodcurdling story about three men being thrust into a fiery furnace because they refused—he had forgotten why—to react in some way to the blare of sackbut, dulcimer, and timbrel. He had not thought about this for years and years but now he remembered it very clearly. It was part and parcel of this improbable evening and even more improbable recruit.

"Time!" called the barmaid, and they drifted out into the street. Under the sting of the night air Rawlins reeled and fell against Pedlar, who clutched him protectively. That was something else about this enormous Swede, Rawlins reflected, he seemed impervious to alcohol. They had been sitting in that boozer for at least four hours and they must have consumed vast quantities of liquor.

"Are we going to walk home?" asked Pedlar.

"Not if I can help it," muttered the sergeant, struggling manfully to collect himself. "There's a camp bus at ten-thirty, goes from the civvy bus depot. Know where that is?"

"No," said Pedlar, "but we'll find it!"

Rawlins let go then and felt himself half-carried through the swirling darkness of the blackout, supported by what seemed to him to be the lower branch of an oak tree.

He remembered feeling vaguely frightened when crossing a road and later feeling shamed by his pitiful condition. After that there was a chorus of voices singing a familiar ditty beginning:

> *This old coat of mine,*
> *To you it may look fine* . . .

but beyond this he remembered nothing at all until Corporal Thompson was shaking his shoulder and shouting: "Sarge! Sarge! We're posted! W.O. says it's an aircraft carrier but I think it's Tangmere!"

Rawlins sat up, bowing his head under a rain of sledgehammer blows. His mouth was parched as he stumbled about his billet, checking his kit and snarling at people who kept popping their heads in his door and asking silly questions. It was not until the detachment was well on its way to Tangmere that he remembered Pedlar. When he did he sat up with a jerk that made his brains rattle.

"Christ!" he muttered. "I wonder what happened to that flippin' Swedebasher?"

And then, because his head was still splitting, and because he wasn't at all sure where he was going, or if he had packed more than half his kit in the wild scramble to get cleared from the camp, he dismissed Pedlar as part of a nightmarish dream, tangled up with tuft-bearded men in pointed hats, who had tried and tried to thrust him into a bakehouse oven, and had almost succeeded in doing so when he was plucked from their grasp by a beaming giant with a lopsided face and hair like old hay.

CHAPTER TWO

There were certain discrepancies, anomalies and in-formalities in Pedlar's enlistment form but the overworked orderly-room clerks, glumly accustomed to backstroking their way across lagoons of paper, sorted it out somehow and added his name to the muster rolls, embracing him in what they called "the transitory nomenclature." They studiously ignored Pedlar's pathetic requests to be taken to Sergeant Rawlins who knew, it seemed, far more about his qualifications to serve in the R.A.F. than did Pedlar himself.

"Should never have touched down here in the first place," grumbled the L.A.C. at Reception. "Bloody shambles! That's all it is, regular bloody shambles!"

He handed Pedlar various documents and told him that he must report to Uxbridge forthwith, adding that, if he ran into any difficulties en route, he was to present himself to the near-est R.T.O.

Pedlar had been going to tell the clerk that he had never heard of Uxbridge, and would not have recognized an R.T.O. should he chance to find himself in bed with one, but at that moment a fresh draft of flight mechanics and riggers surged into the orderly room and the L.A.C. quickly forgot all about the stray recruit. Pedlar hung about on the fringe of this influx until they all went off to the mess hall, when he followed them and had a hearty meal. After this he wandered around the camp until he was arrested by a truculent military policeman while in the act of inspecting the cockpit of a Lockheed-Hudson on dispersal.

Having scrutinized his papers the military policeman told him he had inadvertently committed the one unforgivable sin in the Air Force, namely that of actually looking at an aircraft. He warned Pedlar that if he persisted in this eccentric behavior he might well find himself behind bars for sabotage. The policeman was so disconcerted by the mildness with which this threat was received that he became almost kind to Pedlar, escorting him to a railway siding where, after some further delays, Pedlar entrained for London. Yet he did not go without a protest, pointing out that he was now a member of the Air Force and should have been dressed as such, like all the other men about the camp, but the S.P. explained that newly joined recruits were fitted out at recruit centers and that this was the purpose for which Pedlar had been issued a railway pass to the depot.

He did not go directly to Uxbridge. In his pocket he still had a pound of Gipsy's money and some loose silver, so he spent a pleasant day wandering around London and staring at the traffic.

His father and his eldest brother had once been to London to see a football match and on returning to the hollow they had made some attempt to describe the city's size and appearance, but until then Pedlar had always assumed that they had been joking or lying. The maze of broad, busy streets terrified him so much that his resolution was wavering a little when another S.P. questioned him, inspected his papers, and escorted him to the Underground station, remaining in attendance until he had found a train for Uxbridge and asked a civilian to see that Pedlar left it when they reached the terminus.

This S.P. was himself newly recruited and was still sufficiently civic-minded to recognize an idiot when he saw one.

At Uxbridge the machine soon took charge of him, edging him into a tide of recruits, rubber-stamping his papers, and now and again giving him things to hold.

It was all very easy for Pedlar. He simply followed the general movement to and from various billets, parade grounds, offices and barracks. He was still without a uniform or equipment, but somebody wrote his number on a small slip of paper and told him to memorize it and answer to it whenever it was shouted aloud.

It intrigued him to have a long number as well as a name, but what impressed him even more was the swearing-in ceremony, administered by a tiny monkey-faced corporal who handed everybody a dog-eared New Testament and ordered them to raise their right hands and promise faithfully and unequivocally to protect "the king and his hairs."

Pedlar was fascinated by the wording of this oath. He wanted very much to ask the corporal why the royal hairs needed selective protection, and why it was deemed unnecessary to swear an oath to protect the other royal features, such as the ears, nose and throat. He was denied the opportunity, however, for the squad to which he was now attached was soon hustled out of the swearing-in building and into another building where they were given aptitude tests.

Pedlar was not required to take one of these tests because Sergeant Rawlins had already placed on record his alleged aptitude for transport driving but he watched the others with a good deal of interest as they set about solving little puzzles, or sat at aged Oliver typewriting machines and typed out a passage from a book on natural history.

The ingenuity of the leading airmen in charge of the squads fascinated Pedlar. They were never at a loss. When a man jammed the machine on the first word, the L.A.C. in charge declared that he would have passed the test anyway and gave him one of the discarded sheets of typing that were lying about on the floor, directing him to take it to the sergeant to establish his efficiency on the machine. If any man had difficulty with the puzzles the L.A.C.s leaned over his shoulder and fitted the pieces into place with demoniac speed. All the initiation ceremonies were conducted in this amiable spirit, the staff's sole concern being to keep the stream moving. Every now and again loudspeakers blared and groups of men told each other that this must mean them and they doubled off somewhere, waving papers and shouting encouragement to one another. Hardly anybody directly addressed Pedlar, but he was very conscious of the general spirit of oneness, of being part of a vast, uncoordinated movement surging toward a vague, unidentified goal.

Every few hours the flow carried him into and out of a large hall that smelled very strongly of cabbage, and once he had been issued with a knife, fork, and spoon, collectively referred to as "irons," he was able to do full justice to the food that shirt-sleeved cooks heaped upon his plate.

At some of the places they visited, men in uniform said something unintelligible to him, but when he did not react they were not displeased with him, for at least three of them at once entertained him by executing an eccentric little dance, like a child anxious but unable to visit a lavatory. In fact, all the uniformed men seemed to Pedlar to be keyed up about something, as though the Germans were just around the corner and at any given moment everyone would be packed into airplanes and rushed off to engage them in hand-to-hand combat.

The speed and confusion of it all seemed to worry some of the other recruits in Pedlar's group. One man, a recruit with reddish hair and an orange-tinted moustache, kept muttering: "Bloody panic! Bloody panic!" as he trotted breathlessly from trestle table to trestle table, each piled high with printed papers, handwritten documents, little green cards, typewriters, glue bottles, mugs of tepid tea, and overflowing ashtrays.

Early on the third day in the new camp, Pedlar and a score of others were rushed out of the gates and crammed into a train, already packed with men carrying attaché cases and brown-paper parcels. Everyone seemed extremely anxious to get them to the station in time but the monkey-faced corporal, the very man who had implored them to protect the king and his hairs, must have been misinformed about the time of departure, for when every carriage was full and it was impossible to move along the corridors, the train waited in the siding for two hours before starting with a jerk that emptied the luggage racks and struck the orange-moustached man on the back of the neck, shooting his false teeth to the compartment floor. He was very displeased about this and after they had found his teeth and rubbed them off he put them back and expressed an earnest hope that Hitler would win. The Nazis, he said, might be rough and ready with subject races but they would never treat an Aryan with such indignity.

The train kept going without a halt until mid-afternoon, and everybody got very hungry and restless. Rations for the day had been issued, but few had sufficient elbow room to unpack and eat them. When the carriage doors were opened, men cascaded out, like peas from a stripped pod, but they were soon rounded up and formed into ranks of three, under the direction of the monkey-faced corporal who, in some mysterious manner, had accompanied them. Ten minutes later the group was behind barbed wire again and was herded into a row of tents pitched under an enormous hangar that someone said had once housed a large airship that ran into a hill somewhere and killed everybody on board.

The recruits slept ten to a tent, each man being allotted a slice of ground with his feet pointing to the pole, so that they should have fitted into their sections very neatly, like well-packaged slices of shortbread in a circular tin. This was so only in theory, however, for in practice there were various snags, chief among them being Pedlar's bulk.

Pedlar was given the slice of tent nearest the flap on the up-slope but his feet projected well into the tip of the triangle allocated the man immediately opposite. This man, a patient ex-shopboy from Barnsley, was obliged to swing himself to the left in order to avoid being pinned down by Pedlar, and because the ground sloped to his right the slices below the shopboy contracted hour by hour, particularly when Pedlar, seeking greater freedom, inched closer to the central pole.

By dawn Pedlar was occupying the outer half of the tent and the other nine were sharing the half that remained.

There was a good deal of nagging complaint and Pedlar was always willing to writhe back into his official space, but the nights proved restless for most of the men and after three days the friendly atmosphere in the tent began to deteriorate. Then the man with the orange-tinted moustache, who was something of a barrack-room lawyer, had an excellent idea. He said that life in the tent was endurable only so long as everybody remained still, but this was not practical because every half-hour or so the monkey-faced corporal, or his relief, who looked like a tired spaniel, appeared in the tent lane and bellowed "On paraaade!" as a prelude to the group's setting off on one of its periodic jaunts to stores, the mess hall, the photographer's, or the intake center.

The man with the moustache argued that ten men would never be missed among such a vast crowd of recruits and advised everyone to lie low when the next summons was proclaimed. They all thought this was a good idea until the men in the other tents returned with ten shillings apiece, having been assembled to draw a temporary issue of pay.

The man with the orange moustache never really recovered from the resultant loss of prestige, and perhaps it was because of this that his extreme rashness in volunteering to serve in the R.A.F. developed into an obsession.

He would lie on his back, his hands clasped behind his head, and mutter to himself, hour after hour, and although Pedlar found his monologue very interesting, the other men began to fear for his sanity.

The monologue took the form of a self-accusation, viz.: "Nobody twisted my arm! Nobody said, 'Time to be off, time to be going!' You did it yourself! You went off on your own bat! You said, 'Take me, I'm yours for the duration, do with me as you will, gentlemen!' So now they're doing it! Boy, are they doing it. And it might not be a short war. Hitler mightn't win soon after all and then where are you? Stuck in a tent and chased from apex to breakfast-time! *And you did it yourself! Nobody twisted your arm!*"

When they could stand it no longer the other eight men held a conference in the latrine and elected two of their number to tell the monkey-faced corporal that there was a man in their tent who kept praying for Hitler to make a successful landing in Sussex. The effect of this tipoff was immediate. A squad of Service Police appeared with revolvers strapped to their belts, and the man with the orange moustache was winkled out of his slice of tent and marched off to the guardroom, there to be worked over by the psychiatrist or charged with the spread of alarm and despondency, Pedlar never discovered which.

The arrest of the pro-Hitler recruit should have given the remaining men more space, but unfortunately his departure coincided with the issue of equipment, and that night the group in the upsloping half of the tent were obliged to share about one-third of the area, for Pedlar's issue alone accounted for another three square yards.

The actual issue of gear was a jolly affair. The men were marched into a large store and formed up three deep facing the broad counter, behind which stood a squad of equipment clerks, straining at the leash.

On the command "Move!" the clerks began to claw items from the racks immediately behind them and hurl these items at the files of recruits on the far side of the counter.

For several minutes the air was thick with webbing, mess tins, caps, boots, underclothing, towels and respirators. The leading men in each file were bowled over like ninepins and some of them, struck in the face by the heavier type of issue, such as mess tins and size ten boots, entered into the spirit of the game and began to throw items back at the clerks, so that the corporal had to intervene and arrest half a dozen for insulting the king's uniform. They were ultimately marched into the C.O. with their hats off but no real punishment was awarded them as one of their number displayed two black eyes as evidence in support of the recruits' side of the story.

When everybody was staggering about under kitbags crammed full of assorted accouterments, the group was chased into the tailor's shed, there to be fitted out with greatcoats, tunics, and trousers.

The tailor's method of measuring the men was simple but effective. He paid no attention to their girth, for he had only three sizes—large, medium, and small. His system was to slam each recruit against a wall, hold him there and bring down a sliding rule on the crown of his head, shouting the man's height in inches to an assistant, who stood close by holding a notebook. Unfortunately the tailor was unable to measure Pedlar because the slide rule went only up to six feet three and a half, and having told the corporal that he had nothing to fit a mastodon, he promised to set two of his trainees to work making a special uniform.

The trainees were called in and began to take measurements but the tailor admonished them for wasting the king's man-hours and told them to size Pedlar with their eyes. The result was that Pedlar was the only man in the group who had a tunic that neither enclosed him like a suit of plate armor nor hung about his shoulders like a tent.

It possessed, however, other and more singular defects, for it had been put together by two men with very individual ideas about the measurements. The right flap of the tunic was thus longer by two inches than the left half, and the brass buttons were spaced accordingly, so that Pedlar's massive chest now had a dragged, lopsided effect that matched his slightly lopsided features. When he approached from the front he gave a curious impression of approaching crabwise, but as he himself was quite unaware of this it did not worry him nearly as much as it worried the monkey-faced corporal, who reported sick with double vision.

When everyone was fully kitted out the flight was sent on by train to a coastal recruit center, where they were required to complete their initial training before being posted to various stations.

Pedlar departed from the tented camp with mixed feelings. In one way he had enjoyed his first week in the Service but in another way he was vaguely disappointed. From a material point of view it was clear that the life had a great deal to recommend it. Seldom had he slept so comfortably and never had he eaten so regularly. On the other hand, his loneliness was unappeased for he had not made a friend. He was still, as it were, on the fringe of the community, with a toe over the line that had so far cut him off from all who were not members of the Pascoe clan. -

He was still with them but not yet of them. The bleak looks of passersby had gone and in their place were expressions of easy tolerance, but this did not satisfy the new Pedlar released by the tears shed in the pub opposite the recruiting depot. He wanted warmth. He wanted to be needed. He wanted, above all, *to serve*. All his life so far he had been serving somebody, his parents, his brothers, his cousins, the bereft women of his tribe, and now he was eager to consolidate his service, to surrender himself utterly in exchange for an occasional smile and a pat on the shoulder. He was masterless and to be masterless was to be insecure, in spite of free clothing, bed and board. Somewhere in this eddying mass of blue serge was a master, an officer perhaps, or a sergeant like Rawlins, or possibly someone to whom this cheerful, bustling life was as strange and inexplicable as it was to himself. He knew that soon he would find this man and with him a sense of purpose. Confidently he heaved his kitbag on to the rack of the crowded compartment and entrained for the coast.

2

Corporal Bird was awaiting his monthly shower.

He was a small, well-knit man, with the narrow face and restless eyes of the Cockney.

The outbreak of war, coming toward the end of his fifth year of service, had been a godsend to him. Promotion in Group V of the R.A.F. had been almost non-existent in peacetime. No mere aircrafthand, lacking a trade, could hope to progress beyond the grade of Leading Aircraftman, and it had taken Bird four and a half years to qualify for his "props," the insignia on his tunic sleeve signifying that he had risen one step above the grade of Aircraftman First Class.

When war broke out in September, 1939, Bird had volunteered for a Physical Training and Drill Course and, having qualified, had put up his corporal's tapes and moved on to Blackrock, the coastal resort where most of the recruits went for their initial training. Since then he had proved a devoted contributor to the war against German Fascism. He had taught thousands of men how to salute pilot officers to the front and flight lieutenants to the flank, how to march up and down piers with arms swinging shoulder-high, and even how to perform movements as intricate as arms-raising-sideways-feet-astride-jumping. He enjoyed his work very much, particularly when he got a promising and cooperative squad. So far he had been extraordinarily lucky. The men who came to him were mostly volunteers, attracted by the fly-with-the-R.A.F. posters and they were impatient to be done with the initial training and move on to the flight training schools and operation units.

The majority of them were well-educated and jocular, accepting his comments on their shortcomings with amiability. A sprinkling, particularly those who had served periods in cadet corps during their schooldays, were already half-trained, and for three months' running now Bird's squad had emerged with credit at the monthly passout in the municipal band enclosure.

If things continued like this, Bird reflected, he would soon get his third stripe and then, if the war lasted (which, please God, it would), his flight sergeant's crown and even—although his imagination boggled at the possibility—his pineapple tins, denoting the rank of warrant officer.

Sometimes, during the routine thirties, he had wondered if he might one day be a corporal but never once, not even when he was in liquor, had he dreamed of becoming a warrant officer, of wearing gabardine and shoes and having men address him as "Sir."

He was a very conscientious drillmaster. To Bird there was poetry in twinkling feet and coordinated movement. His heart rejoiced as he saw a line of rifle barrels swing upward and leftward in the slope, and he sometimes gave a little gasp of ecstasy when he saw a squad about-turn with split-second precision. He loved sizing his squads and seeing a rhythm ripple along a slowly descending line of caps.

He had theories about instructing men and always introduced himself to a new batch with a set speech, calculated to inspire in them pride, confidence, and the competitive spirit.

He began: "I'm Corporal Bird, 'Dickie' to me chums but not to you, not yet, see? Later on maybe, we'll see how we go on!

"My job is to turn you lot into airmen in free weeks! It says a munf on the sillybus but it ain't a munf because there's a week's leckshures, so it's free weeks—twenywun days—and I'll tell yer somefin, I'm gonner do it! I'm gonner do it real good, and you're gonner 'elp me!

"I got ambition, see? I'm gonner be a sergeant and when I'm a sergeant I'm gonner say it was Number Two Squad as did it! Now that's the first thing and here's the second comin' up. I'm the easygoin' sort. I don't pick on no one, see? But I don't let no one 'old me up neither! You're a shower right now but you won't stay a shower, not under me, not fer long, see? You're gonner be good, I c'n see that from here! You're gonner be the best mob I ever 'ad! And when the war's over, and you're all back in Civvy Street, you're gonner shoot a line over havin' bin in the Air Force. You're gonner say 'Looker that poor bleeder over there! 'E was on'y in the Navy or the Army! I was in the Air Force, I was!' And every Judy fer miles around is gonner be nice to you on that account, get me?"

At this stage, when he had the incoming recruits thoroughly hypnotized, he would take a smart turn up and down in front of them, as though pondering his next remarks. They would wait, spellbound, watching his smooth, precise movements as he wheeled and coasted. Then they would stiffen, and the ranks would billow a little as he swung round and faced them again, the easy tolerance gone from his voice and manner and a hard gleam in his eye: "Mindjew, I *might* be wrong! We're all wrong sooner or later! You might *stay* a shower! You might be the worst shower I've ever 'ad! Some of you might even try and take the mickey out o' me! You might get bored marchin' up and down like, and you might go to sleep on the job! I don't think so mindjew, but you *might,* and if you do you're all in fer an 'ell of a time! My time is the time o' the dimmest one 'ere, and if he's too dim I'll have to start chasin' yer, and if it comes ter that I will an' all! I'll chase you straight in the bleedin' drink! I'll chase you till yer boots fall orf!" and finally, as though to establish the legality of this particular threat: "*I can!* It's in King's Regs!"

•

Pedlar's squad assembled in Roehampton Road, a long, featureless row, at right angles to the seafront. Nearer the promenade was Number One Squad, and beyond Pedlar's group Number Three Squad, respectively in charge of Corporals Gidley and Frome. It was not until Corporal Bird began to size the squad that he noticed Pedlar and when he did his heart gave a leap, for Pedlar's size terrified him, violating his passion for uniformity and making the men on each side of him look like pygmies.

"Lumme!" he mumbled, half-aloud, "how the 'ell am I gonner fit him in?"

Instinctively he glanced down the road at Number One Squad, and then up the road at Number Three Squad. What he saw gave him an idea and he issued the command "At ease!" and strolled over to Corporal Gidley.

"I got a bloody giant in my shower," he said. "Have you got a couple to match him?"

Corporal Gidley ran his eye along the front rank until his glance rested on a willowy six-footer with thick-lensed spectacles.

"He sticks out a bit," he said. "Give us a short-arse to replace him!"

After the short man and tall man had changed places Corporal Bird went over to Corporal Frome's Squad, where he was able to exchange a rotund man for a tallish, red-faced recruit, who came level with Pedlar's ear. The three tall men now stood in one file, towering above the next trio by nearly three inches. It was the best he could do in the circumstances, but the incident depressed him. He spent half an hour sizing the squad, but no matter what he did the tall file spoiled the even sweep of the caps.

There was a ragged, hopeless look about the three ranks and after endless shufflings and sortings the corporal's exasperation began to spread to the squad. Not one of them Bird told himself, seemed to know left from right, or forward from backward. They just milled around, like a herd of cows sandwiched between two oncoming lines of traffic. The huge man, whom it had been necessary to match by borrowing from the other squads, seemed to march sideways, and the man with thick-lensed glasses appeared to be as good as blind, for he kept reaching out with his hands and reassuring himself by touching a neighbor's tunic.

There was trouble of a different kind at the other end of the squad. The squat, beetle-browed man, whose name on the nominal role was down as "Pope H.," would not stop talking, no matter how often Bird roared at him. He did not seem to be addressing anyone in particular but nevertheless maintained a continual rumble of comment upon the squad's evolutions.

Bird strained his ears to catch the drift of the comments so that he might have something to go upon, hoping then that he could terrify the recruit before he gained confidence in his defiance, but not one mutinous word did he hear and was therefore obliged to ignore the conversation. He did, however, mark down the man for future investigation, nicking a little tick against his name and penciling the letter "B" beside his last three numbers. The "B" stood for "Barbary"—i.e., "deliberately uncooperative"—and the note indicated that here was a man who might give trouble later on. Against the last three numbers of Pedlar Pascoe the corporal wrote "C" for "Clod," and against the name of the tall man with thick-lensed spectacles he wrote "B.B.B.," standing for "Bloody Well Blind."

For the first time in months Bird felt anxious about the intake. Until then he had never really believed the gloomier half of his introductory speech, in the possibility of having to chase men until their boots parted company with their feet, but perhaps, at long last, his luck was running out and he was about to be landed with a bum squad.

All in all it was not a promising beginning and on the way back to the billet Corporal Bird felt more depressed than he remembered feeling for years.

Just how inept the squad was likely to prove he was not yet prepared to say, but the mere presence of a trio like Pascoe, Pope, and a blind man could, as he knew better than anyone else in Blackrock, make nonsense of the carefully timed training schedule.

"Not a bad bunch, mine!" crowed Corporal Gidley, munching away at his brisket of beef when Bird joined him for high tea at the billet. "How did your lot look, Dickie?"

Bird shook his head. "I dunno!" he said, cautiously, "I got me doubts! I got 'em right here!" and he tapped the taut muscles of his stomach.

"Well, I'm right glad you lifted that sightless so-and-so off me!" declared Gidley, with maddening cheerfulness. "Grade Two Vision he was, and oughter be in St. Dunstan's! I bin real lucky this time. I got three real gents, public school and O.T.C. wallahs, what-what? They ought to make things easy for me and I dare say they'll be good fer a quid apiece on passout day, eh?"

Bird looked hard at Gidley and suddenly decided that he had always hated the man.

"I got a Barbary!" he said slowly. "I got a real bloody Barbary! Well . . ." he reached out for the sauce and splashed it savagely on his brisket . . . "we'll see who comes out on top, 'im or me! I'll chase him, I'll chase 'im till 'is boots fall off! I can! It's in King's Regs!"

Corporal Bird's professional eye had not deceived him. In Horace Pope and Pedlar Pascoe he was faced with a drillmaster's nightmare.

There were always methods of dealing with stupid recruits. If they couldn't be bullied or coaxed while out on parade they could always be given the benefit of concentrated private instruction and then so placed in the squad that their errors were limited in scope. An odd man who couldn't learn to drill could always be sandwiched between two competent recruits, but what were you to do with a prize clod who towered inches over everybody else and automatically riveted the eye of any flight sergeant or pilot officer who happened to be looking on? What, for that matter, could you do with a man like Pope, who worked with one eye cocked on the instructor and was obviously a shrewd, semi-professional evader, a man who not only did not care about the Service but deliberately hung on to his individuality, resisting all attempts to be merged into the squad?

In his own, far-off square-bashing days Bird had occasionally encountered such a man and had been shocked by his obstinacy and sheer bloody-mindedness. This kind of joker was civilian through and through, and Bird was well aware that whenever a man like Pope found himself in a uniform he took refuge behind a network of defensive obstruction that was, in the end, absolutely impenetrable. A man like this never did anything really wrong. He was never openly defiant or insolent. He carried out his orders to the letter but in a manner that left no doubt at all in the mind of his instructor that he regarded his N.C.O. as an oafish halfwit, too dull and brutish to earn threepence an hour in civilian life. There was something else, too. Faced with a type like Pope even the keenest drillmasters began to lose confidence and find themselves doubting their own ascendancy over untrained men. A "Barbary" made nonsense of the syllabus and left professional pride in tatters.

The corporal's estimate of Horace Pope was a very accurate one. A market huckster by trade, Pope's appearance in uniform was due to over-confidence on his part, for as soon as war broke out and conscription became a certainty, he farmed out his stall and went to work for a brother-in-law who was operating a small machine-tool firm in Hoxton.

Unfortunately the brother-in-law was arrested for the theft of a quantity of lead piping in November, 1939, and his premises were closed down, whereupon Horace sold his stall and signed on with a contractor engaged in building army camps. He had no luck, however, for the following week the contractor was run over in the blackout. His contract lapsed and his employees were dismissed.

With call-up due at any moment, Horace had rushed to the Labour Exchange, but by this time Hitler had launched his attack on the Lowlands and thousands of patriots in Horace's age group were alive to the need for a duration job in industry.

When his call-up papers finally arrived Horace canvassed his system for chronic disabilities. The canvass was so disappointing that he decided he would have to invent one and on the day of his medical examination he swallowed a vial of bluish medicine, sold to him by a market colleague, along with a guarantee that it would make his heart beat faster than the wings of a trapped insect.

The mixture might well have had this effect but it also made him violently sick. He thus missed his place in the morning queue, coming up for his examination a moment before the lunch break, when all the doctors were irritable and impatient to be gone. Not one of them did more than glance at him and he was passed fit for active service.

He went home almost in tears but Horace's father, a veteran market vendor, showed no sympathy.

"They got you?" he exclaimed, when Horace told him the news over supper. "They actually got you? Just like that? Well, serve yer right! They 'ad me fer six weeks in nineteen-sixteen, but they jumped that one on us. Not so much as a word about conscription in the papers there wasn't, but you fellers have had months and months to look out for yourself, and you still let 'em get you! Sloppy it is! Gives me the fair sick it do!"

And Pope Senior sucked up his jellied eels with the air of a man whose son had disgraced him. Toward the end of the meal, however, when the bowl of eels was scraped clean, he ventured a final comment. "They wouldn't get me," he said heavily, "not if they was fighting in my backyard!"

In a dumb, resentful daze Horace drifted through his first week at the Reception Center, and his experiences there, herded from shed to shed, pushed into endless queues and badgered by the harassed regulars in authority over him, convinced him that escape by some means or other was an absolute priority. After some thought he cultivated the friendship of a gloomy L.A.C., whom he met in the canteen and at once recognized as penniless by the length of time he was taking to drink one glass of beer.

The one preparation Horace had made for life in the Service was to provide himself with loose cash and in Horace's world everything was for sale, even a legal passage back to the world where more money was waiting to be made.

"Can't you buy yourself out?" he asked the L.A.C., after their third pint of a brew that Horace would have liked to have diluted with slops and flung in the brewer's face.

"Not now you can't," said the L.A.C., "there's a war on! Used to be able to, knew chaps who did it, but not now, nobody can, not even group captains and air commodores!"

"Then what about working the old ticket?" pursued Horace.

"Ah," said the L.A.C., "now you're talking! Several ways o' doing *that*, providing you know how. What about another?"

Horace lubricated the L.A.C.'s memory with another and then another, as the man delved into his past, searching out instances of men who had worked their tickets in the piping days of peace.

There was the bed-wetter, he said, who was always granted a discharge in the end but the route was milestoned with misery. It seemed that habitual bed-wetters were watched over by the guard, awakened every hour of the night, and escorted to the latrine by men with fixed bayonets.

"It depends who gets too tired first," said the L.A.C. "The bloke I knew collapsed with exhaustion after a month of it, so it got him out all right but not in a way he planned. Nervous wreck he was and never able to hold himself in fer more than sixty minutes by the clock ever after! No, I wouldn't try bed-wetting, there's a lot easier ways than that!"

"Such as?" prompted Horace.

"Headaches!" said the L.A.C., "headaches that don't answer to nothing! You get sick with a headache, see? They give you a chit, medicine and duty, but you show up next day and it's still there, and the day after, and the day after that, and so on! You have to act up a bit o' course, like you had a permanent hangover that was driving you nuts. I knew one bloke who got out that way but he was never much good after either. He'd talked about his perishing headaches for so long, see, that he'd talked himself into having one like a sledgehammer! No, skip headaches! Let's have another, shall we?"

Under a steady flow of execrable N.A.A.F.I. beer the L.A.C. explored other escape routes. He spoke of sliding kneecaps, of wandering pains in the loins, and of a man who had obtained his discharge by cultivating a distressing twitch, commencing with the face muscles and working its way down to the toes. In all he supplied Horace with eleven pintsworth of information on the subject but apart from the bed-wetting method none of it impressed Horace very much. Whatever established exit route he chose, it seemed, required considerable acting skill and infinite patience, neither of which Horace possessed. The only story that remained in his memory was that concerning a man whose conduct had veered between exemplary behavior and wildly improbable eccentricities, such as waving in trains at Waterloo Station, or appearing on parade in long woolen pants and an officer's cap.

In the end he decided to play a waiting game and work out his own salvation, forming, however, a fixed resolution to study the weak spots in the system, like a determined convict dumped in a newly built jail. He was still in this mood when he came to Blackrock and was drafted to Corporal Bird's squad.

Horace took an instant dislike to Bird. The corporal's initial address, classified by Horace as yards of flannel larded with empty threats, outraged his professional respect for good sales patter. He liked his Blackrock landlady even less, finding himself sharing a tall apartment house with eleven other men and a sprinkling of seaside visitors.

The visitors occupied all the best rooms and drifted about the place licking ice-creams and flirting with girls in pretty clothes. The mere presence of these carefree civilians maddened Horace, and when he discovered that the recruits were expected to clean the landlady's windows, make all the beds, and carry the visitors' dirty dishes down two flights of stairs to the basement to be washed and dried, his resolution to play it safe was subjected to an intolerable strain.

"Lumme, it's ruddy slavery!" he exclaimed to Pedlar, who happened to be the other duty-airman that day. "She can't do this, employ airmen as unpaid skivvies and I'll show her she can't, you wait, cock!"

Horace was unaware that Pedlar's heart had warmed toward him the moment he found himself sharing the same billet. Pedlar, a shambling, awkward creature, had always admired neat, active little men, who made rapid decisions and seemed impossibly sure of themselves.

"I'll do it all," said Pedlar, beaming down at his partner, "leave it all to me, and go out on the pier. This ain't nothing, a few pots to clear up!"

Horace was touched and looked up at the broad, beaming face with mild gratitude.

"You mean that, Pedlar? You'll do it all on your lonesome? Don't you want to go nowhere, after all that frigging about on the prom?"

"No," said Pedlar resignedly, "I got nowhere to go. You go and I'll do it! I'll make a good job of it! Honest!"

He did, too, scouring each dish with loving care and stacking the plates, cups and saucers in neat piles on the long draining board. Mrs. Haggart, the landlady, was agreeably surprised when she popped into the basement an hour or so later.

"Well," she said, grudgingly, "it's the first time it's been done properly! I was about ready to complain to your C.O., all the scamping and dodging that's gone on the last day or two! All right, you can go now!"

"Thanks," said Pedlar mildly, and drifted off, but the incident had a sequel for Mrs. Haggart, recognizing a willing slave when she saw one, canceled the rota system and detailed Pedlar for washing-up duty every day, so that he soon found himself doing most of the housework in addition to an eight-hour stint on the promenade.

"Here, we can't have this!" said Horace, as soon as he heard of the landlady's victimization. "Keep your eye open for me when you come down that dark corner top of the basement stairs. I don't want to break your neck, but I'll soon fix it so as she don't ask you no more, Pedlar!"

Pedlar understood no word of this warning, so that when he descended the basement stairs carrying a heavily loaded supper tray that evening, he did not notice the carpet sweeper that

Horace had placed on the second step and thus fell headlong to the bottom of the flight, smashing every piece of crockery he was carrying.

He rose shaken but unhurt and listened, with interest, to the subsequent screaming match between Mrs. Haggart and Horace, the one bewailing the loss of several poundsworth of china, the other explaining indignantly that all the men had had their inoculations that day, and that Pedlar was therefore quite unfit to carry a loaded tray down two flights of stairs.

Slowly it began to seep into Pedlar's brain that this squat, noisy little man had appointed himself his protector and chum and the knowledge filled him with bliss for here, surely, was the end of his quest, the friend and confidant he sought. It took several days for this conviction to root itself, but when it did the flowering was so sweet that Pedlar wanted to cry again and was even more silent than usual as he shambled along with his rifle at an untidy slope, his enormous boots raising dust on the promenade and drill-field.

From then on he became an even worse recruit, for he did not listen to anything Corporal Bird shouted, reserving all his attention for Horace, who was placed at the other end of the rear rank.

This made things very difficult for Bird. Whenever he gave the command "right wheel" Pedlar trailed off to the left, where he had a less impeded view of Horace. The half-blind recruit, who was immediately behind Pedlar, usually followed his lead, so that every now and again the whole squad would shred away, its members proceeding a few uncertain steps before stopping and looking to the N.C.O. to regroup them and start them off again. Bird did not know what to make of it at all. He had never had a squad that kept breaking up before his eyes and having no knowledge of Pedlar's doglike devotion to Horace he could not begin to understand the cause of the trouble.

By the end of the first fortnight's training Bird was so hoarse that he could hardly make himself heard and was obliged to supplement his commands with wild and piteous signs, like those of a man stuck on the tracks of a train crossing trying to ward off an oncoming express. Sometimes he became physically entangled in the disintegrating squad and was shouldered this way and that, whispering and pleading as he gesticulated, spun and tottered. Other times his men would get mixed up with the following squad, and lose themselves in the eddies, so that the entire parade looked like the rout of a beaten army.

At bayonet practice the following week Bird was pushed a step nearer the cliff-edge.

He had been explaining how to use the bayonet on suspended dummies, hung in a row on an elongated gallows on the far side of the drill-field. Normally Bird enjoyed bayonet practice, for the average recruit put his heart into mad, screaming rushes across the field, the sharp, stabbing lunges at the dummy, the return "present" and the smart trot back to the ranks, but with this bunch something went wrong almost at once.

Pope, the Barbary recruit, lunged his bayonet into the dummy with such violence that its boss became wedged in the heavy folds of sacking. His sullen attempts to extricate it only succeeded in entangling the rifle's fore-sight guard in the tough material, but before Bird could double across and free the weapon Pedlar anticipated him. Gently coaxing Pope's fingers from the butt, he tore rifle and bayonet from the dummy, snapping off the fore sight and bringing the entire frame to the ground. A recruit who did not move out of the way with sufficient speed had his collarbone broken, and both the rifle and frame were damaged beyond repair.

Flight Sergeant Fisher, who happened to be watching the demonstration, at once absolved the recruits, but booked their instructor for slack supervision. Bird retired, gibbering threats and hinting that somebody would be calling for him in a plain van before this particular squad was detailed for passout.

Had he known it, the plain van was not far away and made its appearance at the rifle range the very next day.

The recruits were issued with live ammunition for six shots

at twenty-five yards, and endless precautions were taken to ensure that they pointed their rifles in the right direction and did not fire until given the word of command.

Bird was also careful to detail the man with the thick-lensed spectacles as an ammunition guard, so that he would not be required to fire. While he was doing this Pedlar took his place beside the recumbent Horace and was sighting his own weapon when he heard Pope complain that his rifle bolt was jammed. By this time Pope had accustomed himself to consulting Pedlar on any problem that promised to require the use of brute strength and Pedlar was always happy to oblige. He took Pope's rifle and rolled over on his back in order to get a better purchase on the stiff bolt. In so doing he neglected to make allowance for his movement in so confined a space and rolled on the recruit on his immediate left, just as this man was in the act of squeezing a trigger.

The startled marksman, almost suffocated under Pedlar's weight, let out a wild squawk and automatically elevated his barrel as he writhed and moaned in efforts to free himself. His gun went off twice and one of the bullets cleared the top of the earth ramp by several yards, winging its way across the fields and drilling the bicycle lamp of a warrant officer, nearly a mile away.

The warrant officer, who had been in the act of mounting his machine, was very surprised indeed. He dismounted and stared at the neat hole in his lamp for more than a moment. Then, leaping on his machine, he pedaled away to Station Headquarters, where an enquiry was soon opened under a new file, marked "*Rifle Range Conduct: Reckless Firing by Trainees.*"

Inquiries of this sort usually took years to get under way, but this one was an exception because the guilty party revealed his identity a few seconds after the historic shot was fired. As soon as the men on the firing range had sorted themselves out, and somebody had relieved them of their weapons and emptied their magazines, the taut thread that had been holding Corporal Bird's nervous system together snapped and he began to exclaim and leap about, like a dervish spotted with boiling oil.

At first the recruits thought this was just a routine exhibition of a corporal's displeasure and as such a mere Blackrock side-show, but it soon became very obvious that something had unhinged Bird because he suddenly stopped dancing and began to tear off his tunic and jump on it.

When all the recruits gathered round, anxious not to miss a moment of this unexpected break in the tedium of the schedule, the corporal stopped prancing, sat down, buried his face in his hands and began to whimper like a thwarted child.

Somebody fetched the flight sergeant and after a brief consultation they led Bird away, still whimpering and accusing the men of conspiring one with another to drive him raving mad. They never saw him again, but it was rumored that a day or so later he was declared unfit to give evidence at the formal enquiry at which the warrant officer's lamp was marked "Exhibit A." Perhaps he was only transferred, or perhaps the story that he later bit a medical officer in the calf and was discharged with a hundred percent disability pension was true. In any case his squad was broken up before its members had been transferred out and all belonging to it who were not earmarked for aircrew went into the Non-Effective Pool, located at the other end of the seafront.

Pedlar and Horace were numbered among these strays and quickly became absorbed in the vast group of men whose training had been interrupted by sickness, or some other contingency, and were still awaiting disposal in the Palmfrond Hotel. From the very outset they found the Pool a congenial place to be and soon settled down to its odd but unexacting routine.

"Lumme, it's the best thing that could have happened to us!" said Horace, when their immediate future was made known to them and they were directed to the Palmfrond. "From now on leave everything to me. I've heard all about this flippin' Pool o' theirs and it's a real cinch, Pedlar! If we play our cards right we'll be here for the dooration!"

They were an incongruous pair as they trudged along the promenade, Pedlar carrying both kitbags, Pope supplementing his optimistic comments with expansive gestures, a habit that he had acquired while tending his stall in the Caledonian Market.

Pedlar topped Pope by at least fourteen inches and although Pope was sturdy and well-knit he looked like a starveling alongside his huge, lumbering friend. Pedlar's strawlike hair, shorn to a stubble under the Air Force barber's clippers, stuck out at a variety of angles from beneath the sweatband of his lightly perched glengarry, but Pope had paid the barber an extra half-crown for a civilian haircut, and his black widow's peak, gleaming with Vaseline, curved down to meet his arched, Mephistophelian brows, emphasizing the neat, dapper appearance created by his well-fitting uniform (the result of a substantial tip in the tailor's shop) and his twinkling officer's shoes, authorized by a forged chit describing a mythical bunion, now under treatment.

During their first weeks in the Pool Horace's character underwent a marked but subtle change. He stopped struggling and even began to glimpse possibilities in the Air Force, prospects which his burning resentment at being in uniform had so far prevented him from seeing at all. He became thoughtful and far more affable, obliging toward superiors and tolerant with equals and even civilians. These changes followed a period of Yogi-like meditation on his present situation and his future. He made up his mind to swim with the tide, but with one important proviso—to keep a sharp lookout for flotsam and jetsam.

CHAPTER THREE

Non-Effective Pool was the responsibility of Flight Sergeant Huxtable, a former P.T. instructor who had been taken off the square following a spell in hospital with chest trouble.

Huxtable, now in his early forties, had hopes that his chest complaint would earn him a medical discharge, with a fifty percent disability pension, but so far his ticket had not materialized. He was still under treatment at the Medical Center and was employed, meantime, in keeping track of Blackrock waifs and strays at the Palmfrond Hotel.

In the early days of the war the job had been a sinecure and he had judged himself very lucky to get it. In those days there were only about a hundred recruits awaiting individual postings and he had been able to keep a close check on them when making out his daily strength returns and afterwards spend the remainder of the day in his office, sound asleep in a wicker armchair taken from the hotel sun lounge.

Huxtable, a regular, had two spells of overseas service behind him and his sojourn in Singapore had enriched him with the come-day-go-day philosophy of the East. Every now and again one encounters a man whose character and outlook has been changed by a single incident or a pious phrase. The Earl of Shaftesbury was such a one, pledging himself to succor the lowly, and examples are numerous of impressionable people whose lives have been altered by a single sermon. Huxtable's outlook had been revolutionized by the mildly reproachful reply of a Malay dock laborer, whom he had once found asleep under a tree when the coolie should have been unloading R.A.F. equipment. In response to Huxtable's shrill scoldings the coolie had said: "Job last lot longer than me, white boss!" Huxtable had gone away tremendously impressed by this simple statement of fact and had subsequently applied it to every task he undertook. It made him a very difficult man to drive.

When the Blackrock Training Depot was in the process of being established, and the Non-Effective Pool was little more than a figure of speech, Huxtable had been able to sleep, on the average, about six hours a day. Having dealt with the parade and sent in his daily strength returns, the flight sergeant had retired to a chair and detailed a runner to awaken him for tea break at 1030 hours and 1500 hours. The runner employed had been over-zealous and having checked the time by the hotel clock he jogged his master at 1028 and 1458 hours precisely. Huxtable taught him how to conserve energy by sitting beside him while he slept, and occasionally raising his master's tunic sleeve to watch the minute hand of the flight sergeant's wristwatch, then performing his duty as the hand reached the exact hour.

As the size of the establishment increased, however, the post of N.C.O. i/c N.E. Pool ceased to be a sinecure. Each intake of recruits left behind it a residue of about a dozen men for whom no immediate postings were available. Soon the hotel was like a beehive exclusively populated by drones. Airmen swarmed everywhere. Fat, thin, tall and short airmen. Sick, hale and crippled airmen. Airmen with widowed mothers in charge of understaffed businesses; airmen whose homes had been devastated by bombs; airmen whose wives were expecting twins, and even airmen who had been coal miners and were now homesick for the pits.

All these men had two things in common. To each of them the imperative need in life was to convince Flight Sergeant Huxtable that they had no business to be hanging around doing nothing, and that since there was nothing to do they should be despatched on indefinite leave. If this was not possible then they should be left strictly alone and suffered to serve out their period of exile as best they could, without any undue interference from the Air Force.

Theoretically the Pool was supposed to provide bodies for every chore in the depot. Men from the Pool were required to act as runners, blackout erectors, window cleaners, draft conductors, prisoners' escorts, and perform every other duty that did not appear in the recruits' training syllabus. A stream of orders had, in fact, issued from S.H.Q. to this effect and since there were now nearly two thousand men in the Pool Flight Sergeant Huxtable should not have faced a manpower problem. The fact that he could never assemble enough bodies to fill S.H.Q.'s demands was perhaps the most curious feature of the Pool.

The men were paraded at 0800 hours each morning, assembling in a block of streets immediately behind the hotel. It should have been a simple matter for an old hand like Huxtable to count them and despatch them on the various duties listed for him by units stationed in other parts of the town. He had worked out a foolproof scheme along these lines several months ago but somehow it soon went awry, and now, when he appeared on parade, he behaved rather like a grizzled sheep dog ordered to coax two thousand reluctant sheep into widely scattered pens. Every morning the flock melted away before his eyes. One moment it was ranged before him, twenty hundred strong, and meekly awaiting his dispositions, and the next the streets were empty of all but Blackrock housewives with shopping bags and shrill-voiced children playing hopscotch on the pavements.

This mass vanishing trick was a kind of daily miracle and Huxtable could never really believe that it had indeed taken place. He always returned to the hotel rubbing his eyes and scratching his gray head before beginning the second part of his duties, a daily sorting out of the men anxious to leave Blackrock on one pretext or another.

This was a reverse situation to the one in the open. Instead of melting away the number of men facing him multiplied hour by hour, the tally of supplicants increasing until all the approaches to his office on the first floor were jammed with men, all fighting their way toward the orderly-room table and each trying to attract his attention by waving a letter or a pass, which they seemed to think entitled them to prolonged absences and free railway tickets.

Thus, the scene in front of his trestle table at ten o'clock every morning was like a run on a failing bank. Men kicked and punched one another to get closer to him and the bare boards of the hotel room shook and trembled under their shifting weight. Stray tags of their piteous appeals reached Huxtable from time to time, heartbreaking pleas like "mother all alone!" ". . . wife having her first!" ". . . the old Dad bombed out!" and even ". . . bailiffs in the house!" He had ceased to bring his mind to bear on individual problems, or to make any attempt at all to separate the genuine cases from the spurious. Sometimes he opted for the most colorful yarn-spinner, such as the man who told him that the train engineer who lived next door had taken to sleeping with the applicant's wife but did so only on nights when he was not required to drive an express to Edinburgh. In the spirit of a judge asked to award a prize to the teller of the tallest tale Huxtable awarded this man a fortnight's leave and told him to wire for an extension if his stay at home ran contrary to the timetable of the L.M.S.

Sometimes Huxtable simplified matters by dealing only with the men nearest him, sending them off pell-mell, in half-dozens and dozens. He had no real help, for although he constantly detailed any number of clerks and runners to assist him and to answer the telephone, his staff were just as elusive as the men on the parade grounds and were never with him long enough for him to memorize their numbers or faces.

He had tried writing the names of his temporary clerks and telephonists on slips of paper, so that he could build up a scratch staff and grapple with the muddle, but the slips of paper disappeared from his desk as soon as he had written them and in the midst of the uproar around him he was often obliged to answer the telephone himself and to promise S.H.Q.

that ten men would soon be on their way to unload coal lorries, or fold up ten thousand gas masks in Main Stores. The men never arrived, of course, because everyone in the Pool soon realized that he was nameless, numberless, and therefore un-identifiable. They just said "Yes, Chiefie! Certainly, Chiefie!" and at once disappeared, perhaps for days.

All day long the cafés, cinemas, and amusement parlors were full of Pool men who should have been distributing rations to isolated units, or conveying urgent, secret messages, like the edict forbidding the smoking of pipes in the street, to the widely separated hotels that housed the various squadrons.

It did not take Horace Pope more than a few minutes to size up the situation after he and Pedlar had reported to the Palm-frond the morning after the dissolution of their squad. They were more than an hour fighting their way up the stairs, sur-rounded on all sides by men waving chits and screaming out intimate details of complicated domestic problems. Horace had never read the works of Thomas de Quincy or Edgar Allan Poe, but it struck him that the dreams drug addicts dreamed under the influence of powerful stimulants must ap-proximate the scene on the landings of the Palmfrond Hotel. One had only to change the blue-clad men into maddened imps and malevolent gnomes, or put oneself in the place of the trembling Flight Sergeant Huxtable, in order to understand what a junkie experiences in the throes of a delirium.

"Lumme!" he said to Pedlar, who was slowly cleaving a path toward the flight sergeant by leaning his weight on the packed ranks of the men between them and the table, "I never seen such a shambles! It's like a ruddy Cup Final!"

He turned to the man whose body was pinioning his left arm.

"Does this go on all the time, mate?" he demanded. "And if so, what the 'ell is it in aid of?"

The man twisted his head. "You just reporting, chum?"

Horace admitted that this was so and that they had just been posted to the Pool for temporary duty.

The man chuckled: "Duty?" he said. "You don't do no duty here!" As he said this he lifted his right knee, butting the man in front of him in order to gain sufficient ground to half-face Horace. "This is the Miker's Paradise! All you do is to think up a dodge to get home. Wife trouble, house bombed, shop unattended, anything! Then you smack in a '295,' providing you can get near enough. Once your pass is okayed you hang around until you can take it to S.H.Q. and down there, where things is a bit organized, you slip one o' the clerks a packet o' fags to get it signed by an officer—any officer'll do, there's a shower of 'em down there! Chiefie over there gets through about fifty passes a morning!"

"Don't he ever turn none down?" asked Horace, who was now deeply interested.

"Not him," said the man, giving the airman in front a sharp jab in the buttocks, "he went barmy months ago! If you can get to him he just listens and then signs! Mind them banisters, they give way yesterday!"

They heaved forward clear of the stairs, but Horace kept a tight hold on his informant's tunic and the conversation was resumed in an angle of the landing.

"Suppose you don't put in for a pass? What sort o' jobs do they dish out?" he demanded.

"Jobs!" said the man, shrinking a little, as though Horace had said something disgusting, "you don't want to hang around looking for work, do you? They have a parade every morning, but that don't help 'em much. You give a wrong name and number to the L.A.C. who comes round and then take off down one o' the back alleys! You don't show up here at all unless you want a pass. They can't keep track of you, there's too many of us, and more coming all the time. Blimey, I hope they never get tabs on me, I could do with a year or so o' this! Why, if I was you, just reporting . . ."

But Horace was unable to profit by any further advice the man might have given him, for a renewed heave by the men at the top of the stairs spewed the vanguard into the flight sergeant's office, the press of applicants crashing into the trestle table and scattering papers in all directions.

The lurch had carried Horace to the feet of the flight sergeant, who had been overthrown behind his table and now rose up roaring with rage and shouting that the room was to be cleared.

"I'll take you!" he shouted, grabbing Horace, "and if you others don't clear out I'll close the office for the day! All of you, you listen to me—clear out right away, and gimme a break or I'll slap the lot of you on a charge and close the office for a week!"

The threat of being placed on a charge carried very little weight with anyone within hearing but the prospect of the office being closed, even for a day, sobered the most clamorous. The men shuffled into line and some of them helped Pedlar and Pope to set up the tables and gather up the scattered papers. One of the papers retrieved by Horace was a black-edged letter and Horace read it through, discovering that it concerned an airman called Jacqmar, Number 1050666, who had, according to the writer, died of pneumonia while on leave. The letter had been forwarded from S.H.Q., and was marked *Action, N.E. Pool.*

Horace took it over to a string of typewritten names pasted on the wall behind the flight sergeant's chair and having found "Jacqmar" among the "Js" he obliterated the name under heavy pencil-strokes. "Now, Chiefie, where were we?" he demanded, returning to the table.

The clamor began again but this time Horace spun round and faced the crowd.

"Shut up and keep in line!" he shouted. "How can the Chiefie cope with anything if you don't take your turn? Pedlar! Throw that bunch out, and tell the others they'll only be let in one at a time!"

He turned back to the astonished flight sergeant. "Now you sit down and take it easy, Chiefie, while me and my mate get some organization into this shower! It's N.A.A.F.I. time too, ain't it? Where do you get tea? You could do with a mug, couldn't you, Chiefie?"

It took a great deal to surprise Flight Sergeant Huxtable but Horace's action, in taking it upon himself to erase Jacqmar's name from the list and the bland assurance with which the erasure was carried out, had astonished him so much that he now sat mute and staring. The recruit's sense of purpose and assurance hypnotized the N.C.O. Wordlessly, he reached out and took from him the black-edged letter, skimming its contents and then looking over his shoulder at the crossed-out name on the sheet of "Js."

"You a pal o' this Jacqmar?" he said at last.

"No," said Horace cheerfully, "I never heard of him before, but it's plain enough he's snuffed it, so I struck him off! After all, that's one less to deal with, ain't it, Chiefie?"

The flight sergeant hummed a bar or two of "Shenandoah." Unlike most men he did not hum to express good spirits but to suppress inward agitation. Slowly he became aware of renewed clamor, of the press edging toward his table again, of men closing in on him, waving pieces of paper and making impossible demands upon his concentration. Then as though in a dream, he saw the swart, thickset recruit approach a huge, formless-looking airman, who had been standing listlessly near the door. The smaller man addressed the big one in an offhand manner, as though making a casual remark on the weather or time of day.

"Chuck 'em all out, Pedlar!" he said, and the larger man shook himself like a vast mastiff and straightway went into action, spreading apelike arms and engulfing whole groups of supplicants in the first grab.

For a few minutes the room was a flurry of limbs and then the door was slammed, the gorilla was leaning against it, and the thickset airman was addressing the N.C.O. i/c N.E. Pool.

"Trespassing on yer good nature they are, Chiefie," he was saying, "but don't you worry, me an' Pedlar'll fix all that, you just leave it to us! I been a sort o' clerk, see, and I'll stand by to give you a hand, and ole Pedlar here is the best chucker-outer I know. He never really hurts anyone, gentle as a baby reely, on'y he sort of intimidates 'em and nobody stops to argue with 'im, see? He's bloody dim o' course but you can't have it all ways, can you?"

Flight Sergeant Huxtable at last found his voice.

"What are you after? What do you want?" he said thickly.

"Well," said Horace, "you might say I got a kind o' proposition, Chiefie. It come to me all of a sudden when that mob was pushing and shoving round your table. Me and Pedlar—he's my friend over there—are attached to this here Pool and we could help to get things organized, couldn't we? Tea, for instance! As I was saying it's about N.A.A.F.I. time, isn't it?"

Without waiting for an answer he picked up the empty mug at the flight sergeant's elbow and crossed to the door. Pedlar stood aside, grinning as Horace opened it.

"First bloke back with that filled gets his pass signed!" he said, tossing the mug into the crowd.

He came back, shut the door, and Pedlar resumed his place against it.

"That's bloody marvelous!" muttered Huxtable, half to himself, "absolutely bloody marvelous! Why didn't I ever think of that dodge?"

"Because you got too much to cope with, Chiefie!" said Horace, solicitously. "Now, if you could give me the gen., just the outline o' course . . ." and he pulled up a chair beside Huxtable and began delving among the mass of papers on the table.

2

Flight Sergeant Huxtable did not abdicate his position as N.C.O. i/c N.E. Pool without certain misgivings. The surface of his brain accepted these men, much as a shipwrecked sailor clinging to a spar might allow himself to be lifted into a canoe manned by two painted savages. For all that the flight sergeant remained slightly uneasy and when he asked himself why he could only conclude that his uneasiness stemmed from the vaguely sinister relationship of the two volunteers.

There was something very chilling about the way the big man looked to the other for orders, and the ponderous efficiency with which those orders, whatever they were, were carried out. It was like a Frankenstein monster come to life and perhaps Huxtable's disquiet went a little deeper, perhaps its true origin lay in a suspicion that there were no limits to the power the smaller man exercised over the other. If Pope told Pascoe to get the men in line then he went out and got them in line, herding them together with outspread palms and about an acre of chest, but having watched this performance once or twice Huxtable decided that, had Pope said "Cut all their throats and bury what's left in the parking lot!" the gypsy would have gone about the business with the same casual efficiency and made a clean job of it by garrotting Huxtable himself.

In less reflective moments Huxtable told himself that he was a fool to quarrel with his astonishing luck, for from the moment that these two recruits had inherited his problems life in the Pool had undergone a number of rewarding changes. There was no more pushing and clamoring on the stairs or in the orderly room. Now the men filed in to see him one at a time and there was ample leisure to study their claims and reject the more frivolous. The telephone was answered promptly and Huxtable's papers were always in order. An accurate nominal roll was made out and, after a week or so, fresh alphabetical lists appeared on the walls. Men actually detailed for S.H.Q. chores were tracked down and checked upon as never before, not even in the earliest days of the Pool and as time went on order emerged from the chaos of the morning parades. Pope gathered about him a swarm of minions, who, in return for minor privileges, effectively sealed off the back alleys in the roads behind the hotel, turning back fugitives who were seeking escape to the cafés and cinemas.

Soon Huxtable began to catch up on his sleep, particularly after Pope had found him an adjoining office where he was seldom disturbed. The tea mug arrived sharp on time and with it a couple of biscuits, for which Huxtable was never asked to pay. All the stress ebbed from the flight sergeant's life and yet he remained uneasy, looking over his shoulder for the storm that long years of regular service told him must inevitably succeed a period of calm. Once he had come to accept the curious relationship of Pope and Pedlar Pascoe, a new and unworthy suspicion germinated. He asked himself over and over again why a mere national service man like Pope should go to such extraordinary lengths to smooth the path of a senior N.C.O., a man who was not even related to him, whom he had never so much as seen until the day the pair had reported to the Palmfrond Hotel. What was the angle and where was the payoff? In nearly twenty years of R.A.F. life at home and abroad Huxtable had never once encountered an airman prepared to perform a service without recompense in pay, privilege or kind.

What exactly did Pope and Pascoe gain by sacrificing the freedom of life in the Pool for hard graft in the orderly room?

He found the answer to this interesting query a day or so before his ticket came through and although, by then, he was too late to profit by it it gave him something to think about during his discharge leave. His reflections on the subject were bitter, for his gratuity seemed to him absurdly inadequate in the new world of rapidly rising prices and he wished, with all his heart, that he had met Pope and Pascoe years before. Together, using Pope's astuteness, Pascoe's brawn, and his own position as an N.C.O., they might have made a very good thing indeed out of the Air Force. In the meantime his heart bled for the staff he handed over to his official successor, a Puritan flight sergeant called Hixon.

Hixon, a civilian until September, 1939, had risen meteorically in the Service and would doubtless go much further before the war finished. He was not, however, the kind of N.C.O. to countenance a fiddle, even though Pope's fiddle was, as far as Huxtable's wide experience carried him, as safe and as lucrative as any devised in the history of the Junior Service.

The first glimmerings of the scheme had occurred to Horace when he was gathering up the scattered papers from the orderly room floor.

One of the documents that came into his hand was a posting notice for a man called McTarvish, and Horace noticed (he could not have said why) that this Scotsman had been posted to R.A.F. Station Dyce, near Aberdeen. The juxtaposition of the words "McTarvish" and "Aberdeen" gave him an interesting idea. All the recruits that Horace had encountered during his training period had been interested in the possibility of being posted near home. Some, he now recalled, had even tried to ensure as much by bribing, or attempting to bribe, squad N.C.O.s and S.H.Q. clerks.

Here was one, it appeared, who had been lucky. He might not reside near Aberdeen but at least he was in Scotland, and it at once occurred to Horace that advance information of this trivial fact might be the means of turning an honest penny.

That same day he sought out McTarvish, locating him through the billet book that he found in the flight sergeant's drawer. He went straight to the point, asking the Scotsman how much it would be worth to secure a posting to Dyce.

After some keen bargaining the price of the posting was fixed at a pound. Pope kept the posting note in his pocket for two days and then called on McTarvish again, informing him that, after a great deal of trouble on the part of the flight sergeant, the Dyce posting had been arranged.

McTarvish was far too canny to pay out until he had official confirmation of the news but when the crumpled posting note was presented, and he was told to get himself cleared and call in for his railway ticket, he paid up gladly enough. His clean pound note represented the first dividends of a new company that, had it been officially registered, might have read "Selective Postings Unlimited" on the stationery.

Horace told Pedlar little or nothing of the scheme and Pedlar made no attempt to investigate his partner's reasons for keeping them in the first-floor office of the Palmfrond. He was ecstatically happy to serve and to act as Horace's strong arm and hatchet man. His duties were not arduous. He was a kind of runner-cum-commissionaire, his time being divided between controlling the crowd at the hotel, and seeking out airmen who were prepared to pay cash for a local posting. Every day, immediately after parade, he went out into the highways and byways of Blackrock to locate recruits whose names had been written out for him on a slip of paper. With the impersonal patience of a debt collector or a probationer detective, he ran down the men whose names appeared on the list, afterwards shepherding both willing and unwilling up the stairs to Horace's trestle table. He then shut the door and leaned against it, sometimes listening in an uncomprehending way to the conversation between his friend and the visitor, but more often indulging in a pleasant daydream in which he rescued Pope from a murder party of fanatical stormtroopers.

Greedier men would have abused Horace's key position. Avarice or vanity would have got the better of their judgment and they would have established contact with potential fiddlers at the source of postings, arranging for Cornish airmen to go to St. Eval, and Kentish airmen to find snug billets at Biggin Hill, but Pope was not an amateur. He came from a long line of fiddlers. In his veins ran the blood of Cockneys who had coaxed sovereigns from generations of merchant adventurers, silver shillings from Thames watermen evading George III's imposts on tea during the Napoleonic blockade, and tribute from fugitive Jacobites and zealous, priest-hunting sheriff's officers. His was a commercial not a blackmailing tradition. He gave value for money and he backed only certainties. Thus, he preferred not to meddle with the dispensations of Providence as represented by the Postings Section of R.A.F. Records, Ruislip.

Every posting list that came into the Palmfrond contained the names of approximately a hundred airmen. Among this hundred was an average of about seven posting airmen of the Pool to stations near their homes. It was necessary, of course, to know where these men lived but their Service documents were available and Horace soon built up a system of green cards containing all the information he needed. The accelerated postings of impatient, would-be aircrew trainees was a lucrative sideline but no more. If a recruit was falling over himself to be shot from a rear-gunner's turret, or scattered piecemeal over Germany, then Horace made a note of his name, held back the posting until the man had been located and priced and then turned full pressure on S.H.Q. orderly room. One of the most rewarding aspects of his self-appointed task was the simple gratitude of these eccentric heroes, some of whom shook him warmly by the hand and thanked him over and over again for speeding up their posting by phone calls or tersely worded notes beginning "please expedite!"

When posting notes did not arrive at the Palmfrond and transfers were tiresomely delayed he helped the strays to enliven the monotony of the café and cinema life by the distribution of half-crown weekend passes. He also sold a good line in medical immunity chits that placed Pool men outside the demands of S.H.Q. upon their time and labor.

It was pleasant on the first floor of the Palmfrond through the long, summer days. He had inherited the flight sergeant's wicker armchair and had procured for Huxtable a fire watcher's bed and mattress. There was a mug of tea and biscuits at 1030 hours and 1500 hours. All day long he interviewed happy, trusting men, ushered in, one at a time, by dear old Pedlar, who never seemed to want to sit down but remained bolt upright, barring the door more effectively than any lock, bar or harem eunuch.

In the evenings, when the office was closed, they went to the cinema, bypassing the long queue and going straight into the best seats, for Horace had formed friendships with the attendants at all three motion-picture houses. After the show they usually drifted along to a fish and chip bar, where Horace always ordered the best hake. Later still they stopped by The Sceptre or The Balaclava on the way back to their billet and enjoyed a meditative pint, perhaps two.

Pedlar noticed that the chip vendors and barmaids were always jocular and amiable with his friend but this did not surprise him. Horace Pope was obviously a very great man and it seemed only natural to Pedlar that everybody should go out of their way to smooth his path and make life more comfortable for him. Pedlar himself had no other aim in life. If anything he was happier and more settled in the Pool than was Horace.

CHAPTER FOUR

Flight Sergeant Huxtable discovered the postings racket a few days before he reported to the Medical Board for his final discharge. It was then too late either to censure or participate.

His discovery of the thriving concern came about by pure chance. A Welsh recruit, named Thomas, had paid over a pound in acknowledgment of a posting to R.A.F. Station St. Athan, but there were many Thomases in the R.A.F., and Records must have confused him with somebody else, for they canceled his posting after he had departed from Blackrock and signaled Pool to the effect that, for "St. Athan," they should now read "Benbecula," an island off the west coast of Scotland.

Thomas, recalled on the day of his homecoming to Wales, considered himself diddled and said as much the moment he arrived back at Blackrock. It would have been a simple matter for Records to repost him direct from St. Athan to Benbecula but R.A.F. Records did not operate in this way. The theme song of its clerks was a parody of the familiar hymn commencing "God moves in a mysterious way his wonders to perform," and, as Horace had noted, Records had been performing a striking variety of wonders among the Pool personnel. Nine flight mechanics, posted to Dover Castle in error, and desperately needed on a satellite station only four miles away, were re-routed there via Marston Moor in Yorkshire; an Irish defaulter, apprehended in Belfast, and wanted for questioning in the Isle of Man, was sent via Blackrock to Dungeness, and thence to King's Lynn, before turning up at his original station to face a charge of desertion and go, under escort, to a detention barracks in Somerset. Even here his odyssey did not end. The prison authorities refused to admit him because he was short of a buttonstick, and he was returned to his unit via a depot in the Grampians.

Vagaries of this sort were familiar to all who had anything to do with the administration of the Royal Air Force but they did not interest Thomas, who, failing a speedy return to Wales, demanded that his pound note be returned and that he be given a railway and steamer voucher to Benbecula. Having secured the latter but derived no satisfaction from Horace regarding a refund, he made a blackhearted appeal to the flight sergeant and the bare bones of "Postings Unlimited" were exposed to view.

Huxtable was somewhat relieved to discover that Horace had not, after all, reorganized his office out of the goodness of his heart. Huxtable admired enterprise and having looked into the scheme, and commended Horace's initiative and restraint, he said nothing about it to his successor, Sergeant Hixon, beyond advising him to retain the services of the recruits, Pope and Pascoe, whom he described as "keen types who knew their way around." He then departed, having outraged Hixon's neat, clerkly mind by waving a hand toward the files, wire baskets, spiked chits, and mutilated nominal rolls that littered the room, and remarking: "That's all the bumff! Better leave it to that shyster Pope to clear up!"

For a week or so after taking over the job of N.C.O. i/c N.E. Pool, Hixon had no choice but to follow Huxtable's advice. Several times he tried to get his papers in order, to docket the posting notices and make himself familiar with the constantly changing nominal rolls, but each time he needed Horace's help this recruit seemed to be frantically busy on work of national importance and Hixon, who admired zeal, thought it would be a great pity to clutter up the mind of such a conscientious man.

Horace, for his part, was growing impatient with the new sergeant, for whereas Flight Sergeant Huxtable had left all the paper work to him, this new man kept hovering over him like a worried bank examiner, fussing about official procedure, and asking all manner of tomfool questions concerning the whereabouts of honest airmen, often men who had already paid a fee to be screened from the work of cleaning windows and listing laundry.

Hixon also developed the distressing habit of sitting on posting notes when they arrived, thus making it difficult for Horace to extract the names of those who might be willing to pay for the privilege of going to places to which they were going in any case.

By the end of the first fortnight Horace had conceived a great dislike for Sergeant Hixon and his eager, bespectacled, gently perspiring face. He confided to Pedlar that he would have to square him but before he could decide how to take Hixon into his confidence, and simplify the operation of "Postings Unlimited" at the price, perhaps, of half its turnover, sergeant and underling came into collision over the matter of the mayor of Bruton Spa's file. Abruptly the problem was solved for Horace.

The mayor of Bruton Spa was a protégé of an elderly group captain at S.H.Q. and strenuous, semiofficial efforts were being made on the part of the Spa's corporation to locate, and at once extricate from the R.A.F., a former employee called Oliver Shapley-Stewart.

For many years prior to the outbreak of war Shapley-Stewart had been sitting pretty as supervisor of the Spa Pump Room, a post secured for him by the mayor himself shortly after Shapley-Stewart had pledged himself to marry the mayor's oldest and least comely daughter, Heather.

Shapley-Stewart had, in fact, been one of Horace's first clients, having presented himself for a private interview the moment news reached him along the grapevine that his father-in-law had converted his post at the Pump Room into a reserved occupation and was now hoping to return Oliver to wife and Pump Room.

These efforts, backed by the local M.P., took preference over the routine bleats of other stranded citizens and had already been invested with the distinctive honor of a green confidential file marked *"Case of A.C. Shapley-Stewart, O. Provisional Discharge to Industry."* Horace had seen some correspondence on the matter at S.H.Q. and scenting a modest profit had contacted the ex-Pump Room manager, hoping to cheer him up and get a down payment on the promise of speed. Pedlar located Shapley-Stewart in one of the billets and at once escorted him to Horace's office. On the way Pedlar warned the potential customer that influences were at work to return him to civilian life.

"God help me!" moaned the mayor's son-in-law, wringing his hands.

Horace saw standing before him a plump, earnest little man, dwarfed by his huge jailer. Pedlar invariably took up his position immediately behind Horace's clients, almost as though he anticipated that one of them might make a dash for freedom if the opportunity presented itself.

"Well, mate," said Horace genially, "I got real good news for you! The missis and your pa-in-law are pulling strings to get you out! Takes time, o' course. Bags o' paperwork in a job like this, but it might be done, pervided it ain't blocked this end! Now what say you an' me come to a friendly little arrangement and help everybody get their skates on, eh?"

It was the routine approach, friendly but clinically direct and having delivered himself Horace leaned back in his chair to give his prospect time to weigh the situation.

He was very shocked by Shapley-Stewart's reaction. Instead of looking pleased and excited, the news appeared to unnerve him to the point of hysteria. He gave a long gasp of dismay, his pursey little mouth twitched, and in his prominent blue eyes Horace thought he saw a gleam of desperation.

"What's up, mate?" he asked, as Shapley-Stewart looked fearfully over his shoulder. Mistaking this movement for unwillingness to cooperate Pedlar gave him a friendly little shove in the back. There was nothing aggressive about it, it was just a reminder that Pedlar was still on duty.

"Hold up, Pedlar," said Horace quickly, "something's a bit offbeat here!" Then, addressing himself to Shapley-Stewart, who was now licking his lips and fidgeting with his tunic sleeve, he said: "Cops looking for you, chum?"

"No," said Shapley-Stewart, nervously, "no, no! Certainly not! But I'm not going back there! I'm not, d'you understand? Nothing'll make me, not now it won't! Not now that I've found Emma!"

On the word "Emma" his voice rose to a squeak and Horace at once understood, or thought he understood.

"'Ullo, 'ullo! Bit o' skirt, eh? Who's Emma, chum? Tell uncle! Uncle's here to help!"

"Emma's not 'a skirt' as you put it," said Shapley-Stewart, with dignity, "not in the general way, that is! She's—she's my landlady!"

"Your *landlady*? Well, for crying out loud! 'Ear that, Pedlar? Emma's 'is landlady!" Then, turning back to Shapley-Stewart: "Landlady's daughter you mean?"

"No," said Shapley-Stewart, "just my landlady, like I say!"

Horace tapped his teeth with a pencil, his brain assessing the new situation and estimating its potentialities. Instances of men eager to remain in the Service were not unknown to him but Shapley-Stewart obviously did not belong in this limited category. He did not look like a young man itching to get at the enemy but much more like a defaulting clerk, with the proceeds of forged checks in his haversack.

"Tell me about it, chum," he suggested, "and maybe we can organize something at this end!"

Shapley-Stewart did not need much prompting. After a glance or two at Pedlar, and a nod of assurance from Horace, he poured out his tale. It not only presented lucrative possibilities; it touched Horace's sentimental heart.

In the years leading up to the outbreak of war, it seemed, Shapley-Stewart had been a two-pound-ten-a-week service engineer, in the employ of Bruton Spa Corporation Pump Room and Roman Baths. Here, in the course of his duties, he had made the acquaintance of Heather Potbury, eldest of a long string of unmarried daughters of Alderman Potbury, Bruton Spa's most prosperous citizen, and next in line for mayor. Shapley-Stewart, apart from his aristocratic-sounding name, had nothing very much to offer a mayor as a prospective son-in-law, but the promise of a dowry, plus rapid professional advancement, had so far failed to tempt any eligible bachelor on the corporation payroll, each having been sounded by the solicitous alderman.

Daughter Heather, steamed up by the unexpected marriage of her youngest sister, was raging for a man, any man, and after some hesitancy Oliver succumbed to civic pressure on the part of Papa and near rape on the part of his daughter, who herded Shapley-Stewart to the altar on her thirty-seventh birthday.

Thus, without quite understanding how or why, Oliver Shapley-Stewart found himself Director of the Pump Room and husband to Heather. Heather was spare, sallow and demanding, and Heather's papa was a pompous tyrant. Even so, most men in Oliver's situation would have settled down and made the best of it and Oliver tried. He tried very hard. He was a mild, unambitious little chap and the demands of his dual role prostrated him. Mayor Gorton was determined to make Bruton Spa the most talked-of spa in the country. His daughter was equally determined to make up for lost time. By the end of the year Oliver was a shambling, hesitant wreck, harassed by Pump Room responsibilities by day and exhausted by the performance of marital obligations by night. One might almost have said of him that here was a volunteer expected to man the pumps on a twenty-four-hour shift. Only Hitler's invasion of Poland, and the Bruton Spa recruiting campaign that followed it, saved Shapley-Stewart from drowning his worries in the Roman Bath when the last visitor had been shown round and the maintenance staff had locked up for the night.

He found some kind of relief, even during his training period, for all his decisions were made by others and he could at least enjoy eight hours' unbroken rest each night. Soon he began to put on weight and look about him once again.

Freed from the insufferable weight of corporation responsibilities he soon lost his harassed look and became pensive and relaxed.

He wrote home now and again, maintaining the pose of a hero who had willingly abandoned ease, affluence and comfort for the sterile hurly-burly of Service. Then, after a spell of flu that kept him from being transferred, he drifted into the Pool and from thence into the soothing embrace of Emma Rawlinson, proprietress of the Shangri-La on Ruskin Road.

Emma, a placid widow of forty, made a great pet of Oliver from the day he volunteered to fix a window frame for her. He was a handy little man, fond of carpentry and amateur plumbing, and pathetically grateful, it seemed, for a little mothering. Other airmen came and went but Shapley-Stewart, drifting about in the central eddies of the Non-Effective Pool, stayed on, doing little repair jobs about the house, unstopping drains, laying stair-carpeting and interpreting the war news to the gentle Emma, as they sat in her warm, bright kitchen when all her other servicemen had gobbled their brisket and chutney and were racketing around the town.

After a month or so Emma gave Oliver a room of his own and one night, when she heard him coughing badly, she went to him with cough syrup and sundry other home comforts. Shapley-Stewart found her ministrations very soothing. It was like dismounting from a show jumper and climbing into the saddle of an elderly, retired mare who never lengthened her stride beyond the hand gallop. Pedlar listened to this story with deep and sympathetic interest. Here was something he could understand, the deep, unspoken yearning of a man for placidity, security and warm companionship, such as he himself had discovered in his association with Pope.

Horace listened too. Only one factor nagged him and he tackled it at once.

"How're you for quid?" he demanded, sternly suppressing his characteristic sympathy for all hunted men.

Shapley-Stewart's expression brightened. "Oh, I'm quite okay," he said, "I get my pay made up by the corporation!"

"Well," said Horace, slowly, "I dare say it c'n be fixed. They can't do nothing in this outfit without papers you see and all your papers are right here!"

He tapped the green confidential file marked *"Case of A.C. Shapley-Stewart: Discharge to Industry."* "Now you go back to your Emma, son, and lie low, and if any S.P. stops you you're hanging around awaiting a medical, pending your ticket. Here's a chit to back it up, it says you're excused from parades and on detached duty. How about a quid down and another every payday, so long as you're here?"

Shapley-Stewart, now almost giggling with relief, cheerfully paid over two pounds and put the chit away in his paybook.

"Something'll have to happen to this flippin' file," said Horace, by way of an epilogue to the interview, "but you leave that to me, chum, I'll cope with it!"

He coped with it before Shapley-Stewart was out of the hotel. Resisting a temptation to burn the file he buried it under a stack of nine thousand official pay envelopes in the orderly room stationery cupboard.

"That ought to keep Emma 'appy for a year or more," he told Pedlar. "We don't use more than half a dozen o' them envelopes in a week!" and having thus disposed of Shapley-Stewart's immediate worries Horace turned to the routine business of postings.

It was Sergeant Hixon who, all unknowingly, reminded him that the ex–Pump Room supervisor's second installment was almost due by bursting into the main office one morning and demanding the Shapley-Stewart file, lent to the Pool by S.H.Q. more than a fortnight ago.

"Went back," said Horace, briefly. "Sent it over with a whole lot o' stuff, a day or so after it come here!"

"It couldn't have gone back, S.H.Q. are screaming for it!" said the sergeant, conscious of the contraction of stomach muscles that is peculiar to clerks all over the world whenever a file has been mislaid. "They say it's still here and they want it badly! The mayor of Bruton Spa is coming here on a personal visit, something to do with the discharge to industry of one of his staff who is supposed to be with us!"

"Is that so?" said Horace, with a show of mild interest. "Well, they'll have to get busy, won't they? We got a signature in our runner's book to show they had that file back on, let me see, the twenty-first of the month!"

"Give me the book," demanded Sergeant Hixon, greatly relieved. "Yes! You're quite right, Pope! Here it is, 'SHQ-stroke-P—one—stroke—2109—stroke—DIS—IND!' No mistake about that! By George, I'll take this up with them at once!"

"You do that, Sarge," said Horace, and whistled for Pedlar in order to despatch him at once to Shapley-Stewart's billet with a warning regarding the mayor's visit. This was obligatory. Pope always believed in giving value for money, providing such required no additional outlay of capital.

The sergeant descended on him again an hour or so later. There had been acrimonious exchanges over the phone, S.H.Q. insisting that the green file was still at the Pool headquarters, Hixon stating flatly that it had been returned. He wanted the runner's book to establish his claim that it had, in fact, been signed for.

"What do you make of that signature?" he asked Horace, pointing to the penciled scrawl at the foot of the column.

"Ah, you'd need one o' them Old Bailey 'andwriting experts to cotton on to that," said Horace, sighing. "Might be anything, mightn't it, Sarge?"

The sergeant went away, returning in about half an hour. A thin film of perspiration showed on his pimply forehead. "This is very serious," he said. "No one over there will admit to that signature!"

"No? Then where does that leave us?" queried Horace innocently.

Sergeant Hixon did not make the customary reply to this query. He was a strict Methodist and not given to using that kind of expression. His grimace, however, implied that he might have used it had his upbringing been less rigorous.

The hunt for the confidential file on Shapley-Stewart lasted, on and off, for nearly a week. To Horace, sitting on the outer edge of the volcano, it was as though somebody had reported the presence of an unexploded landmine in the hotel.

He sat with his back to the stationery cupboard, watching a group of nearly a score of pressed men play hunt-the-slipper all over the hotel. A similar operation, the searchers informed him, was going on down at S.H.Q., where all routine work had ceased and everyone, from the group captain downwards, had been enlisted to locate the file containing the papers needed for the mayor of Bruton Spa and his missing son-in-law.

In due course the mayor himself arrived, bowler-hatted and very anxious to please. During the journey to Blackrock he had been feeling vaguely apologetic for intruding his own trivial affairs upon a Service conducting the war with such gusto, but as he sat in the visitors' room adjoining the S.H.Q. orderly room, and watched the search being conducted, his embarrassment grew and grew. He did not know what they were seeking. He did not even know that they were looking for any specific thing, but as he sat there his admiration for the R.A.F. soared point by point, giving him a warm, interior glow born of the certainty of speedy victory over the Hun and the Eyetie. For how, he reasoned, could soulless Fascists compete with the breathless efficiency, the incredible dash and élan, of the men performing before his eyes? As the minutes passed he began to feel more and more of a nuisance to these fanatical airmen. He was accustomed to watching others work. He sometimes took a stroll along Hadrian Street and watched his corporation employees at their daily toil, men who plodded to and fro carrying lengths of sawn timber and bags of tools, who knocked off for tea every now and again, who sucked contemplative, cherrywood pipes as they fiddled halfheartedly with concrete mixers and manhole covers. There were obviously no pipes and tea breaks for the R.A.F. Everybody here worked literally on the double, rushing upstairs and downstairs, bawling directions at one another, cannoning into one another at the entrances of rooms and grabbing the receivers of insistent telephones. Spellbound, he watched officers and N.C.O.s chivvying the slower men, giving them little prods and frank words of encouragement; "Try the Runners'

Room, clod!" "Turn out the adjutant's safe, you great oaf!" and once the thrilling order: "Check the Secret Files, but lock yourself in while you're doing it!"

Motorcyclists, booted and helmeted, roared in and out of the hotel forecourt. Breathless corporals sped past him, hammering on the door of the harassed young officer who had welcomed him and had promised so courteously to attend to his little matter the moment they came up for air, didn't you know?

They never did, at all events not while he was there. Frenzied activity was fraying everybody's temper and the mayor began to wish that they all would ease up a little, light cigarettes, and sip the cooling tea rushed in by menials from the Y.M.C.A. mobile canteen outside.

He grew more and more ashamed of himself for intruding and at last he could stand it no longer. He rose and demanded to be presented to the group captain, to whom he had written in the first place.

"I'm ashamed," he admitted, "thoroughly ashamed! And I beg you to forget all about me until things quiet down a little! Forget all about my little query. Let us postpone it for, say, a month or so, and then I'll contact you again. Or better still, you contact me when you are able to locate Oliver. In the meantime, I can hardly thank you enough for showing me such courtesy, and at a time when it must be clear to the meanest intelligence that you have other and far weightier matters on hand! A parachute landing over the Rhine, perhaps?" and he winked knowingly and withdrew.

He then caught the next train back to Bruton Spa and the group captain saw him no more, for he was promoted to Air Ministry staff a week or so later and down there, where everybody took three hours for lunch and read all the papers, even the advertisements, nobody had ever heard of green confidential files about men due to be discharged to industry.

The search died down and clerks went back to more urgent work, such as making out lists of trainees who had attended all their anti-gas lectures but had not yet had their weekly bath in the Blackrock swimming baths. In time everyone forgot the case of A.C.2 Shapley-Stewart, everyone that is except Horace, who was still sitting with his back to the stationery cupboard, and Sergeant Hixon, his spectacles misted, his forehead glowing like a Westcountry sunset, as he sat drumming clerkly fingers on the trestle table in front of him.

"Amazing thing where that file got to," mused Horace. Then, solicitously, "Here, Sarge, you look all in! Have your tea before it gets cold."

The sergeant shook his head impatiently and pushed the proffered mug aside.

"If only I could decipher that signature in the book," he muttered. "Is it Cherry, Chorley, Chalmers . . . ?"

"It'll turn up, I dare say," comforted Horace.

"No, no, never!" said Hixon, "we've looked everywhere—but *everywhere!*"

There was one place he could not have looked, underneath his own gas mask in the little office adjoining the main orderly room, for when he picked up his gas mask for the weekly exercise the following Tuesday there it was, tossed down no doubt when somebody came in and interrupted him.

He stared at it as though it was a rearing cobra. After a moment or two he touched it gingerly and then whipped his hand away, as if it had burned his fingers. After a moment or so he called Horace, making no comment on the file but pointing down at it, his hand shaking, his face parchment pale.

Horace picked it up. It did not appear to bite him.

"Well, what do you know?" he said cheerfully. "The old green file! I told you it'd turn up, didn't I, Sarge?"

Deep in Sergeant Hixon's subconscious was the utter certainty that Horace, Pedlar Pascoe and the green file were in some way linked together. He did not know how or why, but he knew that it was so and that the loss of the file, and its inexplicable reappearance from beneath his own gas mask, were in some confused and sinister manner connected with this thickset, cheerful little man, who ran his orderly room with such diabolical efficiency. When he could trust himself to speak he said:

"Can you offer any explanation at all, Pope?"

"Yes," said Horace, readily, "matter o' fact I can give you a choice o' two, Sarge! Either you slapped it down there yourself, and overlooked it in the panic, or someone at S.H.Q. came across it and planted it here when none of us was around, if you know what I mean! You'd have a job to prove it though, wouldn't you, Sarge?"

There was silence in the room, save for the labored whistle of Sergeant Hixon's breathing. Finally he said:

"And what do you propose we do about it now, Pope?"

"Well, that's easy," said Horace, "we burn the bloody thing, don't we?"

The sergeant quivered from head to foot and was obliged to steady himself by leaning his weight on the wall. If Horace had suggested that they sit down and mail it to Winston Churchill he could not have been more agonized.

"Bbbburn it? Ssset ffire to it? To a *file*, a confi*dential* file! Are you mad?"

"Not me," said Horace, shrugging, "but begging your pardon, Sarge, I reckon you would be if you took it back to S.H.Q.! We got a signature for it and our conscience is clear. No one can read the signature but that's beside the point, ain't it? That signature don't go for a lot but it'd go for nothing if you turned up with the file and the so-sorry-sir routine! Lumme, I wouldn't like to think what might happen to you and them stripes o' yours! They was looking for it for nearly a week, wasn't they? No, Sarge, there's on'y one thing to do now—burn the perishin' thing!"

The dreadful logic of Pope's advice penetrated Sergeant Hixon's stomach like a steel-tipped rod. The man was quite right. To return the file now would be a tacit admission of having had it in his possession all the time. He would have to tell the group captain, perhaps even an air vice-marshal, exactly where the file was found and then explain, or try to explain, how it came to be there. The least he could expect from then on would be reduction to the rank of corporal and he might even see the inside of one of those terrible military prisons, having been court-martialed and sent there for gross dereliction of duty! As things stood the matter was still very confused and the blame equally divided between S.H.Q. and Pool. No one could say, with conviction, just how the file had gone astray, or who were the culprits.

Hixon thought hard for a moment, then nodded slowly and despairingly.

"All right, Pope," he said hoarsely, "burn it, but after this . . . you understand . . . after this you must go away, you and that hairy ape of yours! I . . . I couldn't stand you about the place any more . . . I couldn't, I'd go clean off my head, you understand?"

Horace nodded sympathetically, for he understood very well. Somehow he had known that the file panic would set a term to his reign at Non-Effective Pool, and an uneasy association with a disciplinarian like Hixon. They could never work together, not after this. There would always be distrust and mutual disdain. From now on he would be closely watched and the exploitation of lucky postings and other sidelines would be a very dangerous undertaking. It was far better to call it a day and go while the going was good.

He took the file and buttoned it inside his tunic.

"Okay, Sarge," he said, "so long as you fix us a couple o' decent postings, mind! We don't want to land up anywhere, do we? None o' those Shetland or Orkney larks for me an' my friend Pedlar! As for this 'ere file, forget it, Sarge! It never happened, see? After all, what's it all in aid of, anyway? Some old fogey trying to pull a fast one on the R.A.F., and get 'is son-in-law back into a cushy civvy job! Lumme, when you come to think of it we done the R.A.F. a good turn be scotching it, 'aven't we? As it is that bloke—what's-his-name . . . Shapley-Stewart—he's still in the mob, still servin' his king and country!"

"Yes, yes . . . go away!" moaned Sergeant Hixon, now writhing with nervous indigestion and desperately in need of a good belch.

Horace went out of the room and Hixon tottered over to his desk, where he began to sort through his papers in a vague and distracted way. After a time he found what he was looking for, some blind postings to the big camp at Heathfield in the

Midlands. S.H.Q. had passed on a demand for a dozen Group V aircrafthands, to be selected from Pool at the Senior N.C.O.s discretion. This would do, he imagined. Pope and Pascoe would be swallowed up in a huge station like Heathfield and he would never hear of them again. Perhaps, if the war lasted long enough, he would forget all about them and the deliberate act of sabotage that he had authorized. He wrote their names into the space under the demand and took it into Horace, who was sipping tea at his table.

"Here," he said, "it's to Heathfield, a good camp. Collect ten other men and don't overlook that dreadful henchman of yours! Get cleared and go away, as quickly and quietly as you can, do you understand?"

"Sure, Sarge," said Horace placidly, and pocketed the posting note.

Sergeant Hixon hesitated a moment longer. He found it almost impossible to put the question into words but he had to know. He couldn't go away without making absolutely sure.

"The . . . the file . . . ?" he quavered.

Horace nodded toward the grate, where a thin spiral of smoke rose from a pile of charred papers. Hixon moved over, picked up a poker, and gave the ashes a stir or two. Then he went quietly out of the orderly room and out of Horace's life.

CHAPTER FIVE

Heathfield was more like a town than a camp. It was a labyrinthine, prewar settlement, set down in the middle of a wide, featureless plain, a vast assortment of hangars, huts, parade grounds and concrete buildings that looked like a background set for "Things to Come," the whole being surrounded by miles of barbed wire, a highway, and a branch railway line.

There were no aircraft in the camp now. It was used as a technical training school for flight mechanics, flight riggers and fitters. It had a staff establishment of over five thousand men and an average population of three times that number of trainees, who came for courses lasting from ten to fifteen weeks.

By wartime standards it was a comfortable, well-served camp, with its own cinema, swimming pool, gymnasium and four N.A.A.F.I.s, one for each wing, the kind of camp where men stayed for years on end, building up their own personal or group-operated dealings or fiddles. War had disorganized these for a time but by now the camp had settled down again, so that there was still some truth in the prewar adage: "There are two Air Forces—the Royal Air Force, and the Heathfield Air Force: occasionally they cooperate."

Horace and Pedlar detrained in a thin, driving rain, and Horace left his helpmate to gather up the gear while he moved across the windswept platform and stared down on the camp from the top of the station embankment.

His eye took in the almost frightening vastness of the establishment; the miles of buildings reaching out across the plain, the smudges of blue that marked the trudging progress of trainee columns going to or from the workshops, the knot of Service Police fussing around the main gate, the lorries barreling along the intersections. Here, he thought, was a big enough oyster if he could find a means to open it. Down there, among all those men and buildings, there must be fiddles galore, but it would surely need time and leisure to explore them all, discard the abortive and develop the most promising.

He had set aside sixty pounds from his Blackrock activities, and the money was snug in the Post Office Savings Bank. He had been tempted to invest it in a War Loan, but had decided against it. The interest was meager and he might, at any time, need capital. His initial disgust at finding himself in the Air Force had disappeared, smothered under a steady stream of profits, and he now regarded his presence in a place like this as an excursion into the commercial avenues of total war.

Pedlar, humping nearly a hundred pounds of gear, joined him at the wire fence and broke in upon his meditations.

"We gonner like it here, Popey?"

Horace pursed his lips. "Dunno," he said briefly, "depends!" And then, because Pedlar's presence close beside him expressed an unspoken plea, "It don't matter where we are, chum, so long as we're together, do it?"

Pedlar's big frame quivered slightly and his broad, lopsided face relaxed into a seraphic smile.

"No," he said slowly, "no, I reckon not!" The smile spent itself and was replaced by a vaguely harassed look. "But we *always* gonner be together, Popey?"

Pope looked up at him and nodded slowly. "You bet," he said, "no one's gonner split us up, not now, Pedlar, not never!"

The worried look chased after the smile and Pedlar braced himself, a movement that made the bulging kitbags balanced on each shoulder look as inconsequent as a pair of dwarf sausages.

"You stick by me and I'll watch out for you," said Horace, by way of sealing the contract. "There's nobody down there who can't be fixed, just so long as we go about it the right way, see? And I *know* the right way. I know *all* the right ways. Come on, mate!"

They made their way down the greasy wooden stairs and along the fence to the main gate. A blue-chinned S.P. examined their identity cards and glanced shrewdly at Pedlar, standing quietly on one side with the two kits on his broad back.

"They issue you with a private porter?" the policeman asked Horace.

"No," said Horace mildly, "but I sprained both ankles on the assault course at the Recruit Center and my buddy here 'as been giving me a hand!"

The S.P. grunted and ran his eye down Horace's greenish buttons.

"Why don't he have a go at your brass," he said shortly, then: "Okay! Report to Reception!"

They moved on down the main lane to a long hut that stood in the shadow of one of the workshops. Pedlar remained outside with the gear while Horace went in and showed his posting note to a red-headed sergeant.

"More aircrafthands for Four Wing?" he mused. "What the hell do they need more down there for? They're twenty-two over-strength as it is! Okay, report to Four Wing orderly room and see if they can find you something to do! Damned if I could, this place is crawling with rookies!"

He stamped the paper and returned it to Horace, at once applying himself to another matter.

Horace was braced by the interview. It was clear that no one was expecting them and they could therefore take their time about reporting. If they could find a comfortable billet and blankets they might wander about the camp of this size for days without being challenged. There was a date on the posting note, of course, but dates could be altered and he could always have remained behind in Blackrock for treatment of his sprained ankles.

"Put the gear in here," he said to Pedlar, "we'll take a look around and find some grub!"

They left the kitbags in the Reception Center lobby and Horace gave a runner five cigarettes to guard it, promising five more if it was intact on their return. Then they wandered down the main road, looking about them, studying the general layout, until they saw a column of men queueing outside a mess hall. They joined the queue and ate a hearty meal, afterward having coffee in the nearest N.A.A.F.I. On the way out Horace picked up a pail and mop, handing the pail to Pedlar and throwing the mop across his left shoulder, riflewise.

"Don't do to be carrying nothing!" he told the puzzled Pedlar. "Whenever you're idling around, carry something . . . pail, file, ladder, bag o' tools, anything! Nobody gets nosy if you're carrying something!"

Pedlar expressed admiration for the ruse but Horace made light of it. "Ancient Britons did it, mate," he said offhandedly. "Betcher they went around with chariot wheels under their arms!"

They carried the pail and mop around until dark, looking in on the swimming pool and cinema, glancing into workshops, studying the transport yard and other centers. Finally, around teatime, they wandered down to Four Wing and reported. Horace said that all the billets looked too organized to gate-crash and they had to have somewhere to park their gear and sleep.

The sergeant at Four Wing echoed the words of the N.C.O. at Reception.

"Remember that demand we put in for bods about a month ago?" he asked a corporal who was stabbing away at a vintage typewriter. "We were four under-strength then and now we're twenty-one over! Get a billet and come back in the morning, you two!"

They found a billet that was occupied by eighteen cooks and butchers. It was a long hut, with ten beds on each side and a little cubicle at the far end where the corporal i/c slept. The quarters were snug enough, but the inmates kept curious hours. They worked in shifts, the first shift going out at 0300 hours, and there were men asleep in the hut at all hours of the day.

Horace, who liked a quiet night's rest, did not take very kindly to the comings and goings of the cooks and butchers. They thundered past his bed in the small hours, making a prodigious uproar on the bare floor. In addition the hut radio was going day and night, the night shift sleeping through the programs of dance music, advertisements, and interminable news bulletins. The sheer repetition of the radio programs got on Horace's nerves, so much so that after hearing a crooner sing "Over the Rainbow" half a dozen times he took an opportunity to tinker with the loudspeaker, effectively silencing it.

A radio mechanic who was called in to mend it started a fight among the cooks and butchers, who accused each other of experimenting with the aerial the previous week. When the set was repaired and going again Horace decided that he and Pedlar must find quieter quarters and at once went in search of them. He eventually found an empty hut down near the transport yard. It was half-full of mattresses and gas masks, but they made a space at the far end and carried along their gear, beds, and bedding. When they were settled in, Horace thoughtfully erected a stenciled notice, taken from a generator shed on the far side of the camp. The notice read: *"No Admittance on Any Pretext Whatever!"*

They slept very peacefully down here. No one came in the hut, not even on weekly inspection days.

They kept away from Four Wing orderly room as much as possible. The surplus aircrafthands attached to the permanent staff were given odd jobs, such as coal-heaving, message running, barrack-room furniture shifting, and so on. For a month or so Horace and Pedlar spent their time in the N.A.A.F.I., or wandering around with their pail and mop. Nobody took the slightest notice of them. At five o'clock every night they presented themselves at the main gate and caught a train for Waxley, the nearest town, where they called in on the cinema and the Y.M.C.A. It was a pleasant, humdrum life and would have suited Pedlar indefinitely, but after a time Horace began to get bored and said it was time that they got in on something and promised to give the matter some thought.

They finally "got in" on Motor Transport. Horace had observed that dozens of lorries came and went on various errands every day and discreet enquiries informed him that they were employed on routine journeys into the surrounding countryside. Laundry had to be collected and delivered, rations distributed to various outlying satellites, and there were a number of occasional trips, such as fetching and returning stage scenery for the padre.

They finally muscled in on the laundry detail, which meant a fifteen-mile journey into Waxbury every day. It was an unexacting job and very popular with the M.T. personnel. Horace paid the existing laundry detail a pound apiece to absent themselves one morning, then presented himself and Pedlar to the corporal i/c and explained that the regular driver and his mate had been posted and that he and Pedlar had been instructed by the orderly room to replace them.

The corporal did not question this. His job was to collect, deliver, and fetch the camp laundry, and one driver was as good as another. They drove around to various points collecting hundreds of bags of laundry and then passed out of the main gate, Pedlar at the wheel, Horace relaxing on the leather cushions of the cab.

The camp laundry was farmed out to a civilian contractor called Gribble, and Gribble's premises were situated in the industrial heart of Waxbury, a large red-brick building with a spacious yard.

While Pedlar was unloading, a squat, heavily-built man, with ponderous calves and a squint, approached and beckoned Horace to climb down. Horace got out of the cab and followed him into a private room, cut off from the office staff by a stout partition and warmed by a bright coal fire. The laundry-man, whom Horace took to be the foreman of the establishment, produced a bottle of gin from a cupboard and poured two generous measures.

"Tonic or orange?" he demanded.

"Tonic," said Horace cautiously, studying the man closely as he mixed the drinks.

"You haven't been to see me lately!" said the foreman solemnly.

"No," said Horace, giving nothing away, "I haven't!"

"Anyone twigged it?" asked the man, tossing back his drink and beginning to replenish the glass.

"No," said Horace, "not as I know of."

It was clear that the foreman took him for somebody else, so he waited for the man to skirmish into the open, his mind exploring various possibilities. The foreman looked at him under black, bushy eyebrows and rubbed his chin reflectively.

"When you didn't come I thought they was on to us!" he said at length. "I suppose you was playing it quiet-like and maybe you're right. No sense in bein' greedy and overdoing it. Good many come a cropper that way, haven't they?"

"Yes," said Horace flatly, "they have and all!" And then, in order to bring matters into the open: "How about having another go right now?"

The foreman finished his gin and hitched his belt.

"Ah!" he said encouragingly, "how much you got in the tank?"

"Round about fifteen gallon," said Horace promptly, "but the price 'as gone up. Getting a bit risky back there!"

"How much has it riz?" demanded the foreman.

"Bob a gallon," said Horace.

The man sucked his teeth. "Okay," he said finally, "we got to get about somehow, 'aven't we? Back her into the garage, same as before!"

Horace went out and told Pedlar to back the van into a large empty garage on the far side of the yard. The foreman walked over and foraged about in the background, presently coming around to the cab with a jerry-can and a length of pipe.

"I'll siphon off three," he said, "while you two take a smoke. You don't need to keep tabs on me, I always play it safe and three won't be missed. Tanner over the odds you said, didn't you?"

"No," said Horace, "I said a bob!" and pocketed a pound note.

They returned to the lorry after an interval of fifteen minutes.

"Well, what do you know?" said Horace, as they switched on and studied the gauge, "I wonder how long they bin at that lark? Bloody thieves them civvies, aren't they, Pedlar? Think o' blokes risking their lives to get that gas over from the States!"

Pedlar said it was a shame and turned the lorry out of the yard. Horace began to hum his favorite tune, "Home in Pasadena." He had no idea where Pasadena was and whether, in fact, the bees in that area did hum melodies but when he was relaxed and happy he always sang or hummed this particular melody.

They trundled blithely through Waxbury and down the main road toward the camp.

CHAPTER SIX

The petrol racket brought in three pounds a week and made Horace feel that he was earning his keep.

The operation was extraordinarily simple. As far as Horace could judge nobody checked on their mileage. Every time they needed petrol they drove to the pumps and three times a week exactly twenty-five percent of their gallonage was siphoned off by the foreman at the laundry.

The foreman was a man after Horace's heart. Never once did he take liberties with the tank but voluntarily rationed himself to a meager three gallons, for which he paid over one pound per siphoning. On Tuesdays, Thursdays, and Saturdays the lorry was driven into the yard, unloaded outside the checking office, and then driven straight out again, but on Mondays, Wednesdays and Fridays it stopped at the garage on the way out and here Horace and Pedlar left it in charge of the foreman for fifteen minutes by the office clock.

Horace would liked to have discovered how the foreman extracted his three gallons, no more and no less, in this comparatively brief space of time but he was never present while it was being done. The foreman always insisted that he and Pedlar walk across the yard for a smoke and in the end Horace had cause to thank him for this precaution, for the foreman was hard at work with his length of hose when Mr. Hubert Gribble, the son of the proprietor, happened to observe him from his throne of vantage in the managerial lavatory.

The lavatory window looked onto the yard and from here, silent and unobserved, Hubert had, in times past, overlooked all manner of misdemeanors and infractions of office rules and factory acts. It was unfortunate for the foreman that, on this particular occasion, Pedlar had driven the lorry forward into the garage, and although the siphoner took the obvious precaution of closing the big doors, a playful gust of wind blew one of them open, so that Hubert Gribble got a quick glimpse of the foreman bent over the petrol tank, with a yard of rubber piping hanging from his mouth.

From where he sat it appeared to Hubert that the foreman was disgorging his entrails. Greatly alarmed, he hardly waited to adjust his trousers before quitting his observation post and hurrying downstairs and across the yard. Panting, and hardly knowing what to expect, he flung back the door and thumped the foreman between the shoulders. The siphoner at once collapsed over the rear of the lorry.

Horace and Pedlar, who had been enjoying their cigarettes outside the main office, saw Hubert emerge from the building and dash into the garage. They threw down their cigarettes and hurried in pursuit, coming up just in time to assist Hubert in applying the artificial respiration he had learned at the local St. John Ambulance classes.

Despite their joint efforts the foreman remained in a poor way. The sudden wallop on the back had caused him to swallow the end of the tubing and when they freed him of that he continued to leak petrol down the front of Hubert's natty tweed suiting. Finally he rose on his knees, gasping and retching, while Hubert stared down at him in dismay. He was a very correct young man and when it was clear to him that one of his senior employees had been caught red-handed in the act of stealing R.A.F. petrol he was outraged. Not for one moment did he involve the driver and driver's mate in the plot, particularly as the foreman, when at last he could speak, gasped out that he had yielded to a sudden temptation. His eight-horsepower car, he said, had been laid up since petrol rationing began and his wife was nagging him unmercifully to resume their peacetime Sunday trip to visit her mother in a neighboring town.

Horace and Pedlar stood in silence while the foreman made his excuses. Pedlar, as usual, looked mildly bewildered but Horace's face was a study of pained reproach. He did not enter the discussion until Hubert declared that he was going to make an example of the foreman, saying that it was incompatible with his honor, as an authorized washer of airmen's shirts, to allow pilfering of this magnitude to go unpunished.

Then Horace spoke up, pointing out that the foreman's dismissal was punishment enough, that one ought to consider his innocent wife and children, and that not everybody could be expected to share Hubert's patriotic outlook. Toward the end of his appeal he mentioned, in passing, that Hubert would not wish punishment to fall upon two innocent airmen, who might even be court-martialed for leaving their lorry unattended, or that anything so unpleasant as theft should cloud the cordial relationship existing between the R.A.F. and the laundry.

This last aspect gave Hubert pause. Having asked Pedlar whether he would be able to cover up the loss of the petrol swallowed or spilled by his foreman, and having been assured that this might be achieved, he went on to ask whether an incident such as this, should it come to the ears of the camp authorities, would result in a cancellation of his contract.

Horace was very adamant on this particular point. He sucked in his breath and shook his head, like a doctor diagnosing an incurable disease.

"It'd be curtains as far as your firm's concerned, sir!" he said respectfully. "My C.O. would take a dim view o' this 'ere and you ain't the on'y laundry around town, are you? No, sir, I wouldn't carry it no further if I was you! After all, you scotched it quicker than any copper could 'ave done, and if I was in your shoes I'd call it a day and let 'im orf with a severe rep!"

The foreman, who was feeling as though he had been

drowned in an oil well, said nothing at all but remained doubled up, either from shame or nausea.

"He'd be devilish hard to replace, devilish hard!" agreed Hubert, "but I'm bound to say you chaps are pretty decent to put in a word for him! It shows a grand spirit, the sort of spirit one associates with the R.A.F. these days. Suppose we discuss it further over coffee in my office?"

They adjourned to Hubert's office and drank two cups of coffee apiece, but there was no further discussion on the subject and they parted on good terms.

Horace was very silent on the way home. He was a man who never failed to profit by experience and it seemed to him that the time had come to hand over the laundry detail to the clamorous Dusty Miller, who had been trying to buy it for weeks. Horace did not doubt but that the channels of honest trade could be reopened at the laundry but there were, it appeared, two very weak links in the connection, the foreman's criminal carelessness, and his employer's earnest patriotism. At any moment one or the other of these links might yield to sudden pressure and nobody could say where the end of the broken chain would lead. All in all, it seemed wisest to sell the laundry detail to Dusty and invest the proceeds in the daily ration trip to Little Bickrington, a satellite camp further afield. He had been pondering the possibilities of the ration trip for some time. Maybe the prospects were not as steady as those of the laundry, but they were fraught with far less risk. By the time they had reached camp he had made up his mind and the transaction was effected in the N.A.A.F.I. that same evening.

The following morning the switch was made. Instead of driving south to Waxley they now drove northwest to Little Bickrington, with the day's meat. It meant starting out an hour earlier but this was no hardship since it gave them time to stop off in Bindlescombe, a straggling village en route.

There was a pleasant old pub in Bindlescombe, the Robin Hood, and here, a day or two after they had taken over the ration run, Horace made the acquaintance of a Mr. Cooksley, the genial and rubicund village butcher. They began by discussing the war and ended commiserating one with the other upon the tyranny of the rationing system.

Mr. Cooksley came out with them to inspect the vast quantity of red meat in Horace's lorry. He realized, of course, that it was not for him, and that every ounce of it was earmarked for uniformed bellies, but it did his butcher's heart good just to look at it and pat it and say how right it was that meat as good as this should be set on one side as the sinews of war and the fuel of democracy.

Cooksley and Horace struck up a warm friendship on the spot. The butcher venerated the Air Force and Horace, for his part, admired Mr. Cooksley's high-minded disinterestedness. Not many professional butchers, he reflected, harassed by rationing regulations and obliged to say "no" to lifelong customers when they called for the Sunday joint, would have been so insistent that the men who were hammering Germany every night should be fed as generously as the U-boat campaign would permit. It was heartening, Horace told Pedlar, as they threaded the narrow roads toward the satellite camp, that here and there one still ran across the odd civilian who was happy to put his regard for the Forces ahead of personal profit. It was a sign, surely, that they were indeed engaged in a People's War and not, as last time, a conflict on behalf of the City stockbrokers.

Pedlar did not understand very much of this homily but he listened to it with the greatest respect. At length, however, he rather shocked Horace by demanding to know whether Mr. Cooksley had in fact bought any of the meat and if so for how much? Horace tut-tutted at this but after another mile or so expressed an opinion that much of the meat they dumped each day at the cookhouse found its way into the pig bins and that this seemed a great pity and should be remedied if the opportunity presented itself.

It was remedied the following morning, a small sack having been inadvertently left behind in the pub after Horace had finished his second pint at the Robin Hood.

Mr. Cooksley noticed the sack within seconds of Horace's

departure. Exclaiming, he picked it up and ran after the lorry, shouting and gesticulating, but the noise of the engine drowned his voice and presently he fell behind, sighing with vexation and telling himself that he would now have to keep the sack in his refrigerator until Horace called again.

After this incident memory lapses on the part of Horace grew frequent. Nearly every time they traversed Bindlescombe they called in at the Robin Hood, and it was not long before they were both on very friendly terms with Mr. Cooksley and were invited to call for tea on their way back to camp.

Mrs. Cooksley, every bit as affable as her husband, fed them and cosseted them, and Horace began a mild flirtation with Iris, the Cooksley's only child, who presided over her father's cash register.

Iris was a hefty, squarish girl, with her father's high complexion and the sort of bust that one might expect of someone who had eaten plenty of good red meat through childhood and adolescence.

Soon they were calling at the Cooksleys every day and it became their private N.A.A.F.I., a regular home away from home. The butcher's wife took a great fancy to Pedlar and they sometimes talked of Exmoor, a place she had once visited on a prewar coach tour. When Pedlar had consumed every morsel of food that she placed before him she let him sit in her husband's rocking chair and listen to the radio, while he waited for Horace to return from his evening stroll with Iris, the daughter.

Iris took to Horace as readily as her mother had taken to Pedlar. A flirtation that had commenced very lightly, with sly nudges, pinches and guffaws in the back of the shop while Father Cooksley was poking about the cold storage shed, soon developed into a steady romance.

Every now and again Horace and Pedlar came over to spend their weekly day off with the family and on these occasions Horace and Iris usually excused themselves after lunch and wandered down the village street toward the belt of woodland bordering the main road.

The butcher seemed not to mind these attentions to his

daughter, seemed, in fact, to take them very much for granted, like the heavy little sacks that Horace was constantly putting down here and there and forgetting to take away again.

Almost every day, Pedlar noticed, Horace overlooked a sack which ultimately found its way into Mr. Cooksley's cold storage shed for safekeeping. At first Pedlar was slightly worried by Horace's absent-mindedness. There might, he reflected, be trouble over short rations at the satellite camp (there had already been trouble between the Transport Pool and the team that had succeeded Pedlar and Horace on the laundry detail), but week followed week, and no one complained, so perhaps Horace had been right, perhaps the satellite cooks did fill swill bins with excess meat, or perhaps the amount that went into the sack each day was too small to be missed.

When it did come the trouble originated from an entirely unexpected quarter. Once more a sudden crisis shattered the rhythm of their lives.

Three months to the day after Horace had escorted Iris on their first evening stroll to the woods Mr. Cooksley stomped into the kitchen, where Pedlar was listening to one of Vera Lynn's Forces' programs, and said something to his wife that caused her to put down her knitting and disappear into the scullery, closing the door behind her.

Pedlar had been puzzled by Mrs. Cooksley's demeanor that evening. She seemed snappish, preoccupied and far from her motherly self. The butcher too seemed vaguely out of sorts. He took off his boots, sat down in the chair his wife had vacated, placed his large, red hands on his thighs and subjected Pedlar to a hostile stare.

"What time are you two due back in camp?" he demanded suddenly.

Pedlar told him at eleven-fifty-nine hours precisely.

"Ah," said Mr. Cooksley, "then that gives us all time for a little heart-to-hearter, don't it? When will Horace get back with our Iris, d'you reckon?"

"Any time now," said Pedlar, still puzzled. "We haven't got the lorry with us and we got to catch the last bus!"

"Good," said the butcher, and lit a meditative pipe, puffing away in stolid silence until they heard Horace and Iris enter by the side door.

Iris came into the kitchen looking rather flushed and at once asked: "Where's Mum?"

"Upstairs," said her father shortly, "and you'd best join her, while I have a little talk with Horace!"

"Okay, Dad," said Iris lightly, and called over her shoulder, "Horace! Dad wants to see you!"

"We're close on time for the bus!" called Horace from the hall. "Shake a leg in there, Pedlar!"

Mr. Cooksley reacted unexpectedly to this warning. He jumped up, took his pipe from his mouth and shouted: "Never mind the flamin' bus! You come in here and see me! What I got to say won't take long, d'you hear?"

Pedlar looked at him with surprise. He had never heard Mr. Cooksley address Horace so sharply and he did not like the sudden change of expression on Iris's face as she skipped out of the room and ran up the stairs.

Horace came in slowly and reluctantly, moving like a boxer, glumly determined to renew the fight after a grueling round. He sat down on the very edge of a high-backed chair, very nicely balanced, as though for a split-second getaway.

"What's cooking?" he asked. "What's all the panic for?"

Mr. Cooksley relaxed somewhat, sitting down again and knocking out his pipe against the fireplace.

"No panic, Horace," he said evenly, "not as I know of anyway, but tell me one thing, are you married?"

Horace looked surprised. "Married? *Me?* Lumme, o' course I'm not married! What give you that idea?"

To Pedlar, watching very closely, the butcher seemed to breathe a little easier.

"That's good," he said, "then maybe there's no harm done! My Iris is in the fam'ly way!"

Pedlar looked quickly at Horace, expecting a lead but receiving none. Horace blinked once or twice and slowly massaged his knees with his palms.

"Yeah, I know it!" he said laconically.

"You *know* it?" said Mr. Cooksley, with evident surprise.

"She just told me," said Horace, looking very glum.

There was silence for a moment. Vera Lynn was still singing about a nightingale she had heard in Berkeley Square but nobody in the room seemed interested in bird-watching.

"Turn that ruddy thing off!" commanded Mr. Cooksley, and Pedlar twisted the knob until it clicked. "Well . . . ?" said the butcher, inadequately Pedlar thought, for he failed to develop the remark.

Horace collected himself. "We got swept away," he said helpfully, "so now I reckon you'll be wanting to hear about us getting married, Mr. Cooksley."

The butcher relaxed. "Yes, Horace m'boy! Something like that, I imagine. The wife carried on alarming o' course, but we won't let that worry us, will we? This has happened before and I dare say it'll happen again. It's just like I said, if you're single there's no harm done!"

Suddenly Horace stood up, his glumness gone. Instead he seemed to Pedlar his brisk and businesslike self. "Matter o'fact we been discussing it, Pop," he said, "and me'n Iris fixed on a fortnight today! Nothing classy o' course, just a registry job, in Waxley. How's that suit you, Pop?"

Whether it was the businesslike statement of fact contained in Horace's speech, or whether it was the easy fashion in which "Mr. Cooksley" had been converted into plain "Pop," Pedlar did not know, but it was quite clear from Cooksley's expression that the butcher was more than ready to welcome Horace as a son-in-law. His familiar affability flooded back across his lobster-pink face like a slow, rosy tide. He jumped up and patted Horace affectionately on the shoulder.

"Spoken like a man!" he declared. "Now you run for your bus, and I'll break the noos to the missus! Don't fret yourself over her, she'll get used to the idea, but pop in tomorrow on your way through and we'll go into the details, eh?"

"Tomorrow's Sunday," said Horace, "there's no ration run."

"All right then, on Monday," said Mr. Cooksley, carelessly. "Make it Monday and I'll tell you something else, Horace. You and me'll get on fine . . . fine . . . ! I always admire a lad who looks out for himself, and you can come into the butchering after the war. We'll open a shop in Metborough and maybe another in Biscombe! It'll work out all for the best, you see if it doesn't!"

"Yes, Pop," said Horace woodenly. "Now come on, Pedlar, we don't want to have to hoof it back to camp!"

They ran out and down the street to the bus stop outside the Robin Hood. The bus was crowded and there was no chance to converse during the journey. It was not until they alighted at the end of the long road leading to the main gate that Horace spoke again. He said: "Pedlar! We got to get posted and bloody quick!"

Pedlar had been thinking something like this all the way home, but his hour-hand brain movement had faltered and petered out among the uncertainties and improbabilities of arranging an authorized flight from the locality.

"You don't get posted just like that, Popey," he argued. "Besides, Mr. Cooksley'll show up in camp even if we did, wouldn't he? I dare say someone'd soon tell him where we'd gone!"

"Ah," said Horace bitterly, "he'll show up all right, but he's gonner find it dicey looking through the nominal rolls of a camp this size for a bloke called 'Horace,' ain't he?"

Pedlar pondered this throughout the remainder of their walk to the gate, finding in it further proof of Horace's greatness. For months now they had been calling on the Cooksleys. Week after week Horace had been walking Iris through the deep, green woods beyond the village. They had sat for hours in the butcher's kitchen, exchanging confidences and small talk, yet all this time Horace had never disclosed his surname. He was just "Horace," the airman who drove through the village with the satellite's meat.

"Won't someone in camp tell 'em who you are?" asked Pedlar.

"No!" said Horace. "We sticks together in this mob, don't we? I 'ad mothers come to me back in Blackrock, looking fer Alberts, 'Enrys and 'Erberts, but it never got none of 'em very far!"

All this, however, was of little use unless they were posted within days, and Pedlar's brain soon returned once more to the principal problem of getting clear of Heathfield and winning a head start over butcher and daughter.

Doggedly his mind probed various possibilities, operating like a mastodon giving battle to a small, elusive animal. This camp was no Blackrock. It was not a recruit center, where men were posted the moment they completed their initial training. It did not even possess the fluidity or anonymity of the Non-Effective Pool, where men like Shapley-Stewart could get lost for months. It was a regular camp, with a regular permanent staff of which both of them were now members. Snug in their gas-mask store, immune from weekly inspections, and in receipt of whatever income Horace derived from off-the-ration petrol and off-the-ration meat, they had, indeed, taken out insurances to stay put. Only a month ago Horace had purchased semi-immunity from a sudden move, paying the orderly room sergeant in charge of blind postings the sum of two pounds. Furthermore, Four Wing personnel was no longer twenty-one aircrafthands over-strength. All the other odd bods had been posted long ago, and it was extremely unlikely that authentic postings containing the names of Pope and Pascoe would arrive like foot-of-the-gallows reprieves within the next few days. Glancing sideways at his friend Pedlar realized that Horace appreciated all these difficulties and was himself testing each of them, like a long, long row of rope ladders.

"We'd better have a word with Sergeant Gillespie," he said finally, as they walked slowly down the main avenue of the camp. "No time to lose. Do it now. You make up the beds and get the cocoa from the cookhouse. I'll be along in about ten minutes!"

Pedlar did as he was told. Part of his duty each evening was to make up the beds and fetch supper from the cookhouse, two pint mugs of cocoa and whatever was going, usually sausages and mash, or fried bread and beans. Supper was not on the airmen's menu but theirs was an offshoot of a little arrangement that Horace had made with the corporal i/c cookhouse, supper every night in exchange for a bi-weekly lift into town on the ration wagon.

Horace was gone much longer than ten minutes and Pedlar had to put his supper to warm on the stove. When he came in it was clear from his expression that the visit to Sergeant Gillespie had had negative results.

"Ruddy 'opeless," said Horace moodily, as he probed the congealed sausages. "They don't reckon on any more blind postings for a month or more! Can you beat this outfit? We was overstaffed a few months ago and now we're ruddy well understaffed! Gillespie said he could fix it in about four weeks but not before. Lumme, I'll be coming up fer me perishin' silver wedding before he gets round to it!"

"What are we goner do then, Popey?" asked Pedlar.

"I dunno; stall I reckon . . . tell the old so-and-so the Registry Office 'as a waitin' list. That'll keep 'im quiet for a week or so, but after that . . . I'll think o' something. Goo'-night, Pedlar!"

"Goo'night, Popey!" Pedlar replied, and heaved himself lower in the bed.

He did not sleep, however. For the first time in their association Pope was clearly at a loss and Pedlar, morbidly sensitive to his friend's moods, was disturbed by Horace's air of defeatism. With a huge effort he forced his brain to survey the problem objectively. They could wangle a couple of blind postings, that is, postings without names handed out to whoever happened to be without protection, or under orderly room displeasure, but not, it seemed, for a month or so. In the R.A.F. that meant at least six weeks, even with constant pressure. But Horace was pledged to marry Iris in a fortnight! He talked of stalling but Pedlar had formed a conviction that Mr. Cooksley would not prove an easy man to stall. His manner that evening had been clear-headed and determined, and Pedlar had no doubts but that, even if he was disposed to delay, he would be pushed from behind by Mrs. Cooksley and Iris.

It was not as if they could avoid the Cooksleys while they were looking for an escape route. They were obliged to pass through the village every day and if they failed to call on the family suspicion would be aroused at once. They had one day's grace—tomorrow; on Monday they were expected to attend a family conference and once that took place all possible lines of retreat would be closed. It followed then that, if they were to escape at all, it would have to be within the next thirty-six hours and an authorized posting was a wild improbability. Airmen in their position did not have that kind of luck. Only men desperately keen to stay put were likely to be posted off at random to an outlying camp, to the Western Isles, or overseas.

Overseas! Pedlar's slow current of thought snagged on the word. If they could get an overseas posting they could move fast. Pedlar had known men who had been whistling their way about the camp lanes at 0800 hours and almost on the boat by teatime. When overseas postings came in there was always a panic. The customary clearance procedure was speeded up and unheard of liberties were taken in navigating the official channels. Men had even been known to leave for Africa without a chit signed by the Stores L.A.C., declaring that they had handed in their frayed ties and soiled denims.

When a man was going overseas the only thing anybody bothered about was his health. He was bundled down to the M.O., passed fit, and bundled out again. Before he knew what had hit him he was on the train for a personnel despatch camp, still bleating that he was due for leave, that his wife was expecting twins, or that his old mother was expecting an operation for the removal of gallstones. Surely an overseas posting would do the trick and although one could never be sure, it seemed reasonable to suppose that some were always available, or that two men, *volunteering* for service overseas, would be accepted without question, and packed off as a couple of eccentrics who did not deserve a billet in a cushy camp like Heathfield.

There and then Pedlar made up his mind what to do and for once he decided to act without consulting his friend. It would come, he reasoned, as a pleasant surprise for Pope when he was sipping his mug of tea in the morning. He would wake up and discover that his problem had been solved overnight and that his slow-thinking buddy had shown the kind of initiative that Pedlar so much admired in Horace. Horace was still asleep when Pedlar rose, dressed, and hurried across to the S.H.Q. orderly room.

Officially there was no Sunday in wartime. Sunday was supposed to be just another day, with a church parade or two for those unable to dodge the column, and then work as usual, but civilian habits died hard and there was always an atmosphere of somnolence and Sabbath calm about the camp on a Sunday morning. One could always tell that it was Sunday without looking at the calendar, for almost everyone seemed to take their day off on a Sunday and the mess halls were often more than half-empty at breakfasttime.

Pedlar did not stop for breakfast, promising himself a call at the cookhouse on the way back to the billet. He marched straight down the main road to Station Headquarters near the main gate and presented himself to a yawning corporal clerk who was sorting mail at the registry table in the orderly room. Pedlar recognized the clerk as a member of the orderly room staff called Reeves.

"Me and my friend want to get on the boat!" he said, without preamble.

The corporal's jaw dropped. He stared at Pedlar over his pile of mail and for a moment or so he was far too astonished to speak. Finally he said: "You trying to be funny, cock?"

"No," said Pedlar placidly. "Me an' my friend—A. C. Pope, Four Wing, that is—we want to go overseas, and we want to go now! Right away!"

Corporal Reeves pushed the mail to one side and groped for his mug, steadying himself with a deep swallow of lukewarm tea.

"What's your trade?" he demanded suddenly.

"We haven't got a trade," said Pedlar, "we're A.C.H.'s, Group V. We bin attached to the Transport Pool ever since we come here and we're brassed off! We want to see the world. You must have something for chaps like us, you're always coming around Transport Section looking fer blokes for the boat. Why, I seen chaps hide in the bog every time you show up! Whenever they see you they know you'll nab someone or other!"

The corporal considered this and was obliged to admit its authenticity. It saddened him to reflect that all over the camp his comrades had come to regard him much as the inhabitants of an eighteenth-century fishing village regarded the boat-swain of the local press gang. He only had to drift into the N.A.A.F.I. for men to break up their conversations, stop half-way through the recounting of a joke, and melt away in all directions. It was not his fault that he had become a pariah. Overseas postings were coming into S.H.Q. orderly room every day, and should have been handled by an officer, but the officer either wasn't there when he was needed or, if he was, he detailed the warrant officer to find four or six men for a draft. The warrant officer considered this rooting-out business below his dignity and passed it on to the flight sergeant, who at once sent it through to the orderly room sergeant.

The sergeant was a very amiable soul. He hated having to listen to the wild pleas of the men he detailed, so he had formed the habit of taking his N.A.A.F.I. break whenever the order filtered down to him, and on the way out of the room detailing a runner to instruct Corporal Reeves to find the necessary number of men and tell them to report for clearance and M.O. inspection.

Reeves was unable to pass the buck any further down the line. He was living proof of the R.A.F. adage that the corporal carried the can. He had tried handing it on to the senior L.A.C., but nobody took any notice of L.A.C.s, and when men were detailed by one they only said, "Wrap up!" and got on with whatever they happened to be doing when the L.A.C. had approached. They couldn't say "Wrap up!" to a corporal without sealing their doom or, if they were lucky enough to wriggle out of the posting, getting themselves placed on a charge, so instead they poured out their pitiful appeals and Reeves was sometimes obliged to threaten them with instant arrest if they didn't stop pleading and accompany him back to the orderly room where they were interviewed by the sergeant.

Reeves always considered it grossly unfair of the sergeant to answer the victims' renewed pleas with a curt: "Sorry, pal, but you been detailed! *I* can't do anything about it! Corporal Reeves detailed you, didn't he?"

When these conversations were going on Reeves sat at his registry desk and busied himself with mail, reflecting bitterly that this system of passing on the can had converted him into a cross between a police informer and a professional hangman, with whom no one would associate.

And now, here was this great, bumbling-looking airman actually presenting himself at 0800 hours on a Sunday morning and begging to be shipped overseas! There was a kind of atonement in the man's request and the corporal's heart warmed towards him.

"What's your name?" he demanded gently, and when Pedlar had given his name and number, "How about your friend's?"

"He's called Pope," said Pedlar, and recited Horace's service number.

The corporal wrote down the names and numbers and thumbed through a tray marked "IN," selecting a sheet of flimsy paper that Pedlar at once recognized as a posting note.

"You're dead lucky," said Reeves, "we got a panic demand for two A.C.H.s in this morning's mail. Get yourselves cleared and report to M.O. at 1100 hours. There's no embarkation leave and if the M.O. passes you you'll go straight off to the Personnel Despatch Center and get your kit and inoculations up there, okay?"

"Okay," said Pedlar, beaming, and took the clearance chits, one made out in his own name, the other in the name of Horace.

"That's all," said the corporal, "see you later."

"Thanks, Corp," said Pedlar, and only just stopped himself saluting.

He called in at the cookhouse on the way back and filled an enamel jug he had with him with tea. Then he crossed to the gas-mask shed and gently awoke Horace, who sat up yawning and groped for the butt he had placed on the ashtray beside his bed the previous night.

Pedlar smiled down at him, drunk with achievement.

"You don't have to start worrying, Popey," he said, noticing a crease form under Pope's widow's peak as he reached out for his tea, "it's all fixed."

"Eh?" said Horace sleepily. "What's fixed?"

"Our postings," Pedlar told him, "it's all buttoned up! I just bin down S.H.Q. and done it! They give me our clearance chits and we got to see the M.O. at 1100 hours!"

"What you burbling about, Pedlar?"

"The postings! Us! I give the corporal our names just now and we'll be out of here by tonight!"

"Out of here?" echoed Horace. "Don't be screwy, we won't get posted for more'n a month. I told you so, didn't I?"

"Ah, but that was at Four Wing," said Pedlar impressively. "I fixed it at S.H.Q. It's overseas!"

Horace hiccoughed into his tea and the hiccough made him cough violently. He spilled half his tea over his blankets, slammed down the mug and writhed this way and that, beating his chest, his face horribly contorted. When at last he had ceased coughing he could barely speak and his voice was reduced to a nasal wheeze but he signaled violently with his hands. Pedlar could make nothing of his signals and bent lower to catch his whisper.

"Overseas, you said? You did say 'overseas,' didn't you?"

"That's it, Popey! The corporal down there was shaken a bit, but he didn't raise no objections. It's all fixed, like I said."

The impact of Pedlar's confirmation breached Horace's defenses, projecting him out of bed in a single bound. He clutched Pedlar's tunic with such force that the big man staggered back a pace without, however, losing his gratified expression.

"You went down to S.H.Q. and stuck in our names for overseas?" roared Pope, levering himself up and down on Pedlar's lopsided lapel. "You give 'im our names? You . . . you *volunteered?*"

"That's it," said Pedlar, his smile fading, as it began to dawn on him that Pope was not merely excited but for some reason hysterically enraged.

"It was a good idea, wasn't it?" he faltered. "It'll get us out

106

o' camp, won't it? It was what you wanted, wasn't it? It *was*, wasn't it, Popey?"

"Why you great, clumsy, hamfisted gorilla!" bawled Pope, releasing his hold on Pedlar's tunic and sitting down on his rumpled bed. "You've booked us on the boat! You've signed our bloody death warrants, you clod! *Overseas! As a volunteer!* Lumme, they'll have the photographers out to take pickshers of us! They'll have a band march us to the gangplank! No one's never volunteered for overseas! It's like . . . like . . . signing on for the wrong end of a perishin' firing squad!"

"I thought you'd be pleased, Popey," said Pedlar, with infinite pathos.

"*Pleased!* For crying out loud! You want me to jump fer joy because you gone and set me up as a ruddy torpedo target? Why, half the blokes who get posted overseas don't get no further'n Gib! After that they splash around in the bloody Bay o' Biscay and I can't even swim! Can *you* swim?"

"No," said Pedlar, "but you get issued with lifebelts, I seen pictures of 'em wi' lifebelts on!"

Horace made a hopeless gesture, signifying the utter hopelessness of reasoning with a man who used the promise of a lifebelt as an argument in favor of attempted suicide.

After the initial explosion he felt weak and incapable of further discussion. Fear clawed at his stomach. His mouth felt parched and the remains of his tea was left to go stone cold. Wearily he began to pull on his trousers while Pedlar stood by, a picture of wretchedness.

"I'm sorry," he repeated, "I thought it was a good idea, honest I did, Popey!"

A particle of his pathos communicated itself to Horace. He looked up, studying the broad, earnest face and pleading eyes. There was something infinitely touching about the way Pedlar stood there, like a huge bull-calf awaiting the slaughterer's axe. His hands dangled listlessly, his thick, pudgy fingers curled and uncurled with nervous tension. All the rage and fright ebbed from Horace, leaving him hollow, helpless and used up.

"Okay, okay, Pedlar," he said. "Go and get some fresh tea

and see if you can rustle up some slices o' toast and a blob o' marmalade. I'm not going overseas on an empty stomach, that's for sure! Maybe I'll think o' something while you're gone, maybe we can pass it off as a joke or something!"

Pedlar went across to the cookhouse and Horace finished dressing. When Pedlar returned they made a silent breakfast after which Pedlar tidied the hut, while Horace slouched over to find Corporal Reeves and explain to him that his buddy, Pascoe, had a ghoulish sense of humor and had been playing a practical joke on him, but that he, Pope, considered it very indecent to joke about such a grave matter and had therefore come right over to straighten things out and scrub the voluntary postings.

Corporal Reeves heard him out but bleakly.

"Well, I don't know whether it began as a joke or not," he said, "but it's no joke now, chum! I've just sent off a signal to Records with your names and numbers, so you can laugh it off on the boat! In the meantime, get cleared and don't forget the M.O. It's Sunday and he don't like Sunday sick parades!"

It was, as Horace had suspected, quite useless to attempt to undo Pedlar's act. News that two of the permanent staff had actually volunteered for an overseas draft spread out from S.H.Q. like a heath fire. Men discussed it gravely over their tea, biscuits, and the *News of the World.* It had reached the officers' mess before midday and the Four-Wing adjutant, learning that the volunteers were his bodies, donned a mantle of virtue, discussing the news with the air of a proud parent whose no-good sons had unexpectedly distinguished themselves by an act of heroism.

"You don't have to snoop around *my* wing looking for good types," he told the newly arrived photographic officer, as they played a quiet game of snooker in the games room. "My bods are mad keen to get overseas! Matter of morale y'know. It's the pep talks I give 'em every other Thursday!"

Even the M.O. received Pedlar and Pope with affability.

"Thank God I wasn't called over here on a Sunday to look at a bunch of malingerers," he said heartily. "Volunteers! That's what I like to hear about! Chaps who really want to get into the war, instead of loafing about at home dodging parades, going sick, and putting W.A.A.F.s in the family way! There now, I hardly need to look at you, do I? Cough! That's right! Now give me a sample in the bottle—I thought so—sound as a bell, both of you! Well, the best of luck, troops, and I wish I was coming with you!"

Horace made no response to this speech. By now he was in a state of profound apathy. He moved here and there in a half-daze, proffering his grimy clearance chit for signatures, undressing, dressing, and answering questions in a toneless voice. His brain was still numb with shock and remained so, even after Pedlar had packed their kitbags and stowed them aboard the train. He hardly spoke during the long, dismal journey up to Keston Point, the Personnel Despatch Center on the coast, whereas Pedlar, smarting under a sense of bewilderment and injustice, made no effort to reopen the subject of the posting.

Popey was displeased when he should have been pleased and did not, it seemed, prefer this alternative to a shotgun wedding with Iris. Why this should be so Pedlar did not understand. As long as they were together it did not matter to him where they went. One camp or country was as good as another but obviously Popey did not feel this way about it. He wanted to escape from Iris and her father but not, it appeared, by steamship. He had stopped abusing his friend but he made no effort to restore friendly relations, sitting steeped in depression, avoiding Pedlar's anxious eyes and saying nothing when tea and sandwiches were pressed into his hands at the junction, or comments were made upon interesting sights to be seen through the carriage windows.

In this way they arrived at the railway station nearest to the P.D.C. and were gathered into the lorry that met every train, even the Sunday trains. Ten minutes later they were filing through Reception, filling in more forms and answering more questions. Pedlar had to answer some of the questions on Horace's behalf, for his friend did not seem to hear the demands for information barked at him by permanent staff men, whose job was to sift the stream of woebegone airmen parading before them. Pedlar shepherded his friend into a bare-looking hut near the parade ground and coaxed him out of his restrictive webbing equipment.

"You take it easy, Popey," he said gently, as he lifted Horace's unresisting legs on to the mattress. "I'll go and get something from the N.A.A.F.I. and take a look around."

Pope nodded but said nothing. Even now he could hardly believe that he was here, actually inside a dreaded P.D.C., and due, within a matter of days, hours perhaps, to hump his kitbag up a gangway and sail to some embattled corner of the world, where he might encounter real live Germans or Japs, firing real live bullets at him. It was a comfort, perhaps, that he would never get that far, that soon, in the middle of the night he would grope his way on deck as torpedoes tore their way into the ship. Then, together, he and Pedlar would take the plunge and the waves would close over them once and for all. There was comfort, he reflected, a tiny, microscopic crumb of comfort, in the fact that Pedlar could not swim and would drown alongside him, and perhaps his vast bulk would carry him to the bottom a moment or so in advance. It would have been too hard to bear if Pedlar had turned out to be a strong swimmer, capable of keeping himself afloat until rescued and leaving the victim of his lunatic action to drown.

Pondering this Horace went to sleep, lulled by the radio and the desultory conversation of a school of pontoon players at the end of the hut.

When Pedlar returned Horace looked so peaceful that the gypsy did not want to disturb him, so he covered him with two greatcoats and sat down on the adjoining bed to eat some biscuits.

The pontoon players took no notice of them. They had just been issued with an advance of pay and were absorbed in the game. As from far away Pedlar heard their calls: "Deal me another! and Another! Bust!" The radio played "Scatterbrain," and Horace slept.

Horace's black mood had disappeared by midday the following morning. It was impossible to remain depressed at Keston Point P.D.C. Far too much was going on, and the atmosphere of the camp was charged with a brittle, nervous excitement, rather like that of the prison of the Conciergerie at the height of the Terror.

The strain of waiting to go on the boat had the oddest effect upon discipline. It was not so much relaxed as wafted away on the sea breeze and the camp was thus a grotesque parody of the kind of establishment suggested by Whitehall propaganda efforts. Everybody in the camp was on the brink and once they got used to the idea depression from which all had suffered on passing inside the wire gave way to harsh jocularity and a devil-may-care panache of men caught up in an adventure that had no predictable outcome.

Little was to be feared in the way of reprisals from officers and N.C.O.s. Anyone who felt like it could stamp, shout, rave, dance or bawl themselves blue in the face, for there was no means of enforcing commands. Men reasoned that no punishment in the book was worse than being shipped overseas and a charge against them might even result in a cancellation of the posting. It was not that they were openly mutinous. They did not defy the hoarse and harassed N.C.O.s when they were shepherded into batches of a hundred or two hundred and marched here and there about the camp. They did what they were told but in their own time and fashion, shambling rather than marching, and exchanging audible and jocular remarks, such as the curious facial likeness between the escorting sergeant and a Barbary ape featured in the newspapers after its escape from Regent's Park during an air raid. Parades melted away without the formality of the "dismiss," the men aimlessly dispersing when somebody rang the N.A.A.F.I. bell for break. Airmen lit up on parade, that is, all save the rank facing the N.C.O. in charge, and when this happened the hapless fellow in charge could be seen prancing about screaming, "No smoking! No smoking I said!" as a cloud of tobacco smoke drifted up from the ranks screened by the men in front.

Everyone abandoned the tiresome business of button and boot cleaning. Nobody saluted officers, or, if they did, saluted with a curious irony, infinitely insulting in its quivering perfection.

There was nothing the permanent staff could do about this regrettable slide into slaphappy chaos. The guardroom was already qualifying as a Black Hole of Calcutta, and prisoners awaiting trial leaned out of the barred windows and made rude noises at passing wing commanders who drove heedlessly by in big cars. Jankers' squads, booked on trivial offenses, threw potatoes at one another instead of peeling them, or fenced with the long, pointed sticks they had been given to spear the rubbish lying about the camp.

A strong group of N.C.O.s, whose own future was secure, might have restored a certain amount of order, but the morale of the permanent staff was in very poor shape. Its numbers were constantly decimated to fill gaps in drafts as, here and there, a man wriggled off the hook, grabbed his railway warrant and fled. Even the orderly room staff was not safe from these last-minute substitutions. The clerks hardly had time to get to know one another before they were themselves inoculated, kitted out, and marched off down the road to the embarkation point at Slipsands.

This made everyone very irritable and jumpy. Clerks scamped their duties and stayed out of sight as much as possible, like civilians caught up among the garrison of a besieged city who might, at any time, be told to man the walls and beat off attacks.

Horace and Pedlar attended a parade on the first morning. It was called, someone said, for the purpose of a short-arm inspection and proved to be such a happy, uninhibited assembly that Horace cheered up almost at once.

A lean flight sergeant, with a nervous tic in his left cheek, had been ordered to prevent the parade from dispersing until the M.O. was ready, but the task was beyond his powers. He kept marching round and round the billowing ranks, jabbing men in the chest and the back and shouting, "Keep still! Fall in!" When these orders had no apparent effect he shouted piteously that he would "walk in the sea till me hat floats!"

Pedlar felt very sorry for him but was nonetheless fascinated by the N.C.O.'s steadily twitching cheek and unconsciously began to practice it, an endeavor that, together with his height, singled him out for special attention and seemed to annoy the flight sergeant very much.

"You're mocking me!" he roared, prodding the immovable Pedlar with his knuckled hand. "You're bloody well mocking me, you big Swede! I'll slap you on a charge! I'll walk in the sea till me hat floats!"

This double threat delighted the men near Pedlar and they abandoned their loose formation and surrounded the twitching couple.

"Let him alone, Chiefie!" shouted an L.A.C. "Stop making fun of the afflicted!"

This sally was greeted by roars of approval and even the front ranks turned about and began to circle Pedlar and the flight sergeant. There were ribald shouts of: "Victimization!" "Send 'im to the M.O.!" and "Sending blokes overseas with the twitch!"

Horace stood quietly by, fascinated by the scene. The chorus of catcalls, and the pressure of the men on all sides of him, at last drove the flight sergeant into a frenzy. He waved his arms and spun about, screaming commands and leaping this way and that, his tic accelerating to an alarming rate. Just then someone across the square shouted "Tea up!" and jangled a bell. The parade suddenly lost interest in Pedlar and the flight sergeant and began to surge toward the N.A.A.F.I., carrying the struggling flight sergeant along with it.

"Blimey!" said Horace, "this is some camp, ain't it, Pedlar? I wouldn't mind stopping here a bit! Never seen such a shambles!"

Fortified by the tea, the men were easier to handle when the parade reassembled. A glaring bullfrog of a warrant officer had now replaced the twitching flight sergeant, and the men were marched over to the M.I. Center for their short-arm inspection. Here they were examined by a laconic flying officer, who walked slowly along the inward-facing ranks, but made no comment upon the assorted display. After that they all went along to the equipment shed and were issued tropical kit, which they carried back to their billets and by then it was time for dinner.

The same happy-go-lucky atmosphere prevailed inside the mess hall. When a young pilot officer put in an appearance and asked "Any complaints?" in an anxious and squeaky voice, five-hundred airmen rose as one man and gave him a generous broadside, flourishing sausages impaled on forks and expressing all manner of opinions regarding the obscurity of the cook's birth and ancestry. Impressed by this enthusiasm the pilot officer went so far as to sample a sausage, masticating it slowly, while the men nearest him quieted down, awaiting his comments.

He finally swallowed the sausage with a gulp and said: "Ha! Ha, yes! Indeed!" after which he hurriedly withdrew into the kitchen, from whence he effected an escape into the parade ground and was seen no more.

Three or four days passed in this way and then Horace's group was issued with a generous advance of pay and told that they would be embarked in the next forty-eight hours.

The news sobered Horace, who had been enjoying himself in a modest way. Half his mind was still groping with possibilities of escape but the various avenues he had explored had proved culs-de-sac. In sober tones he suggested a last night out in the old country and that evening they booked out of camp and hitched into Slipsands, a largish port possessing a disproportionate number of hostelries.

It was in one of these, The Steam Packet, that Horace first discovered his friend's astonishing capacity for beer. He had, of course, shared many pitchers of beer with Pedlar at Blackrock and Heathfield but had never noticed that the gypsy's capacity for beer was as vast as everything else about him, or that his outstanding abilities as a toper might be turned to profit.

When they first entered the pub a group of Australian air-

114

men were there, engaged in some kind of contest around the upright piano.

A big navigator was playing a version of "Underneath the Spreading Chestnut Tree" and at his elbow stood an auburn-haired air-gunner, also Australian, who was holding a pint mug filled to the brim.

At the command "Now!" the pianist struck a long chord and then sailed into the chorus, the other men roaring a parody of the song that went:

Here's to Ginger, he's true blue!
He's a Digger through and through!
Drink it down-down-down-down-down-down-*DOWN!*
Drink it down, down, down, down, *dooooown!*

On the opening chord the air-gunner had raised his glass to his lips and on the last "down" but two he had crashed an empty tankard on the piano top. The feat earned him a round of applause from all present.

"Lumme, that's ruddy marvelous!" said Horace admiringly. "I seen some quick drinking in me time but never that quick! He muster downed it in fifteen seconds dead!"

Pedlar was far less impressed. "Giddon, I could drink it much quicker'n that!" he said mildly.

Horace gave him a shrewd look. "You could? You mean that, Pedlar?"

"Ar!" said Pedlar. "There's nothing to that, Popey! Nothing!"

Horace was impressed but slightly skeptical. "You sure, Pedlar? You absolutely sure?"

"Yes," said Pedlar modestly, "fact is, I don't get no flavor if I don't mop it back quick! You seen me, haven't you?"

"Come to think of it I 'ave," said Horace thoughtfully, "but I didn't take no special note. Here, half a tick . . ." and he got up and approached the air-gunner, who had returned to the bar for a refill.

"That's pretty good, Sarge," he told the Australian, "but I got a pal here who could knock three seconds off your time!"

"Yeah?" said the pianist. "Care to bet on it, cobber?"

"That's the idea I got in mind," said Horace, and taking a pound note from his breast pocket he laid it on the bar.

The Australians, scenting a contest, at once gathered round. Beer was purchased and Horace placed both tankards on the piano top, ordering Pedlar to take up his position on the far side of the pianist.

Solemnly the chorus was chanted and the mugs were lifted and emptied. The air-gunner knocked a second off his previous time and finished on the last "down" but three, but in spite of this improvement he was well behind Pedlar.

The gypsy had emptied his tankard before the choir had reached the end of the third line.

The Australians proved good losers and at once suggested a second contest, with stakes double or quits. Pound notes piled up on the bar. All the English airmen backed Pedlar and the Australians reinvested in their air-gunner.

"I get better as I go along," he told them, rocking on his heels.

Everybody in the bar gathered round, but the air-gunner pleaded that as he had been heavily engaged before Pedlar appeared on the scene he was entitled to a moment or two in the open. There were cries of protest from the Englishmen but Horace held up his hand.

"Fair enough!" he said, and as the Australian and the pianist left he whispered to Pedlar: "Play to lose this one mate and we come up on the next!"

It was almost a dead-heat but Horace conceded the match and then proposed a third and final round, with a jackpot of five pounds, loser to pay for the beer.

"Win this one, cock!" he told Pedlar, as the men crowded round the stakeholder to get their money on, and Pedlar won it with ease, returning his empty tankard to the piano top before the choir was halfway through the chorus and the air-gunner still had a gill of beer in his mug.

"Now I seen everything!" said the navigator, but he spoke too soon, for the air-gunner suddenly crumpled up and fell across his shoulders, doubling him up and driving his face against the piano keys. At that moment an air-raid siren began to wail and the barman shouted: "Beat it, lads! It's gone time and the civvy police'll be round!"

The Australians ignored him, as they ignored all orders. In any case they were too busy extricating the navigator from beneath the unconscious air-gunner. The navigator's face had struck the keys with considerable force. He had lost a tooth and his lip was bleeding. When they got him out he kept dabbing his mouth with a khaki handkerchief and shouting "The bahstah'd! The bahstah'd!" over and over again, but Horace had no opportunity to discover whether his abuse was intended for Pedlar or for the air-gunner who had fallen on him, for at that moment aircraft zoomed over and the first stick of bombs fell in the docks area, about a hundred yards away. The pub rocked and glasses crashed to the floor, customers following them as splinters from shattered windows flew in every direction.

It was probable that the Australians had not heard the siren because the sergeant at once exclaimed: "Jesus! It's the mucking war!" and made a sudden rush for the exit. Before he could reach it the second bomb fell on a warehouse immediately opposite and it seemed to Horace that the world about him disintegrated. The pub windowframe fell out in a single piece and half the ceiling came down, extinguishing all the lights and filling the bar with reeking dust.

As he dived under the large wooden bench on which Pedlar had been sitting he heard the third and fourth bombs detonate farther down the road and wondered fleetingly if he was dead. Then, after a moment's comparative silence, he heard Pedlar's urgent voice coming from very close at hand and felt the gypsy's huge hand grope across his face.

"That you, Popey? You okay, Popey? Where are you, Popey? Say something, Popey!"

Popey said: "Pipe down, Pedlar, I got an idea!"

He had, too, a stupendous idea, but he wanted a moment or two to shape it and view it impersonally.

It is true that after the first shock of arriving at the Personnel Despatch Center he had soon recovered confidence in himself, but he was still far from being his optimistic self, a man

117

ready and eager to match himself against the machine that had caught him up and was tossing him here and there without purpose or design. He had enjoyed watching the demonstrations of high spirits and the gusty indiscipline of the camp, but had taken no active part in the ragging.

Most of the time his mind had been occupied with ways and means of extricating himself and, if possible, Pedlar, from this slow, grinding process that threatened to reduce them to the status of ordinary airmen, humping kitbags up a steep gangway to a troopship and waiting passively to be taken halfway across the world and set down somewhere within easy reach of Germans and Japs.

Somewhere, *somewhere* he told himself over and over again, there must be a chink in the system, a fissure wide enough for two men to wriggle through and back into the world of opportunity. He was aware by now that if they had arrived at this camp a year ago, or even six months ago, they would have soon found a way out of it, probably within forty-eight hours, but by this time Authority had had leisure to sew up the loopholes. All the hoary old pleas, a wife's pregnancy, an aged, failing mother, a neglected business, a torn cartilage that resulted in headlong tumbles on parade, had grown blue whiskers. Each failed to scale the outer defenses of the orderly room and accumulated, like dishonored checks, in the clerk's wire baskets, spilling over onto the floor and drifting about under the boots of the men who popped in from time to time to see how their applications were getting along.

It was as though the P.D.C. staff, worn down by an interminable siege, had now retreated into the citadel, double-locked the gates, posted sharpshooters on the walls, and turned indifferent backs on the rabble outside. Horace had circled the walls a dozen times without finding so much as a hair-crack that offered a promising foothold.

Now, as the dust settled in the shattered bar, and men began scrambling over him in the dark, cursing and calling to one another, he saw at once how this unlooked-for incident might be used as a scaling ladder. He spat plaster from his mouth, gingerly checked his body in order to make sure that he was not a real casualty, and then called softly to Pedlar, who was rummaging round on his hands and knees shouting "Popey! Popey!" in the pleading tones of a mother whose child has disappeared in the blackout.

"Stow it, Pedlar," he said suddenly and irritably, "I'm okay! Come over here and mind the flippin' glass, it's all over the place!"

Pedlar grunted with relief and scrawled across to him where he sat behind the bench.

"Lumme, Popey, that was a near go, wasn't it? I thought you'd bought it proper that time! I did, honest, I thought you was gone!"

By this time the Australians had found their way into the street and an ambulance clanged past.

In the beam of its headlights they saw that the structure of the taproom was still sound and that damage had been limited to blast. Everyone else, including the barman, appeared to have scrambled out into the street and hurried off in the direction of the docks where several hits had been registered.

"Listen, Pedlar," said Horace, speaking quietly and very slowly, "if we play our cards right this is our *out*, get me? I heard our draft was for the boat day after tomorrow, but if it is then you an' me'll be missing, see? We're casualties! We copped it, the night the docks was pranged, understand?"

"No," said Pedlar anxiously, "not really, Popey. I'm okay and you weren't hit, were you? If you was I could . . ."

And he began to scramble up but Horace grabbed him by the sleeve.

"Sit down, Sloppy, and lissen! This is our chance, see? We *copped* it! They don't put air-raid casualties on the boat, do they?"

The bare outline of Horace's plan finally got through to Pedlar. "You mean we both do a bunk, Popey?"

"No!" growled Horace, "I don't mean nothing of the sort! Where's the sense in that? The S.P.s would have us in no time and besides, I'm game to stay in the ruddy outfit so long as we stay on my terms! I mean we mump! We let on we're proper shaken up! I'm deaf in one ear, see? And you?" He thought

119

hard for a moment; "You're so shocked you've lost your perishing memory! Lumme, that ought to come natural enough! You don't know who you are, nor what you're doin' here. You just look bloody stoopid all the time and leave all the talking to me, get me?"

"What'll happen to us then?" asked Pedlar, but without apprehension, for he trusted Horace implicitly.

"We'll go to a civvy hospital and it might even be days before they trace us. If we act up enough we'll still be in bed when the boat sails and after that . . . I dunno, maybe they'll transfer us to Sick Quarters for observation, and then we'll be attached to permanent staff at the camp, or posted somewhere else. Now mind what I said! You don't remember nothing till I say you do and you leave all the gab to me, understand? There might even be a pension in this if we play our cards right!"

There was a bustle outside as more ambulances arrived and emergency lighting was rigged up in the street. The Australian observer looked through the shattered windowframe and seeing them gave a yelp of recognition.

"Jesus, it's that human sponge and his sidekick!" he shouted, and when they made no response to his hail he fetched an ambulance man, who ran in and demanded their names and numbers.

Horace parried his questions, standing up and staggering about with both hands pressed to his ears.

"I'm proper shook up," he said. "Sort've all muggy in me napper! And as for 'im"—he nodded toward Pedlar—"there's something funny about him . . . seems kind of shell-shocked, don't you, mate?"

"You'd better get in the ambulance and come up to the hospital for a checkup," said the ambulance attendant. "Anyone else cop it in here?"

"No," said Horace, still massaging his ears, "they all went out, I think, but what's all that water rushing? Burst main, is it?"

"Water? What water?" asked the attendant.

"That roaring sound—like perishin' Niagara!" said Horace. "I never heard nothin' like it! 'Ere!"—with great urgency—"we'd better get out of here before we're drowned, mate!" and he seized Pedlar by the arm and began to drag him toward the gaping window.

The attendant scribbled something in a notebook and then became excessively gentle.

"Here, let me help you chaps! . . . Hi there! . . . Couple of R.A.F. types need help! Put 'em in the balance, Buster!" and a dozen hands reached out and guided Horace and Pedlar through the door and out into the street.

"Sure you can walk?" asked the ambulance man, as they stumbled over piles of debris toward the open space, where a row of ambulances were parked.

"Don't you bother with me," said Horace stoutly, "you look after my mate. He's the worst, I reckon, he don't say nothing sensible! I'm okay, 'cept for that perishin' waterfall!"

"I think it's ear trouble," said the attendant sympathetically.

"No," said Horace firmly, "I can drink any amount o' beer. Besides, we'd only sunk a couple o' pints when the bomb dropped, hadn't we, Pedlar?"

Before Pedlar could reply they were stowed in the ambulance and tucked round with blankets. Nobody climbed in after them.

"That's fine," said Horace approvingly, as the doors closed and the vehicle moved off, "keep it up, mate, and we're almost 'ome!"

They were very busy in the out-patient's ward at the big hospital on the hill, and for more than an hour Horace and Pedlar sat side by side on a bench, while doctors and nurses bustled in and out, making notes and calling patients' names in arrogant, hectoring tones. Horace began to feel that they might be overlooked.

"Pedlar," he said, "sing something, loud as you can!"

Pedlar did not question the order but began to sing "This Old Coat of Mine" at the top of his voice until a student nurse,

121

wheeling an empty trolley through the ward, stopped and shouted: "Keep quiet there! How dare you! I say, how dare you?"

"No good nagging 'im, Nurse," Horace told her, with a side-long grimace, "he's clean off his chump, I reckon! Shock, the ambulance man said. You'd better fetch him some 'ot sweet tea and I'll have a cup meself too, but first do something for me, will you? Turn all them perishin' taps off, before we get flooded out!"

The nurse looked more flustered than ever. Pedlar continued to sing, beating time with his hands. He saw that he was pleasing Horace and was prepared if need be to sing all night.

"Make him stop singing and I'll get some tea," screamed the nurse, and then: "What taps are running? And where?"

"Like a waterfall," said Horace dreamily, "just like a flippin' waterfall!" He tapped his ear significantly and nudged Pedlar. "That's enough, mate," he said sharply, "you don't sing that kind o' song in front o' ladies!"

Pedlar stopped singing and the student nurse hurried away and fetched a doctor. Ten minutes later Horace and Pedlar were in bed, side by side, and the nurse, smiling now, brought them mugs of hot sweet tea.

They remained in bed for the better part of the week, their identities having been established after a tiresome amount of phoning on the part of the hospital staff. The delay was occasioned by Horace's thoughtful destruction of their identity cards a moment or so before they were seen by the house surgeon on the morning after the raid.

The doctor was an earnest young man, fresh from Edinburgh, and once Horace had made up his mind that he was a fool things went very smoothly for them. The doctor was very interested in neurology, and spent a good deal of his time during morning rounds trying to coax Pedlar to talk. For a long time he was unsuccessful. Pedlar looked happy enough, propped up in bed and beaming genially at everyone who brought him food, drinks and radio earphones, but he followed Horace's initial instructions so literally that Horace began to fear he was overdoing it and might get whisked off to a neurasthenic center at any moment.

On the fifth day, when the doctor was standing between their beds, Horace volunteered some gratuitous information about his friend.

"He's been talking, Doctor," he said hopefully. "He asked for the bottle in the middle o' the night!"

"He did? That's splendid," said the doctor, rubbing his hands, "we'll have another go, shall we?"

He sat down on the edge of Pedlar's bed and twinkled at him.

"Well, old man, are we going to have a little chat today?" he asked pleasantly.

Pedlar looked interrogatively at Horace, who nodded encouragingly.

"Say anything," the doctor said encouragingly, "say anything that comes into your head, old chap! We want you to get used to the sound of your own voice again, you see, so say anything at all!"

The sister and a staff nurse joined the group and they all looked fondly at Pedlar, who licked his lips and grinned.

"Pope!" said Pedlar obligingly, and everyone relaxed a little.

"There now, that's very interesting," said the doctor. "He's a Catholic no doubt!"

"No," said the staff nurse, "he's got 'C. of E.' on his identity disc, look!" and she lifted the disc from the bedrail.

They were all rather crestfallen at this but Horace chimed in. "Pope's my name," he volunteered, "and him saying it had made me remember who I am!"

The doctor leaned forward and patted Pedlar's shoulder.

"We've found out all about you, old chap," he said, "and I expect you'd like one of the nurses to drop a line to your mother, wouldn't you?"

Pedlar stopped smiling. "No," he said, with considerable emphasis, "I'm buggered if I would!"

The doctor tut-tutted and the staff nurse smothered a giggle.

"He don't get on very well with his mother," said Horace,

feeling that some explanation was necessary. "He never writes to 'er and she never writes to him!"

"I see," said the doctor dryly, and then, "Your hearing seems to be improving today!"

"I'm glad to say it is," said Horace cheerfully. "The waterfall has stopped and all I'm getting now is a lot o' popping, like a motorbike going up an 'ill in the distance!"

The doctor stood up and gave the sister some instructions about the patients, before moving off down the ward.

"That's about it for now," said Horace, when they were all out of earshot. "You c'n give over acting daft, Pedlar, and we'll shift over to camp Sick Quarters. There's no sense in pushing our luck. We missed 105 Draft and if we play it right we'll be downgraded and that'll keep us off the next perishin' draft and the one after that!"

"Anything you say, Popey," replied Pedlar. "Anything you say!"

They were moved over to the camp Sick Quarters the following afternoon and spent another fortnight there under observation. The popping in Horace's ears faded to a crackling, "like dead leaves rustling in a wood," and on discharge from hospital they were temporarily downgraded, just as Horace had predicted.

Their case presented the P.D.C. orderly room with a vexing problem. They could not be added to a fresh draft owing to the change in their medical category and ordinarily they would have been reposted to Heathfield, a prospect that somewhat alarmed Horace, until he learned from an orderly room clerk that Heathfield now had its full quota of aircraft hands and that a direct application for a fresh posting had been made to Records on their behalf.

In the end they went off to Craddock Wood, a small maintenance unit, deep in the Northamptonshire woods.

It was late spring when they set off on their cross-country journey and the warm temperature and general mildness of the atmosphere must have communicated itself to Horace, for he hummed softly to himself while Pedlar stowed their kitbags on the carriage rack.

"This time," he told Pedlar, "we'll try an' get really dug in. The longer you stay in a camp the less likelihood there is of you being winkled out and now we got to get dug in for the duration, see? I'm fair sick of humping that perishin' great bag all over the auction, like we bin doin' ever since we come unstuck in that Pool at the Recruits' Training Center!"

Pedlar did not answer that never once during their odyssey had Horace's kitbag rested on its owner's shoulders, or that as often as not, Horace's respirator was dangling from Pedlar's own by a strap. As long as Pope was taking care of things nothing mattered. Everything would turn out all right and as far as he cared the war might go on forever and ever. He put his feet on the seat opposite, closed his eyes and dozed, and from across the compartment Horace studied his friend's big, lopsided face. As he did so there came to him, for the very first time in their association, a conscious acknowledgment of the gypsy's homage, and with it something altogether foreign to Horace—a vague and slightly irksome sense of responsibility for the big, helpless Swede. He shrugged it off, but it returned again and again as the train rattled southeast across the country and finally he was obliged to accept it as a condition of their present situation.

Having done this he was able to relax while Pedlar snored. He puffed slowly at his cigarette, promising himself a long, cooling beer at the first junction.

CHAPTER SEVEN

Number 2130 Maintenance Unit was situated deep in the Northamptonshire Woods, some four miles from the nearest village. It had little connection with the R.A.F. and none at all with the war then being waged against German Fascism.

Far back at the beginning of the war, when the M.U. had been used as a depot for aircraft parts, it had been a busy little community, with convoys coming and going and wide-awake security men picketed in the glades alongside the approaches from the railhead, at Smedley Junction, but since then global events had overtaken and passed Craddock Wood, the decline commencing about the time of Dunkirk. Its stocks of spare parts were for types of aircraft no longer used in the air war, its staff had dwindled to a rump, and long rows of Nissen huts were empty and falling into decay. The civilian security guards went elsewhere, to lie in wait for bonafide visitors behind other clumps of trees, screening other and more important depots.

The camp should, of course, have been closed down and left derelict, but nobody at the Air Ministry had remembered to give the necessary orders, so it continued to exist as a kind of ghost camp, with weeds sprouting in its avenues, its farmhouse S.H.Q. half-hidden in nettles and undergrowth, its small permanent staff slouching about the clearings like the miners of a gold rush town years after the local vein has been played out. It was now used as a depot for unwanted packing cases and for all the contribution it made to the war effort of the Grand Alliance it might just as well have stocked chain mail or arrowheads.

For all that Craddock Wood continued to function and had even developed a bizarre life of its own. It was now something like Pitcairn Island, years after the civil strife had passed but years before the island was rediscovered by mariners, and it probably owed such vitality as it possessed to its patriarch, Squadron Leader the Rt. Hon. Oswald Tankerlieu, affectionately known as "Kindly," ever since a facetious corporal (once a gagman in the music halls) had acknowledged the helping of turkey traditionally served by the officers on Christmas Day with a "Tankerlieu-Kindly, Sir!" a quip that had delighted everyone within hearing, including the C.O. himself.

The Rt. Hon. Oswald Tankerlieu was as much an anachronism as the camp he commanded. He might have been hand-picked for the job of presiding over No. 2130 M.U., for everything about him was archaic. The youngest son of the third generation of Tankerlieus to make a living out of chutney, he had passed Army Entrance Examination at the ninth sitting, after spending two years at a crammer's in Rottingdean. That was before the First World War, when cavalry still existed, and in due course Oswald had been assigned to a regiment of Dragoons and had spent the First World War preparing to exploit infantry breakthroughs that failed to materialize. As M.U. 2130 was now, as it were, a camp-in-waiting, Oswald was admirably suited to command it.

One way or another he had been waiting all his life. He had waited, booted and spurred, for the breakthrough at Neuve-Chapelle in 1915, and was sitting erect on his charger, ready to gallop forward and wheel behind fleeing Hun, in the successive Somme battles of 1916. He had developed a severe bout of sciatica while awaiting orders to advance on Passchendaele in 1917, but had recovered and actually ridden forward a mile or two in the final advance that preceded the Armistice of 1918.

Then, when at long last he was moving at a steady trot, the

cavalry was disbanded and he had waited in various camps for half-pay retirement, or a transfer to the Tanks, or to the R.A.F. He had never liked tanks since one had frightened his horse at St. Quentin in 1916, hurling him fully accoutered into a shellhole of slush, so that when they finally presented him with a choice he opted for the Royal Air Force and was sent to a flight training school.

Here he waited about until he was on hand to crash three aircraft and kill an instructor. After that he waited in hospital for his transfer to the Administrative Branch.

He did not take kindly to Admin. He could never remember the number of forms, or the correct legal procedure to be followed at the taking of summaries of evidence. He served on a number of court-martials and courts of enquiry, contributing to some very remarkable decisions, decisions to which time-serving men still refer in billet and N.A.A.F.I. when talk harks back to the halcyon days of the prewar R.A.F. Then the Second World War broke out and he and his unit were at once shipped off to France.

Throughout the period of the phony war Oswald waited for Hitler to advance and throw him into the Channel, but during the interim period he enjoyed himself, accounting for at least a bottle of cognac a day and organizing concerts to which the French villagers were invited and at which Oswald himself sang songs of the previous war. At his rendering of "Keep the Home Fires Burning" a gray-headed officer from an adjacent field artillery battery was so moved that he had to be assisted back to his quarters by a pair of anxious bombardiers.

Oswald was a merry, unexacting soul, fanatically conscious of Britain's military past, and very active in his interest in the welfare of "the cheps," a collective noun that he applied to everyone below the rank of "s'arnt." He had been, in fact he still was, a very keen sportsman. Sporting phrases colored his everyday speech. If a document was mislaid (and a document grew as many legs as a centipede as soon as it entered Craddock Wood) he told his adjutant, or the orderly room corporal, "to put a ferret in and flush it out!" He referred to all administrative difficulties as "hairy fences" and usually summoned his runner by a sharp toot on a hunting horn that always reposed on the top of his "In" tray.

He was small, wiry and slightly bowlegged, with a florid, narrow face, bisected by an enormous cavalry moustache. His flushed complexion, and the swathe of black hairs that grew along his nose toward gray, arching eyebrows, misled many people into thinking him a martinet. He was anything but this. The only thing that really irritated him was administrative detail, referred to by him as "bumff, pure bumff!"

The administrative weight of No. 2130 M.U. was shouldered by Corporal Gittens, a former auction-room clerk, who had his own and highly original ideas about R.A.F. procedure.

Gittens was sometimes assisted, but in a half-hearted and vacillating manner, by the adjutant, Flying Officer Trumper, a glum, moon-faced young man who had been on the point of taking holy orders when war broke out but had changed his mind and was now regretting it.

Trumper, born and raised in a suburb, was awed by the C.O., who conformed to his idea of a real country gent, but he was a conscientious young man and could never quite reconcile the squadron leader's accent and manner with his hopeless irresponsibility. The C.O. never seemed to care, for instance, how the airmen looked on parade. He himself was always faultlessly dressed but the men could straggle about like a flock of tramps in search of Salvation Army soup for all he seemed to care. He never pulled them up or dressed them down, not even when they lurched past him without bothering to salute. He found it far less exacting to think of them all as "good types, jolly good types," although Trumper had a growing suspicion that this was not really so, that in any properly run camp any one of the men would have been pounced upon by the Service Police and wheeled in with their hats off before they could shout "Jankers!" Trumper said nothing of his private misgivings, however, but he continued to worry over his incoming mail, most of which was absolutely incomprehensible to him.

He also answered the telephone for Corporal Gittens, who usually ignored it, particularly if he was deep in a paperback Western.

The corporal was much addicted to Westerns and owned a great stack of them. His absorption with pioneers like Wild Bill Hickok and Wyatt Earp encouraged him to wear the only offensive weapon ever seen in Craddock Wood, namely the C.O.'s Webley pistol. He was never without this and sometimes used it to shoot rats.

There were a great many rats at No. 2130 M.U. They lived among the pyramids of crates that had accumulated from the steady flow of empties arriving at Smedley Junction every Friday. Nobody knew why these crates continued to arrive, where they came from, or what was to be done with them, but they continued to pour in in batches of about fifty a time, until every glade and clearing in the camp was stacked with them, large oblong crates that looked like unplaned coffins, most of them stuffed with shavings and cotton waste. The pyramids of crates gave the woods a macabre look, as though somebody was expecting a bloody battle or a devastating epidemic of plague in the district.

The arrival of the boxes each Friday was the only event that maintained the link between No. 2130 M.U. and the R.A.F. as a whole.

The train carrying the boxes was met at the junction, where the crates were unloaded, put onto lorries, driven up to the wood, unloaded, and afterward abandoned.

Apart from this weekly chore there were one or two half-hearted parades, some desultory litter-clearing, meals always on time, a lottery session every evening, a concert or two by an E.N.S.A. team who arrived, performed and fled, and a great deal of card-playing, skylarking and free love in and around the pyramids of crates. For the rest nothing much happened and nobody wanted anything to happen.

Shortly before Horace and Pedlar arrived at the camp there had been a sensational change in camp personnel. Two dozen airmen had been posted away and replaced, nobody could imagine why, by a draft of forty-eight W.A.A.F.s, all newly joined recruits.

The male survivors of the purge welcomed the change. Hitherto those who sought female company had been obliged to hitchhike into Smedley and hang around the Y.M.C.A. canteen and street corners in search of women, but now there were nearly enough girls to go around and the woods, as well as the endless corridors of crates, afforded ideal cover for the development of warm and mutually satisfying friendships.

This epidemic was encouraged by the C.O. himself. For some time now he had been the frequent guest of a middle-aged widow at Craddock Hall, a large Georgian house that lay in the shallow valley below the wood. Odds were being laid in camp as to whether the widow would bring Squaddy Kindly to the boil before the Air Ministry woke up to the continued existence of the camp and posted him somewhere else.

The advent of the W.A.A.F. contingent complicated matters for the squadron leader, the sole officer among the W.A.A.F. party being a spinster in her late thirties. Her sole object in abandoning an ailing father in the Cotswolds, and enlisting in the W.A.A.F., had been a reckless determination to find a husband. Any husband would do and she booked into the camp with a blithe heart, but after a few sterile exchanges with the moon-faced would-be parson she had changed direction and swooped down on the C.O. like a starved bird of prey.

Now in addition to being a keen sportsman the squadron leader was a very accommodating man and for a time he did his very best to keep both widow and the section officer reasonably happy, but as spring advanced across the woods he began to feel hunted and tried hard to persuade Flying Officer Trumper to take the section officer off his hands.

He had heard that the widow was, as he put it in a letter to his brother, "very comfortable indeed," and had more or less made up his mind to propose to her and then apply for a discharge. He was over fifty now and had been waiting for something like this to turn up for a long time. He was happy

131

enough where he was but who knew what disconcerting information might appear in the next mail, uprooting him and posting him off to the Far East, or maybe to a real camp, where they had proper parades and both officers and airmen were expected to have haircuts and polished buttons.

The rest of the men took the W.A.A.F. party in their stride or rather in their shuffle. The occupied billets, always unkempt, now degenerated into rural slums and huge stacks of boxes began to spill over on to the parade ground. Then the food began to deteriorate, as L.A.C. Tovey, the cook and butcher who had supervised the kitchen for as long as anyone could remember, fell madly in love with the brunette assistant sent to help him and spent most of his time in the woods, or on the racks in the flour store. Other N.C.O.s and airmen cultivated similar friendships and a succession of long sighs and sudden giggles could be heard from behind almost every clump of trees or stack of boxes at any time of the day or night.

Slowly the social pattern of the camp began to change. None of the married men at Craddock Wood applied for living-out passes, or for what Corporal Gittens in the orderly room referred to as passionate leave. Soon there was an Arcadian air over Craddock Wood and it would not have seemed very surprising if, on taking a stroll down the main avenue between the sagging, weed-screened huts, one could have heard the toot of the merry, merry pipes of Pan, or seen an airman attired as a shepherd chasing a blue-uniformed nymph across the box-strewn parade ground.

As far as could be judged only two people in the camp were dissatisfied with this happy state of affairs. One was the ex-candidate for the priesthood, who sat in the boxlike adjutant's office adjoining Squaddy Kindly's headquarters, and the other was Section Officer Flora McNaughton, the C.O. of the W.A.A.F.s who, as the bluebells began to sprout along the whispering glades, was conscious of the fact that rank alone prevented her from taking glorious advantage of this idyllic situation. As an officer she could hardly join in the fun available to other ranks of both sexes, whereas the irritating old roué in command of the camp, who would have done very well to go on with, was clearly in search of richer pastures lower down the valley.

The adjutant, a self-effacing man, concealed his anxieties, taking refuge in a study of Peake's *Commentary on the Bible,* but Section Officer Flora was not a self-effacing woman. She had not, after all, exchanged the boredom of village life in the Cotswolds for a commission in the W.A.A.F. simply in order to watch other people enjoy themselves and after a month or so at Craddock Wood the sense of deprivation began to boil up inside her and she had to let off steam somehow. She took it out on the W.A.A.F.s, ordering daily hut inspections, then morning and afternoon parades, and then an orgy of brass cleaning and kit inspections. She informed her sergeant, who was in love with the equipment corporal, that she intended to clean up this pigsty of a camp and install a sense of order and discipline into the ranks of the female personnel. The sergeant did not take her very seriously at the time but then, once you had settled down among the crates, it was impossible to take things seriously at No. 2130 M.U. Craddock Wood.

Horace discovered all this within an hour or so of his arrival. He and Pedlar hung about Smedley Junction until they could hitch a lift three-parts of the way to camp, and then trudged on up the hill and into the woods via the unoccupied guardpost, situated at the commencement of the trees.

The wire gate of the camp precincts was not only open but hanging on a single hinge. There was a shed that did duty for a guardroom and Horace went in and hollered, but nobody showed up and they began to wonder if they had arrived at the right place.

"Seems funny," said Horace. "This place is like a flippin' morgue! Can you see anyone around, Pedlar? I never been in a camp that didn't have one S.P. on the gate!"

Pedlar put down the kitbags and advanced into the undergrowth. He had not moved a dozen yards before he trod on somebody who reared up and told him to look where he was going. The man he had stepped on was an L.A.C., and on looking a little closer Pedlar also saw a tousled W.A.A.F., who blushed, sat up, brushed some leaves from her skirt and said: "My! My! It must be Mr. Garth himself, Nobby!"

"I don't care if it's Tarzan," growled Nobby, "I don't go for Peeping Toms, big or little! Why didn't you holler, Lofty? Why do you want to sneak up on a feller?"

Pedlar explained mildly that he and A.C. Pope were new arrivals, posted from the P.D.C. up north, and the L.A.C.'s face cleared at once.

"Is that all? New here? Well, you're dead lucky! You don't know how lucky! This is a scrummy posting, mate! Amble down to the orderly room and get yourselves fixed up. You can't miss it, straight down the path and fork right!" And so saying he extended a hand to the W.A.A.F., yanked her to her feet, put his arm round her waist and led her deeper into the woods.

Pedlar returned to Horace and described the encounter.

"Sounds our cup o' tea," said Horace. "Come on, get the bags and let's find something to eat!"

They moved off down the path to the farmhouse which they mistook for a ruin on account of its high screen of docks and nettles. Inside, however, they unearthed Corporal Gittens, his feet on the table and a forgotten cigarette drooping from his lip, as he pursued Billy the Kid across Texan plains. He attended to them reluctantly.

"Posted here? A.C.H.'s? That's funny, we haven't had A.C.H.'s posted to us since I don't know when. Let's see your posting note."

They gave him their posting note and he shook his head doubtfully.

"Don't like the smell o' this," he said. "It means someone's still keeping track of us. We had the W.A.A.F.s, o' course, but that don't mean anything. Brass don't know what to do with all them W.A.A.F.s. Gotter send 'em somewhere. We haven't had an airman posted here for months."

Horace was a keen believer in careful reconnaissance.

"What's the matter with this dump?" he wanted to know. "Why wasn't there no guard on the gate?"

"What's he supposed to guard?" demanded Gittens. "A bloody great pile of empty crates?"

"Is that what you deal in here," asked Horace, "just crates?"

"That's all we want," said Gittens aggressively, "and don't you two go looking about for anything else! Best camp in the outfit this is! A dippy adjutant, a C.O. who don't believe in bull and stays outside the wire all day, plus forty-eight Judies who don't ask silly questions about whether a bloke's got a missis an' kids, like they generally do! What more could you want?"

"Nothing!" said Horace, "except regular grub, I guess."

"Ah," said the corporal, "you've put your finger on our weak spot there! Was okay but not lately. That was before Dai Tovey got stuck on that nifty little brunette in the cookhouse. Grub's been pretty grim since then. Dai's got too much on his mind, I reckon. Still, you can't have everything, can you?"

"No," said Horace mildly, "mostly you can't, Corp! Where do we sleep?"

"Take your choice," said Gittens, already returning to his paperback. "There's a dozen billets to choose from. Find one that don't leak and isn't too far from the coke dump!" He sat down, replaced his feet on the orderly-room table and forgot about them. They ventured a question or two but he ignored them. He was already riding with the posse along the banks of the Rio Grande.

There was, in fact, one W.A.A.F. in camp who was not as disinterested in the background of male personnel as Corporal Gittens implied. Horace and Pedlar heard a good deal about her during their first night in the M.U.

They took the corporal's advice and sought a billet within easy reach of the coke dump, but Horace also took care to choose one that was just as near the cookhouse. By this time Horace's entry into a new camp had developed into a drill. First he found a strategically situated billet and then he went to work on what he called the "key fiddles," that is, the Orderly Room, Transport, Equipment and Mess. Only when amiable relations had been established in all four spheres of influence could life in a new camp become tolerable, let alone profitable.

The billet he chose was a hut whose sole occupant, up to that time, had been L.A.C. Dai Tovey, the Craddock Wood cook and butcher.

Tovey, who had in peacetime been chef at the Owen Glendower Luncheon Rooms in Newport, Monmouthshire, was a thickset man with bowed shoulders, pleading eyes and the enormous personal resource of the much persecuted Celt. He had a curiously hunched walk, half furtive, half plodding, and when he crossed from billet to cookhouse he looked as though he ought to have been carrying a coracle on his back. Like every Celt he was an incurable romantic. He had a musical, singsong accent and an amiable disposition. Far from resenting the new arrivals' intrusion into his privacy he welcomed Horace and Pedlar as an audience for the airing of his personal problems. At that time he had problems of considerable complexity and each of them revolved about L.A.C.W. Evelyn Smithers, the W.A.A.F. cook, who was his official helpmate at the cookhouse.

L.A.C.W. Smithers, it appeared, was not merely Dai's *fille de guerre*, cheerfully reconciled to the sharing of his exile in the woods until it pleased Records to post one or both of them elsewhere, but a girl who had marked out the Welshman as her own. She was also a girl of unusually strong character, so strong that Dai had not yet dared admit to the existence of a plump wife and three children in Newport. Yet it was not this evasion that worried Dai.

Sooner or later, he said, Evelyn would discover his status, as every W.A.A.F. always discovered such facts. Horace himself had had firsthand experience of their resolution in this field when he had worked in the orderly rooms at Blackrock. W.A.A.F.s were always drifting in and hanging round in order to get a quick look at a man's Personal Service Record and see whether the space marked "Married or Single" had a penciled "M" or an "S" in the column. A married airman's claim to be unattached was routine flannel and a W.A.A.F. girlfriend's discovery of the truth an ultimate certainty. What distressed Dai far more was the demands L.A.C.W. Smithers made upon him now that their relationship had scaled Olympus and begun its humdrum descent into the plains.

"She's nothing but a slip of a girl and I could sit her on the palm of my hand, I could!" he explained, as the three of them lay in the billet, smoking and listening to a radio Forces concert of old-time waltzes, "but, man, she's got a fiery furnace inside her and calls on the stoker all the time! Mind you, it's not complaining I am," added the cook, "except that a man has his work to think of, don't you know? Seventy men and forty-eight girls there are in the camp, and only me and her to cook for them! And I take a pride in my work I do, but it's heavy work it is, heaving at all them great slabs of meat and sacks of one thing and another! 'Dai,' she says to me, suddenlike you know, when I'm opening a gross of herring, or brewing the ten-gallon tub of tea, 'Dai now, don't you love me no more?' Don't I love her no more, you understand? With me sandwiching my slap and tickle between the night-shift supper and day-guard breakfasts! It's dreading going on leave I am! Gwynneth will think me a writeoff, she will!"

The cook sighed and stretched himself, his arm swinging down and crushing his cigarette butt on the floor. "Ah, but that's beautiful music, that is! Always been partial to Strauss, I 'ave! Sometimes it reminds me of . . ." but Horace and Pedlar never heard what "Tales of Vienna Woods" did for the Welshman, for he dropped off to sleep in the middle of the speech and at once began to snore like a Snowdonian torrent.

This conversation had an immediate sequel. In the morning Dai Tovey suggested that Horace and Pedlar attach themselves to the cookhouse staff forthwith. He seemed to have forgotten his lamentations of the night before and went off to work whistling "Bread of Heaven," after telling the other two to come round and join him and Evie in the kitchens as soon as they had finished their breakfast.

Horace was rather disappointed when he met the L.A.C.W. He had always favored broad-hipped blondes, heavy, sleepy-eyed women, like the butcher's daughter at Heathfield, whereas Evie Smithers was small, dark and intense, with hair that made open mockery of W.A.A.F. regulations and not only cascaded over her overall collar but looped saucily over one violet eye, in excellent imitation of the current Veronica Lake vogue.

They helped the two cooks to prepare the camp's midday meal but during the morning Dai and the girl disappeared. Dai returned from an hour-long N.A.A.F.I. break beaming and sweating, and shortly afterwards the L.A.C.W. came back and went about her work with a quiet smile but with what seemed to Horace an unnecessary amount of clanging oven lids and rattling crockery.

Several days passed uneventfully and Horace and Pedlar slipped into the cookhouse routine. Nobody bothered them and they never attended a parade. No N.C.O.s came ranting into the kitchen, demanding to know why they were not at such and such a place at such and such a time, or why the ovens weren't polished, or the floor scoured. Queues of men appeared at the serving counter at regular intervals and were handed plates of stew, potatoes, corned beef, beans, slabs of cheese and other food. Pedlar did all the washing up and such scouring as Dai Tovey felt was necessary. Taken all round the work was unexacting.

Then, about a week or so after they had arrived at Craddock Wood, there was a minor explosion in the kitchen. Soon after breakfast one morning Section Officer Flora McNaughton sailed in, her sergeant at her heels, and began to rate Dai for the lack of variety in the fare, demanding to see the menu for the following day. Dai turned sulky. He never prepared menus but concocted and served up whatever came into his head, and he was not to be intimidated by a shrewish W.A.A.F. officer.

"It's answerable to the C.O. I am, Ma'am!" he told her sourly. "It's been cooking here close on a year I 'ave now, and yours is the first complaint I've had, isn't it?"

"How dare you talk like that to an officer!" blazed S.O. Mc-Naughton. "I'll have you on a charge, and this L.A.C.W. alongside you! Get this filthy place cleaned up and send me a copy of tomorrow's menu by 1200 hours, do you understand?"

"Nay, I don't that," said Dai, his accent thickening under

138

the stress of emotion, "for look you, there's no catering officer in this camp, isn't there, and I'm answerable to the C.O., so you put your ole moan into him, don't you?"

As this was strictly the case, and the W.A.A.F. officer was well aware of it, she beat a fighting retreat and Horace watched her bustle across the crate-strewn parade ground toward the farmhouse H.Q.

Her sergeant remained behind, pouting and muttering. It was clear that she had aligned herself with the rebels.

"There goes a first-class cow!" the sergeant remarked pleasantly, "and she'll make all the trouble she can, mark my words!"

"What's got into her lately?" the L.A.C.W. wanted to know. "She was a piece of cake when we first came here!"

"Not now!" grumbled the sergeant. "She's all burned up and leads me a hell of a life. She tried to get Squaddy Kindly to order you on our morning and afternoon parades, but he said you were too short-handed and wouldn't wear it! It was different when he used to run her into Smedley shopping every other morning. Nothing but sweetness and light she was, but it narks her to see the rest of us taking it easy, with her left out in the cold because the only other officer here is that drip of an adjutant who's always got his nose in the Bible! Well, it was good while it lasted! Me? I'm for a posting now she's gone sour on us!"

"Why don't someone sweeten her up?" suggested Horace, who had been an interested spectator of the scene and had formed his own conclusions about the section officer. "I never seen a camp like this, and everyone ought to lean over backwards to keep it so! Lumme, it's a ruddy rest cure this is, and it's worth a bit o' trouble to keep it ticking over that way until someone in Whitehall rumbles us!"

They sat around the scrubbed table and the discussion became general.

"What Sarge means is that Flora needs a man," said L.A.C.W. Smithers simply. "She can't chum up with any of the enlisted men, like we can, and the C.O.'s going strong with the widow down at the Hall."

"Well," said Horace thoughtfully, "I never knew a skirt yet who cared what grade a bloke was, so long as he went about it the right way. I'll give it a go, just to keep everybody happy!"

"You mean you'll 'ave a go at putting sugar in her tea yourself, man?" asked Dai incredulously.

"Not me," said Horace modestly. "I would, mindjew, but she's not my cup o' tea, nor me hers! I'll 'ave a word with my pal, him over there washing dishes."

They looked across at Pedlar, splashing away at the big sink. He was wearing nothing but trousers and an undershirt, and his shoulder muscles rippled as he heaved at the trays of dirty plates stacked on the drain boards.

The W.A.A.F. sergeant pursed her lips. "Well, he's husky enough," she said, "you never can tell. Detail him for S.H.Q. guard on Thursday. That's her night for duty and she sleeps in H.Q. I'll fix you for duty clerk, so as to keep an eye on both of them. Would that help?"

"Sarge," said Horace approvingly, "I know how you come by them stripes!" And they left it at that.

About 2300 hours on Thursday night Section Officer Mc-Naughton carried her small attaché case into the squadron leader's office at S.H.Q. and rang for the duty orderly to go over to the cookhouse for her thermos of cocoa and beef sandwiches. She took one turn as duty officer each week, the C.O. and the adjutant sharing the remaining six nights. There was a bed permanently made up in the C.O.'s room, and so far nothing untoward had ever occurred at No. 2130 M.U. during the night, so that both duty officer and duty clerk, the sole custodians of the building between 2000 hours and 0700 hours, went to bed at the usual time and got up with everyone else in the camp at reveille.

If there is such a thing as an ordinary woman then Flora McNaughton qualified. At thirty-seven she was medium-sized, brown-haired and brown-eyed, with good if rather heavy features. She was neither plain nor pretty, fat nor thin, distinguished or undistinguished in any way whatsoever but just

140

the kind of woman who always gets left behind to look after father. All her brothers and sisters had married and provided her with a tribe of savage little nieces and nephews, to whom she occasionally ministered as doting aunt, but they had never grown really fond of her and considered her a bit of a frump. She was not a frump, not yet, for frumps are resigned to being regarded as old maids and this was not true of Flora McNaughton. She was still fighting back and her presence in uniform at an R.A.F. camp was, one might say, the gesture of an undefeated spirit, a kind of sally on the part of a garrison reduced to half-rations.

Flora was a romantic and for many years past her romanticism had been fed and watered by the late Jesse Boots, through the medium of a Boots "A" subscription. She read, on an average, three boy-meets-girl novels a week, and her enlistment in the W. A. A. F. was a final (and so far her most desperate) endeavor to go out and find a romantic experience, the essence of which was to be desired by some man, any man. She felt that she could put up with any other tribulation in store for her, and maybe a whole lifetime of boredom in the Cotswolds after the war, if only, *during* the war, something romantic happened to her before she was too old to appreciate it. So far nothing had, but she had far from abandoned hope.

Standing orders at Craddock Wood prescribed a night guard at the main gate but the corporal in charge slept in the hut and every two hours the sentries, one on the gate and the other in the farmhouse garden, came off duty and posted their own reliefs.

Nobody ever checked on the sentries and they usually spent their spell of duty dozing against a wall, or sitting in the sentry boxes reading paperbacks by flashlight.

When she had unpacked her little attaché case Section Officer McNaughton inspected the guard. The corporal, duly forewarned by the W.A.A.F. sergeant, was ready to receive her. He turned out his half-dozen warriors with Buckingham Palace precision and honored her with a resounding "present." Flora was both touched and flattered by this compliment although she was aware that she was not entitled to it. It was something that had never happened before and it gave her a cozy glow of self-esteem.

"Carry on, Corporal!" she chirruped, returning his smart salute, and the corporal snapped: "Yes, *Ma'am!* Detail—slope *arms!* Right *turn!* Quick *march!* Lef'ri, lef'ri, lef, lef, lef . . ." as the six men marched away down the winding path toward the main gate.

She watched them until they were out of sight and paused on the porch to light up a cigarette. It was a calm, quiet night, bright with stars. A light wind came soughing through the woods and she thought of her home in the Cotswolds, and how pleasant things might be if this had been a real camp, teaming with gay and robust young men but no other commissioned W.A.A.F.s.

She sighed audibly, and at that moment a squat, beetle-browed airman stepped smartly out of the shadows behind the rainwater barrel and saluted.

"Night duty clerk reporting, Ma'am! Permission to check on blackouts?"

"Why, yes, I suppose so," said Flora, thinking that this must be something new in night-duty routine. "Doesn't the day clerk see to that?"

"C.O.'s orders," said the airman, saluting again. "Special detail checks on blackouts every night from now on! C.O. came round last night and spotted chinks in S.H.Q. Said it looked like a Christmas tree, beggin' your pardon, Ma'am! I got to check up here, then tour the whole camp!"

"I see," said Flora very affably, for she was still glowing from the effect of the guard's airmanlike demonstration. "Well, perhaps you'd better go round and have a good look, airman!"

At this moment another figure materialized from around behind the rainwater barrel, a huge, shambling airman, carrying a rifle and fixed bayonet. Section Officer McNaughton noticed that it was the tallest and broadest airman in camp and the largest airman she had ever seen. He stood, she estimated, some six foot four in his socks and his shoulders looked as wide and as beefy as those of a circus strongman.

142

"I thought the guard corporal had marched all his men down to the gate," she said, addressing Horace, who was standing stiffly to attention.

"This one's special!" said Horace.

"For S.H.Q.?"

"Yes, Ma'am!"

"Is this the S.H.Q. sentry?" she asked Horace.

"He's volunteered to patrol all night!"

Flora McNaughton looked mildly surprised.

"All night? But that's nonsense. Sentries are relieved every two hours, aren't they?"

"Not this one," said Horace, "he's a keen type and it's like I said, he volunteered for the job, didn't you, Pedlar?"

"Arr!" said Pedlar coming swiftly to attention and slapping his rifle butt. He then stared at the officer so fixedly that she felt herself blushing.

Almost imperceptibly the night began to assume aspects of gentle unreality to Section Officer McNaughton. She summarized the unusual occurrences. First the strange, soldierly behavior of the main guard, then the camp blackout check, and now a man who had (she could hardly credit it) volunteered to act as guard over S.H.Q. and for four times the period laid down by standing orders, the man who stood staring at her as though he had never before seen a woman in uniform.

The faint but unmistakable scent of wildflowers came in from the woods and Flora McNaughton suddenly felt pleased with herself and most pleasantly relaxed. She said:

"Very well, airman. It does seem as if things are smartening up a little round here. Look after your blackouts and then dismiss!"

"Ma'am!" said Horace and marched noisily into the farmhouse, passing rapidly from room to room, reappearing almost immediately, saluting, and barking: "All blackouts in position, Ma'am! Wishing you good night and an uneventful spell of duty, Ma'am!"

"Er . . . thank you," said Flora wonderingly, as Horace saluted again, wheeled about and marched off, his arms swinging, his back as erect as a flagpole.

"I wonder if that peptalk I gave the squadron leader is responsible for all this?" she mused, as Pedlar sloped arms and paced slowly across the yard. "It does seem to have jolted them a little!"

She puffed slowly at her cigarette and watched the sentry cross in front of the soft beam of light issuing from the open door. He was certainly a magnificent specimen, huge but somehow not ungainly. There was a manly spring in his step and it seemed to her that he was taking his duties very seriously indeed, turning smartly at the end of his beat and bringing down his feet with a snap that caused an owl to hoot on the edge of the woods.

Watching, she became very curious about him. Was his presence here the result of some quirk of gallantry on the part of the C.O., who had come to the tardy conclusion that it was unsafe to leave a woman unguarded all night? Or had it something to do with the new decision to despatch the duty clerk on a tour of the camp that would occupy him at least two hours if he was to carry out his check conscientiously?

She shivered slightly in the night breeze and thought of her thermos flask and sandwiches. Carefully extinguishing her cigarette, she went into the office and took off her tunic and shoes, sat on the bed and poured herself a cup of steaming coffee from the flask. Sipping it, she heard the sentry's footsteps crunch on the gravel as he passed the heavily curtained window. On impulse she got up and, pulling aside the heavy felt, rapped on the pane. Pedlar checked his stride, came back and pressed his face to the glass. Flora held up the flask, pointing and beckoning.

She heard him move round the building and stomp up the steps to the corridor. Suddenly she wanted to giggle and had some difficulty in checking herself. It was, she reflected, all rather cozy and picnicky, like a scene from her childhood in the Cotswolds.

When Pedlar saw the section officer beckoning him from the C.O.'s office he was not particularly surprised. Pope had persuaded him that the section officer needed the attentions

144

of a man and everything Horace said would happen did happen.

Over their long association Pedlar had acquired an enormous respect for Pope's swift assessments of the men and women whom they had encountered in their travels, so now he crunched swiftly round the building and up the steps, holding his rifle and bayonet at the trail.

"You want something, Ma'am?"

Flora found herself blushing again and turned aside, pouring coffee from the flask into a mug, her own mug.

"Well, I . . . er . . . I thought you might like something hot and . . . er . . . perhaps a sandwich, airman," she said lamely. "It must be rather chilly out there! Here, help yourself!"

"Thanks," said Pedlar briefly, and taking a sandwich disposed of it in two enormous bites.

The section officer sat down on the edge of the bed and watched him eat. She was fascinated by the rhythmic chomp of his jaws. They operated like the steady crunch of a dredger and as soon as he had disposed one sandwich he reached out for another.

"I'm afraid that's all there is," said Flora at length.

"That's okay, Ma'am, I'm not all that hungry," said Pedlar.

"I dare say we could get some more later on," suggested the section officer. "Is there anyone on duty in the cookhouse?"

"Popey'll get some more if you want any, M'm," said Pedlar, bolting the last of the pile and emptying the mug of coffee.

"Who's Popey?" asked Flora, after an embarrassed pause.

Pedlar looked at her with surprise.

"Popey's my pal," he said, "the one who was here just now."

"You mean the duty clerk?"

"Arr," said Pedlar, shifting his position slightly in order to scratch his thigh, "that's Popey!" Then, almost defiantly: "We bin together since the start!"

He was not in any way abashed in her presence. To him she was not a woman but a straightforward task, set him by his master. He was not in the least curious as to why Popey

145

wanted him to be specially nice to this W.A.A.F. officer. Probably she had done Popey, or was about to do Popey, a good turn, or perhaps Popey had designs on her himself and wanted her warmed up like a dinner.

Suddenly recollecting his duty he beamed down on her and his wide smile caused Flora McNaughton to shiver slightly and then color once more. This time, however, she did not turn away but asked directly, and in her best, on-parade tone of voice:

"I confess I don't quite understand all this! We've . . . er . . . never had an S.H.Q. sentry before, but I remember you very well. You work in the cookhouse, don't you? But I don't remember 'Popey'! That's a strange name, isn't it?"

She did not give him time to answer either question but continued: "He told me you volunteered to patrol all night? Whyever should you do a thing like that?"

"Well, I suppose because you were here," said Pedlar still beaming.

Flora McNaughton swallowed hard and sat down on the very edge of the bed.

"Because . . . because *I* was here? You mean . . . you decided among yourselves that as there was a woman doing duty officer she should have a sentry posted?"

This was much too complicated for Pedlar. He wrinkled his forehead, scratched his thigh again and said:

"Popey thinks you're smashing, M'm!" Then, feeling that he ought to associate himself with this statement, he added: "Come to that, so do I! *Smashing!*" He repeated the word with emphasis, so as to make quite sure there should be no mistake about it.

The section officer could find no adequate reply for this. She sat very erect on the extreme edge of the bed, her hands along her plump thighs, her wide mouth slightly open. She was aware, of course, of her duty, and realized that she ought to have done one of two things, laugh openly and then dismiss this huge, insolent bumpkin, or, if she felt herself unable to regard the matter so lightly, deprive him of his rifle and bayonet and summon the corporal of the guard from the main·

146

gate. He would then, no doubt, be placed under close arrest, pending a charge. What the nature of the charge would be, or how it would be worded when it came before the C.O., she was not absolutely sure but it would probably entail severe penalties.

She was unable, however, to adopt either course. After the initial shock of his confession she was conscious of a tide of warmth stealing over her, engulfing her from head to foot, suspending the dictates of reason and restricting her movements. She knew that she must be flushing furiously and also that she must seem an utter fool in front of this man, but this knowledge did not help her to pull herself together and neither did it cause her to leap from the bed and bundle him out of the office, or shout for help, or make some excuse and slip past him into the passage and thence to the yard.

These alternatives presented themselves like a series of speeded-up film pictures, but they were gone before she could apply her mind to any one of them. She just sat very still on the edge of the bed, luxuriating in the delicious glow that his stupid words and his undeniably harmless expression had produced in her.

At last she managed to say something and was alarmed at the unwonted gentleness of her voice.

"Where . . . where *is* the duty clerk, airman?" she asked.

"Popey? Oh, he's around. D'you want him?"

"Nnno," said Flora slowly, "I think I . . . er . . . I remember now, he's touring the boundaries to check on blackouts . . . C.O.'s orders," she ended, almost in a whisper. Then, recklessly silencing a mutter of caution before it could utter more than a syllable, "What's your name? And what part of the country do you come from?"

She told herself that she only asked these questions to gain time and perhaps also to give the impression that she found him stupid and harmless. She knew quite well, however, that she was lying and lying very cheerfully, for as the warm tide began to recede another wave broke over her, this time a crashing, thundering wave of downright recklessness. For months now, and for years and years before that, she had wanted most desperately for something exciting to happen to her, something like the kind of thing that happened to every woman at least once in her lifetime in all the subscription "A" novels she had borrowed from Boots. Even as she sat facing this strange and apparently infatuated giant, she recalled one particular story about a schoolmistress from Manchester who went off on her first Continental holiday at the age of thirty, there to be wooed by a gondolier under Italian stars. She even recalled the title of the book, *Venetian Encounter,* and how it all ended, with the gondolier turning up at the Manchester school years later when he was nothing more than a bittersweet memory. Remembering this she smiled, and Pedlar, greatly encouraged, stopped scratching and propped his rifle and bayonet against the filing cabinet.

"My name's Pascoe," he told her; " 'Pedlar' Pascoe they call me!"

" 'Pedlar'? Why Pedlar?"

"We've all got names like that in the hollow," said Pedlar.

"The hollow? Where on earth is the hollow?"

"Up on Exmoor. You know Exmoor?"

At this point in the exchange a breathless Section Officer McNaughton almost overtook the speeding Flora and managed to gasp, "Fool! Fool! Send him away before you make a complete idiot of yourself!" but Flora put on a spurt that carried her out of earshot and smiled up at the airman, saying, in tones that were never employed on parade:

"Yes, of course, I *love* Exmoor, I think it's my *favorite* place! I used to go there a great deal before the war. Well, fancy that, you come from Exmoor! Is the hollow a village, then?"

No, Pedlar told her, not a village, but an encampment of the Pascoes from time immemorial. It was their home, he supposed, if people like the Pascoes could be said to possess a home, and Flora was intrigued for she had known from the very beginning that there was something romantic about this man and now it turned out that he was a gypsy, a real, live Romany! Leaving Section Officer McNaughton on the far side of the horizon she plied him with dozens of questions about gypsy life. How they fared in winter? What they made and sold? How many brothers and sisters he had? Was it true that they gathered herbs and brewed secret medicines? Pedlar answered her freely. He was accustomed to curiosity on the part of people who lived ordinary lives in ordinary houses, people who went to and from work on trains and buses, and had never slept a night in the open or sat musing over a fire of greenwood.

He could never understand this curiosity. The life he had led, up to the time of his enlistment, had never seemed odd or romantic to him. Mostly it was a matter of shifts and evasions, of damp couches and half-cooked food. Popey, however, had told him to be very nice to this pop-eyed, talkative woman, so he set himself to be nice, describing the hollow in detail, telling her little things he recalled about his father and brothers, and generally going out of his way to be unusually sociable and informative.

All this time he continued to stand in front of her, while she remained sitting on the edge of the bed, and this was how he was able to catch a fleeting glimpse of Horace through a chink in the blackout, which the officer had pulled aside when she had summoned him.

Horace, he noted, now had his nose pressed to the pane and was shining his flashlight under his chin in order to identify himself. Pedlar saw him crook his finger urgently and deduced from this that Popey must want to speak to him. Then Flora noticed his distraction.

"What is it, Pascoe?" she said, and turned her head, but Horace jumped back out of sight and as he did so Pedlar's eye fell on the empty coffee flask.

"I'll get you some more coffee, M'm!" he said briskly, very pleased with himself for thinking of such a good excuse to get out yet leave the way open for a speedy return, "I can brew it myself, I won't be five minutes, M'm!"

"That's very kind of you," said Flora, still a little shocked by the vague caress in her voice, "but there's really no point in my not going to bed. Nothing ever happens on night duty, does it? And if it does there's always the telephone. I *would* like some more coffee, however, and then I think I'll hop into bed!"

"You do that, M'm," advised Pedlar enthusiastically, and there was something about his heartiness that started the warm tide rolling in again. At this point a finger-shaking section officer appeared on the skyline and although still a long way off hailed Flora so loudly that her voice carried across the enormous distance between them, causing Flora to add, with a sigh:

"We . . . er . . . we had quite a pleasant little chat, didn't we?"

"Yes," said Pedlar calmly, "and we'll have another when I get back!"

Then, abandoning his rifle and bayonet, he nodded twice and clumped out of the room.

This should have been the signal for Flora McNaughton, daughter of Major McNaughton, late Royal Horse Artillery, spinster, reader of hopelessly romantic fiction, and holder of a commission in the Women's Auxiliary Air Force, to gasp with relief, bolt the door, phone the main gate guard, and report that she was being pestered by a common airman, who talked to her as if she was a newly enlisted A.C.W.2 and a very broad-minded one at that! She did not bolt the door, however, and for a moment or two she did not even get up, but sat musing, her hands loose on her lap, her mind a maelstrom of conflicting currents of thought.

Was this an elaborate legpull? Was this airman Pascoe a kind of half-idiot, acting, from the standpoint of a cretin, normally and naturally? Had she really made an impression on him and his friend, the duty clerk? And, if so, what kind of impression? What might a woman infer from that single, currently popular adjective, "Smashing"?

Before she had made any progress in sorting out these queries she got up and was almost surprised to find herself undoing the grippers of her skirt. She stopped, quite horrified, at the third gripper and then the wave of recklessness swept over her again and she giggled and said aloud: "Oh for Heaven's sake don't be so *stuffy*, Flora! You've always been stuffy and here, for once, is something amusing! You're being fussed over by a gypsy in uniform, who finds you pleasant to look at and easy to talk to! Get under the blankets and have him give you the coffee on a tray!"

There was a circular tin tray on the desk and she put it within easy reach, with her own mug in the center. Then she wriggled out of her tight skirt, took off her tie and unbuttoned the top button of her shirt, afterwards worming down between the heavy brown blankets and propping her back with the canvas bolster. To make everything look perfectly natural she picked up her current novel and opened it at its celluloid marker. After a moment's reflection she put on her horned-rimmed spectacles and fixed her eyes on the page. She sat like that for nearly five minutes before she realized that she was holding the book upside down.

Horace slipped out of the shadows and accosted Pedlar before he was halfway to the cookhouse.

"Where you off? I thought you was going strong!" he demanded, falling into step behind him.

"So I am," said Pedlar, "I'm getting her some coffee, that's all."

"Ah, that's the style," said Horace approvingly. "So she does go for you, like I said, eh?"

"Well, I dunno," said Pedlar uncertainly. "We done a lot o' talking and she keeps going red in the face, but she don't seem to mind me being there. You know, Popey, I reckon you'd do this better'n me. You got a way with women and I 'aven't!"

"You're doin' okay, Pedlar," said Horace encouragingly. "Slip in and brew up the coffee and I'll see you when you come out. And don't be too long neither! We don't want her to cool off now we got her interested!"

Pedlar went into the cookhouse and Horace lifted his head and sniffed the night air, noticing a strong and pleasing scent from somewhere close at hand. Then, in the slanting light of the kitchen bulb, he spotted the source, an old lilac tree growing at the rear of the cookhouse that had been made out of one of the barns. Switching on his flashlight he prowled round the tree, plucking a few sprays of the blossom, inhaling their scent and murmuring "Ahhh, luvly!" Presently Pedlar came out with the coffee, a large lidded container of it, and in his free hand

151

was another plate of beef sandwiches. Together they walked quietly back to S.H.Q. and at the door Horace said:

"Give her these! Tell her to put 'em in water and leave everything else to me!"

"How am I gonner carry 'em?" protested Pedlar. "I got something in each hand, 'aven't I?"

"Open your perishing great gob," said Horace, and when Pedlar obeyed he thrust the stalks of the lilac sprays between his teeth.

Thus it was that Pedlar kicked open the door of the office and presented himself to Section Officer McNaughton, a jug of coffee in one hand, a plate of sandwiches in the other and his face screened by a big bunch of lilac held by strong, white teeth.

Flora gave a little scream and dropped her book. Pedlar set down the provisions and gathered up the lilac, thrusting the bunch at her rather like a duelist presenting a rapier.

"They smell nice," he said briefly. "We'd better put 'em in water, but don't forget to hammer the ends, they last longer that way!"

Flora McNaughton giggled again but this time there was hysteria in the sound. He looked so unspeakably droll, standing there pushing lilac in her face. Nobody, as far as she could recall, had ever given her flowers, but it was pleasing to reflect that no woman in the novels had ever been presented with a bouquet of lilacs in such wildly improbable circumstances. By a gypsy airman! In the middle of the night! And while she was sitting up in bed!

Then the scent of the blossoms swept over her, bringing with it an extraordinarily powerful impression of the past, of growing up in the trim house behind a wall of Cotswold stone, the soft whine of a lawnmower in the background and a wide, hot sky overhead. Suddenly she found herself crying and in a swirl of terrible embarrassment she leaped out of bed and gathered the lilac in her arms, burying her head in the bunch and inhaling great gulps of the heavy perfume.

Pedlar did not seem to notice her embarrassment, only that she appeared very pleased with his bouquet and for this he chalked up another infallibility mark for Popey, whose nose was again pressed to the blackout chink.

"Where did you find them?" said Flora, when she could trust herself to speak.

"There's a big old tree outside the cookhouse," Pedlar told her. "I often go out an' take a sniff at it. Sometimes it freshens you up like, especially when the smell o' cooking gets a bit too much inside."

He took the sprigs from her and picked up a dummy hand-grenade that the C.O. used for a paperweight. Methodically, as one who had done it many, many times, he hammered the stalks, while she sat down on the edge of the bed and watched him, forgetting that she wore only her shirt and pink under-slip. The rush of tears had cleared her brain but it had not restored her of sanity. For Flora McNaughton time was now fully suspended. She had ceased to be a W.A.A.F. officer, performing a spell of night duty in an obscure R.A.F. camp in the Northamptonshire woods. She was simply Flora, the heroine of a story, for whom a big ungainly gypsy gathered lilacs.

Then, without warning, the light went out. Neither of them knew that Horace had stepped inside S.H.Q., tinkered expertly with the fuse box in the passage and slipped out again. Pedlar thought the bulb had blown and grunted as he struck his thumb with the dummy hand-grenade. Flora thought the sudden rush of darkness was the end of the story and that she would now wake up and become a Section Officer on night duty again.

"I got a match somewhere," said Pedlar, standing up and sucking his sore thumb, but before he could find his matches Flora had begun to grope around for the duty officer's flash-light that she had last seen on the table. Her hand touched the can of coffee and the lid rattled.

"Watch out, M'm, don't go knocking the coffee over!" he warned her and suddenly she began to laugh for joy as the situation whisked her back into dreamland. He found his matches and struck one. In the light of the flare he saw her standing by the table, shaking with silent laughter. She looked almost alluring and her figure seemed to him far less tubby stripped of its skirt and heavy brass-buttoned tunic. Her head was thrown back, emphasizing the strength of her neck and large, firm breasts.

Then the match went out and Pedlar acted on impulse. He put down the hand-grenade, took a step forward, gathered her in his arms, and kissed her hard on the mouth.

She made a token struggle but it was no more than a wriggle. She gasped "No!" and then "No, *no!*" the moment she could speak, but he continued to hold her and although Flora McNaughton was a well-built woman, with legs muscled by long tramps in the Cotswolds, she could not have broken from that embrace had she been ten times as strong. In any case, her vitality began to ebb after a few seconds and her knees suddenly gave way, so that he supported her wholly. The scent of the lilacs seemed to fill the room and after inhaling it again all that was left of Section Officer McNaughton soared away like a savagely bounced ball. In her place was a woman held fast in the bearlike embrace of a gondolier, a gypsy chief, the wicked squire's son, and a dozen or so brown-faced, lean-jawed and impeccably groomed young men in Savile Row dinner jackets.

The office itself underwent a similar magic-carpet change, becoming a moonlit terrace at Cannes, the boat-deck of a deep-sea liner, and a patch of shadow under the Bridge of Sighs all at the same time. When his pressure eased a fraction she instantly renewed it, throwing her whole weight against him and in the delirium that accompanied this movement she even forgot his romantic name.

"Airman," she gasped, as her toes sought the floor, "put me down and take off your boots!"

CHAPTER EIGHT

In the weeks that followed the wooing of Section Officer Flora McNaughton, Horace sometimes wondered what might have happened at Craddock Wood had she remained for more than a week or two after Pedlar's triumph. As it was she soon disappeared, to be replaced by a tiny little flight officer who fell hopelessly in love with her own broad-shouldered sergeant and was thereafter content to leave all decisions to the N.C.O.

For a brief spell, however, life at the camp went on very much as usual. The C.O. spent most of his time at the hall, the adjutant remained immersed in Peake's *Commentary on the Bible,* Corporal Smedley ran the orderly room efficiently in the intervals between cattle drives to and from Dodge City, and a fresh consignment of crates arrived every Friday.

In the meantime Horace had to admit that Pedlar had made a sensational success of his difficult assignment. There were no more morning and afternoon parades for the W.A.A.F. personnel and although Section Officer McNaughton frequently appeared in the cookhouse she never once stormed at L.A.C. Tovey or L.A.C.W. Evie Smithers, or made a single adverse comment about the monotony of the diet, or general sloppiness of the kitchen. Her attention was concentrated solely upon Pedlar, who was usually washing up clad only in undershirt and trousers. She would take her stand by the sink and gaze at him for minutes on end, occasionally saying something in a low voice.

After one or two of these visits Horace formed the habit of making tactful withdrawals, busying himself in the flour store or, if this was already occupied by Dai Tovey and Evie, crossing over to the N.A.A.F.I. Unlike the N.A.A.F.I.s in other camps, this establishment was open all day, not merely at specified intervals.

The silence and secrecy of the relationship between the gypsy and the W.A.A.F. officer piqued Horace, who was very curious to know what had happened after he had fused the lights. He never did discover this. Pedlar proved exceptionally reticent on the subject and without understanding why Horace found himself becoming slightly jealous of the section officer and was secretly delighted when Pedlar returned from the orderly room one day with the news that she was posted.

Horace took this opportunity to question Pedlar about her, but when he wanted to be evasive the gypsy could be as uncommunicative as a clam.

"She's just posted," said Pedlar flatly, "told me so herself!"

"Well, that let's you off the hook, mate!" said Horace a little huffily, and then, ingratiatingly: "Come on, Pedlar. What *did* 'appen that night I fixed things so nice for you?"

"You *know* what happened, Popey," said Pedlar gravely, "and in any case, she says it's not right to tell!"

"What? Not even me?" said Horace indignantly.

"No, Popey, I reckon not," said Pedlar quietly.

He looked so troubled for a moment that Horace's impatience evaporated. As his affection for the gypsy returned he murmured, without rancor:

"Well, strike me pink if it don't look to me as if you'd fallen for the old girl! Okay, what you say is okay by me! We don't want to blab it all over the camp, so tell her you'll pick her up in the station jeep and see her orf the premises tomorrow!"

He went away rather sobered, reflecting that perhaps Pedlar was not as simple and uncomplicated as he appeared to be. It was clear that some hidden spring in Pedlar's bumbling soul had been touched by the encounter, and that he did not want the subject of this association with the W.A.A.F. officer made the subject of barrack-room jests.

The next morning Pedlar took Flora to the junction in the jeep and was away most of the day. While he was gone Horace was approached by Tovey, the cook.

"Me'n Evie need a break," he told Horace. "D'you reckon you and that big Swede o' yours could cope in the cookhouse over a long weekend? We'd make the menus out for you and leave all the stuff ready."

Horace had never admitted an inability to cope to anyone.

"You go," he said, "me an' Pedlar'll cover up for you!"

So they went, with genuine passes signed by the adjutant, and their brief absence led directly to what came to be known as "The Tapioca Riot."

Dai and his camp follower departed on the Friday noon and throughout Friday and Saturday Horace and Pedlar cooked and served the meals planned and prepared by Tovey. Sunday was a meatless day, so they eked out with cheese and beetroot, but when neither of the cooks showed up on Sunday night they were faced with the necessity of inventing something for Monday's lunch.

On Monday morning, with no menu planned for the day's meals, Horace decided to play for safety and settled for Irish stew and tapioca pudding. Dai Tovey was very fond of Irish stew and Horace had often watched him prepare it, so that the main part of the meal offered no problem.

Neither substitute, however, had seen Tovey make a tapioca, and this was unremarkable, for Tovey hated tapioca pudding, having once lived with an aunt who had compelled him to swallow large, gooey helpings of it every weekday. As a rule Tovey only served meals for which he had a personal preference. As it happened Horace was very fond of tapioca pudding and the prospect of making one appealed to him after he had discovered a large bin of seed-pearl tapioca in the store.

"Very filling it is," he told Pedlar, "blows you out does tabby-oker! If Dai don't show up until 1159 hours it'll keep 'em going, an' stop any back-answers!"

They rolled out the bin, filled the large saucepans with water

157

and looked up tapioca pudding in Dai's rarely consulted cookery manual.

"It says here two ounces for four people," said Horace. "We gotter do some multiplying. How many on strength?"

"I cut ninety-seven slabs o' cheese yesterday, so it's ninety-seven I reckon," Pedlar told him.

"Say a hundred," said Horace. "That means two hundred ounces. Weigh it out while I look for the sugar. We got no eggs, but I dare say a few packets o' powdered egg is better'n nothing. We got no lemons either, but this ain't the Ritz, is it?"

Pedlar said it wasn't and Horace returned to the book mumbling, while Pedlar ladled out an estimated two hundred ounces of tapioca and distributed the mound evenly among the saucepans. It looked very sparse and lay on the surface of each pot like a light shower of snow.

"Don't look thick enough to me," said Horace, "got no body in it! Stick in a bit more, while I add the sugar an' egg."

Pedlar added a generous handful to each saucepan but the mixture still looked as thin as prison soup. He went on adding handfuls until Horace told him to stop.

"Maybe it'll thicken up when we add the milk," suggested Horace. "One and a half pints for four—that's about thirty-seven pints for a hundred—slop it in and let it simmer."

"There's no room," said Pedlar, "it'll overflow."

"Well, pour some of the ruddy stuff away and make room for the milk," snapped Horace, whom anxiety was making irritable. He began to feel resentful against Tovey and Evie for overstaying their pass.

Pedlar poured away about a third of the mixture and topped the remainder with milk. In a few minutes the pudding began to thicken and Horace brightened up a little.

"Coming on okay," he said, with a surge of confidence. "Stick in a bit o' salt and keep your eye on it while I 'ave a look at the stew. Keep stirring, it says so in the book."

He went over to the other ovens and tasted the stew, smacking his lips and looking critically at the roof. Pedlar added salt to the tapioca and began to stir, moving along the line of pans and giving each of them a lively poke as he passed. He noticed that Horace was right, and that the puddings were indeed thickening very satisfactorily. On his second stirring trip he had some difficulty in moving the stick around the pans and on his third tour the stick had to be jammed in the center of the pan and lunged to and fro, like an obstinate gearshift.

He called across to Horace: "Better come an' have a look, Popey! It's getting hard to stir!"

Horace finished what he was doing and came over, peering into each saucepan and jabbing the mixtures with Pedlar's wooden spoon. They did not look much like tapioca puddings but more like overcast skies, with heavy rain in the offing, or enlarged photographs of the moon.

"We can't water 'em down now," he said. "On'y thing to do is to keep 'em fluid. Gimme another spoon and I'll work from this end."

They abandoned everything else and went to work on the six pans. It was work that demanded plenty of muscular exertion. At first they were able to stir to and fro but after a few minutes it was only possible to push the spoons up and down. In the meantime the surface coloring changed to a kind of primrose yellow and the puddings took on a mottled, leprous appearance. The smell was not unlike that of glue.

Men began to drift in for their midday meal and Horace abandoned the tapioca in order to serve the stew. A queue formed at the serving counter, the men rattling their irons and shouting for service.

Corporal Smedley put his head in the kitchen door and sniffed: "Christ, what's happening in there?" he demanded. "You chaps frying skunk?"

"Tabby-oker pudding," said Horace with dignity, "but it's not quite done yet."

"Don't hurry with it, I can wait," said the corporal, and carried his stew to a table.

Some of the other airmen made a blunt comment or two on the smell but Horace ignored them, dishing out all the stew and telling a batch of late-comers that they could fill up on the afters, of which there promised to be a surplus.

He then closed the door and hurried back to Pedlar, who

had taken the saucepans from the stove and was endeavoring to upend them into a shallow serving pan. He shook and banged one saucepan until a handle came away in his hand but the tapioca remained set in a heavy, gray mold. Horace fetched a large meat knife and cut the pudding round the edge. After some vigorous shaking it slid out and struck the pan like a soggy football. He performed similar operations on the other puddings and then began to hack them into portions.

"You tried it, Pedlar?" he asked anxiously.

"Yes," Pedlar told him, "and it nearly give me lockjaw. Don't you eat none, Popey," he added solicitously, "you give it all to them greedy buggers outside!"

Twenty or thirty greedy buggers were now rapping on the door, and Pedlar crossed over to it with the pan containing the chopped-up puddings.

He arranged the serving trays on the counter. Standing in line the puddings now looked rather like a promenade, after a heavy pounding by southwesterly gales. The men stared at them in quiet wonder and Horace felt called upon to do a little advertising.

"Tabby-oker!" he said, smacking his lips. "Luvly!"

The first dozen men took him at his word and heaped pudding on to their plates. There had been insufficient stew to go round and they were still hungry. Horace watched them anxiously, hating to admit failure. The man sitting at the end of the table nearest the serving area filled his mouth and swallowed. He choked and leapt to his feet, pressing both hands on the table edge, held semi-rigid in a fierce bout of coughing.

"Jesus!" he gasped at length, and then again, after a slow beating of his chest, "*Jesus!*"

Horace backed away from the serving door but in his alarm and concern he forgot to close it. In a last-minute attempt to seal himself off from the mess hall he took a single step forward but at that moment he saw Pedlar engaged with a civilian, over near the ovens. He was so surprised to see a woman in civilian clothes inside the kitchen that he forgot all about the open door.

The first thing he noticed about the woman was her hat. It

was a large black straw, decorated with cherries. The cherries were not uniform in size but started out as large as plums on the right, tapering off to cherries as small as peas over the left ear. They seemed all to be suspended by stalks, for as she nodded her head, in earnest conversation with Pedlar, they bobbed and danced and Horace was reminded of the rows of service bells that he had seen in old-fashioned kitchens. It was as though someone was pulling all the bell-ropes at once. He studied the hat for a moment and then lowered his gaze to the wearer.

She was short and plump, with a broad, florid face, gold-rimmed spectacles and the beginnings of a double chin. She was dressed in what was obviously her best and carried a handbag as capacious as a lawyer's briefcase. Her legs were short and very thick about the ankles. She might have been about forty to forty-five.

Horace went over and looked interrogatively at Pedlar, who had been accosted by the woman while chopping up the last of the tapioca pudding. Pedlar still held the meat knife in his right hand and Horace thought he looked very puzzled.

"She's asking after Dai," he told Horace. "I've told her he's not here today!"

"Where is he, then?" demanded the woman, "I've come a long way to see him, I 'ave, and I'm not going back until I do!"

Horace might have noticed that she used the same singsong accent as Dai and from this fact alone he could have drawn helpful conclusions, but he was preoccupied with the reception his puddings had received and less than half his mind was at the visitor's disposal.

"He's on a dirty weekend with Evie," he said shortly, "and you oughtn't to come in here like this! Civvies aren't allowed in the cookhouse, and I dunno how you got in anyway. How did you get in?"

"Through the door," said the woman, "same as anyone else would, and if I'm not allowed here I'd like to know who is!"

It crossed Horace's mind that she was the wife of the farmer who had occupied the camp premises before the war and the guess disarmed him, so that he was totally unprepared for her next action. She leveled her umbrella at him and suddenly became alarmingly aggressive.

"Who's Evie?" she wanted to know, "and what's this about my husband being away with her?"

She drove home the question with a sharp jab of her umbrella, the brass ferrule striking Horace on the bare skin, where his shirt was unbuttoned. The jab was painful but loyalty to the cook helped him to keep his temper. He had grown fond of Dai Tovey in the last few weeks and had taken an instant dislike to this sour, inquisitive woman and her cherry-laden hat.

"Look here," he temporized, playing for time, "how do I know you're his missis? He never said nothing about his missis coming here, did he, Pedlar?"

Before Pedlar could reply Mrs. Tovey had laid aside her umbrella and flung open her handbag. From its vast interior she pulled out some letters, addressed to her in Dai Tovey's handwriting.

"I'm wasting me time here," she snapped, closing the bag again, "I'll go and see the officer!"

"No! Don't do that," said Horace, his mind now wholly centered on the immediate problem, "he's a bad-tempered old so-and-so and he's got it in for Dai, anyway. You don't want to land him in trouble, do you? Fact is, he shouldn't be off duty, he ought to be here but he . . . he's doing this W.A.A.F. Evie a good turn, see?"

Mrs. Tovey was interested in spite of herself. Pedlar was also interested, as he usually was in his friend's masterly improvisations. He always paid close attention to Horace's spontaneous fabrications. They seemed to sprout from Popey's mouth like fairy beanstalks, overshadowing and distorting the entire universe. He laid aside his meat knife in order to devote his entire attention to the argument.

"Well," said Horace, "it's like this, Mrs. Tovey. We've had a girl working in here with us, nice little thing, name of Evie, and she heard yesterday that her 'ome was wiped out by a bomb, Liverpool way it was. Well, naturally, she was cut up. Mum, Dad, little sister, all gone, you see? She was for dashing off to find out what happened and find out if there was any 'ope for her kid brother, the on'y one they fished out of the ruins, and me an' Dai, well, we didn't like to see her go off alone, not in the state she was in, so Dai said to me, 'You take over, Horace, and I'll go along with her!' Get me?"

The effect of this story upon Pedlar was impressive. The corners of his wide mouth turned down and he looked, for a moment, as though he was going to burst into tears, but it did not have the same impact upon Mrs. Tovey. Her expression remained hard, hot and bothered, so that Horace was encouraged to redouble his efforts.

"I did say your old pot an' pan was off on a dirty weekend," he went on, "but that's a kind of figure o' speech with us chaps. When a bloke goes on seven days to his missis we always say he's on 'passionate leave,' but when he goes anywhere else— *anywhere*, mindjew—we always say he's off on a dirty weekend! Kind of wartime slang, d'you see? Now old Dai and that W.A.A.F., there's nothing narsty about them! He's not that type, and come to that nor's she, is she, Pedlar? Respectable kind o' girl . . . not the usual sort at all! . . . Shut up out there, I'm busy!"

The last remark was not part of the story but was addressed to the airmen clamoring beyond the open serving door. They had congregated there in a group and were banging on their plates and shouting abusive remarks into the kitchen.

Mrs. Tovey turned aside to look at this demonstration and as she did so Horace looked over her shoulder and his jaw dropped, for Evie and Dai entered the kitchen from the S.H.Q. side. He made a wild signal in their direction, but Evie, who was in front, did not seem to understand it and walked right up, beaming at the group.

"Hullo, Horace," she said cheerily, "we've had a smashing time! How are you coping?"

Mrs. Tovey swung round from the door and looked the W.A.A.F. up and down. Horace had to admit to himself that Evie did not carry herself like a girl who had just lost mother, father, sister and home in an air raid. She looked serene and affable, and as Dai drifted up she said: "We've had a whale of

163

a time, haven't we, Dai darling? We popped up to Blackpool and we've brought you both a surprise!"

She turned aside to forage in her haversack and in so doing caught a sidelong glimpse of Dai. The Welshman was standing beside her, hands loose, mouth agape, staring and staring at his wife.

"Well, for crying out loud, Gwynneth! What are you doing here?" he exclaimed.

Gwynneth was more than equal to the occasion. "Checking up on a whoremaster I am!" she snapped. "Him as I married, now, isn't it, Dai Tovey?"

It was now Evie's turn to gape. "Married!" she shrieked. "You and my Dai! *Married!*"

"Yes," said Mrs. Tovey, with great composure, "he's my husband he is, and now I suppose you'll ask me to prove it, like this one did and so I will, see!" and she grabbed a handful of tapioca pudding from the tray beside her and hurled it in Evie's face.

She was only standing six feet away but she missed nonetheless, for the big handbag, suspended from her forearm, spoiled her aim. The missile passed over Evie's left shoulder, sailed across the kitchen and through the serving door, striking a disgruntled L.A.C. below the ear and exploding like shrapnel, so that every man about him received a warm, glutinous spatter.

The L.A.C. yelped with surprise and then called upon his comrades to witness the dastardly assault, pointing out that the kitchen staff did not stop at serving up atrocious fare but had now taken to hurling it at them if they complained.

By way of instant reprisal he grabbed a double handful of tapioca from the serving trays, kneaded it into a snowball and flung it through the door in the general direction of the group standing beside the ovens. He was a better marksman than Mrs. Tovey, and the missile was more concentrated than hers. It struck Horace in the mouth, jarring him so sharply that for a moment he thought his front teeth had been displaced.

His shout of rage was the signal for a free-for-all. The dozen men near the serving door rushed at the trays placed there by Horace, and the cooks, using all the tapioca that remained to be served, spiritedly returned their fire. The smaller group had the best of it, for their attackers were massed together at the door.

One of the first tapioca bombs to enter the kitchen accounted for Mrs. Tovey's hat and precipitated her into temporary alliance with the garrison. For several minutes there was chaos. Tapioca-smeared airmen, having exhausted the contents of the trays, ran back to the tables and snatched ammunition from the plates. A.C.2 Berens, a member of the sanitary squad who was said to be able to eat and enjoy anything placed before him, was only halfway through his pudding when an airman shouldered him aside and grabbed all that remained of his dessert. Pedlar, eager to avenge the direct hit on Horace, rushed the serving door like a wild bull, grabbed two airmen by the collar, yanked them over the counter and rammed their faces into the congealed grease left in the stewpan.

In the very midst of the battle Flying Officer Trumper entered the mess hall but his appearance went unnoticed in the mêlée and he was violently jostled by Corporal Gittens and afterwards by L.A.C. Seaforth, who was prancing about in front of the kitchen door swearing at the cooks in Gaelic.

Trumper plucked sleeves at random and shouted, "I say, I say . . . !" but as soon as the combatants realized that an officer was present they made off, using both exits. In a few seconds Trumper was alone in the tapioca-strewn mess hall, rapping on the zinc counter of the servery and still shouting "I say! I say!" in the agonized voice of a man who is morally obliged to appear outraged but is satisfied that the opportunity to exercise authority no longer exists.

"It's disgusting, absolutely disgusting!" he squeaked at length. "Like a lot of animals! Like a lot of wild beasts! You'll hear all about it! You'll learn that the C.O. won't tolerate this kind of hooliganism! Come over heah, L.A.C.! D'you hear me? Come over heah, and explain what was occurring when I came into the mess!"

Dai Tovey, thus directly addressed, brushed tapioca from his best blue tunic and slowly approached.

Whenever challenged by authority, even such a token authority as that wielded by F.O. Trumper, Tovey took refuge in the traditional servility of the outnumbered Celt.

"It wasn't beginning it we didn't!" he whined. "They set upon us, they did, and that's God's truth, now, and isn't it, Horace? It's just back from pass I am, sir! Me and L.A.C.W. Smithers here, and they'll all bear me out in the matter, as anyone here can say . . . !"

He turned toward the ovens for corroboration but broke off, passing his hand across his brow when he discovered that three of his four witnesses had disappeared and that he now shared the kitchen with the hatless Gwynneth. His wife was engaged in scraping tapioca from her skirt with Pedlar's meat knife.

"Who is that civilian lady?" asked the adjutant, "and what on earth is she doing in there?"

Tovey licked his lips and mumbled that the civilian lady was his wife. As he said it the aged music-hall joke occurred to him, as did the tag "Officers and their ladies, N.C.O.s and their wives, other ranks and their women," allegedly printed on all prewar invitations to R.A.F. socials.

"That's her," he reiterated. "That's my wife, sir, and it's come down on me sudden, she has!"

In order to head off any possible investigation as to the cause of his wife's appearance in camp, he added: "Housing trouble, sir!" and left it at that.

The adjutant did not quite know what to make of this and gained time by clicking his tongue. Even then he could think of nothing to say but: "It's all rather irregular, isn't it, L.A.C.?"

Dai Tovey suddenly recovered his nerve and agreed that it was most irregular, but that his wife had been obliged to visit him on account of being put out of her house in Newport, Monmouthshire, and that he, Tovey, intended to put the matter before the R.A.F. free lawyer as soon as she had explained to him how scurvily she had been treated by the local council.

"There's a wonderful lot of liars, they are!" murmured Gwynneth half admiringly, as she continued to scrape the tapioca from her skirt. "Lie so easy they do! Just drips from them it does!" but either the adjutant did not hear her or decided that he was already out of his depth. He could not, moreover, meet the steady gaze of Dai Tovey's brown, pleading eyes, so he gave a little cough, promised half-heartedly that he would discuss the whole thing with the C.O., and left the building with long, hurrying strides.

Tovey relaxed and turned his melting gaze upon Gwynneth.

"*Cariad bach!*" he exclaimed, opening his arms and advancing toward her. "*Cariad bach!* It's good to see you, it iss!"

But Cariad bach gave no answering smile. Instead she laid down the meat knife and picked up her umbrella, holding it bayonetwise, in the "on guard" position.

"Now, Cariad bach! Gwynneth my love . . . !" began Tovey, but with far less certainty in his voice than when he had been addressing the adjutant. He saw then that it was useless to argue and wheedle until she had had time to cool down after the tapioca battle. Afterwards, he told himself, when she had got her breath back, and given him time to invent a more probable story than the one he had told the adjutant, he would be able to talk her round, as he had cajoled her so easily in prewar days. In the meantime it would be best to leave her alone, to let her wander disconsolately among the glades of the camp, while he dug up Horace and Pedlar Pascoe and found out how much she already knew.

It was all sound enough reasoning, but he was too slow off the mark. Anticipating a shrewd jab with the ferrule of the umbrella, he misjudged his line of flight and ran between the ovens, so that he had to pass too close to her.

He almost succeeded in escaping for he was very quick on his feet, but as he darted by Gwynneth deftly reversed her umbrella, thrust it between his legs and anchored herself on the oven rail. By this means Dai was brought up very short indeed, for Gwynneth, one might say, had gone to the very heart of the matter.

"*Gwynneth!*" he squealed, "*Cariad bach . . . !*"

It was less of a protest than a reproach.

CHAPTER NINE

A day or so after the tapioca battle Horace decided to wash his hands of the cookhouse and apply for leave. He had no wish to become involved in Dai's domestic troubles and his dismal failure to make tapioca puddings had shaken his confidence in himself. Moreover, Craddock Wood, as a camp, was beginning to bore him, for although entirely lacking in stress and military bullshine, it had, as far as he could see, no commercial possibilities. He was not irked, as so many airmen were irked, by an oppressively military régime, or by the insistence of those in authority over him that he should play a personal part in the overthrow of Hitler. By now he had come to terms with the R.A.F. and had made up his mind that, for as long as he was closely watched, he would play along with the Service, obeying orders, keeping himself presentable, occasionally going where he was told, even saluting if he failed to see an officer in time to slip between huts. In extreme cases, and if there was absolutely no help for it, he would even attend a parade.

In the meantime, as he repeatedly reminded himself, he must keep a sharp outlook for Pope and after Pope for Pedlar.

To Horace there was nothing unusual in this attitude.

Everyone was watching out for themselves and this, in Horace's view, was a healthy outlook. Manufacturers were watching out for Government contracts, the wholesalers for their meager flow of supplies, officers in all services for allowances to which they were not entitled and promotions they did not deserve. Even seaside landladies were watching their minimum scales and making up ration deficiencies at the expense of billetees.

The flood tide of propaganda set in motion by patriots at the Ministry of Information (who were, Horace assumed, engaged in watching out for propagandists) had not yet wetted Horace's feet. He listened to the news bulletins without hearing them and when he read a newspaper he turned first to the cartoon strips, then to the sport pages, and finally to the nearest litter basket, for he was essentially a tidy man. He no longer speculated on ways and means to escape from the R.A.F., for it was, he had decided, a far more free and easy outfit than the army or navy. In the army, he understood, they actually put a gun in your hand and despatched you to places where you were almost certain to meet Germans, Italians or Japs, with guns in their hands, and orders to use them. In the navy they put you in ships and sailed you round enemy-occupied coasts, thus multiplying the natural hazards of storm and wreck by inviting torpedoes and bombs from the air.

The fact that many thousands of unfortunates were facing these risks every day, and that many of them were getting killed and maimed in the process, saddened him somewhat but did not stir his conscience. Most of these poor wretches, he reasoned, had not gone into the danger zones of their own free will, but had been despatched there by somebody higher up, whereas those who had volunteered for active service plainly deserved all they got.

It is true that Horace sometimes wondered whether the prospects of personal enrichment in wartime were more promising to civilians and it sometimes depressed him to listen to the stories of men in the billets, who spoke of brothers-in-law and cousins now making money hand over fist in civvy street. He was not blind, however, to the advantages of operating within a military system, where almost everyone in authority was not only stupid but almost incredibly trusting. During his market days Horace had often found himself face to face with the curious system of laws that governed civilians and had sometimes found them very difficult to circumnavigate. Outside, in the big callous world, controls were much tighter, and minions of the law far more wily and experienced. Inside the Service the regulations were archaic, and the people charged with enforcing them were either red-capped amateurs or gentlemen of honor. Horace preferred to deal with men of honor. They took so much for granted. In addition, the uniform itself was a kind of armor against too much interference or inquisitiveness on the part of civilian policemen and officials.

So far he had shown a credit balance in the R.A.F. His wants were few. He was fed, clothed and housed at public expense, and his profits from a series of small-scale fiddles were stacked away in the post office. For the rest, life was supportable, particularly with Pedlar at hand to clean buttons, carry gear, make up the beds and clean the quarters. He sometimes reflected that if he had weathered the war as a civilian he might have earned more money but he would have had to have paid most of it out again for board, lodging and transport. How many wage-earning civilians had a personal manservant and bodyguard maintained out of the public purse?

Notwithstanding this he was finding life very dull at Craddock Wood and he badly needed a change. When he told Pedlar that he was going on leave the gypsy had looked dismayed. Pedlar had no intention of returning to the hollow, at any rate not while the war lasted, and he hated to let Horace out of his sight. He had a morbid conviction that if he did he would never see him again and the prospect of soldiering on alone terrified him.

In the end Horace decided that he might as well take Pedlar on leave with him and asked Corporal Gittens for two passes and railway tickets instead of one. Before they left Horace took a stroll round the camp and inspected the growing stacks of crates. There were now nearly twice as many as when they had arrived at Craddock Wood and they were piled every-where, in the glades, in the camp lanes, behind the billets, in what had been the farm outbuildings, and all round the edge of the parade ground.

Horace studied the pyramids a long time, thoughtfully rub-bing his chin and screwing up his eyes. Then he sought out Sergeant Wallace, nominally in charge of the crates and offi-cial keeper of the tally book.

"How many d'you reckon there are around, Sarge?" he asked.

Wallace was a keen snooker player and spent most of his time in the N.A.A.F.I. He was not the slightest bit interested in crates, his own or anyone else's.

"Boxes? In this dump? God knows! I lost count months ago. There were over two thousand when I took over. Must be double that now. Why? You falling over yourself to nurse 'em?"

"Yeah, I might at that!" Horace told him, "but not till I get back from leave."

"Why?" said the sergeant suspiciously.

"Oh, I dunno," said Horace airily, "it gives a chap something to do and I like something to do. I never was one for laying about, Sarge."

Sergeant Wallace considered this remarkable phenomenon, an airman actually seeking work. Then his mind ranged about looking for the inevitable angle but finding none.

"Okay," he said finally. "Look me up when you get back and you can start counting 'em. I'm supposed to keep returns of the damn things but the chap before me cooked his returns every week and then I stopped sending mine off to Group. No-body ever bothered but they might one day. We could at least get the book up-to-date!"

"Thanks, Sarge," said Horace, and went his way, Pedlar in tow.

"I got half an idea about them boxes," Horace confided when they had boarded the London train at Smedley Junction. "Seems to me timber must be in short supply somewhere and

171

there's no sense in leaving so much of it to rot. Waste that is! Helpin' Jerry, you might say!"

"Arrr!" said Pedlar noncommittally.

He had long since abandoned all attempts to make sense out of Popey's initial confidences. If Popey had anything in mind he would think and think about it, and then, having come to some decision, he would either do it or abandon it without an explanation. It had been that way with the Pool, the petrol, and the meat fiddles. He was not in search of Pedlar's opinion when he talked like this but simply thinking aloud and Pedlar had discovered that any supplementary comments annoyed him.

Horace remained silent and preoccupied during the journey south. Once or twice he took out a stub of pencil and made some rapid calculations on the margin of the magazine he had been reading. Pedlar did not, as was usual with him during a train journey, drop off to sleep. He was too keyed up and excited at the prospect of revisiting London, this time in Popey's company, and as the train entered the outer suburbs he was again staggered by the sheer area of the place, the miles and miles of terraced houses, the thousands and thousands of lines of washing, the volume of heavy traffic glimpsed when the railway lines ran parallel with roads.

At first he was surprised that Popey did not seem in any way impressed by the spectacle and then he remembered that Popey lived in London and would be accustomed to its immensity and bustle. Perhaps, he reflected, it was just being born here that made Popey so clever and resourceful, and so penetrating in his judgments of people. He folded his arms and continued to look steadily from the window. Alone in a place like this he would have been scared almost to death but with Popey everything would be all right. With Popey around London was just another camp.

At King's Cross they took the Underground to the Minories. Pedlar was speechless with wonder at the rushing trains and the whispering tunnels of sound, at the moving staircases and the uncanny skill with which Popey threaded his way through the maze of underground passages and seemed to know exactly where they were going. At one fork in a tunnel Pedlar's curiosity overcame his habitual reserve.

"Don't you never get lost down here, Popey?" he asked.

"Lost?" Horace stared blankly at him for a moment and then grinned. "Oh, I forgot! You on'y been to the Smoke once, haven't you? No, I don't get lost, no one don't! If you keep a butcher's on them lights and keep on going you're bound to come up somewhere. 'Ere we are, a few more steps and there's the Tower, where Bloody Queen Mary 'ad 'er napper chopped off!"

Unconsciously he took on the role of guide, pointing out various landmarks and features of his city.

"That there's the Thames and that's Tower Bridge. See that span between the towers? They built that fer people to walk over when the bridge was up to let ships go under, but they soon stopped that lark! Took people more time to climb up an' down than to wait and besides, they 'ad so many stiffs on their 'ands! People who was browned orf took orf from it, see? Take a look at that little round air-raid shelter? Well, it ain't an air-raid shelter! It was the entrance to a subway under the river!"

"For divers?" queried Pedlar.

Horace chuckled. "Divers? Lumme that's rich! I must save that one fer Pop! No, a subway under the river, fer people to cross before the bridge was built. 'Apen'y a time it was, on'y my old man says he never paid up in his natrule! They 'ad an old feller each end to take the money and Pop used to walk up slow and then make a dash for it! Over there's the Minories. You won't know what Minories are, will you? Well, it's where they make all the tosh! Every half-dollar an' tanner you 'andle comes outer there, some time or other. 'Ere, watch your step, mate, you ain't in the flippin' woods now! Down here and first left, that's where we hang out, or did, last time I 'eard. Christ, the geography's changed a bit around here since I was 'ome!"

He piloted Pedlar past a large area of desolation, past huge mounds of rubble sown with rosebay willow-herb, now a playground for strident-voiced children. In a narrow thoroughfare called Crispin Court he turned in at a seedy, half-shuttered shop and called: "Anybody home?"

Nobody was, so they went upstairs to the flat over the shop and Horace directed Pedlar to make up a bed on the floor in his own room at the back.

They ate baked beans and made tea and while they were eating Horace's sister Lil came in and looked at Pedlar with interest.

"Er-*ummmm!*" she said appreciatively, but Horace frowned and made no attempt to introduce his friend. Lil had made passes at various friends of Horace's in the past and afterwards something had gone wrong with the association.

"Lay off, Lil!" was all he said, and mopped up the last of his beans with a piece of bread.

Later on Horace's father and his brother Charles came in, bickering among themselves about a load of lead that one or the other had located but failed to acquire. They glanced at Pedlar and Horace but offered no greeting. Pedlar reflected that they were just as offhanded with one another as was his own family, back in the hollow.

Presently Horace asked his father a question: "Jellybelly Nell still around, Pop?"

"You bet," said Pop, "and cleaning up so they tell me! Dunno what her fiddle is! Can't be bananas, can it? She still got the fruit stall in the market tho' but it must be a cover for something, if I know Jellybelly!"

"Okay, we'll go see her," said Horace and got up, signaling to Pedlar to follow.

They went out and boarded a bus. Ten minutes later they were walking through the empty arcades of Covent Garden. Hardly anyone was about, but the stalls were stacked with empty boxes, smaller and flimsier boxes than those at the camp. Horace found a ragged moustached man eating a raw carrot and asked him if Jellybelly Nell was around. The man snapped off a length of carrot, chewed it and waved the green stem over his left shoulder. They passed behind him and into a draughty, glass-roofed room. Jellybelly Nell was sitting on a backless chair in front of a large, brassy-looking till.

"Watcher Nell!" said Horace affably, "how's tricks?"

"Bloody awful!" said Nell, but genially. "Can't get nothin' to sell with them U-boats, blarst 'em! Gives you the fair sick it do! Ain't seen a noringe in weeks and as fer fancy stuff—bananas, pineapples an' suchlike, we 'ave to look at pickshers of 'em to remind us wot they looked like!"

This was not verbal window dressing for the fruit vendor held up a poster advertising bananas. Pedlar realized how Jellybelly acquired her name. She was one of the fattest women he had ever seen, with elephantine shoulders, a bosom like an oncoming paddle steamer and a belly as vast and taut as a wineskin. Her face was so wide and so creased that nose, mouth and eyes were lost in it, and when she grimaced these features seemed to dart about looking for one another. She had hands like sliced hams and forearms as thick as Pedlar's own.

Horace was obviously on very familiar terms with her, for he sat down on the edge of the table that supported the till and offered her a cigarette.

"This is my buddy, Pedlar," he said, "and we're on leave. I'm here to talk business. What's your fiddle, Nell?"

"What's yours?" she demanded, her smile fading.

"Now, now, Nell," said Horace, in a bantering tone, "you don't want to talk like that to an old pal like me! I wouldn't have come over soon as we got in if I 'adn't 'ad it in mind to put something good in your way! If you don't sell much fruit now, and I don't see how you can, then you must have a fiddle. Pop said you had one and Pop's always got his ear to the ground!"

Jellybelly considered this for a moment, cocking her head to one side and looking like a coquettish hippopotamus.

"All right, Horace," she said magnanimously, "it's toys!"

"Toys?" Horace was surprised and incredulous. "How do you mean? Toys!"

"Kids' toys, like those in there," said Nell, nodding her head toward a tea chest that stood in a corner behind her.

Horace went over and took a look. Inside the box was a jumble of crudely made toys, each constructed of unplaned wood. There was a toy lorry, a toy crane, and two or three toy engines. He reached down and took up one of the engines, whistling through his teeth.

"You sell these? People actually buy 'em?"

"You find better," said Nell, shrugging her shoulders, so that she now looked for a moment like a whale coming up to breathe. "All a question of supply an' demand luv, supply an' demand! What makes the world go round, come peace, come war? Supply an' demand!"

"But Lumme, I could knock one up like this meself!" protested Horace. "A bit o' wood, few nails, a cotton reel for the chimbley, an' Bob's your uncle!"

"I'm not saying you couldn't," said Nell tolerantly, "but first you got to get the idea, then the timber, and then tap the right market!"

Horace inhaled deeply and looked hard at her, spirals of smoke trickling slowly from the corners of his mouth.

"Is timber *that* hard to get? *This* sort o' timber?"

"That's the rub, dearie," Nell told him. "We did well to start. Used up all our boxes. When we'd used our own I sent Lennie and Leopold around the stands half-inching others but soon we come to a full stop. S.T.O.P.—*Stop!* No more boxes, no more engines! Simple as that!"

"But you could pick up this sort o' timber anywhere, Nell!" protested Horace, still unconvinced.

"You could? You tell Lennie that and he'll crown yer for it! We tried everywhere. You don't *find* timber no more and you can't buy it without a ruddy license!"

"If it's not a rude question, 'ow much would you get for this?" asked Horace.

"It's a bloody rude question, but I'll tell yer dearie," said Nell. "That sells at five-and-a-tanner wholesale, ten bob retail. Got refugees makin' 'em we 'ave, bob a dozen or thereabouts. Larse Christmas we 'ad stalls outside some o' the camps. We cleared four thousand of 'em and could have sold twice as many again. No one makes kids' toys now. It's like I said, Horace, supply an' demand!"

"Then I come to the right shop!" said Horace shortly.

"Come an' have a cup o' char, Nell, while Pedlar here minds the till for you!"

"Is he good at minding tills?" said Nell heartlessly.

"He'll do anything for me, won't you Pedlar?" said Horace.

"Arr, I will that, Popey!" said Pedlar readily, and moved round behind the trestle table, while Nell heaved herself up and waddled in the wake of Horace.

They were away about half an hour, and when they came back they seemed to be in excellent spirits. Horace was laughing and slapping Nell on the back. Each time he slapped her her huge body quivered and she lunged back at him with the ram of an elbow. Horace had purchased some beer and they all drank a bottle. Then Horace said that he and Pedlar were going to do the town and that they would return to camp and get things fixed up before their leave expired.

"The sooner the better," said Nell gaily. "Christmas'll be here in no time an' before that every kid 'as a birthday, don't he?"

"How about a bit in advance, Nell?" demanded Horace. "Me an' Pedlar are scant."

The affability faded from Nell's face so rapidly that it was like a noonday sun disappearing behind a swirl of pasty clouds, but she opened her till nevertheless and took out a roll of pound notes. She handled them like explosives.

"I don't really hold with advances," she said, "but seeing we done business before, and you're one o' them Brylcream boys we've all heard so much about, here's five! Gawd help you son if I don't hear from you by Saturday! I'll foller you if I 'ave to get in a barrage balloon to do it, so help me I will!"

"I bet you would an' all," said Horace lightly. "Remember Paddy O'Bannion, an' them leeks he promised you?"

At the mention of Paddy O'Bannion and his leeks Jellybelly Nell seemed to liquefy before Pedlar's astonished gaze. Her face retreated into her shoulders and then her shoulders slipped down like a melting blancmange over and beyond the vast buttresses of her breasts. As though fearing she would disappear altogether her thick, beringed fingers made a wild grab at the edge of the table and finding it, held on, checking the overall metamorphosis and sending it back, like a receding wave. For a few seconds Pedlar thought she was having a seizure but then a thin, bronchial wheeze told him what was happening. Jellybelly Nell was laughing and this always happened to her when she laughed.

They said goodbye and went out into the Strand.

Pedlar noticed that Horace was in high good humor. He whistled softly and held himself very erect. His eyes were clear, and his chin challenged the sullen lions in Trafalgar Square.

"Lumme, we landed right on our feet!" he told Pedlar. "I went round there thinking Jellybelly might be short of a few fruit and veg. crates and here we are in the toy business! Funny how things happen like that in wartime. Who'd have thought Heath Robinson stuff like hers would have sold? Well, we'll have a night out, Pedlar, and then get back. No sense in kicking our heels down here with all that tosh lying about in camp!"

"How you going to get hold of them boxes, Popey?"

"Oh, I'll figure a way," Horace told him, "but first we'll have something to eat, a few beers and then a show, eh? You never bin to the theater 'ave you? No? Then you got a treat coming to you, chum!"

They moved up Haymarket and across Piccadilly into Soho. Horace took him into a Greek restaurant for a meal and afterwards into an adjoining pub, where they had three beers and two gins.

"Just in time for the final show at the Windmill," he said, as they went and joined a moving queue outside the theater. "This is it! 'We never closed!' And I don't wonder, neither, when you come to look at them pickshers outside!"

They went into the best seats and Pedlar enjoyed the show although, deep down, he was the slightest bit shocked by the display of static nudes.

"I thought they on'y showed that kind of thing in Paris?" he asked Horace on the way out.

"Ah, there's a big diff'rence," said Horace. "Over there they dance around like it, but here they gotter stand still! There's hell to pay if they so much as lose their balance!"

Pedlar pondered this all the way home and all the way through their fish and chip supper. It seemed to him a very fine distinction, so fine indeed that he could make no sense of it, and presently addressed Horace as though he too had been pondering the matter for the last hour.

"What's the diff'rence?" he asked suddenly.

"Eh?" said Horace, his mouth full of hake.

"Them Judies we saw, the ones like statues! Why's it okay if they stand still and not if they flop about?"

Horace swallowed his fish and regarded Pedlar paternally.

"I don't reckon I could ever make you understand, Pedlar," he said, "so forget it, son, and concentrate on them crates at the camp!"

Pedlar took him literally. Half the night, reclining on his bed of leather cushions at the foot of Horace's bed, and all the way back to camp in the train, Pedlar concentrated hard on this particular problem, going over it stage by stage, with a line of thought for every eventuality.

At last, as they rattled into Smedley Junction, he spoke.

"We'll have to build up a dump right here on the siding!" he said suddenly.

Horace was delighted with him. It was as though he, Horace Pope, had been given the task of coaching an exceptionally stupid pupil for a very difficult examination and after a period running into years, all occupied in knocking facts and figures into his pupil's head, had entered him with the gloomiest forebodings and watched him pass with honors in all subjects.

"You're coming on!" he exclaimed. "You're coming on wonderful! That's the right answer and I never come near it! I been sitting here working out how we could get crates already in camp down here on the lorry, and that means we'd have to choose between cutting in the Transport section or risking half-inching a lorry. We won't bother with the crates already delivered, we'll go for the noo ones as they come in. Lumme, it's brilliant—bang on!" and he thumped the gratified Pedlar on his broad back as the train drew into the platform.

It was Thursday night and the next load of boxes was due to arrive the following morning.

"Lucky we squared it with Sergeant Wallace before we went," he said. "We'll tell him we'll cope with tomorrow's lot and he can concentrate on his snooker!"

Sergeant Wallace was delighted to be relieved of his Friday morning chore and told Horace to fix it with Transport and use Pedlar as his driver.

"That pal of yours looks as if he could carry the boxes up here on his lonesome," he said approvingly. "The A.C.2 Transport gave me was useless. Couldn't even hold one end, while I pulled from the tailboard. I had to do it all and me an N.C.O.!"

They drove down to Smedley and met the goods train. There were two wagons full of crates and Pedlar set about unloading both, while Horace went off and found the goods yard foreman and signed for a total of thirty-four.

"Some of 'em have got to go on to Smoke for tool kits," he told the railwayman, "so there's no sense in taking 'em up to camp and lugging 'em back again. When do you have a goods train for town?"

The man consulted his book. "Day after tomorrow," he said. "Are they carriage forward?"

"That's it," said Pedlar. "The party who gets 'em'll square up for 'em. That's my orders!"

"All right," said the foreman, "stack 'em alongside the coke dump. They'll be going from that siding and here's some labels to fill out. I'm up to my neck in it and you chaps never seem to have nothing to do!"

"Leave it all to me," said Horace, and took the labels back to the siding where Pedlar had already loaded half the crates on to the lorry.

"You're getting quicker an' quicker on the uptake, Pedlar," he said enthusiastically. "A year ago you would have piled 'em all ready for Jellybelly and expected us to drive up with an empty jalopy and answer a lot o' silly questions! How many you got aboard?"

"Seventeen," Pedlar told him. "Is that enough?"

"Plenty," said Horace, "I had a look at the tally book last night and went back ten weeks. The numbers vary, see? The most we ever had in one day was fifty-two and the least four-teen. All we got to do now is to enter seventeen against today's date and the ruddy Fraud Squad wouldn't cotton us!"

As far as Horace could see the fiddle was foolproof. Every time a supply of crates arrived they were halved, one consignment going back on the lorry, the remainder being stacked alongside the coke dump for onward transmission, carriage forward, to Jellybelly's address in Covent Garden. In the first month a total of one hundred and three crates had gone to make toy railway engines and forts.

Horace received an enthusiastic letter from Nell enclosing twenty pounds and saying that her refugee craftsmen found the crates far more suitable than the wood previously given them and that their work had shown a corresponding improvement.

She was now able to get as much as fifteen shillings whole-sale for an engine and over a pound for more complicated models. Did Horace think that he could step up deliveries, so that she could enter the scooter market?

Horace wrote back saying that this depended on his supply, but before she had time to reply a goods train arrived with seven truckloads of crates, totaling more than a hundred.

There had never been a delivery on this scale and for a moment Horace was stunned by the array. Ordinarily it would have meant half-a-dozen trips with the truck, and once in camp it would have been difficult to know where to find space for the boxes. Pondering this he decided to take advantage of the situation and told Pedlar to take a single truckload of twenty crates and leave the remaining eighty-eight on the siding.

Sergeant Wallace had never bothered to check the delivery notes himself and because Horace made a habit of doing this he earned the busy foreman's gratitude. The railwayman came down to look at the towering piles of boxes and shook his head doubtfully.

"We got no room in Sunday's goods for that lot," he told a crestfallen Horace, "they'll have to accumulate and go by driblets!"

Horace never believed in pushing his luck.

"Okay," he said, "it's not my worry. Can I build up a dump down here if any more come along?"

"Why not," said the railwayman, "there's plenty o' room isn't there?"

It was a spacious yard but the goods foreman did not bargain for deliveries on the scale of the next three weeks. Soon a fortress of crates had been erected on the siding and the boxes threatened to cover the entire station area.

Horace's main fear was that someone from the railway should take it upon themselves to ring through to the camp, and demand clearance. If this happened he had a story ready. With only one lorry available he would be able to claim that a buildup was inevitable, but any such emergency would surely lead to an examination of the tally book and perhaps a count of boxes in camp. Then someone would be sure to want to know what had happened to the five hundred or so already converted into trains, trucks, scooters and kiddicars.

On the last Friday in May the bottom fell out of his world. He and Pedlar were unloading boxes in a camp glade when the adjutant came down the path, followed by a harassed-looking Sergeant Wallace.

"Hi there! A.C. Pope! Come over here!" called the sergeant.

"Hullo! Something's up!" Horace told Pedlar. "Stay here while I give it the onceover!"

He scrambled over a barricade of crates and saluted the adjutant.

"Lovely mornin', sir," he suggested hopefully.

"Never mind the flaming weather, A.C.!" snapped Wallace, who had been dragged away from the N.A.A.F.I. in the midst of a sensational snooker break, "we've had a signal in about the boxes! They're needed, all of 'em, and in a hurry!"

Pedlar's stomach cartwheeled but he kept his head.

"*All* of 'em?" he said, trying to sound more surprised than alarmed.

"Eventually, yes," said the adjutant briefly. He snatched the tally book from Wallace's hand and adjusted his spectacles. "According to this we've got over three thousand lying around.

We'd better start counting at once and then I'll see the C.O. about despatching the first five hundred. We've got until 2359 hours to get them off. The incoming train with the tool kits is there now and it has to be emptied by 1800 hours. That gives us a bare six hours!"

Horace understood nothing of this but was struck by the sergeant's dismayed expression.

"That's absolutely impossible, sir!" he protested. "These crates are lying all over the place and it'll take at least forty-eight hours to collect and transport five hundred to the station. Why didn't we have more warning?"

"We did," said the adjutant somberly, "we had more than a fortnight!"

"But I never heard a word about this until you came into the N.A.A.F.I. ten minutes ago, sir!" wailed Wallace.

"That," said the adjutant bitterly, "is neither here nor there! The fact remains that either we pack and despatch five hundred crates of tool kits by 2359 hours tonight or we're in trouble, real trouble, all of us, d'you understand?"

Squadron Leader Tankerlieu did not spend much time in his office at the farmhouse. He could be found there but one day in three, the day he slept in as duty officer. When the C.O. moved in the adjutant moved out, retiring to a drafty cave that had once been the woodshed adjoining the farm kitchen. Corporal Gittens occupied the orderly room proper, a long, stone-floored room that had been the farm dairy. Gittens had made himself very cozy in here, commandeering several thick-nesses of coconut matting from empty billets and stacking mountains of sawn-up railroad ties in the alcoves. He was fond of his creature comforts and kept a good fire, summer and winter. His motto, as he was always glad to tell anyone, was "Any damned fool can be uncomfortable!"

Even when the C.O. was on duty he did not spend much time on administration. Most of this was carried out by the corporal, who, on this account, stood high in Tankerlieu's regard. The squadron leader was fond of a good book and was much addicted to Sapper, Dornford Yates and other action authors. Such forms and documents as Gittens placed in his "In" tray he attended to just before he went to bed on the nights he slept in the office. The work usually occupied him about twenty minutes, sometimes less, for Gittens always held back any papers that could be used as camp currency. Certain leave passes and appeals for reclassifications to higher grades fell into this category. Gittens liked to keep a sheaf of these in reserve, and put them in for signature when he needed the cooperation of the men who had submitted them. Nobody minded this judicial blackmail, it was the way things were run at Craddock Wood. If the C.O. wasn't available when these little bargains had been struck then the corporal signed the papers himself. He was expert at forging the C.O.'s signature on passes, warrants and transport chits and Tankerlieu himself would have sworn to one of Gittens' signatures in court, possibly disclaiming his own casual scrawl.

The C.O. kept a large documents tray on his desk. This was divided into six compartments, three of which were marked "In," "Out" and "Pending," the others being unlabeled. He used the unlabeled trays for his tobacco and pouch, his novels, checkbook and private correspondence.

It would be unfair to suggest that Tankerlieu never rummaged in his "Pending" tray. He sometimes needed a paper clip to scrape out his pipe bowl and this was where the paper clips were kept. He examined his "In" tray when he was drinking his nightcap of cocoa, just before climbing into bed. He did not mind dripping cocoa onto leave passes and airmen's documents but he had too much respect for Sapper and Dornford Yates to risk soiling their pages with cocoa splashes.

Nobody at Craddock Wood ever discovered how the original Command signal came to be mislaid. It was never afterwards found and it is very probable that it fell from tray to floor when one or another of the airmen awaiting a pass came into the C.O.'s room in his absence and rummaged about until he found what he wanted. The office was cleaned out two or three times a week and in this way the signal would have been stuffed into the wastepaper basket and later burned in the S.H.Q. incinerator.

The first intimation that anyone had of the urgent demand for boxes, and of the arrival of the special train containing tool kits for Operation Overlord, was a second and more urgent signal demanding prompt acknowledgment of the first.

This second signal arrived at Craddock Wood on the last day of May, 1943, and Corporal Gittens, at once relating it to all the newspaper talk there had been about the Second Front, decided that it was sufficiently urgent to be placed before an officer at once.

He went into the office and handed it to the adjutant, now deeply immersed in *The Life of Archbishop Cranmer.*

"Signal here, sir," said Gittens casually, "looks like a bit of a flap at Group!"

Flying Officer Trumper read the signal. He then removed his glasses, read it again and at once forgot all about Archbishop Cranmer.

"Where's the original?" he demanded.

Gittens had been prepared for this and opened his registry book.

"Came in on the seventeenth," he said, "you give me a signature for it!"

"Did I?" murmured Trumper. "Did I really? That's odd, I don't seem to remember a thing about it! Let me see!"

He examined the signature carefully and distress showed on his pale face.

"We'd better have a look for it in the files," he said.

"I've looked," said Gittens blandly, "and it's not in the files! Thing like that wouldn't be, sir, it'd be in the greens or reds if it was anywhere."

The red files were marked "Secret" and the green files were marked "Confidential." Both were maintained by officers and kept locked in the safe.

"Very well, Corporal," said Trumper, slightly relieved. "I'll look into it but this is very urgent, so you'd best contact the C.O. Do you know where he is right now?"

"I got a pretty good idea, sir," said Gittens and left, ringing through to the Hall on the orderly-room phone.

After some delay he located the squadron leader who had been feeding the peacocks down by the weir.

"Signal? Tool kits? Sounds like a lot o' nonsense!" said Tankerlieu testily. "Can't the adj. cope with it?"

At this stage Trumper barged into the room and snatched the receiver. He had searched through every red and green file in the office and found nothing more interesting than airmen's statements about unfaithful wives and a brief letter from Command, dated June, 1940, dealing with the proposed manufacture of pikes to replace the wastage of rifles at Dunkirk. Even in the stress of the moment Trumper had been struck by the second paragraph of this letter, which read: "Para 2. *Airmen are expected to sell their lives dearly.*"

"I say, sir! Trumper speaking! This is a real flap if you don't mind my saying, sir! The train with the tool kits is due in this morning and has to be loaded and on its way by midnight!" he said all in one breath.

"Good God!" said Tankerlieu. "What a bloody panic!" And then, resignedly, "Okay, I'll toddle over. Hold everything!"

There was nothing to hold except the second signal, so Trumper put this carefully away in his pocket and went back to steady his nerves by contemplation of Cranmer's courage at the stake. Gittens, confident that he was now in the clear, did not need Cranmer's stimulus. He simply winked at his registry book and returned to his paperback, an epic entitled *Wagon Train West.*

It was not, however, a propitious morning for a jog along the Santa Fe trail. A few moments later the C.O. roared up in his two-seater and went into the office, shutting the door and conversing in low tones to Trumper.

Followed by a good deal of banging about, opening and shutting of drawers and then a phone call to group H.Q., Gittens was tempted to pick up his receiver and listen in but on reflection he thought the less he knew about the matter the better. He had the adjutant's signature and was therefore in the clear. Presently the C.O. emerged, looking rather flustered and after him F. O. Trumper, looking like Cranmer on his way to the stake. The C.O. began searching through the open files and Trumper disappeared across the parade ground, making a beeline for the N.A.A.F.I.

"Bad business this, Corporal," said the squadron leader. "Looks as though we've put up a black taking no action on that signal, providing there was one of course!"

"Yes, sir, I'm sorry, sir!" said Gittens sympathetically. He rather liked old Squaddy Kindly and was distressed to see him so ruffled.

"We'll cope, we'll cope!" said Tankerlieu, "but there's no dam' sense turning the place upside down for a bit o' paper is there? Thing is, let's get cracking! Let's get the dam' things off and then settle down again, what? We can always look for the confounded signal afterwards!"

"That's the general idea, sir," said Gittens approvingly. "Shall I inform the camp, sir?"

"Do it myself!" said Tankerlieu, bracing himself, and went into his office to draft a public announcement.

The loudspeaker announcement reached Horace and Pedlar while they were still talking to Trumper in the glade. Half the able-bodied men in the camp were ordered to assemble on the parade ground and stand by in readiness to march down to the Junction to pack tool kits, and the other half were to assemble boxes from various parts of the camp and stack them ready for the transport that the C.O. promised to assemble.

"Transport?" said Wallace lightly, "he's had that, sir! We've only got three jalopies and there's the only one available!"

He indicated Horace's lorry and the adjutant, already very pale, turned sea-green.

"Where are the other two vehicles?" he demanded huskily.

"Camp cricket team's taken one over to Little Norton—you authorized it, sir—and the other one is U.S., with its engine stripped," said Wallace.

"Great God!" shouted the adjutant, "this is disastrous! We won't be able to transport more than twenty boxes at a time, so what on earth is the use of marching half the camp down to the Junction?"

"No use at all, sir," said Sergeant Wallace, "you'd do better to let me, Pope and Pascoe load up as many as we can take and I'll make a start until the main body arrives with more crates. They're not all that heavy. Two men can carry one between 'em!"

"But it's four miles to the station!" objected Trumper.

"So it's four miles," said Wallace carelessly. "You can't despatch tool kits in brown paper, can you, sir?"

"By George, I believe you're right, Sergeant!" said the adjutant, with a gleam of hope. "I'll double back, get the men collecting crates and tell the C.O. the procedure!" and he rushed off up the path toward the parade ground, where men were beginning to collect in response to the summons.

Wallace looked after him dispassionately.

"Bloody Volunteer Reserve!" he said contemptuously. "Never was no good an' never will be! Start loading up and make it quick, for Pete's sake!"

Horace and Pedlar loaded crates into the lorry and as he worked Horace's mind explored the situation, probing here and there into various possibilities, weighing risks and watching Wallace out of the corner of his eye.

It was clear that the crate fiddle was done for and that from now on all the boxes that arrived at the Junction would be carefully checked, even if boxes did indeed continue to arrive. There remained the huge stack of boxes already at the siding and it was the immediate future of these that engaged his attention. When they had twenty-two crates aboard, and he was wedged between Pedlar and the sergeant in the driver's cab on the way to the station, he finally delivered himself, speaking slowly and carefully, with a thought for every word he uttered.

"Sarge," he said, "I . . . er . . . I didn't want to say nothing in front of the adj. in case we dropped you in it, but as things've turned out we're in the clear, all three of us! Fact is, we're more'n that, we're in clover!"

"What the hell are you talking about?" snapped Wallace. "I know we're in the clear! You heard me tell him so, didn't you?"

"Ah," said Horace, "but you don't know *how* clear, Sarge!

You got a bit of a shock comin' to you in a minute or so but don't you worry, it's a pleasant shock as things've turned out this morning!"

The sergeant opened his mouth to demand an explanation but at that moment Pedlar, who had been driving fast despite their top-heavy load, swung into the station yard and pulled up with such a jerk that crates cascaded from the lorry and saved them the trouble of unloading.

They climbed out and Horace pointed to the rows and rows of boxes stacked in front of the coke dump.

"I sorter've expected a flap like this, Sarge," he said, "so I kept a few by like! There's enough to go on with over there, wouldn't you say?"

The sergeant gaped at the dump and for a few moments he could not speak. Presently he looked hard at Horace and said: "Tell me, how . . . how'd they get there? How'd they come to *be* there?"

He passed his hand across his eyes as though he doubted the actuality of the boxes and suspected a mirage.

"Well," said Horace easily, "you know how it is, we only got the one lorry and that takes twenty a time. They bin coming in fast lately, so me 'n' Pascoe unloaded 'em, took a vanload now and again and let the others accumulate!"

"What about the book?" demanded Wallace. "Are they all entered in the book?"

"Why no," admitted Horace, "naturally not! Matter o' fact, I was gonner tell you we was building up a dump down here, but somehow I forgot, or you was too busy. Playing snooker I dare say," he added respectfully but with the faintest hint of reproach. "Meantime, I reckoned you'd want the book to tally with the number in camp!"

Wallace, with years of regular service behind him, did not believe this story for a single instant but his service had taught him to look for something more saleable than truth. He could recognize an out when he saw one and it occurred to him, even before his mind had begun to investigate the nature of A.C. Pope's private fiddle, that the mere presence of a large pile of boxes within two strides of the siding containing the tool-kit wagons would stop an enormous amount of investigation on the part of Group, Command, and perhaps even the Air Ministry into the true state of affairs at Number 2130. M.U. God alone knew why these men had disobeyed his orders and neglected to convey all the boxes up to the camp, but what might have happened if they had not done so, and the tool kits, urgently demanded by signal, had remained on the siding when the goods train left Smedley Junction at midnight?

"Get hold of the civvy in charge down here," he said grimly. "We'll sort this out before that clod of an adjutant gets here!"

Horace doubled over to the station buildings and found the foreman.

"We got a rush job on, chum," he told him. "You any spare bods around?"

"For you?" said the foreman, winking. "Why o' course I have, son! Fred! Jimmy! Give the Brylcream boys a hand unloading that train, will you? It's your war too, ain't it?"

The first column of airmen arrived in a welter of dust and perspiration after covering the four miles between station and camp in just over forty minutes. This batch was unencumbered, and soon discovered that Sergeant Wallace, Horace, Pedlar and the three railwaymen had made good use of the interval. Already four trucks of tool kits were unloaded and twenty-five crates were packed and waiting to be manhandled back into the train.

An hour or so later the adjutant arrived with the first of the crate carriers. This party was sadly done up. It came over the hill like a long line of native porters accompanying a gigantic safari. They dropped their boxes with cries of despair and sat about in the dust of the yard, pleading for rest and refreshment.

"C.O.'s farther back!" gasped F.O. Trumper, "keeping the chaps up to it!"

He sat down on a crate, wiped his forehead, and waved his hand vaguely in the direction of the ribbon of road leading down from the woods. Horace paused for a moment to look down the station approach.

"Lumme!" he said to Pedlar, "just looker that! Like one o' them films where they all go looking fer flippin' King Solerman's Mines, ain't it?"

The line of airmen reached all the way up the hill and beside them, running up and down, was Squaddy Kindly, uttering short barks of encouragement at the string of carriers.

Slowly F.O. Trumper recovered his breath and his eyes fell on the diminished pile of crates near the coke dump, and thence on the neat stack of loaded boxes piled beside the rails.

"Who . . . who brought all those boxes down?" he demanded of Wallace. "What are they doing there?"

"Better see A.C. Pope, my driving team," said Wallace shortly. "He dumped 'em there, I didn't!"

The train went off right on time with its full complement of cases and Squadron Leader Tankerlieu, who had quite enjoyed himself after the first hour of anxiety, was seated before his office trays. Corporal Gittens opened the door and announced A.C. Pope and A.C. Pascoe, in his best orderly-room manner.

"A.C. Pope, A.C. Pascoe!" he shouted, "lef' right, lef' right, lef, lef, *halt!* Right *turn!* Sir!" and he executed a quivering salute.

"Good types, good types!" murmured the squadron leader. "Saved our bacon, what? Jolly good types, eh, Corporal?"

"Due for reclassification to A.C.1, sir! Overdue as a matter o' fact, sir!"

"Really?" said Tankerlieu. "Good show, good show! Fix it up right away, eh, Corporal?"

"Sir!" yelled Gittens, wheeling about and executing a salute that almost destroyed his balance. Salutes did not come easily to Gittens, he had been at Craddock Wood a long time now but early in the war he had worked in other camps, and for other officers, and he knew how to impress when circumstances demanded. The stone floor rang under his boots as he stomped out into the orderly room and began looking through the files for the necessary service record sheets.

As they emerged into the evening sunlight outside. S.H.Q. Horace looked thoughtful and resigned.

"Funny thing!" he said to the silent but attentive Pedlar, "they always baffles me, they do!"

"Whot does, Popey?"

"Officers!" said Horace generally. "They comes from good 'omes, goes to slap-up schools that costs 'undreds a year, land good jobs in civvy street and pick up more'n you an' I ever will, but when it comes to sorting something out and getting to the bottom of it they're just clods, ain't they? Plain, pea-brained clods! And that's a fac'!"

"Arr," said Pedlar affirmatively. He seldom commented on Pope's philosophies. It had been a hot, tiring day, probably the most hectic in the history of the camp. " 'Struth, I'm dry Popey! How about a N.A.A.F.I. beer?"

"Better'n sweet Fanny Adams!" said Horace listlessly, and added, after a pause, "Just about I reckon!"

They drifted over to the N.A.A.F.I. The parade ground looked empty and desolate without its ragged ramparts of boxes.

CHAPTER TEN

Horace was able to take a very detached view of D-Day. Possibly alone among the enlisted men of the Royal Air Force he had never wasted much time speculating upon the course of the war or its duration in terms of months and years. He thought of it only in terms of time, effort and financial yield, much as a civilian contractor might have done when committed to providing so many Nissen huts, or so many gross of army boots. If he thought about the Normandy bridgehead at all then it was how this new enterprise would affect his own and Pedlar's retirement from the stress and strain of total war in a comfortable backwater like Craddock Wood, for the invasion backwash had begun to splash the silent coverts of Craddock Wood and there were stirrings in the undergrowth that promised change.

Nobody understood how this came about. Perhaps the missing signal had made someone far away in Air Ministry, or elsewhere, aware of M.U. 2130's continued existence. Mail began to arrive and with it sporadic postings. Strength returns were demanded with what Corporal Gittens considered impossible arrogance. The C.O. spent less time feeding peacocks at the Hall and the adjutant less with Peake's *Commentary on the Bible*. Now and again an eccentric airman cleaned his boots.

"Pedlar," said Horace one morning, about a fortnight after the crate crisis, "they've rumbled us, I reckon! Someone's found the flippin' file on this dump and stuck an 'action' slip in the perishing thing! One o' these mornings old Squaddy Kindly and the rest of his shower will get out o' bed an' find a fryin'-pan full o' scrambled eggs on the ruddy doorstep!"

By "scrambled eggs" Horace meant gold-braided officers of group captains or above, men the Americans would have called "top brass." They had acquired this name from their impressively braided headgear and their appearance in a place like Craddock Wood was certain to have the same effect as that of foxes descending on a chicken farm.

The certainty of a showdown grew within Horace as the days passed and the radio news bulletins became cluttered with phrases like "buildup," "pincer movements," "counter-attacks" and warnings about secret weapons. He became very thoughtful and a day or so after he had voiced his forebodings he came into their billet near the cookhouse and shook the sleeping Pedlar by the shoulder.

"Get weaving, Pedlar!" he said shortly, "we're posted! I just fixed it with Corporal Gittens in the orderly room and lumme, I must be slippin'! Cost me half a quid, it did! Everyone's on to this posting fiddle nowadays! It ain't what it was when we first thought of it, back in Blackrock!"

Pedlar asked no questions but at once began to assemble their gear, while Horace doled out a little more information.

"It's like this Pedlar, old son," he said, for he had never for-gotten Pedlar's brilliant summing-up of the crate situation and nowadays he was far more ready to explain things to his partner. "It's like this here, Pedlar! I c'n see a red light when it's winking at me and inside of a month this whole outfit'll fold up! And do you know where it'll go? Right! On the boat, and if you asked me again I'd say it won't be the flippin' cross-Channel steamer but the slow boat to China! Now we don't want that, do we?"

"No," said Pedlar happily, "not if you don't, Popey!"

"Germans is bad enough!" mused Horace, locking his hands behind his head as he sprawled on his bed and watched Pedlar convert their concertina'd kitbags into long, taut sausages, "but when it comes to the flippin' Japs you c'n look fer me

among the missing, chum! I never was after no medals, an'
when you're up against blokes who reckon they're a lot better
off pushing up the daisies then you've more or less 'ad it
'aven't you? I mean, it don't give you no sporting chance, do
it? And as for trade—" he now spoke of his real and deeply
rooted prejudice against the East—"there's too much flippin'
competition in them parts! Every other bloke wants to sell you
something, so I've heard! Can't compete with 'em neither, too
much cheap labor!"

"Where we goin'?" asked Pedlar casually, "just anywhere, or
somewhere special?"

Horace looked at him with mild reproach. "If I lay out half
a quid on a posting, mate," he said mildly, "you can take odds
on that I ain't settling for a posting that might land us in an
Overseas Pool! 'Ave a bit o' sense, Pedlar, I'm not barmy!
We're going to a camp the Yanks've took over, a place down
your way so they tell me. Dartmoor I think it was. Yes, that
was it, because the minute I heard it, I said to Gittens 'It's not
the flippin' great jug they got down there is it?' and he said
he reckoned it was just the oppersit, because any Yank camp
was bound to be a piece o' cake on account of there being no
bull. He said that seeing it was you an' me we ought to do
well in a place like that, because even the A.C. Plonks in
Yank camps get more'n a quid a day!"

"Arr," said Pedlar, and contentedly left it at that.

Squadron Leader Tankerlieu was very sorry to see them
leave. Ever since the tool-kit incident he had held them in the
highest esteem, as conforming to his estimates of "thoroughly
good types, wallahs with a keen sense of the community spirit
an' the good of the Service, don't you know?"

"Good Lord, we can't have this, can't have this!" he protested, when Horace presented their clearance chits for his
signature. "Can't we send somebody else? Somebody skulking
around doing nothing?"

Horace scented the prospect of being killed by misplaced
kindness.

"Kind o' compassionate posting, sir," he explained hastily.
"Me an' A.C. Pascoe 'ave got our 'omes down that way an' we

put in fer this posting months ago, sir. Pascoe's got an old mother laid up with arthritis. Can 'ardly get about, sir, and as fer me, well, we was all evacuated from Smoke in the Blitz, sir, and now we got a fam'ly business down there and me sister's written saying she can't cope unless I can do the books on me day off, sir!"

"Really? What kind of business?" inquired Squaddy Kindly, not because he was interested but simply because he liked Horace and wanted to sound pleasant.

"Quarrying," said Horace firmly, mentioning the only industry he could think of as being synonymous with Dartmoor. "We . . . er . . . we supply all the stone fer the big clink down there!"

"Really?" said the squadron leader, with a flicker of genuine interest, "I always thought the convicts dug it themselves?"

"No, sir! They just cart it away, sir!" said Horace. "We got the contrac' for blasting. You can't trust them deadbeats wi' dynamite," he added, supplying a touch of color to the story.

"No," said Tankerlieu, "I suppose not!" and he signed their chits with his usual flourishing scrawl.

Horace left S.H.Q. breathing heavily. "Lumme," he told Pedlar, "I thought fer a minute he was gonner squash the postings and keep us handy for a trip across that flippin' jungle! Come on, let's get out o' this dump quick! It's got the perishin' Indian sign on it it 'as!"

They trailed southwest all that day and when the sun was setting over the open moor they had reached a small, isolated public house on a crossroads in the middle of nowhere.

Pedlar sniffed the familiar moorland air and shook himself.

"Funny," he said, looking round with interest, "this reminds me of home somehow. Where do we go from here, Popey?"

They had hitched a ride from the nearest railhead, but the driver was by no means clear where the American camp was situated.

"It's over there somewhere," he said, waving his hand toward the setting sun, "but I don't go any farther, I'm heading for Plymouth. Maybe you'd best ask the chap who keeps that one-eyed boozer over there but I'd sooner you than me, chum. Gives me the creeps this part o' the moor does, I'm always glad to get it behind me!"

They humped their kitbags along to the hostelry pointed out by the driver and one glance round the bare, dismal-looking taproom confirmed Horace that the driver possessed accurate information of the locale. The pub was called The Last Chance and nobody could have quarreled with its title. A huge green log smoldered on the open grate and the room was hazy with smoke. Round the walls hung the naked skulls of foxes and stags, looking as ancient as trophies of Elizabethan hunting forays. The calendar, advertising a popular soap, had evidently failed to persuade the landlord to use it, for dust rose in clouds as they tramped across the bare floor and rang the hand bell on the edge of the bar.

Propped up beside the bell was a moldering card that said: "*Ring for Service.*"

Nobody came forward to answer the summons, however, and they had ample leisure to inspect the shelves that flanked the inside of the bar aperture. There were nine bottles of ginger beer, an empty gin bottle, some lime juice cordial, a stuffed otter, a number of pewter tankards, and a copy of Old Moore's Almanack for the year 1938.

" 'Struth!" muttered Horace, genuinely shocked by the landlord's apparent apathy, "this place ain't just dead, it's putrefying!"

He gave the bell a dozen energetic shakes and roared "Anybody 'ome!" at the top of his voice.

The bell jangled away and lost itself in echoes. For a moment or so there was perfect stillness in the bar. Then an unseen person coughed and they heard a shuffling step in the dark interior behind the barroom door. The door opened slowly, as if pushed by somebody desperately unwilling to appear and a man about seventy appeared. He was in shirtsleeves and his arms were coated with bran mash. He looked as if he had once been portly but had lost a great deal of weight very quickly, so that his flesh hung in creases, particularly around the jowls. His hair was very sparse and gray and he wore steel-rimmed spectacles on a shiny bottle nose. The spectacles seemed always to be on the point of sliding down the nose and slipping over the ragged, nicotined-stained moustache to the floor, but either they were more firmly fixed than they appeared or an occasional volley of loud sniffs on the part of the wearer checked the descent and hitched the bridge of the spectacles higher up the nose. The sniffs were at one with the innkeeper's appearance and manner. They were despairing protests against life in general.

"Was veedin' the hens out back!" he said at length. "Didden 'ear 'ee, maisters!"

Horace studied the man with dismay, unable to rid himself of a feeling of frustration and intense irritation. He had the hereditary respect for the public-house dormant in every Cockney, particularly a Cockney who has worked the markets and grown up in the teeming streets of the southeast. For generations the pub had been the center of Papal life, of all its social encounters and hours of relaxation. Every Pope met his or her friends in pubs and everybody was always happy and relaxed in a pub. It therefore followed that a pub, even a pub stuck in the middle of a desolate moor, should be a place of cheerfulness, staffed by someone who stepped forward briskly and came more than halfway to match the mood of customers. The air of abject surrender that clung to this man and his establishment annoyed Horace, much as a crusading clergyman might have been annoyed by a visit to a slack and slovenly-conducted parish. Deep down in his heart Horace cherished an ambition to one day stand where this man was standing, that is behind a bar, facing thirsty but potentially friendly people.

He collected himself and addressed the innkeeper with false heartiness.

"Me and my mate are on our way to the Yank camp," he said breezily, "but before you give us the drill on 'ow to get there draw us a pint. We're parched, ain't we Pedlar?"

"Arr," said Pedlar, "we are that!"

The man did not respond to this cheery advance but moved

toward the nearest cask with painfully protracted movements. He walked like a man in a slow-motion film, or like a lazily operated puppet, lifting his arms as though they were leaden and his feet as though he were crossing a pool of molasses. Horace watched him, fascinated, and then, with ironic emphasis, he said: "No hurry, chum! We got all night to drink it!"

"Aye, you 'ave that," said the innkeeper unexpectedly. "You'll not get over to Torboggin in the dark. End up in a bog you would and no one to hear you gurgling!" He stopped, his hand on a barrel, and looked hard at them.

"'Er went that way, but serve 'er right! She would 'ave it us'd do well down yer, what wi' all they tourists and whatnot, and everyone goin' in fer they motey-cars! Then the war broke out . . . hee, hee! . . . and there warn't no motoy-cars! On'y army lorries an' they was always in a gurt long line, like sea-sarperts, and never stopped, not one of 'em!" He sniffed four times in succession, drew the liquor and returned facing them.

"Yer's your zider. Us abben got a drop o' beer in the place! Brewery stopped zending, long since! Hee! Hee!" and he concluded with another high-pitched chortle that was as much a part of him as his intermittent sniffs.

Horace, although intrigued, was unable to catch the full drift of the story.

"You mean you lost yer missis in one o' these bog holes?" he demanded incredulously.

"Us zertainly did!" corroborated the innkeeper, with great satisfaction. "Us zertainly did, maister!"

"Is . . . er . . . is she still in it?" asked Horace, almost reverently.

"Well, I dorn zee where else 'er could be, maister," said the innkeeper, chuckling. "Stands to reason, don't it?" He leaned his skinny forearms on the bar. "We had an up-and-a-downer in yer one night, 'bout the bizness 'twas mostly, but all manner o' things come into it mind! Then 'er jumps up and says 'Trowbridge!'—that's my name and she never used no other— 'Trowbridge," she says, 'I'm fair zick o' zittin' yer along o' you, day after day, night after night! Bain't no joy in it, nor profit neither! I'm going along to Maud Snellgrove's fer a bit o' gossip an' a cup o' tay!' "

"Who's Maud Snellgrove?" Horace wanted to know, his interest thoroughly aroused. He was an avid reader of Sunday newspapers and it seemed to him that chance had brought him face to face with a rural and undetected Crippen. "Is she your neighbor?"

"The nearest," conceded Mr. Trowbridge. "Well, as I was zaying, 'er goes off with the bull's-eye, outer that door and that's the last I ever zeed of 'er as God's me witness, same as I tell Officer Gorfin, and all them other nosey-parkers who come round yer astin' a lot o' damfool questions! Mind you, us 'ad a good look around come morning," he concluded, with an air of having performed a good deal more than his duty.

"Well that was jolly decent of yer mate!" said Horace. "Go on!"

"Well, there warn't no trace! Just the bull's-eye, which I vound in the road 'bout a furlong downalong!"

"Just the bull's-eye?" commented Horace. "Is that all?"

"That and 'er tammy!" said the innkeeper, and suddenly turning his back on them he tugged open a drawer in the bar dresser and took out a small black lantern, much corroded around the lens, and with it a faded blue beret with a large bobbin on the crown.

He laid the two relics of the late Mrs. Trowbridge on the bar and Horace handled them gingerly.

"Well, chase me across the flippin' bog holes!" he murmured, "I've never heard the beat of it, have you Pedlar? Wasn't there no enquiry? Didn't they 'ave bloodhounds up here, same as they do when a convict breaks loose?"

"Bloodhounds? *Fer my Em?*" Trowbridge spoke as though Horace had suggested calling in Interpol to solve the mystery. "Giddon with 'ee, 'course they didden! Bloodhounds? Hee-hee! What would us want wi' bloodhounds, maister? Suppose us'd ad found her, and pulled her out o' the bog? Now what could us've done about it then, eh?" and he gave three quick sniffs, his spectacles shooting about an eighth of an inch up his nose.

"Well," said Horace heavily, "I see what you mean, Gaffer. You would have been put to all the expense o' burying her somewhere, wouldn't you?"

The innkeeper nodded enthusiastically. "Ah, youm right there maister," he admitted, "but I can't zay as I thought on it at the time." He then dismissed the tragedy with a fusillade of sniffs. "Now be 'ee gonner bed down in yer for the night? One of 'ee could take the zettle over be the vire an' I could bring in my Em's camp baid for the big 'un, yonder."

He nodded toward the silent Pedlar, who had been sipping his cider over near the smoking fire.

"'Er dorn 'ave much to zay, do 'er?"

"No," said Horace thoughtfully, "he's the strong, silent type." He braced himself and made a decision. "Maybe we'd better ring through to the camp and fix up some transport, Pedlar. Where's the blower?"

"Eh?" said Mr. Trowbridge, cupping his ear.

"Blower! Telephone!" said Horace, who did not relish the innkeeper's hospitality and felt, moreover, that he needed a hot meal.

"Hee-hee!" chuckled Mr. Trowbridge, "us abn got no telephone yer! Us did 'ave mind, once, but they cut us off, long zince! I could give 'ee some stew and some eggs. Bit o' bacon maybe, an' some homebaked bread. Nothing fancy mind! Us don't run to it!"

"No," muttered Horace, "I'd bet on that, mate! Well, Pedlar, what's it to be? Do we stay here for the night and push on in the morning? Or do we take a chance wi' them bog holes?"

Pedlar did not answer immediately. Then Horace noticed an abstracted look on his broad, lopsided face, and also that his glance roved about the parlor, from the open fireplace to the door, then to the bar, then back to the fire again. Horace was struck by his look of puzzled concentration.

"She's there all right!" said Pedlar suddenly, and gave a little shiver. He then turned to the landlord, who was leaning forward, his hands on the bar counter.

"She never stopped talking did she? She talked and talked and never sat still while she did it?"

"That's Em!" said Mr. Trowbridge, but without the faintest show of surprise.

Horace blinked three times and looked from one to the other.

"What's all this?" he demanded. "You two know each other?"

"No," said Pedlar slowly, "we never met before but he's a moorman an' so am I, so I reckon it amounts to the same thing, don't it, Mr. Trowbridge?"

"Aye, it do that!" said Trowbridge offhandedly. "I'll zee about the supper an' get that camp bade in!"

He left very abruptly and Horace scratched his head.

"I don't get this, Pedlar," he said. "What do you mean, moorman? It gives me the creeps this place do! Let's push on to the camp, never mind old Crippen and his flippin' bog holes, I can't spend a night in this dump. I got shivers runnin' up an' down me back already!"

Pedlar smiled. His smile was warm and reassuring.

"Aw, you don't want to worry, Popey!" he said. "He'll be all right while I'm around and it's true what he says about the dogs. Gipsy, my Ma that is, came up from Dartmoor and people do disappear in them, just like he says. But we'll be okay here. Don't you worry, Popey!"

"But that missis of his, and the way he talked about her! Lumme, it was so perishin' cold-blooded!" protested Horace. "Besides, he's off his chump, isn't he?"

"Not really," said Pedlar. "You get that way on the moor. His wife was a terror, so don't you waste no sympathy on her!"

"Don't talk so barmy!" snapped Horace, "you didn't know her, did you?"

"I didn't 'ave to," said Pedlar simply, and smiled again, absently yet mysteriously.

Horace felt that he was being pushed further and further out of his depth. Always it was he who had done all the talking and made all the arrangements but now the balance of their partnership had suddenly shifted. Ever since Pedlar had spoken to the landlord he seemed to have grown remote yet authoritative. He now reached out his foot and stirred the

202

smoldering log with his boot. A bright flame sprang up making the room cozier and more inviting.

"We'll do all right here, Popey," he insisted, and then, ducking under the bar flap and reappearing the far side, "what you need is a lot more o' this scrumpy! It's not a bad brew. Tasted a lot worse I have!"

While Horace continued to gape at him and wonder at his sudden mastery of the situation, Pedlar drew another tankard of cider from the barrel and handed it across the bar. Horace took it, without comment.

I'll never really get to know this bloke, never! he said to himself, raising the pewter tankard to his mouth.

Pedlar was correct in his surmise. They not only "did all right" at The Last Chance that night, they did very well indeed. Gaffer Trowbridge might have been a hopeless landlord but he was no mean cook and the supper they ate in front of the revived fire was the best that Horace had eaten since prewar days. They had eggs, bacon, fried bread and a rich, savory stew that Pedlar said was flavored with herbs gathered on the moor.

Gaffer Trowbridge made up the camp bed that had once belonged to his wife Em and they drank a big pot of tea and then several more pints of rough cider. The cider soon went to Horace's legs and he found difficulty in moving about the room, but his spirits revived under the double impact of good cheer and unexacting companionship, so that he did not find it surprising when he heard Pedlar and the innkeeper conversing in a jargon that was completely alien to him and put it down to effects of the cider.

Presently, while they were still talking, he stretched himself on the settle and slept. The last thing he remembered of that evening was Pedlar draping him in his greatcoat and putting a kitbag under his head, and as he did this he murmured: "You won't get a head on this stuff, Popey. No one never does!"

Pedlar was right about this too, for when Horace sat up and tried to remember where he was, it was broad daylight and his head was surprisingly clear. In addition he had an excellent appetite for the eggs and bacon that Pedlar brought in on a tin tray.

"I been out across the moor, Popey," Pedlar told him briefly, "and I can take you a shortcut over the Tor and down the valley. It'll save us about four miles I reckon!"

Horace said nothing. It was taking him some time to accustom himself to this new Pedlar Pascoe, who seemed so much at home in this desolate spot. He ate his breakfast in silence and then took out his wallet.

"What do you reckon we ought to give that gaffer?" he asked.

"He wouldn't take anything," Pedlar told him. "He's kin!"

"You mean it's all on the house? Just because you and him can natter Chinese to one another?" asked Horace, greatly astonished.

"We'll pay him back some other way," said Pedlar.

"What way? How?"

"You'll think of something, Popey!"

"Me? *I'll* think o' something? Such as?"

"Maybe to get this place known a bit and get him some trade wi' them Yanks, perhaps!"

Horace scratched his head again but said nothing.

That was the very beginning of it, the first small seed of the Dartmoor Fiddle.

It took Horace some considerable time to settle down at Torboggin, the American air training base.

Perhaps he was still bemused by the strange encounter between Pedlar and the innkeeper, a man Horace still thought of as a country Crippen, hiding some sinister secret about his late wife, Em. Or perhaps he was becoming a little punch-drunk by his migratory life of the past few years, a constant change of scene that was midway between nonstop travel and settled residence, yet neither one nor the other.

"I'm fair sick of livin' in a ruddy kitbag!" he told Pedlar, a week or so after they had settled into the tiny R.A.F. section of the half-built camp. "I'm flipped if I wouldn't like to settle down somewhere and know where everything was and who was what!"

"How about here?" asked Pedlar, whose gypsy background armored him against constant change of scene.

Horace looked out of the door of the billet and stared down the teeming valley, buttressed by its two towering crags. One runway was almost finished. New and half-erected huts stretched away to the river bank, half a mile distant. Men loafed about in various stages of undress, picking their way between concrete mixers and bulldozers and slopping through spongy pools of peat water in their airmen's fur-lined boots, the clumsy footwear that even ground staff affected among the Americans of the 9th U.S.A.A.F. It all looked so temporary, transitory and disorganized. Horace shook his head gloomily.

"No," he said at length, "give me Smoke, or even that last place. Maybe I'm getting homesick, or maybe it's because I can't figure out a way to make it pay. Cards is no good. These flippin' Yanks can wipe the floor with anyone at poker and none of 'em want to play nap, solo or euchre!"

"They got a kind o' dicing game," Pedlar suggested, cast down by his friend's ennui. "Why don't you have a crack at that, Popey?"

"Crap? Never no more!" said Horace emphatically. "I 'ad a go when you was on guard duty night before last and them flippin' Kaffirs left me skint! Got through five nicker in as many minutes! Flippin' voodoo, that's what it is!"

"Arr," said Pedlar sagely, "the colored ones go for that, I was talking to 'em in the P.X. the other day. They really go for that, Popey!"

He became very thoughtful after this conversation and the following evening he disappeared. Horace ranged about the camp looking for him. He felt forlorn and alien without Pedlar beside him, lost in a mass of gum-chewing foreigners, with their displays of boisterous horseplay and unfamiliar expressions, "Hiya!" "Howya!" and "No kiddin!" Half-closing his eyes as he watched a game of baseball Horace felt thousands of miles from home and, what was worse, a hopeless amateur. The feeling of inferiority was new to him and he did not like it at all and from this it was a short step to disliking everything about the Americans, their stridency, their ceaseless energy, their coal-scuttle helmets that reminded him of Germans, but most of all the prodigality of their spending. It was very painful to him to see wads of notes being thrown about here, there and everywhere, without being able to coax some of them into his pocket or Pedlar's.

"There must be a fiddle somewhere," he told himself for the hundredth time, as he watched a crap game going on behind the showers. "There must be one of *my* kind of fiddles, one that'd make the time pass a bit quicker!"

There was, of course, but once again it was Pedlar who proposed it.

He came into the billet about 2300 hours that night and Horace, who had gone to bed half-dazed with boredom and loneliness, was inclined to be surly.

"Where you bin?" he demanded truculently.

"I been havin' a chat with Gaffer Trowbridge down at the pub!" said Pedlar, sitting heavily on Horace's bed. "It's funny, Popey, he doesn't get 'em in down there at all. It's only four miles, and these Yanks can always scrounge transport but they don't come that way, never!"

"It ain't funny at all," mumbled Horace, who felt very neglected and was not disposed to worry himself about a half-witted old rustic whose company, it seemed, Pedlar preferred to his own. "What's old Crippen got to sell except that tall story about 'is missis falling into a bog hole?"

"That's just it!" said Pedlar earnestly. "If a thing like that got around I bet half the camp would want to go down and hear all about it. These Yanks go for that kind o' thing, don't they? Look at the papers and magazines they read. It's all blood an' thunder, isn't it?"

"They might go once," said Horace reluctantly, "but the place ain't lively enough for them, mark my words!"

"You could figure out some way to make it so," persisted Pedlar. "Gaffer says he'll go halves with us on the takings!"

Horace sat up, his crustiness gone.

"That what you went down there for?" he demanded. "That

206

what you had in mind when you said I needn't pay 'im nothing for that feed and lodge he gave us?"

"Something like that," said Pedlar noncommittally.

"Lumme, you're deep, Pedlar," said Horace, unable to keep respect from his voice. "Most people take you for half-dippy but not me, never no more, Pedlar! You're the cagiest one in the outfit bar none and sometimes even I can't hold a candle to you!"

Pedlar almost blushed. Praise from Horace always made him wriggle.

"Oh, just an idea," he said apologetically.

"And a perishin' good one!" said Horace enthusiastically. "It just needs me to work it up a bit! Now you get into bed and 'ave a good sleep Pedlar and leave me to give this idea o' yours a good going-over!"

Pedlar climbed into bed and was asleep in less than a minute. His snoring did not disturb Horace. He was accustomed to it and, in any case, it was at least two hours before he was ready to sleep. By then he had things worked out pretty thoroughly and his confidence in himself had returned with a rush. The measured whine of Pedlar's snores was its theme song.

Horace Pope was not an inventor but an improver of other people's inventions. He had the happy German and Japanese knack of seizing upon a patent, turning it over and over in his hands, taking it apart, reassembling it and then making more profit out of it than its originator.

It had been this way with most of his fiddles and Horace always thought of them all as fiddles, unashamedly so. Fresh fiddles were very hard to come by in the summer of 1943. By then almost everybody in the country lived on fiddles of one kind or another, and Horace did not, like some of his competitors, possess the advantages of high rank or capital to develop them.

Of all the fiddles he had practiced since he had joined the R.A.F. only four had proved profitable.

In his post office savings account were the proceeds of the postings, the petrol, the meat and the crate fiddles, but the total yield of these ventures was not impressive, certainly not so when measured against the profits of men who had evaded military service, or those who supplied the bricks, mortar, concrete, fencing, huts, food, clothing and the accouterments that had been lavished upon Horace and his comrades. All the same, Horace's profits did exist and could not really be considered the gross total resulting from his efforts. After all, he had spent freely as he went along, buying himself off fatigues, keeping the boat at a safe distance, watering down the zeal of officious N.C.O.s and Service Policemen, or looking after his own and Pedlar's creature comforts in cookhouses and main equipment stores. He had, one might say, kept his head above water yet still managed to show a modest profit and until his arrival at the predominantly American camp of Torboggin he had been more or less satisfied. It was everyday intercourse with his Transatlantic allies that set him brooding, for to Horace the very affluence of the average G.I. was an affront and a challenge.

These men, he reasoned, did not think in terms of sixpences. They lived well, far better than the officers at some of the camps in which Horace had served, and yet they always had money in their pocket. Wads of money! The kind of money Horace had sometimes seen on market associates, like Jelly-belly and her boys! It made him doubt himself every other Friday when he stepped up to the trestle table, saluted, bawled "Sir!" and scooped up three pounds fifteen shillings as a fortnight's retainer fee in the R.A.F.

His mind had been busy for some time now looking for a successor to the highly promising but ultimately abortive crate fiddle at Craddock Wood and Pedlar's hint that they might exploit the possibilities of The Last Chance struck a responsive chord in him. It was at least an idea and for want of a better one he went to work on it with the industry of a beaver building a dam.

He had been disgusted by the seediness of the pub when he had stayed there one night on his way to camp. It had struck him then that a lonely public house, situated within four miles of a camp housing several thousand men, should have shown signs of wartime prosperity, but after making the acquaintance of Gaffer Trowbridge he had realized that the reason for the pub's failure was not far to seek.

A man who stocked nothing but rough cider and still took five minutes to answer a bar-counter bell-tinkle did not deserve to prosper. What The Last Chance needed was reorganization and drive. With drive, he told Pedlar the following morning, it could be converted into "a littl' golmine."

All his adult life Horace had been looking for a "littl' gol' mine." He was not interested in a goldfield, in the treasure of the Incas, or, indeed, in vast riches and their attendant responsibilities. All he wanted was a small but steady source of income, for which he was not expected to work. Yet it was extraordinary how elusive little goldmines were.

He went about shaping his plan as a man solves a large and complicated jigsaw puzzle. He knew what the finished picture would look like, and he had several one-color corner pieces in his hands. In the back of his mind he actually began to think of the problem in this light. The corner pieces from which he would ultimately assemble the picture were already labeled, viz. Real Liquor, Publicity and Women, or, as he identified them, Beer, Ballyhoo and Barmaids, in that order.

The easy straightforward pieces were liquor and women. Horace knew enough about the public house trade to appreciate that once a demand had been established, the kindly brewers would jostle one another to supply it, and The Last Chance was a free house, a very strong suit when brewers and landlord got down to business.

On his next day off he and Pedlar went into the nearest city and they made one or two calls upon brewers. He found them all very accommodating gentlemen and at length encountered one who listened very patiently indeed to his story regarding his maternal grandfather's little hostelry on the moor.

"Been let go you see?" said Horace apologetically, as though the brewer was already the prospective purchaser of The Last Chance, and he, Horace, was the tenant who had almost destroyed the brewer's faith in beer. "I come back from the desert an' pay a call on my ole granfer, see, an' what do I find?" He spread his hands helplessly, indicating to his attentive audience that his grandparent's lack of enterprise was a source of acute distress to him. "I find the place has all but gone to pot, see? Granfer don't care . . . too old, too lazy, stuck out there talkin' to hisself you might say and all ambition gone! He don't care about making the place pay, see? Just wants a roof over 'is head, 'im, 'is ole dog, an' 'is flippin' chickens!"

"Then why on earth doesn't he put it on the market?" demanded the brewer, more than half his mind grappling with the arithmetic attendant upon the purchase of a badly run-down inn.

Horace looked faintly shocked. " 'Ere, 'ere, come orf it, mate!" he protested. "The war ain't gonner last forever is it? And he's willed it to me, ain't he Pedlar?"

"Arr!" affirmed Pedlar, who, as usual, had not followed Horace's line of reasoning very far but was nevertheless completely absorbed in his selling technique.

" 'Course, there's no knowing what I might do when I get out o' this lot and take over," said Horace expansively. "I'm all fer cashin' in an' emigrating after we put paid to 'Itler. No future in this country fer chaps my age! I shall be looking round for a purchaser the minnit I get my claws on the place, but I can't do nothing right now, can I? Nothing to sell, not like it is. Fact is, that's why I'm here! That's why I askin' you, in yer own int'rests as well as mine, to start deliveries again!"

The brewer pulled himself together and stopped adding up sums in his head. He became brisk and businesslike.

"Look here young feller-me-lad," he proposed, "I don't know your circumstances at all but there must be something in what you say. That place ought to be able to cash in on the nearness of Torboggin camp. Other places have done and I don't see why that one doesn't. Suppose we agree to supply you? Could you run to a month's check in advance and give me first refusal when you decide to sell out?"

"I can't get nothin' out o' the old man," said Horace cautiously, "but I might slap down a hundred on me own, that is, providing *he* don't know about it! Independent old cuss he is! Wouldn't take kindly to charity, would he Pedlar?"

"I reckon not," said Pedlar loyally, "he's a moorman, like I said!"

The brewer suddenly became very affable.

"I appreciate you dropping in to get my advice on this," he said, patting Horace on the shoulder. "After all, anything we can do to help an R.A.F. boy we'll do gladly. *Gladly,* you understand?"

Horace was accustomed to this attitude on the part of civilians and was not impressed by it.

"It's a question of each of us helping the other, mate," he said dourly. "You sell your beer an' put in a word fer me about the shorts, which no one can't lay hold of now without a pull on the old strings, and I get granfer back in production. Moot-yall! That's what I call it, moot-yall!"

"Quite so," said the brewer, slightly deflated, "just as you say, mutual!" and they got down to preliminaries.

"Well," said Horace to Pedlar, when they had made arrangements for a month's supply of beer and had emerged into the street, warmed by the brewer's hospitality, "that takes care o' the beer and if I know that pot-bellied old shyster he'll work it so as I get shorts from somewhere! Now we got to stock up in barmaids!"

"From around here?" asked Pedlar, still mystified.

Horace looked at him affectionately. "Pedlar, old son," he said gently, "now an' again you get a ruddy inspiration an' that's a fact! It's on account of you being simple-minded I reckon, and not havin' to keep thinking round the ol' Johnny-Horner, like I do. But when it comes to gettin' down to real business and working out a fiddle, you ain't got a clue, mate, not a clue! *Barmaids?* From round *here?* Lumme, all you're likely to find round here is milkmaids with showers o' freckles an' long flannelette reachmedowns! They ain't likely to keep the till ringing wi' Yanks, are they? Wot we need is a couple o' streamlined types—you know—the kind that wobbles when they walk and gets everybody wolf-whistling when they turn around and reach up for something on the top shelf! I know what I'm looking for but it ain't gonner be easy to get 'em out o' Smoke, an' snuggled down be'ind the counter at that dump! Might even 'ave to go up there an' talk 'em into it meself!"

In the event, Horace did not have to go to this trouble to recruit staff calculated to interest the fur-booted, zip-jacketed defenders of democracy whom he relied upon to patronize a rejuvenated Last Chance. He had underestimated his own powers of persuasion on the telephone and most of that afternoon he was closeted in a booth, working through a penciled list of probables.

Flossie, his favorite at The Balaclava, was on the point of marrying an American first-lieutenant, and Alma, at the Golden Ram, was steadily improving her position with the landlord, whose wife had evacuated herself to Windermere early in the blitz, but although she rejected the offer she was very helpful and reminded Horace of the Routledge sisters, Myra and Vi, who were, she said, dissatisfied with their wartime jobs in a canteen and wanted to go back to the pub trade.

Horace had a long talk with Myra, whom he vaguely re-called as a pneumatic blonde with impulsively generous in-stincts. By the time he had finished talking Myra saw herself sitting in the back seat of a chauffeur-driven Dodge saloon, threading its way through slow-moving Manhattan traffic. As she confided to the equally bemused Vi, after they had handed in their overalls and told the canteen manager to go fry 'is own bloody chips, "Three thousand of 'em to choose from! And no competition for miles around! We won't deserve to better our-selves if we don't make something of this, and it's nice of old Horace to remember us! I always did like Horace. He's a little man an' I always go for little men! They always got more tech-nique than huskies!"

If Myra and Vi had had their way they would have boarded a train and arrived at Torboggin with the dawn but Horace in-sisted that he needed a weekend in which to make the pub worthy of its new staff.

The basic problems had been solved but one thing still bothered him, how to break down the prejudice that the Americans entertained for this particular hostelry? Many of them had called in there while driving to or from the junction, but none had been able to stomach Gaffer Trowbridge's rough cider. It was not an American drink. By going to the legs instead of alerting the faculties like Scotch, or rum and Coca-Cola, it destroyed their confidence in their ability to hold liquor. Cider had none of the satisfying body of golden English beer, which went down very well if it was topped off with a whisky chaser, and even the Westerners among them compared the drink unfavorably with their traditional applejack. In addition the atmosphere of the pub deflated them. There was no one to rib, no one to brag at, no one to confide in. Gaffer Trowbridge himself they had already written off as a short-changing creep and, taken as a whole, The Last Chance was at one with their dismal natural surroundings, a wilderness of naked rock, coarse heather, weed-covered pools and eternal drizzle.

Horace considered this prejudice carefully and arrived at the conclusion that the only way to awaken interest in the premises was to make a bid for the sensationalism latent in all Americans. What was needed, he felt, was to front-page the pub as it were, and get it talked about in and around the camp.

It was Chuck, the big transport sergeant, who unconsciously suggested the initial line of publicity.

Chuck was a big, friendly extrovert from Nebraska, who fitted exactly into Horace's thought-pattern of the American male.

He had, it seemed, done everything that Hollywood attributed to Americans. He had been an oil-man, a truck driver, a chucker-out in a Las Vegas dive (hence his name) and even a cowboy of sorts, or so he claimed. He spoke exactly like the men Horace had seen sliding from horses and crashing through the swing-doors of saloons in Westerns, and he walked like one of these men too, with slightly bowed legs, hands loose with fingers spread, as though to claw at the butts of six-guns. Horace rather liked him, not only because he was amiable but because he conformed. Horace liked people to conform. It kept them nice and predictable.

Chuck was the kingpin of the Transport Yard, to which

Horace and Pedlar were attached as units of the R.A.F. caretaker wing. It was he who allocated the jobs and Horace had therefore made himself agreeable to the big Nebraskan from the day of his arrival at Torboggin. He had encouraged Chuck to talk about Paleyville, the sergeant's home town, and Chuck, a victim of successive waves of homesickness, was touched by the little Cockney's interest in Paleyville and in three of Paleyville's youngest citizens, who stared, solemn-faced, from the family portrait that Chuck carried round with him in his breast pocket.

Chuck was never tired of exhibiting this picture. Several times a day he would take it out and thrust it under the nose of whoever he happened to be addressing.

"Get a load o' them, Mac!" he would say. "Jes get a load o' them three, brothers! Ain't they cute now? *Ain't* they now? *Ain't* they just?"

And because many of Chuck's compatriots were also family men a long way from home they would always give the picture a dutiful glance and agree with Chuck that the trio was indeed cute, cute enough to eat. Then Chuck would glow with paternal pride, tuck the wallet back into his shirt pocket, rub his hands together and say: "Okay fellers, let's go!" as though everyone about him had been delaying the war by exchanging family photographs.

Horace never overlooked a characteristic such as this. It was, after all, an armor-chink, and a man who lived on his wits was well advised to study armor-chinks. Day by day he cultivated Chuck by demanding, at irregular intervals, to see the picture of Chuck's family. After a month or so of this treatment the sergeant was eating out of his hand although not, it seemed, to the extent of organizing a party to The Last Chance.

"That dump? That broken-down outfit?" he exclaimed, when Horace had suggested they have a party in the pub one evening. "Not likely, brother! I seen that dive and it gives me the shakes!"

"Ah, but that's the point, Sarge," said Horace, with the air of imparting a closely guarded secret, "O' *course* it gives you the shakes! That's on account o' the murder! This proves

214

there's something in my theory about atmospherics, don't it, Pedlar?"

"Arr!" said Pedlar, "it do that Popey!" and because he had been carefully briefed on the subject, added: "Funny how that hound of his *knows!*"

Chuck became interested in the conversation.

"Knows what?" he asked.

"Why about the murder," said Horace, with a solemn wink at Pedlar.

The circle round the stove shifted uneasily. It was largely composed of Negroes, chief of whom was Wiltshire, the sergeant's man Friday.

Wiltshire was like Chuck inasmuch as he conformed exactly to the film-fed Englishman's conception of the American Negro. He was tall and well-built, with curiously bulging cheeks that made him like a bugler forever on the point of blowing a despairing Last Post. His eyes rolled when he talked or laughed, showing an almost alarming expanse of white. To see him, or, more particularly to hear him talk, conjured up a vision of steamy plantations, steamboats, Mississippi gamblers and one-horse towns hemmed in by cottonwoods. Because of his status with the Transport sergeant he was the acknowledged leader of all the other colored men attached to motor pool. Horace cocked an eye at Wiltshire before going on:

"Common knowledge round these parts," he said casually. "Thought you would have heard about it by now!"

"Well, we hain't!" said Chuck, rolling his gum, "so shoot!"

"Well, he had a missis called Em," began Horace, looking down at the floor and giving the impression that he would have preferred not to pursue the matter.

"Who had?" demanded Chuck, still only casually interested.

"That Gaffer, the chap who runs the flippin' joint! Trowbridge his name is, and they lived a cat an' dog life, or so I heard. Nagged him to death she did, mostly on account o' there being no trade. Well, one night off she flounces, says she's going to see a farmer along the road, but that's all bull if you ask me. That's on'y 'is story, the one he saved fer the cops!"

By this time Horace was sure of his audience. There was a pause and he held it while coal rustled in the stove.

"Yeah?" said Chuck at length. "What then?"

"She fell down the bog hole! They found 'er lantern and her titfer—'er *'at!* I seen that meself, but they never found her! *Hooshhhh!* Gone! *Hoooshhh!*" and Horace made a very realistic sucking noise, suggestive of the moor's claim on the late Emma Trowbridge.

The Negroes all looked at Chuck, waiting to see how he would take it and reserving their own reaction until they got a lead from the sergeant through Wiltshire.

"So what?" said Chuck at last. "So another broad disappears after a fight with her old man? Maybe that lantern and hat was a blind. Maybe she's alive now, beating it up with some other guy somewheres! They didn't hang him did they? He's still around, ain't he?"

Horace laughed, unpleasantly so, and the Negroes ceased staring at Chuck. Heads came round like a row of black dolls as they transferred their attention back to him.

"Maybe," said Horace, musing, "but that ain't what the hound thinks!"

"What hound?" said Chuck. "You never said nothin' 'bout a hound, brother!"

"I was coming to that," said Horace, with a touch of testiness, "give me time, Sarge! She had a hound, a big one, a Golden Labrador bitch it was—*is!*"

"Yeah? Does that hound talk?"

"I reckon it does," said Horace quietly. "I reckon that's about it, Sarge!"

Wiltshire's eyes bulged but he said nothing and pretended to stoke the fire.

"You kiddin'?" said Chuck after a pause.

"No, Sarge, I ain't kiddin'," Horace told him. "That hound don't talk like a man but as good as! Sharp at ten-twenty-five every night, that was the time she went out the door, that hound snuffles to go out and the Gaffer moves pretty smart to let 'im out, I can tell you! That Gaffer don't fool around any with that hound and soon as he does, soon as he opens the door, away goes the dog over the moor like he's got his eye on winning the White City Dog Derby!"

"Maybe he's got a bellyfull," suggested Chuck hopefully.

"If he has he don't stop for no lampposts," said Horace, "even if there was any around, which they're ain't! Over the moor he goes, till he comes to the soggy patch where they found 'er 'at! And then he stops dead! *Dead*, see? And then he throws up his head and *wow-wow-wow-wow-weooow!*"

Horace had learned the deathwatch howl of a dog from Pedlar, who could imitate all animals and had sometimes relieved the monotony of drill during their recruits' training by introducing cats, dogs, barnyard fowls and even sows at suitable intervals. The strong strain of Cockney mockery in Horace had made him an apt pupil and now he was almost as good at dog-howling as was Pedlar. At all events, the effect of this particular howl was remarkable. The circle round the fire scattered as though a bomb had exploded among the coals. Wiltshire, eyes rolling madly, leaped nearly three feet in the air, upsetting the stool on which the coffeepot had been resting. Steaming coffee poured over the corporal's feet and he let out a howl of pain. For a moment or two there was pandemonium in the garage.

"You stinkin' sonovabitch!" roared Chuck, ashamed at being caught off guard so easily. "You didn't have to make that god-dam racket, did you?"

Horace was very contrite. "I . . . I . . . didn't mean to scare nobody," he said haltingly, "I was just telling you!"

"Well, tell us without all the goddam trimmings!" said Chuck, settling himself again, as the circle re-formed round the stove. "When did all this happen? Was it before we come here?"

"Before you come here?" echoed Horace. "Why, Sarge, it was about the end o' World War One, more'n twenty years ago! Twenty-five to be exact. They reckon she didn't go into that bog on her own. They reckon she was dumped there, after he'd knocked her off, but nobody couldn't never prove nothing, so it all fizzled out and soon enough everybody had forgotten, everyone but the dog that is."

Chuck looked very thoughtful for a moment. Then he said:
"What you say that hound was, Mac?"

"A Golden Labrador," said Horace.

"And this happens every night you say?"

"Every night at ten-twenty-five by the boozer clock!"

"Well," said Chuck heavily, "I figure that dog must be mighty long in the tooth! If this happened twenty-five years ago, and he was a pup at the time, it still makes him rising twenty-six, and I never heard of a dog livin' that long, did anyone here?"

He appealed to the Negroes who brightened up very considerably, shaking their heads in unison.

"Dat's a mighty good age fer dat breed o' houn'!" said Wiltshire, "a mighty good age, suh! Dem kin' o' houn' doan usu'lly live more'n fifteen year at the mos' and that's for suah, Mister!"

Horace had overlooked this point but he was equal to it and even turned it to good account.

"That's the rub!" he said. "No one can understand that any more'n you can! That dog's as spry as he was time o' the murder! He don't age at all and even the vet they called in give it up! And *that* ain't all, neither! When he gets out to the place where she went down and start a wow . . . a howling, he kinder shines, like he'd been frisking about in white paint, but when he comes back he's just brown and silky!"

This embellishment checked the confidence engendered by Chuck's challenge. For a long time nobody spoke; then Wiltshire said:

"You seen all dis, Mister, or you jus' heered 'bout it?"

"I seen it," said Horace recklessly. "The night I come here and stopped off at the pub. He's seen it too, ain't you Pedlar?"

They all turned toward Pedlar, who had been sitting on the fringe of the circle, an attentive listener but in no way a contributor to Horace's dramatic narrative.

"Arr!" he affirmed, "I seen it, jus' like Popey says!"

Pedlar's confirmation was received with great respect. Even Chuck seemed more than half convinced.

"You b'lieve in ghosts, Wilt?" he asked of the big Negro.

"I doan *disb'lieve* in 'em, Sergeant," said Wiltshire guardedly.

"Fact is, I never stays aroun' long enough to make up mah mind whether they is or isn't, and dat's for sure, Mister!"

Chuck looked thoughtful for a moment. Finally he stood up and slapped his thighs.

"Well, fellers," he said, with what seemed to everyone forced breeziness, "I figure there's on'y one thing to do 'bout this! We gotter prove it, one way or the other! We got to go down that boozer and wait around till it's 2030 hours and see that hound go a-yowling! What you say to that, fellers?"

They had very little to say about it. He was the sergeant, and his big, breezy personality inspired a limited amount of confidence in them. All the same, it was apparent that they were not falling over one another to join the expedition and Horace had a bad moment wondering whether he had over-played his hand. Wiltshire voiced the general opinion of the group when he said, hesitantly:

"I doan reckon it pays to go sniffin' aroun' dat sorter thing, Sarge! If it was me, Ah reckon Ah'd let on to myself I hain't heered nuthin' 'bout that houn' business!"

"Aw shucks!" said Chuck, looking round for support, "we'll make a party of it, the whole motor pool, tomorrow night! There's one thing tho', we'd have to take along our own liquor. I couldn't watch out for no ghost-hound on that belly-rot he serves up down there!"

"But he's selling real home brew now, Sarge," said Horace encouragingly. "I had a pint myself there, day before yester-day, and it ain't half-bad."

"Okay," said Chuck, "then it's a date! We'll take the liberty wagon and I don't want none of you backing down on me!"

They finished their coffee and talked of other things but without much enthusiasm. It was clear that Horace's story had made a very deep impression upon them and the party broke up early, men drifting off to their billets. Horace stifled his ju-bilation until he and Pedlar were alone in the lane that lead to their section's quarters.

"Lumme, it worked fine, didn't it?" he said. "They swallered it, hook, line and rattling chains, Pedlar! Now all we got to do is to fix it right. After tomorrow it'll get around like a fire in a candle factory. All the camp'll hear about it and they'll all want to see it. We can't work it every night o' course, but maybe we won't need to, not once we got Myra and Vi installed down there! Which reminds me, I gotter see the Gaffer meself before tomorrow night. We'll nip down there tomorrow morning and talk it over. There didn't ought to be no snags about that side of it!"

There were no snags. Gaffer Trowbridge, though aged, deaf and defeated, retained his peasant avarice and as soon as it was clear to him that this talkative, bustling little airman was interested in attracting American customers he became fairly cooperative. He was somewhat dismayed by the prospect of importing two barmaids and demanded to know who was expected to pay them, but Horace painted such a rosy picture of the immediate future that he reluctantly agreed to a basic salary of two-pounds-ten-shillings per week for each girl, providing they performed all household chores except the cooking, which he himself undertook to look after.

Horace's commission was left in abeyance.

"I'll settle for a lump sum when you sell out," he said, adding: "It'll surprise you, Gov! It'll knock you cold, you see if it don't! You ain't ever seen them Yanks put it back and they ain't short o' ready, none of 'em! 'Struth, if you'd have had me around a year ago you'd have been well on the way to retirement now! You could have sold this place to any brewery in the country! There's one thing tho', you don't want to mind what them Yanks say to you, Gaffer. They're terrors for kiddin'! Just let on you're a bit deafer than you are, see? Just keep on dishing it up and don't let 'em get your rag out!"

"They can zay all they've a maind to so long as they pays for it!" said Mr. Trowbridge, philosophically. " 'Sticks'n zones'll braake they bones but naimes'll never 'urt 'ee!' as my old Em used to zay!"

"Yerse," said Horace thoughtfully, "but if you'll take my tip you'll lay orf Em for the night. We don't want to get the place a bad name, do we?"

"Us zertainly don't!" said Mr. Trowbridge, intelligently for him, "us wants to work it up an' zell it!" Suddenly he recollected his duty. "Yer! What be I thinkin' of? I got to veed they vowls," and he shuffled out into the kitchen regions leaving Horace to finish his beer alone.

The party set off in two liberty wagons at about twenty hundred hours the following night. It was Sunday and there was little doing in camp, so Chuck's motor-pool section was joined by about a dozen men who were enlivened by the prospect of a ghost-hunt.

To some extent the story had already gone the rounds and had gained in the telling. Some of the men who jumped from the lorries outside The Last Chance were surprised to discover that Gaffer Trowbridge was senile rather than sinister. It is very disheartening to the do-gooders of this world that the majority is eager to believe the worst of mankind. To many of the men, Gaffer was already a local Bluebeard, a cold-blooded monster who, in the course of his long stay at a lonely pub, had efficiently disposed of a large number of wives by dumping them into bogs and producing hats and lanterns to prove how they got there. Despite this they all trooped cheerfully into the bar and called loudly for beer, regarding the landlord with considerable curiosity as he pulled at the creaking handles and shuffled to and fro behind the counter.

His appearance disappointed them somewhat. All the older men had visualized him as a kind of Lon Chaney, humped, wall-eyed and repulsively servile. The younger generation, who had never seen *The Hunchback of Notre Dame,* favored the more sophisticated type of maniac, wooden-faced, stiff-jointed, with prison pallor and perhaps a flat, disembodied voice.

Gaffer Trowbridge did not say very much and what little he did say they could not understand, but his unintelligibility did not surprise them at all, the G.I.s having lived in an oral fog ever since they landed in Britain. Whereas the English people they met seemed to follow every word they uttered without any difficulty, the G.I.s could make very little of their mother tongue as spoken from Channel to Hebrides. They did not realize that, whereas Hollywood had conditioned the British to American speech since the early thirties, few Americans among the Expeditionary Force had seen more than half a dozen English films. By now, however, they had accepted Westcountry talk as native patter, like the aimless jabber of coolies, or Polynesian fishermen, and Gaffer's broad vowels and buzzing "r's" aroused no comment.

The dog surprised them all. It was without a single characteristic of the traditional hell-hound but excessively friendly and soft to touch. It was obviously delighted with the rush of customers and the size of the fire, which Horace had built up early in the evening. It pattered about and tried vainly and pitifully to lay its big head on a friendly knee, looking up with mild brown eyes, pleading to be patted and scratched under the ears. When it behaved like this to Wiltshire, he leaped back as if the dog had been a cobra and his eyes had rolled like those of a man in an epileptic fit. His sudden movement repeated the previous night's performance, this time upsetting the corporal's beer and wetting his knees.

"Goddam you, Wilt!" complained the irritated N.C.O., "what the heck do you keep in your pants? Fourth o' July firecrackers?"

"Ah doan aim to let that houn' touch me, Mister!" said the unrepentant Wiltshire. "No suh! Ah ain' gonna let dat houn' lay a hair on me nowhere!"

The other colored men understood this point of view. Whenever the dog came near them they backed away in a widening circle, crossing behind the settle and the tables, but keeping their eyes fixed on the cause of their distrust. In the end the dog returned disconsolately to Horace, who sat in the chimney corner slowly sipping his beer and keeping an eye on the clock. The dog flopped down and laid its head on his boot, occasionally lifting an eyelid at the unfriendly Americans.

By nine-thirty the bar was full and the atmosphere was considerably less tense. A tide of strong local beer and the drowsy heat of the huge fire began to obscure the principal reason for the gathering. Some of the Americans, particularly those who had been lacing their beer with hard liquor from hip-flasks, began to liven up and one of them demanded of the sweating landlord "just how he had beaten the rap?" If Mr. Trowbridge heard and understood, which is very unlikely, he must have taken Horace's warning to heart, for he made no comment but only grinned toothlessly and said: "Us iz thirsty, bain' us?" and called upon Horace to help him serve.

Horace, strangely tense, obeyed the summons unwillingly. On the previous occasions they had been down there the Gaffer had made very free with Pedlar, who helped himself to cider whenever he or Horace wanted any, but Horace had never yet crossed beyond the bar-flap and tonight he seemed nervous and preoccupied.

Chuck, flushed and hearty, commented upon Pedlar's absence.

"Where's that Hobo?" he demanded.

Chuck always referred to Pedlar as "The Hobo." Having learned that the big airman was a gypsy, Chuck at once thought of him in terms of the American equivalent, a homeless vagrant who rode brake-rods and indulged in wild, Saturnalian revels in hobo camps.

"Sick in billets!" Horace told him. "At least, that's what he lets on. Fact is, I reckon he's yellow, like some of the men you brought along."

"Man, I had to boot most of 'em along," said Chuck, "but this was a screwy idea if you ask me. Nothin's gonner happen, brother. You were just kiddin', Limey, and I got to admit I fell for it!"

"I ain't guaranteeing nothin'," said Horace obstinately, "but it happened the night I was here, sure enough!"

"Then let's get the Gaffer warmed up," suggested Chuck, who, as virtual host of the party, felt it obligatory to provide entertainment. "Let's get him to tell his story! Maybe it's good for a laugh!"

"Don't you say nothing to him till it happens," warned Horace. "If he gets wise as to what we come in for he'll lock the dog up and all we'll hear come ten-twenty-five is a perishin' lot o' yapping and whining! I tried that on 'im second time I come down here but he closed up. Lumme, if you was in his shoes would you want witnesses?"

223

"No, I guess not," said Chuck thoughtfully. "You sure got somethin' there, Limey! We'll play it soft till zero hour, like you say!"

One of the Americans had brought along a portable radio and they switched it on. Above the buzz of conversation and the constant yells for service, Vera Lynn once again did her melodious best with "Someday, Over the Rainbow," and later on the party could have learned, had they been interested, that the R.A.F. had bombed Wilhelmshaven and that a German counterattack at Mortain had been foiled by rocket-firing Typhoons.

Despite increasing conviviality, however, the main object of the gathering was not overlooked. At ten-fifteen Horace made an unobtrusive exit, while Chuck was engaged in a noisy argument with a sergeant cook about the time it took a B-47 to fly from Chicago to San Francisco.

Horace slipped across the yard and whistled at the entrance of a shed adjoining the tin-roofed latrine.

"You there, Pedlar? You all set?"

Pedlar emerged from the shadows. He carried the late Mrs. Trowbridge's lantern and although it was lit, and glowed pale orange, its radiance was not entirely due to the flame but to the casing itself which had been smeared with luminous paint. On the very crown of Pedlar's big head was perched Em's beret and over his shoulders he had draped a regulation issue blanket, also generously daubed with luminous paint.

"You look okay!" said Horace approvingly. "You'll scare the flippin' pants off 'em! Now cross over the stone wall and get ready to nip across the moor, the minnit I let the dog out. Don't forget the whistle, neither. In about ten minutes!"

"Okay, Popey," said Pedlar affably, "I know what to do. Soon as they come out I'll cut across the moor and back to camp. They won't catch on, don't you worry! I'll be back in billets long before they've clocked in and I'll go in under the wire, like you said."

"Fine," said Horace. "It's foolproof I reckon. Now get weaving and keep out o' sight if any of 'em come out to piss!"

He went back into the bar and found Chuck, who was getting so heated about the air route from Chicago to the coast that he had almost forgotten the object of the party.

"Stand by to let that hound loose soon as it starts pawing!" he told the sergeant.

"Okay, okay!" said Chuck and reluctantly abandoned the argument, drifting across to the door where Wiltshire and several of the other Negroes were gathered. Horace saw him nod and wink, as their gaze flickered between the door and the dog, now stretched out before the fire.

Suddenly it whimpered, sat up and began to scratch itself. In some mysterious way the movement communicated itself to most of the twenty-odd men in the bar, even those who were not attending. Conversations ceased abruptly and Gaffer Trowbridge was so surprised that he turned aside in the act of drawing a pint and let the beer gush to the floor.

"Bain't time, be it?" he asked Horace.

"*Shhhh!*" said Chuck viciously, and kept his eyes fixed on the dog.

Then everybody heard it, a low, penetrating whistle from some way off, not particularly shrill or piercing, but sustained, distance-carrying and wavering between two flattish notes.

The whistle mopped up the stray ends of conversation between men furthest from the fire and there was complete silence in the room. The dog cocked its head to one side and stopped scratching. Then, but without haste, it padded across to the door, snuffling and panting. Raising one paw it stroked the door and Chuck, at a nod from Horace, flung the door wide open and stood back. The dog went through the exit at a fast trot and everyone in the bar except Gaffer Trowbridge let out a long, satisfied sigh as the tension broke.

"Jeese!" shouted Chuck, stumbling in pursuit. "Jeese! It's a-happening!"

They piled out into the yard, jostling and shouting and the foremost, Chuck among them, saw the dog take the low drystone wall at a bound and scud across the moor toward the curving ribbon of road.

Horace, one of the last out of the pub, fought his way through the stragglers to Chuck's side, reflecting as he ran that never in his entire life had he seen a public house empty so rapidly.

"Can you see him? Has he gone?" he shouted, plucking Chuck's sleeve.

The foremost of the men were brought up short against the stone wall and for a moment, not knowing the geography of the yard, they dithered uncertainly, bunching into the angle of the wall and the shed. Horace was jostled clear of the sergeant and found himself beside Wiltshire. The Negro was screaming and jabbing a finger over the wall toward the open moor that lay bathed in moonlight as far as the shadow cast by the tor.

"Dere she is!" gobbled Wiltshire, "and dere's de houn' a-headin' for her! Mercy, Mistah, Ah whisht Ah never . . ."

Horace was unable to hear the rest of Wiltshire's protest. It was lost in a chorus of shouts and oaths as the men lining the wall saw the strange figure rise up in the near distance and heard the first notes of an unearthly yowl.

Pedlar had positioned himself beside the road about a hundred yards from the nearest building. He was standing quite still and the dog was crouched at his feet, its muzzle lifted skyward.

"Lumme, he's a real scorcher is that flippin' Gypsy!" murmured Horace to himself. "We couldn't have done no better with the real Em!"

Then, once again, he was swept aside in the stampede, this time toward the parked lorries. Men rushed at him in a body, knocking him down and running over him as they fought one another to reach the vehicles. Before he had picked himself up he heard an engine revved and by the time he had struggled to his knees the first vehicle was swinging round, its headlights full on, the beam sweeping the moor as it lurched across the cobbles and screamed round the angle of the gatepost.

Because the mass exodus was not in the program it took him completely by surprise. What he had envisaged was something quite different, a cautious advance on foot, a hesitant reconnaissance that would give Pedlar ample time to fade out, double across the moor and gain the shadow of the great rocks at the foot of the tor. Never for a moment had he anticipated a mad, headlong panic to escape.

"Half a tick, half a tick . . . !" he protested, flinging himself against the shed door just in time to avoid being run over by the second vehicle.

Nobody heeded him. The second vehicle executed a reckless U-turn and took the gateposts so sharply that it carried one of them along with it. Then, in the beam of its headlights, Horace saw something that made his stomach contract and he dragged a wail of despairing protest from his lungs.

"Hold on, Chuck! *Fer Chrissake! Hold on!*"

If Chuck heard him he gave no sign of having done so. Alone of the score of men who had followed the dog out of the pub the sergeant had not boarded either lorry. Instead he had braced himself, vaulted the wall and headed straight for the blanketed figure. In the last wink of the headlights as they swung sharply south, Horace saw Chuck's flame-spurting revolver and heard the volley the sergeant fired as he bounded over the spongy peat.

Horace remained standing by the wall, mouth open, all protests stilled. He saw the sergeant check his rush and crouch, fumbling with his gun. He saw Pedlar's luminous blanket drop to the ground as the ghost of the late Mrs. Trowbridge galloped away across the moors.

There may have been more shots but Horace heard none. What he did hear was the sound of someone running on the road and an isolated, indistinct shout above the dwindling roar of the vehicles toward the south. He stood for a moment, indecisive, muttering under his breath, repeating the same words over and over again—"Trigger-'appy bahst'd! Trigger-'appy bahst'd!" Then, when he thought he heard someone splashing across the moor toward the inn, he made a great effort, doubling round the buildings and circling the road to join it again about two hundred yards from the pub.

It seemed to Horace a much longer distance than it was, for he kept stumbling over tussocks and in and out of shallow pools. When he gained the road again he was soaked through and breathless. He walked along uncertainly until he reached the scattered boulders at the foot of the tor, calling softly: "Pedlar! You there, Pedlar? You okay, Pedlar? It's 'Orace, mate, *'Orace!*"

He was so sick with anxiety that his voice quavered and when he received no reply his appeals became increasingly piteous. "*Pedlar!* Lumme, you ain't dead, are you Pedlar? It's *'Orace!* Where are you, Pedlar?"

He stumbled up and down the road for nearly half an hour and then, to his infinite joy, a voice answered him from behind one of the largest rocks. Recognizing it as Pedlar's he almost sobbed with relief. He ran forward, gasping, as the gypsy shambled forward into the starlight.

"He plugged me!" said Pedlar, almost smugly it seemed to Horace. "He plugged me, right through the backside, Popey!"

Horace was outraged.

"'Struth! Honest? The trigger-'appy bahst'd! I'll fix 'im somehow! Can you get back to camp? The wagons've gone off and we'll have to hoof it!"

"Aw, it's nothin'!" said Pedlar, "nothin' at all, Popey! Did I make a balls of it?"

His voice sounded anxious and pleading and it crossed Horace's mind that the relationship between them was a very odd one indeed, for here was Pedlar, with a .45 bullet wound in his backside, actually apologizing for it when he was surely entitled to express the wildest indignation at the turn of events.

"You did fine!" said Horace generously. "You scared the pants off the others, all but that flippin' sergeant! I ought to have known about 'im! He carries that flippin' artillery of 'is everywhere he goes and I reckon he thought this was too good a chance to miss! Trigger-'appy bahst'd!"

They fell into step and walked along the starlit road. Presently Pedlar noticed that Horace was limping.

"You okay, Popey?" he enquired anxiously. "He didn't plug you, did he?"

"Not 'im!" grunted Horace, "but them other crazy sods

nearly ran me down! I'm wet too, I 'ad to make a wide sweep round the moor to get back to the road. I wasn't taking no chances with that crazy man!"

They walked on in silence for a moment. Then Pedlar said:

"D'you reckon we've got the place talked about, like you said, Popey?"

"We have that," said Horace grimly. "Maybe we've even overdone it a bit! Lumme, you can't predict nothing wi' Yanks, can you? You never know what the crazy so-and-sos are gonner do! No wonder Old Monty's a bit nervous of 'em, like the papers say! Still . . ." he reflected a moment or so, "it'll work out okay, I reckon. It'll be all over the camp by morning and you can bet your bottom dollar everyone'll be down there tomorrow night!"

"We goin' to play ghosts again, Popey?" asked Pedlar and the sheer pathos of the question caused Horace to catch his breath.

"Not on your flippin' Nelly!" he said, when he had recovered from his astonishment. "They'll all have their flippin' artillery 'andy, and anyway we'll have the counter-attractions by then, won't we? Them broads, Myra an' Vi, will have moved in and that'll keep their minds occupied on indoor games, if I know the Yanks!"

As they neared camp he began to cheer up a little. It might, he reflected, have been a great deal worse. The main plan had certainly succeeded. The Last Chance was a sensation and a rousing welcome for the girls was now assured.

There would, of course, be some sort of reckoning with Chuck, especially if he had recognized the fleeing Pedlar, but his reckless employment of the gun had put him in the wrong and he would certainly want to keep that part of the story a secret from the officers. At worst he would calm down if offered a cut in the proceeds, and for the rest of the journey home Horace's mind was occupied with assessing the smallest amount he could offer as a bribe for the sergeant's long-term cooperation.

Pedlar's wound, when they examined it by flashlight, was

229

not very serious, a long, shallow graze along the fleshy part of the thigh, just below the left buttock. It was still bleeding a little and Horace patched it with Vaseline and plaster.

"Do you reckon the sergeant'll look in when he gets back?" Pedlar wanted to know.

"You bet he will!" said Horace and he was right, for in less than half-an-hour Chuck walked nonchalantly into the billet. He had not even had to do the journey on foot. Once out of immediate range of the spirit world Wiltshire's loyalty had re-asserted itself and he had compelled the lorries to stop, crowded all the fugitives into the second vehicle and returned with the empty one, driving at about six miles per hour.

When Wiltshire had first landed in North Africa a year or so before he had driven a five-tonner across an open patch of des-ert swept by Rommel's shell-fire but this, measured in terms of heroism, was a trivial accomplishment alongside his voluntary return to the pub. He did not approach nearer than fifty yards but stopped, and called until the sergeant joined him.

Chuck was curiously elated. He stood at the foot of Horace's bed, hands on hips, a light, cheerful smile playing at the corners of his mouth.

"You guys sure took me for a ride!" he mused, balancing on his heels. "You guys sure had me fooled for a minute or so!"

"We still got everyone else fooled," Horace told him, "but you didn't oughter be so flippin' 'andy with that gun, Sarge! You almost holed poor old Pedlar, and he could make trouble about that if he'd a mind to! There's laws about usin' guns in this country!"

If he had intended this as a veiled threat it did not intimidate the sergeant. Chuck continued to smile and balance himself on his heels.

"It was just a bit of a lark," added Horace, disconcerted by the sergeant's expression and poise. "If Old Pedlar c'n take a bullet in his backside without putting in a moan I reckon you chaps can take a joke, can't you?"

"Sure thing!" said Chuck, with what Horace thought exces-sive affability. "Sure thing, Mac! No hard feelin's! No hard feelin's either side, huh?"

Horace breathed easily again. "Matter o' fact there was a bit more to it, Sarge. Me an' Pedlar reckoned this was a good way to put that boozer on the map! I'm all fixed to do a deal with that Gaffer, soon as we've worked the place up and got a brewery interested. I got some real bits o' glam coming down as barmaids tomorrer and if we all play our cards right there's a litt'l golmine down there. Tell you what, if you don't let on about what happened tonight there might be something in it for you, providin' you're interested that is!"

"You don't say!" said Chuck, still very pleasantly.

"I do," confirmed Horace, "but I can't say 'ow much o' course, not until I fixed a sell-out price with a brewery!"

"But suppose our fellers don't go there no more?" said Chuck.

"Oh, they'll go there all right," said Horace confidently. "People always go places where they get the shivers. On'y yewman nature that is! We'll have the bar chock full from tomorrer night on!"

"Not if the dive is placed out o' bounds we won't!" said Chuck. "There'd be redcaps on duty at the crossroads and everyone'd be turned back!"

"Sure, but who'd do a thing like that?" demanded Horace, outraged.

"Well not me for one," said Chuck, "because it wouldn't be in my interests feller, seein' as I've now fixed myself a swell deal with the Gaffer!"

Horace jumped out of bed. "*You* fixed yourself a deal? *You* have?"

"Uh-huh!"

"You mean, on your own? Without us?"

"You know somethin', feller?" said Chuck yawning, as if he was getting rather bored with the discussion, "I always do things alone! Always have! Why? I'll tell you, Mac. You do things with other guys and what happens? It's mussed up! They don't see things your way, and before you know where you are you're ketched on a snag somewheres! You leave all this to me, Mac! I figure I c'n handle it okay, me and the Gaffer that is! It's like I told him, I can keep his place full, or

231

I can fix it so as nobody goes within a mile of his dive. I got it all worked out and them broads you signed on, they'll be mighty good winder-dressing, wouldn't you say?"

"But law lumme!" protested Horace, outraged at such perfidy, "it was my idea to start with, wasn't it?"

"I guess so," said Chuck, yawning again, "but it's always some guy's idea to start with! Look at inventions and such-like? How much dough did the Wright Brothers make out o' their flying machine?"

With this gem of philosophy he walked abruptly out of the billet and Horace sat down on the edge of his bed, his mouth puckering, his body wracked with speechless indignation.

"Yanks!" he said finally, and again: *"Yanks!"*

And then, as his rage boiled over and enveloped him like a cloud of scalding steam: "Trigger-'appy bahst'ds! It was our war to start with, wasn't it? Wasn't it now? Our's an' Jerry's, so why do they always have to horn in on everything?"

CHAPTER ELEVEN

On the last day of the old year, in a flurry of thin, driving sleet that masked the windscreen faster than the wipers could clear it, they were lurching along a second-class road that was not, as far as Horace could discover, shown on the greasy map issued to him by the transport officer at Lille.

More than an hour ago he had decided that they were lost and that the American unit for which their consignment of tires was intended would be unlikely to receive them until the war had moved on into the east, and the Argonnes were as far from the reek of battle as had been depots like Craddock Wood and Torboggin, in England.

Not knowing where he was or where he was going did not worry Horace in the least. Since landing in France he had been out of touch with the war most of the time. Back in R.A.F. camps there had always been the news bulletins that one heard, whether one liked it or not, over the N.A.A.F.I. radios, and one could hardly miss the flaring daily headlines announcing disasters and triumphs in Russia, at Tobruk, or on the Normandy beachheads. Over here, wandering aimlessly across the endless plain of France, passing in and out of half-demolished villages and over the untidy battlegrounds of July and August, one might as well have been campaigning in the craters of the moon. It might have been different had they been attached to a static unit, with officers and N.C.O.s who had some notion of what was going on and what it was all about, but from the moment of leaving the *Dakota* on the airstrip near Caen in October, they had been embodied into what was hopefully labeled "No. 6 Flying Column," a unit recruited from British and American base supply groups.

This column had long since shredded away, leaving them with a lorry and an Eisenhower pass instructing all Allied troops "to afford the bearer such aid and assistance as he requires in the performance of his military duties." With this pass, and the truck that went along with it, they had become uniformed nomads, ranging about France and Belgium like a couple of furniture removers employed by a slightly shady business that specialized in moonlit flits.

Having no base from which to draw rations or pay they had subsisted upon French charity, eked out with two large crates of American K rations. More often than not they slept in the lorry parked in a convenient farmyard and here they sometimes set up their stand, exchanging bars of Sunlight soap for bottles of cognac, or packets of Lucky Strikes and Chesterfields for French loaves and goat's-milk cheese. Pedlar in particular had become very partial to goat's-milk cheese and consumed enormous quantities of it as he drove the truck here and there among the backwash of the Allied advance.

By mid-autumn they had settled to the life and now they much preferred overseas service to that in a British camp. Even in the best of those camps, in places like Craddock Wood and the northcountry recruiting depots, there had always been at least one officious adjutant or sergeant who wanted buttons cleaned and kit inspected. Over here nobody took any notice of them at all and even when specific instructions had been issued to them to call here or report back there, a sudden lurch or eddy in the pattern of the war made the carrying out of the order impossible. At the end of almost every road in France was a river and the bridge that had once connected the banks had either been bombed by the R.A.F. during the pre-D-Day blitz, or destroyed by the Germans in their retreat into Holland. It was, as Horace once said, a fiddler's paradise, for they were accountable to nobody. It was not even necessary to invent long, rambling stories to account for their interminable delays in getting from one point to another. Under these circumstances one simply said: "Had to go a long way round!" and left it at that.

There were certain other advantages in being attached to a flying column, particularly one that had flown out of sight and out of mind. Opportunities to sell and exchange were endless, presenting themselves in every village and at almost every crossroads.

During the past three months their lorry had carried a wide range of war matériel from one dump to another. In the back of the vehicle they had, at various times, slept on tires, K rations, P.X. supplies, blankets, bridge-building gear, ammunition and jerry-cans of petrol, but these things were not their personal stock in trade, neither was paper money, British, American or French, their currency. They used more negotiable symbols, like cigarettes, soap and small packets of coffee bought and packaged by Horace at Lyons before they took off in the *Dakota* for the Continent.

It sometimes seemed to Horace that money, as such, had ceased to have any purchasing power. During the first week or two in France he had accumulated a fat pile of French notes and he still kept them clipped together in the lining of his respirator, along with a smaller wad of pound notes and five and ten dollar bills, but he hardly ever used them. The people he met were not interested in paper money. They wanted things, and things that they had been deprived of during four years of German occupation. In exchange they were often willing and occasionally very eager to part with small articles of personal adornment, watches, brooches, rings, bracelets and earrings.

Horace knew about such things. In his market days before the war he had operated a stand alongside a dealer called Bernstein, who specialized in geegaws of this sort, not all of them stolen, and from Bernstein Horace had learned a great deal. He could assess the market value of a trinket at a glance.

Under the floorboard of the tool-kit recess Horace kept a small canvas bag that weighed, perhaps, two and a half pounds.

It represented thousands of kilometers traveled and many hundreds of bargaining hours conducted in a queer mixture of basic English, American slang, and *la-plume-de-ma-tante* French, the latter having been acquired by Horace within a few days of his arrival in France.

For years now Horace had been astonishing Pedlar, but his friend's meteoric mastery of a foreign language held, for Pedlar, pride of place in Horace's accomplishments. A demonstration of this mastery never failed to delight Pedlar during their encounters with the locals. If a French pedestrian jumped aside, and shook his fist at them when the truck swished within inches of him, Horace was equal to the occasion. He would lean out of the offside window, wag his finger and shout: "Touché! Alley à la bloddy trot-wire!" and the Frenchman always seemed to understand. If they wanted an omelette at a farm and the patron seemed disinclined to welcome them, Horace would hold up a sliver of soap, or a single Lucky Strike, and say, very deliberately: "Moi et mon camarade want les grosse omelette! What gives, Ma? Okey-doke? Fumer? Bocoop le twa-lette?" In some mysterious way this announcement always converted the Frenchman's attitude from one of indifference or hostility to enthusiastic cooperation. In less than ten minutes they were sitting at the farmhouse table making inroads into a vast omelette.

Pedlar liked best, however, to stand beside Horace when he had gathered about him a small crowd of potential customers and was giving them the benefit of his Caledonian Road litany, suitably translated. It was what Horace called his "softener-upper" or his "warmer-upper," and Pedlar heard it with a kind of ecstasy in which his veneration for Pope found dumb but tender expression.

"Dames ett Messers," Horace would begin, "vous ate lucky! Regardez la bon merchendise! Tray bon! Tray marshay! Voila! Nous avons soap pour le twalette, et beaucoup de drags pour les fumiers among you! Nous avons le petty tins de soup, self-'eatin' some of 'em, pervidin' vous ate tray slick avec les coups de mains!"

After this he would turn aside and address his assistant.

"Show 'em the self-'eatin' soup, Pedlar, and I 'ope ter Gawd they can 'eat the tins without breaking the 'andles off, like I do!" Then, back to his audience again: "Gather round mes amee! Chance of a vee-time! You don't know it yet, but I'm here to diddle yer!"

More often than not, while this was going on, Pedlar's face was lit by a wide, slightly lopsided beam of amiability but notwithstanding this he seldom laughed out loud. Popey's epilogue, however, appealed to him as a supreme piece of irony, and no matter how many times he heard it it never failed to produce a short neigh of triumph that directed the customers' attention to the huge, rugged-looking man who stood so silently beside the uniformed huckster. Once they had noticed him they went on staring. Viewed as a pair Horace and Pedlar were irresistible. To the casual onlooker they must have looked like a vast eunuch, bodyguarding a talkative sultan.

Then, his patter over, Horace would move among the crowd, laughing and joking with the air of a man who was aping the salesman but had no serious intention of offering wares. For all that he would usually sell everything on display and when the money had been counted move among them once again, this time as a purchaser of trinkets.

Sometimes, if anything good showed up, or if the French were inclined to be stubborn over prices, he would disappear into the lorry, carefully close the canvas flap and unearth his respirator, extracting from it some more money. He went through this same performance at every village and hamlet they entered but he never did business in the towns, where there was a strong likelihood of meeting other servicemen.

He was naïvely proud of his enterprise and integrity. "After all," he told Pedlar, "everyone over 'ere, from Air Marshal downwards, is on the fiddle but where's it all done, and *how's* it done? I'll tell you! Down some flippin' cellar and mostly through one o' the wideboys and 'im a collaborator most likely! That ain't my way! Never was and never will be! Out in the open I am, fair and square, and look what we got to show for it! Lumme, we muster bin screwy to waste all that time dodging postings in the old country! Export trade and a starved consoomer market! That's what we ought to 'ave plumped for from the start of it! We'd've bin flippin' million-aires by now!"

Pedlar understood very little of all this yet, in a modest way, he had always considered himself a fifty-fifty partner in the firm of Pope Enterprises Limited.

"How we gonner get it all out?" he once asked Horace. "They search your kit, or so I've heard! They're coppin' chaps all the time, aren't they?"

Horace never met trouble halfway. "We'll think o' some-thing when the time comes," he promised, and Pedlar was quite confident that he would. After all, he always had. He wasn't just anyone. He was Popey.

The sleet turned to snow as the slushy road ran between two high, wooded ridges, empty and desolate under the cheer-less sky.

"We never ought to have let ourselves be shoved orf the main pavé," grumbled Horace, almost disappearing under the turned-up collar of his faded greatcoat. "We ought to have stuck out fer our rights and barged on through that rabble!"

Pedlar said nothing. He never argued a point with Popey and he realized that Horace was only rumbling away because he was cold and hungry. He must have known that an east-bound truck could make no headway against the torrent of vehicles that had come plunging out of the hills that morning. Even Pedlar, who so seldom queried things, had been struck by the speed and volume of the column, and by the tense, pre-occupied look on the faces of some of the drivers, particularly the Negroes.

Back at the last depot there had been talk of a New Year push, a blood-and-guts breakthrough to shove Jerry right out of France and back to Berlin, but they had not taken this rumor very seriously. For a long time now the depot wise-acres and the barrack-room lawyers, British and American, had been talking about Hitler's imminent collapse, and Hitler's overdue assassination, but the war went on and on, at least, people said it went on, for so far neither Pedlar nor Horace had so much as seen a German if they ruled out the forlorn columns of prisoners they had overtaken on the roads during the autumn.

It was clear, however, that something exciting was happening up front. In the last few hours they had met dozens of laden trucks, and quite a few tanks and armored troop carriers, all rolling, clanking and grinding in the same direction. Even on this inferior road, that was little more than a track, they were passing groups of men, heads down in the sleet, all trudging stolidly in the same direction.

"I don't get it," mumbled Horace, as they swerved through a pool to dodge another of these heedless files. "Either they're on a bum steer or we are! Pull up at the next crossroads and let's ask someone for this flippin' ammo dump. 'B.6' it's marked on the map."

The road now ran between two high bluffs forming a miniature pass. The rock faces on each side were sheer and crowned with timber, growing thirty to forty feet above the track. At this point a lonely-looking service policeman walked out of the snow flurry, waving his hand.

"Lumme, here's another of 'em!" said Horace. "No wonder they call 'em Snowdrops! What's he after I wonder? A hitch somewhere I reckon!"

He had continued to speak disparagingly of the Americans ever since his final encounter with the transport sergeant at Torboggin. The thought of Chuck's revenue from a rejuvenated Last Chance, staffed by glamor that he himself had conjured up, and flowing with liquor that he had tapped, made Horace grind his teeth with rage and think very tolerantly of Germans and Italians.

Pedlar pulled up and the American corporal dashed sleet from his eyes, looking up challengingly.

"Where you guys goin'? You aiming to run smack into the Krauts?"

"We got to dump this load o' tires at an ammo dump called B.6," Horace told him shortly. "It says so here!" and he thumped his grimy map.

The Snowdrop laughed unpleasantly.

"Brother, you're 'way outa date! There ain't no B.6! Guys that was building it up lit outa here yesterday. Ain't you heard about the breakthrough?"

"We was just told to dump tires at B.6," Horace repeated, but he began to look anxious nevertheless, for the tide of men and vehicles heading doggedly west now began to make sense. "You mean, you chaps aren't pushing Jerry no more?"

"Pushin' 'em!" The S.P. spat out his gum. "Brother, them Krauts have started pushing us! And how! They're 'bout a mile up the road, and there's only half a company between them panzers and this crazy man standing right here!"

"Christ!" said Horace fervently, and his subconscious made such a pronounced right-about-face that he automatically turned round and cricked his neck. "Get to hell out o' here, Pedlar! Go back the way we come!"

But it wasn't the best place to turn a two-ton lorry, laden with tires. They would either have to reverse for about a hundred yards, and turn at a spot where the right-hand cliff descended to the level of the track, or drive on, hoping for a turning-space round the bend.

"Which do you want me to do, Popey?" asked Pedlar patiently. "Go back or try it farther on?"

The Snowdrop answered the question. "You do like I say, brother!" he growled. "You stay put and wait for me. I gotta make a recky up the road. Orders just come through on the wire. I got to c'lect that vanguard out front and then get to hell outa here. I was aimin' to hoof it myself but now you turned up we'll make it double-quick! You stay put and wait for me, or I'll bust you for desertion when I get outa this! You could git stood up against a wall for that, brother!"

He hitched his submachine gun, straightened his helmet and plodded away up the track. Horace called after him in tones of great urgency:

"How long you likely to be, Corp?"

"Time it takes to say hello-goodbye!" shouted the Snowdrop, pausing. "What do you figure? I'm stayin' to celebrate New Year with them goddam Krauts?"

He disappeared round the bend and Horace climbed out of

240

the lorry and walked aimlessly round to the hood. Ahead of him, slightly right, was a woodman's shack built of rough-hewn logs where the left-hand cliff formed an overhang. He crossed over and looked in. A smoky fire burned there and on an ammunition box stood a pint mug. Beside the fire, on a flat stone, was a dixie half-full of coffee.

While he was poking about in the hut Pedlar joined him, having first gone round to the rear of the truck to examine the chances of a straight reverse.

"Snow's piling up behind them wheels, Popey!" he said mildly. "I reckon I'd better put the boards under right now!"

"You do that," said Horace quickly. "We don't want to get bogged down in this shambles. If that bloke ain't quick I'm gonner take a chance and get out of it while there's still time! I'll 'ave his flippin' coffee on'y road!" and he edged the dixie on to the fire and crouched, holding it by the handle.

At that moment, as Pedlar turned to go back to the lorry, they heard a burst of tommy-gun fire from the woods just ahead. Horace jumped so violently that he almost fell into the fire but Pedlar stood quite still, scratching his head.

"Just hark to that!" he said wonderingly, "just *hark* to it!"

Horace made up his mind. The chance of being reported by a stray American policeman for disobeying a mere corporal's order was, he decided, extremely remote, whereas the chance of being overrun by Germans and actually shot at while he sat in a reversing lorry was now a good deal more than a probability.

"Get that flippin' jalopy movin'!" he told Pedlar. "Never mind about the boards!"

Pedlar hesitated. He had never previously questioned an order of Popey's but he was inclined to question this one. Out ahead, no more than a hundred yards or so away, was a half-company of Americans engaging the enemy. The American corporal had made it quite clear that he expected them to wait, in order that the truck might be used as a means of conveying men away from the Germans, but here was Pope ordering the exact opposite. Pedlar thought very hard for a moment. Then he said:

"We can't do that, Popey. We can't run off an' leave 'em!"

"What?" snapped Horace, amazed at the prospect of mutiny from such an unexpected quarter. "What you say?"

"We gotter wait, like he said, Popey!" said Pedlar, but kept his eyes on the ground.

There was a short silence, broken by another stutter of small-arms fire, and suddenly Horace knew shame. All his life he had been told to look out for Number One. All his life he had concentrated upon Number One. Ever since he was a child he had been running into trouble of one kind or another and sliding out of it, his escape hatch kept open by nimble feet, a glib tongue, and a deeply rooted conviction that those who neglected to watch out for themselves soon went under and were walked over by the next man, or the man after that. His instinct now was to hurl himself bodily into the lorry, compel Pedlar to reverse, and roar down the track until they could turn and regain the main road. Even then, he told himself, they would probably be caught up in that column of retreating armor and might be shelled, or bombed from the air, but this was bearable if it was endured *en masse*. It was a hideous, unthinkable prospect to suffer out here alone, with only the unaccountably heroic Pedlar for company. In spite of this, however, he felt shamed and shame put a clamp on his tongue. He tried to say something but no clear words emerged, only an indistinct mumble.

Pedlar left the hut without looking at him and began foraging in the back of the truck for boards.

Alone in the hut Horace made a big effort to pull himself together but had only partially succeeded when some confused shouting was heard from the direction of the woods. He ran out into the open then and saw a little cloud of Americans, eight or nine he estimated, running down the track toward the lorry.

Even in the first few seconds of seeing them Horace noticed that their new uniforms contrasted oddly with the stained, bulging look of the clothes and equipment worn by the troops he had seen that morning. These fugitives looked as if they came hotfoot from a passing-out parade. Their helmets and boots were brand-new. Their camouflaged capes looked as though they had just been unrolled at a recruiting depot.

The leader, a bronzed young man of about twenty-five, at once accosted him.

"You!" he shouted, in what Horace would have called a toffee-nosed accent, "Do you know the way to the main highway?"

Horace was mildly surprised, both by the question and the man's tone.

"Lumme, o' course I do," he replied, "it's straight back and we're all headin' for it, aren't we? Is this all there is?"

He tried to sound casual, for the spurt of shame still smarted inside him and made him want to swagger a little.

"Eight!" said the man briefly, and Horace now noticed that he was a lieutenant. "Reverse that vehicle! I'll get my men aboard!"

"How about the Snowdrop?" asked Horace.

The man stared at him. "Snowdrop?" he asked carefully.

"The Nark! Copper! Corporal!" interpreted Horace, as Pedlar showed up beside the driver's cab.

The man blinked rapidly. "These are all that survived!" he snapped. "Reverse the truck at once, driver!"

Horace shrugged and climbed in, Pedlar entering from the other side. The officer got in after them and the other men, seven in all, scrambled over the tailboard. Horace noticed then that the officer was eyeing him tensely and that he kept his submachine gun braced across his knees.

"Lumme, he's more scared than I am and that's saying something!" Horace told himself, as Pedlar put the gear in reverse and arched his thick neck over the edge of the side-screen.

The heavy vehicle began to move and skidded for a moment, its rear wheels reversing madly; then it moved on again.

At that moment the service policeman appeared round the bend. He was running hard, shouting, and shooting off a burst as he ran. Some of the bullets smashed into the windscreen and Horace ducked to the floorboards. As he did so the lieutenant beside him shouted something in a strange, guttural tongue. The exclamation lit a fuse that had been smoldering inside Horace ever since he had noticed the uniforms, the lieutenant's oddly cultured voice, and his obvious bewilderment at the use of the word "Snowdrop." Suddenly he knew and the knowledge made him gasp.

"Jesus!" he cried aloud, "they're Jerries! We're stowed aboard with a lorryload o' flippin' Jerries!"

The next lurch of the truck shot him forward and he struck his forehead against the dashboard, the sharp pain driving out every other sensation. Then, as he bobbed up, he felt a surge of maddened irritation that directed itself, for want of a specific target, at the young man who had pushed him into the cab and made him a sitting target for yet another trigger-happy Yank. The man, however, was now no longer beside him for the lorry had skidded again and he had jumped out of the cab as Horace ducked. He was standing beside the truck, his submachine gun at his shoulder as he directed a long burst at the service policeman. Raising his head above the edge of the dashboard Horace saw the American Snowdrop stop, stagger, and finally roll over on his side, his mouth wide open. His helmet, dingy white against untrodden snow, had been shot away from his head.

Horace had never seen a man die and the spectacle shocked him so deeply that a kind of cramp seized him and his teeth began to chatter. He sat quite still for several seconds, slumped helplessly on the broad seat and then his right hand, resting on the leather cushion, touched something cold. It was the heavy spanner that Pedlar had been using to tighten bolts on one of the hood stays earlier that morning and as Horace's fingers closed on it he slid along the cushion toward the near-side swinging door.

"Why you murderin' flippin' bahst'd!" he screamed, and as he said it he swung the spanner at the lieutenant's neck with all the force he could muster.

The man coughed and then slid down the side of the lorry without another sound. Horace gaped down at him, the spanner still in his hand and at that moment the truck gave one more lurch, swinging sideways against the cliff.

244

Horace did not notice the impact. He had suddenly realized that he had signed his own death warrant and terror made him move with the speed of light.

He shouted: "Hold up! Hold up! They're Jerries!" at the struggling Pedlar, now heaving and heaving at the steering wheel. Then, before Pedlar had given any sign that he heard or understood, Horace jumped down on the body of the lieutenant and snatched up his gun, swinging it round and pointing it obliquely at the taut canvas hood.

Horace had never before handled a Thompson submachine gun. He had fired a few rounds with a service rifle and, once or twice, tried his hand with a .45 revolver, but he could not recall ever having hit anything. He pulled the trigger hard, however, and the gun went off. To Horace it seemed as if he was holding a powerful hose and the din was shattering as a stream of bullets ripped into the canvas and ricocheted madly from the iron stays of the canopy. Then Pedlar was beside him, looking down at him with his familiar lopsided grin, his mild, blue eyes alight with worship and tenderness.

"Popey!" he sighed. "*Popey!*"

He shook himself, like an impatient dog who has been told he is going for a walk, and bending down grasped the dead lieutenant by the shoulder and turned him over, prodding him here and there, as he had once prodded the tapioca puddings in the cookhouse at Craddock Wood.

"Why you've broke his blinkin' neck, Popey!" he said approvingly. "And as for them others . . . I don't hear nothing, do you?"

They listened, standing quite still as the snow powdered their shoulders. There was no sound at all from inside the lorry, and presently Pedlar walked round to the tailboard and glanced in. Seven pseudo G.I.s were sprawled in an untidy heap across the stacks of tires. They lay in grotesque attitudes, like a group of dolls flung together in a corner. Some of them might well have been killed by the burst of the S.P.'s tommy gun, after the bullets had shattered the windscreen, but Pedlar, in his exalted mood, decided that the entire squad had fallen to the burst Horace had fired through the canopy. In any event they were dead, all seven of them, and Pedlar looked at them with quiet pride.

"Lumme!" he exclaimed, in unconscious imitation of Pope, "he's knocked 'em off! He's knocked 'em *all* off!" and as the magnitude of the achievement caught up with him he let fall the flapping canopy and ran round to the front to where Horace was still leaning on the radiator, staring down at the dead lieutenant.

"Popey, they're all dead!" he shouted. "Every last one of 'em! Dead, Popey! You knocked 'em off! *All* of 'em!"

Horace turned quietly to one side and was sick.

A timeless interval passed.

Standing beside Horace Pedlar waited, patiently and hopefully. Then, when Horace at last stood upright, he took him gently by the arm.

The snow was falling much faster now. It lay thickly on Horace's bowed shoulders and had already half-covered the dead lieutenant alongside the hood. They went into the hut and Pedlar saw that the dixie was bubbling. He poured some of the coffee into the mug and handed it to his friend. Horace sipped it gratefully, holding both hands round the mug, and looking past the anxious Pedlar through the doorless aperture.

"Pedlar," he said at last, "we're in a right bloody fix, chum!"

Pedlar nodded. He was not much concerned with their situation or the certainty of advancing Germans. He was far more disturbed by Horace's physical distress.

"You feel okay now, Popey?" he asked. "You feel a bit better?"

"I'm okay," said Horace breathlessly, "but we gotter get out of here, Pedlar! We gotter get out pronto! Can you shift that flamin' lorry, d'you reckon?"

"I could if I could move 'er so as to get chains on," Pedlar told him. "We'll have to ease 'er free o' the bank, and then try and jack her up I reckon."

"Jack her up?"

"Yeah, Popey. To get the chains on."

Horace put down the mug. "Okay! Let's start now," he said,

and they passed out of the hut and walked down the track to where the truck was slewed sideways into the bank.

The rear wheels had plowed themselves into a deep drift. Pedlar wedged two planks under the foremost treads of the offside rear tire, climbed in and revved up. The boards catapulted across the churned up snow and after a single heave the lorry settled deeper into the drift. Pedlar climbed out and rejoined Horace.

"It's no go, Popey," he said, "we need a tow."

Pope gave him a shrewd, sidelong glance and the ghost of a grin puckered the corners of his mouth.

"Yeah? Well the only one we're likely to get is a hitch-up to flippin' 'Itler's staff car!" he said.

The coffee had done much to restore him. His nausea had passed but in its place was a kind of desperate recklessness, not altogether due to fear but also to an odd sense of pride. Odd, inconsequent thoughts passed through his head, one of them, the oddest perhaps, being the caption from a nursery rhyme that he had once seen in a book on his stall. It had been printed under a crude picture of the little tailor, the character who became a giant killer and had read: *"Seven at one blow!"*

The memory pleased him and he savored it for a moment. Seven at one blow, but they had turned out to be flies! He, L.A.C. Pope, had just killed eight men, counting the phony lieutenant! Was there a single man in the British Forces who could boast of such a fantastic achievement? He doubted it; he doubted it very much. Eight ruddy Nazis, in less than a minute! Seven with a tommy gun and one with a spanner! It was absolutely bloody marvelous!

Pedlar was now standing beside him, awaiting instructions. But what instructions could he give? The lorry was stuck. Any fool could see that, and even if another vehicle made a miraculous appearance it was very doubtful whether it could tow them clear for the truck had wedged itself right across the track that ran between the overhanging bluffs. There was no room for a vehicle to pass from the west and it would be a desperately awkward job if tackled from the German side of the woods.

The thought of rescue from this quarter made Horace glance anxiously down the road toward the bend. He could see the blurred hump that represented the dead Snowdrop, and beyond that a flurry of whirling snowflakes obscuring a bluish smudge of close-set timber. They could begin walking west, he supposed, but how far would they get in this weather? It was at least ten miles to the main road and it would be dark within an hour or so.

Staying here and surrendering was surely preferable to wandering about in pitch darkness and blinding snow, with the temperature well below zero. They would need phenomenal luck to follow the track under present conditions and with only a flashlight to guide them whereas, over in the hut, there was at least moderate shelter and a fire. They had rations in the lorry, but Pedlar would have to find them, for Horace at once decided that nothing would induce him to forage about among all those stiffs. They also had plenty of cigarettes and their blanket rolls, and remembering this Horace made his decision. They would bivouac in the hut, build up the fire, get something to eat and trust to luck. If Jerry showed up, as was surely almost certain, then they could come out with their hands up, shouting the First World War cry of *"Kamerad!"* and if a stray party of Yanks showed up and rescued them, so much the better.

"Pedlar," he said at length, "we'll have to dig in here for the night! Get some rations, some fags and the blanket rolls while I make up that flippin' fire! Right now all I want is to get warm!"

Pedlar climbed into the truck, and as he crossed over to the hut Horace heard him thumping about under the hood. He found some dry wood under some sacks and made up the fire, replacing the dixie which still held about a pint of coffee.

Presently Pedlar came in with the blankets and some K rations, which included a packet of Chesterfields and some tins of self-heating soup. There were also some tiny bags of coffee, some chewing gum and a handful of boiled sweets.

Before sorting out the kit Pedlar carefully wiped his hands in the snow and Horace pretended not to watch him. They soon had a bright fire and a meal of sorts spread out on one of the blankets.

"Might be worse I suppose," said Horace, as he poured soup into Pedlar's dixie. "Not much, I reckon, but a bit! We mightn't have found the fire!"

They munched on in silence. Horace's thoughts were too confused to find expression and Pedlar's were too simple to need expressing.

Presently Horace said: "You bin a flippin' good pal, Pedlar! We might get separated now, so don't you forget that, son! You been a flippin' good friend!"

Pedlar made no reply. The mere thought of permanent separation from Pope was more chilling than the temperature.

The light began to fade, not very appreciably because the whiteness all around them still gave the illusion of day. It was only inside the shed that it seemed to be growing darker. A high wind came soughing up the pass and made the flames gutter. Horace shivered and got up.

"I'll find something to block this flippin' door-'ole," he said. "You'd think they'd have made a perishin' door while they was about it, wouldn't you, but ain't that just like the French?"

Pedlar got up too. "I'll come," he said, as though terrified of letting Horace out of his sight.

The drowsy spell beside the fire had calmed their nerves and they walked boldly into the open. The next moment they were flying across the snow between the hut and the lorry, whipped on by a rolling burst of fire that made the pass echo with wave on wave of sound.

They finished up side by side in the narrow angle formed by the cliff and the ditched truck, but a steady stream of bullets still played around them, snicking into the tattered hood and smacking against the metal of the front end and windscreen.

"Christ!" said Horace, spitting out snow, "the bleeders must have been watching for us! They knew we was 'ere all the time!"

His emotions boiled and he had to fight to control the violent trembling that gripped him. Then he noticed that Pedlar was no longer beside him and his desperate fears found an outlet in a wild, despairing shout.

"Pedlar! Where the 'ell you gone, Pedlar?"

"I'm up here, Popey!" said Pedlar's voice, and Horace marveled at its steadiness. "I'm getting tommy guns . . . there's a whole bunch of 'em here!"

"Christ!" thought Horace, "he means to fight the bleeders! He means to start a flippin' battle, just the two of us against the whole ruddy army! He's nuts! He'll get us sliced up in little pieces! They'll serve us up, like a flippin' dog's dinner!"

"We gotter pack it in, you clod!" he called back with frightful urgency. "We gotter wave an 'ankerchiff or something and *show 'em* we're packin' in!"

There was silence for a moment as the firing died away. Horace found himself hanging on Pedlar's reply.

"We can't do that, Popey," Pedlar called back, at last. "They won't take us prisoner, they'll just bump us off, like they did that Snowdrop!"

Horace considered this for a moment and finally had to admit to himself that it was more than likely. In circumstances like this Nazis would surely not bother to make two miserable ground-staff airmen their prisoners, especially when they found out what had happened to their vanguard. They might even accept their surrender and shoot them afterwards. Stories with this kind of ending had circulated the depot during the autumn push, when men who had been engaged in the June and July fighting told bloodcurdling stories about the Nazis' ruthless methods of conducting war.

He was saved from further speculation by the arrival of the first grenade.

It was lobbed out of the undergrowth that grew on a shelving part of the cliff, almost opposite the entrance to the hut and burst with a shattering roar on the casing of the front hood.

The lorry rocked, and Pedlar came tumbling out of the back, a tommy gun in each hand. Horace grabbed one without a word and pushed it forward round the edge of the ditched wheel, squinting along the barrel and pressing hard on the trigger, his face screwed up as he awaited a repetition of the long, stuttering rattle that had made him a giant killer.

There was no rattle and Pedlar's arm came over his shoulder to flick off the safety catch.

"Now how the 'ell did he know about that?" Horace asked himself, but before he could speak the second grenade was lobbed at the truck, exploding in the drift alongside the near-side wheel, the one farthest from where they lay.

Before the roar had died away Pedlar was standing upright and as the sound of his fusillade merged with the echoes of the grenade Horace saw the bomb thrower fall out of the bushes and slide down the bluff onto the snow, rolling to within a yard or so of the snow-mantled body of the American policeman.

"Lumme!" he said aloud, "it's just like the flippin' pick-shers!" Then, his voice shaking with excitement: "Keep it up, Pedlar! For Chrissake keep it up!"

Pedlar not only kept it up, he improved on his performance and with such devilish speed and accuracy that Horace was left speechless with amazement. It did not seem possible that a man so big and cumbersome could move with such precision, running alongside the blind side of the lorry, doubling across the track on the hut side of the bluffs, and firing from the hip as he stooped, ducked and twisted. He did battle with the rapidity of a mongoose.

Horace took no part in this action but lay crouched under the half-buried wheel, watching the little spurts of snow, where the bullets of men perched on the bomb thrower's ledge were aimed at the gypsy but each burst missed Pedlar by yards.

Once he was under the overhang, and crouched between two sizable rocks, they could not get at him and they must have realized as much, for suddenly there was a wild stampede from the cliff and four helmeted figures made a dash down the slope toward the cover of the woods.

Pedlar fired one more burst, dropping one and wounding another who fell, rose again, and then hopped out of sight, moving like a terrified frog.

"Get over to the hut, Popey!" Pedlar called from his vantage point. "They can't get you there or they'd have done it while we was inside!"

It was not until much later that Horace reflected upon the sheer unexpectedness of this logic, logic that stemmed from a man whom the R.A.F., and indeed himself, had always written off as an amiable halfwit. His own brain was working coolly now and he had even forgotten to be terrified. He reached up and threw back the loose flap of the canopy. Inside, just beyond the hinge of the tailboard, were three more tommy guns of the type he held. He clawed them out one at a time and looped them carefully over his left shoulder.

"Okay, Pedlar!" he shouted. "I got three more guns! Give 'em a long burst while I make a dash for it!"

He caught a fleeting glimpse of Pedlar's head and shoulders as he heaved himself out of the drift and dashed across the track. There was more firing but whether it came from Pedlar's gun or from the weapons of the men in the woods he did not know. In seven seconds he was inside the hut and a moment later Pedlar had joined him, flinging down his gun.

"I'm out of ammo, Popey," he said apologetically, "gimme one of them guns!"

Horace gave him one, at the same time sparing a thought for the curious safety of their shelter. It was clear that Pedlar was right, and that the enemy could not bring fire to bear on the corner under the overhang. As long as the enemy remained in the shelter of the woods their line of vision was completely blocked by the bend in the track and they could not fire down from above on account of the jutting rock. They could, he supposed, circle the bluff opposite, and come at the hut from the western side, but either they had not had time to achieve this movement or there existed some obstacle on the far side of the cliff that prevented an outflanking movement.

"Lumme, what a carry-on!" said Horace, and was amazed at the feeling of elation that prompted this comment. Against all probability he was, it seemed, actually getting a big kick out of the battle. Their success had uplifted him and their survival amazed him. Successful resistance, he told himself, was now a kind of challenge, a challenge they had never met before. There was just the two of them, the old firm, against God knew how many Germans. It was, as he had reflected while under the truck, just like a Western film, the kind of situation he had watched at the Odeon on so many Saturday nights in peacetime, or at the camp cinema during their four-year pilgrimage through the R.A.F. The Nazis were the encircling Indians and he and Pedlar were the sole survivors of a wagon train, or a body of U.S. Cavalry, shooting it out in a rockstrewn gorge and so far getting the best of it.

Gleefully he totaled up the casualties. One with the spanner, seven in the truck, the bomb thrower, the one shot by Pedlar in the dash for the woods, and the one who had been winged and had hopped out of range. Ten and a half! Bloody marvelous!

Then fear flooded in again, as he realized it was almost dark.

"They'll rush us the minnit it's dark enough!" he said suddenly. "We don't stand an earthly, Pedlar!"

"We do if we get some light!" said Pedlar very slowly, as if the effort of exploring this possibility demanded an enormous expenditure of thought. Then: "I know! We gotter set that lorry alight, Popey! We gotter make it blaze, so as we c'n see 'em!"

"'Struth you're a flippin' genius, Pedlar!" said Horace. "It's like I said, you always come up with the ideas and then I 'ave to make something of 'em! Now wait . . . there's bags o' petrol in that lorry. There's more'n fifteen gallons in the tank and two jerry-cans in the back. There's tires too! They'll burn like nobody's business, and there's them Jerries too, with ammo all over 'em!"

He thought hard for a moment, sucking in his thin cheeks and making a low hissing noise.

"I got it! Them sacks!"

He put down his gun and rummaged in the corner of the shed. The fire was still blazing brightly and he kicked a half-burned stick of wood from the stones on which the fire was

253

built. Then, bending swiftly, he threw some folds of sacking over the chunk and rolled it round and round, picking it up and fanning it until the smoldering sacking glowed red.

"You let me nip across and chuck it in the engine!" said Pedlar. "Them bullets have ripped half the casing away and it won't take me two ticks!"

Horace considered this but finally shook his head.

"No, Pedlar old son," he said, "you let me do it and that ain't 'eroicks, son! You're a lot handier with that gun than I am, so you can make 'em keep their perishin' heads down while I put a match to it! Hey up! I'll be over an' back in twenty seconds!"

He justified his boast with a couple of seconds to spare. Pedlar stood in the doorway, firing at random, while Horace hurled himself across the track and flung the burning chunk into the half-exposed engine.

It fell down beside the chipped cylinder and continued to smolder. He gave it a single thrust home and then ran round the lorry and back across the track, hurling himself through the doorway with such velocity that he sprawled flat on his face. He picked himself up at once and peeped round Pedlar's bulk to watch the effect.

For a horrid moment or two nothing happened. Then there was a soft puff of flame, followed by a subdued *woof* as the petrol in the carburetor ignited. Within seconds a bright streak of flame had shot from the hood and the glow had spread across the snow, making the darkness of the circling woods more intense but lighting the space between the hut and the bend far more adequately than they had hoped.

"Okay!" said Horace picking up his gun. "Now let 'em try an' nip across that little patch! We'll have it looking like a knacker's yard in no time!"

Nobody tried to cross the space, for the truck burned brighter and brighter and soon the whole of the little gorge was lit up.

Every now and again there was a spattering explosion from under the canopy, as the flames reached the ammunition carried by the Germans. Then the tires caught alight and a column of flames shot up to twenty feet or more.

They stood close together just inside the doorway, watching and waiting as the hours passed. Twice they made up the fire and once made some more coffee. They stood touching one another, peering and peering across the winking snow. They ate nothing, preferring to chew gum and smoke.

Toward dawn, with the lorry still burning, Horace grew careless and abandoned the watch, moving closer to the fire. He seemed very thougtful. Suddenly he spun round.

"Pedlar!" he said, his tone was as somber as an undertaker's, "I've just thought o' something! My flippin' respirator and our little old bag o' trinkets was in that flamin' lorry!"

Suddenly he reeled and his voice rose an octave. "You know wot we gone an' done? We made a perishin' great bonfire of all our capital!"

CHAPTER TWELVE

General Darius Leonidas Burnside Potford had established his emergency headquarters at what had once been a small bacon factory, situated on the main road, about a mile west of the junction of the track used by Horace and Pedlar when they had branched off to avoid the westbound traffic.

He had arrived to command Operation Beaver Dam and his function was to stop the retreat, build up a reserve, and then commence pushing in the opposite direction.

There was, of course, a good deal more to it than that. His orders had exhorted him to "coordinate demoralized personnel, regroup stragglers and, above all, inculcate offensive morale," but had Supreme Headquarters been a private individual, faced with the prospect of paying for a telegram at so much a word, the message would probably have read: "Stop the rot! Ike."

Supreme H.Q. could not have found a better man for the job. The fluid situation in this sector of the Ardennes made a direct appeal to the General's sense of the romantic and he surged forward with zest, completing his first assignment by the simple method of building a formidable roadblock a mile or so west of his headquarters and creating a vast cul-de-sac. This block, without any further help from him, soon provided him with a plentiful supply of demoralized personnel and stragglers, all anxious to be regrouped, if not inculcated with a new spirit of the offensive.

Darius Potford was a professional soldier with nearly thirty years' service behind him. He loved soldiering and he loved soldiers, especially dead ones. He was probably the only field officer in Europe at that time who continued to find an element of romance in warfare, and this had a great deal to do with his background and a little to do with his imposing list of given names.

He was called Darius after his grandfather, who had founded the Potbury military tradition in 1865, when he accompanied the Army of the Potomac all the way from the Wilderness to Appomattox with a canteen wagon. He must have done rather well out of it, for when he set out in the New Year his capital had consisted of the cart, two mules and twenty-seven words of basic English, two of which were "pay" and "now." When the Federals disbanded, in the late summer of total victory, he was able to send little Xerses, his eldest son, to an expensive private school and from thence to a military academy. That year Darius changed the family name.

Xerses had later campaigned as a soldier against stray groups of unrepentant Apaches, and after that had fought in the Spanish American War. He retired with the rank of colonel and at the age of ten his eldest son, Darius, was earmarked for the army and could already tootle six military calls on the bugle that his father had brought home from Cuba.

Darius was too young to see active service in World War I, but he saw World War II a long way off and set about preparing himself for it in an original way.

He read military history by the yard, one might almost say by the ton, for the memoirs of Grant, Sheridan, McClellan, Sherman and Breconridge alone weighed several hundreds of pounds and he had finished with these long before he was twenty. He then began working backwards, ruthlessly and methodically, from Grant to Napoleon, from Napoleon to Marlborough, from Marlborough to Gustavus Adolphus, and so on, right back to the Punic Wars and the struggles of the

Greek city states against his namesake and his father's namesake.

He was such an expert on the use of the chariot against phalanxes, and on the employment of the giant catapult in siege warfare, that they soon put him on the staff and made him a lecturer on modern field tactics.

He could draw wonderfully accurate diagrams of crossbows on the blackboard and when it was sultry in the lecture rooms, and the students wanted forty winks, someone was always deputized to sidetrack Darius into the byways of primitive artillery, or the offensive power of Hannibal's elephants.

He could talk for an hour on Bonnie Prince Charlie's advance south, or Cromwell's Dunbar campaign. He was very popular indeed with the students, particularly the more comatose among them.

Darius was still lecturing when the shockwave of Pearl Harbor washed him to Washington, and after a spell of marching and countermarching in North Africa he was moved on to Normandy. Here, in due course, he found himself saddled with Operation Beaver Dam in the Ardennes.

His superiors in Washington thought him a useful public relations man, for he could always dress up the dull, routine communiqués and make them sound like Crusader war cries. His immediate juniors thought of him as a talkative old fuddy-duddy. His men thought of him as an easygoing screwball.

Having completely blocked the road, and thus effectively stopped the trek westward, General Darius had no clear-headed notion of what to do next. All traffic outside his headquarters at the bacon factory was now at a standstill, and if the Germans were still advancing from the east they must be nibbling away at the tail of the procession, a task that would occupy them some considerable time for it was a very long tail.

Fortunately there was no prospect of air attack on the static column. By this time Allied air superiority was unchallengeable, so General Darius Potford sat in his office, called for a map and his adjutant, and set himself to study the next phase of the operation, i.e., the building-up of a reserve.

This did not take him more than a moment or so because

the reserve was already there, a ten-mile queue of armor, troop-carriers and bewildered infantry, all practically motionless and right outside his window. He passed swiftly on to the third and final paragraph of the H.Q. signal, the one urging him to reassume the offensive.

"Gregg!" he said to his aide, who was holding down the corners of the map in order to prevent them from snarling the general's pipe, tobacco pouch and coffee flask, "we gotter turn all these boys right-about-face! Facing the other way, understand?"

The adjutant said "Certainly sir" and looked indecisive. Active service alongside Darius had made him very jumpy. "I'll go tell the colonel!" he said, and hastily left the room, just as Darius levered himself up and walked over to the window, hands locked behind him, head slightly outthrust. Only the studious would have realized that he was now Napoleon, during the Danube crisis of 1809.

Colonel Churt, the Chief of Staff, was a Texan, a big, beefy man, recalled from retirement and noted, even among Americans, for his contempt of anyone born north of Kansas or east of Arkansas. His favorite expletive was "Cock!" borrowed from the British, who were now training in Texas.

"You'd better go see him, Colonel," said the adjutant nervously, "he's right on the brink again!"

Churt said "Cock!" sighed, hitched his belt, stroked the long black hairs on his nose and got up. The adjutant at once buried himself in papers.

"Goddammit," thought Churt, as he picked up a map and crossed the room, "what can you expect of a goddam schoolmaster from New Brunswick?" but he saluted respectfully enough. He had known more tiresome generals. At least this one could be steered, providing one had plenty of time and patience.

"There's a cat-road leadin' off the main route about here," he told Darius, indicating the branch off the main road. "I talked to some o' the units that came out that way yesterday. It's snowed up, I guess, but a single troop carrier could make it, maybe!"

Darius studied the map, his eye resting on the point indicated by Churt's blunt, nicotine-stained forefinger.

"There's high ground thereabouts," he said thoughtfully, "we could counterattack from there!" He added: "Like Wallenstein did," but not aloud.

At that moment the adjutant popped his head in the door. "Straggler from Wartski's mob here, sir! Made it on a motorbike. Lootenant!"

Churt brightened up. "Show him right in," he said, without a glance at the general.

A well-wrapped and deferential lieutenant marched in and stood to attention, while Churt fired a salvo of questions at him. Where did Wartski's flank companies make their last contact with the enemy? When had he, the motorcyclist, last seen Wartski? How long had it taken him to get here? What was the state of the roads? How much armor had he passed between the end of the cat road and headquarters, and so on.

The lieutenant, who was very cold and hungry, was rather rattled by this interrogation but answered as best he could, and was pleased to note that the general greeted every answer with a sage nod.

"Okay, okay!" said Churt, by way of dismissal, and rubbed vigorously at his nose.

"We better do like I say, General! Maybe some of Wartski's mob are still holed up down there and maybe that's why we haven't been rolled up already! Thought it was kinda funny, things being so quiet this morning! Couldn't figure why the Krauts didn't use that road and come at us on the flank. Maybe they are being held, or more like the road's blocked by snowdrifts. I'll go take a look!"

Darius raised his hand. It was Napoleon cautioning Marshal Ney to await a masterly reassessment of the situation.

"You take over here, Colonel," he said mildly. "I'll go take a look myself! You get the counterattack mounted the minute you hear from me over the field wire. D'you follow me?"

Churt just stopped himself saying "Cock!" He was a man of very wide experience in the handling of men and vehicles and he needed no one to tell him that it would take at least forty-eight hours to sort out, regroup, refuel, feed and stiffen up the bewildered units that were now stomping and cursing along three miles of road outside the bacon factory. He knew that everybody would have to wait for the tankers to come up, for rations to be issued, for the idiotic roadblock higher up to be dismantled and, above all, for the arrival of someone with a far more intelligent grasp of the situation to take command, but he was old and wise in the eccentricities of generals and kept all these opinions to himself.

If Darius wanted to seek glory in the cannon's mouth (who the heck first thought up that screwy phrase?) or freeze to death in a jeep while rooting around for stragglers from Wartski's group, then he was very welcome to do it. In the meantime he, a sane, severely professional Texan, would stay in the warm, awaiting the arrival of a high-level decision based on the latest developments in the field, not a rehash from one of this screwball's history books.

"Okay, General," he said, and went out, rubbing his nose.

Darius had grasped the essentials while listening to the motorcyclist. He knew exactly what he was going to do and how he was going to do it. Already he had formed an accurate picture of what was happening a few miles down that cat-road, the track pointed out to him on the map by Colonel Churt. He could see it all, for it had happened so often in the past. A few desperately brave men, the wreck of poor Wartski's battalions, rallied by some noble spirit, a junior officer perhaps, holding at bay the entire German army as it made frenzied flank attacks up the cat-road. This strange lull had nothing to do with the weather. The weather had been as bad or worse than this when the Germans attacked, yet they had made phenomenal progress, driving a spearhead of armor into the heart of the American advance and halting it in hopeless confusion.

But the sound of gunfire had died away hours ago, and there was no evidence of a renewed surge to the west on the part of the columns outside. Instead there was a sense of cessation in the battle that almost heralded a truce. Someone, some gallant band of survivors, was holding that pass and bearing the entire brunt of the attack until help could come

from the west. And now he, Darius Leonidas Burnside Potford, was about to arrive with that help. *Leonidas!* How wonderfully apt! Leonidas bringing aid to Leonidas at Thermopylae, the Thermopylae of the Ardennes! The general almost
purred with pleasure, reflecting what a wonderful headline
this would make for the papers back home and what a glorious
chapter when he came, at long last, to set down his memoirs,
"From Baltimore to Berlin."

2

Horace's watch, the one that he had bought for thirty
shillings from Smoothie Salomon on the day before Smoothie
went up the line for five years on twenty-seven charges of
housebreaking, said that it was almost ten o'clock.

It had been light since eight, after what had seemed like a
week of black nights spent in watching the lorry burn, glow
and finally smolder outside the hut.

The blazing truck had served them well. Not one shot had
been fired at them during the night and the woods beyond the
bend in the track were very still. It had stopped snowing
shortly before dawn and now the whole world was crisp and
sparkling, encased in ice that glittered like a million crumbs
of glass under the reluctant sun hanging above the farthest
trees.

The fire in the hut had burned very low, for there was no
more wood to replenish it. Pedlar was on his hands and knees,
blowing at the embers and trying to coax a flame strong
enough to heat the coffee. It was their third brew and Horace's belly felt distended with coffee but his legs and hands
cried out for warmth. He was stiff with cold, and from stamp-
ing up and down as he hung about round the open doorway.
He felt as though he had walked fifty miles through snowdrifts and, as if they had not had a surfeit of trouble, they
were now out of cigarettes, all their reserves having gone up
with the lorry.

A heavy, sickly smell hung over the pass and Horace wondered if it stemmed from burned tires or fried Jerry. The thought made his stomach heave and Pedlar, hearing his violent hiccough, looked up, his big, lopsided face red from exertion.

"You okay, Popey? You gonner be sick again?"

"No, Pedlar, I'm okay, just bloody cold, mate," said Horace gently.

There was real tenderness in his voice and he looked down at the gypsy as he had never looked at him during their long association. They were no longer master and man. They were equals who had survived battle with the German army and now, it seemed, the enemy had abandoned all hope of bypassing the hut or the charred lorry that blocked the track.

Yet the silence outside was almost as alarming as the shooting had been at sunset. The only sound that came to him was the steady drip of moisture and an occasional siss of snow cascading from boughs in the woods.

At first he had thought that this sound originated from German jack-boots, creeping stealthily toward the hut, but now that it was broad daylight he discovered its true cause. He picked up his gun and sidled forward an inch or so, cocking an eye at the extremity of the bend in the road, peering into the stiff, winking underbrush that straggled up the cliff. Not a sign. Not a movement out there.

"Pedlar," he said, in a little more than a whisper, "Pedlar, they've scarpered!"

The gypsy did not seem as surprised as he should have been. He got up and brought the dixie across to Horace.

"It's on'y just warm," he said, still with the familiar note of apology. "Best I could get it, Popey."

"I can't drink no more," said Horace, and belched to prove as much. "I don't want to *see* no more coffee for the rest o' me natchrule! You drink it, mate!"

He shuffled cautiously into the open, bending double and stopping to look around at every step. The twisted chassis of the lorry was red-hot and round it, where the snow had melted, the earth was scorched a seaweed brown. Pieces of charred equipment lay about, some of them only half-burned, and there was an untidy bundle under the cab door, all that remained of Horace's first kill. Horace glanced at it and looked away, quickly. Then he forgot about it and thought once more of his respirator containing the thick wad of notes and of the little canvas bag in the tool kit that had represented the bulk of their European takings.

He whistled through his teeth and hummed a bar or two of his favorite, "Pasadena." How much had gone up with that truck? Five hundred nicker? A thousand? He didn't know, he was too tired and too cold to begin reckoning. Instead he crept around behind the tailgate and poked about until he found a twisted piece of metal, the remains of the tailgate hinge. It had fallen clear of the blaze and was still warm. He picked it up and raked dismally among the litter, turning over nothing but glowing pieces of material and odd shapeless lumps of fused metal.

Presently the stench made him retch again and he flung down the piece of iron he was holding and trudged back across the snow to Pedlar, now standing with his gun at the ready just clear of the entrance.

"No go, Pedlar!" he said, "not a flippin' sausage! Well, that's that I reckon! We're back where we started!"

"Aw, we'll make some more, Popey!" said Pedlar, briskly for him, "we'll make some more, soon as we get clear o' this!"

"Christ! I 'ate this flippin' place!" said Horace suddenly and with immense bitterness. "I 'ate it! *Ate it!* Let's get moving! For Gawd's sake let's get back to the pavé!"

Pedlar glanced up and down the track, weighing their chances.

"Suppose they worked round the back and we run smack into 'em?" he asked, but patiently.

"I don't care!" snarled Horace, "I don't care if we run smack into flippin' 'Itler 'imself! All I want is to get out of here! *Now!*"

"Okay, Popey!" said Pedlar pacifically, "we'll get out, just like you say, Popey!"

He went into the hut and gathered up their blankets, throwing one across his shoulders and draping the other across Horace's. He did this very carefully, as a mother might prepare her little boy for school on a winter's morning. Then he hitched two spare tommy guns to his left shoulder and picked up a third weapon. They marched out, turning their backs to the sun.

They had progressed perhaps fifty yards when Pedlar stopped suddenly and held up his hand. Horace stopped too, his heart giving a leap.

"What is it?"

"Transport!" said Pedlar briefly. "Coming toward us!"

Horace listened carefully.

"I can't hear nothing," he said.

"It's coming all right," Pedlar told him, " 'bout a mile off!"

He looked carefully on each side of the pass and Horace awaited his decision. Ever since the first burst of firing from the woods Pedlar had made the decisions, even though he appealed to Horace for orders from time to time. Somehow, during the last twelve hours, the balance of their relationship had shifted. Whenever he forgot about Pedlar for a moment or two Horace's terror began to drown him like a swiftly rising tide, but the moment Pedlar crossed his line of vision or said something, his confidence flooded back and he knew, with complete certainty, that they would get out of this, that normal existence would soon begin again and that once this happened the pendulum would swing back once more and the partnership would settle into the rhythm of years gone by. He accepted this cheerfully, rather as a first-class passenger might place himself in the charge of a professional deckhand throughout the duration of a disaster at sea. Once the rescue ship showed up, once they were all warm and dry again, the deckhand would be thanked, tipped and perhaps altogether forgotten in the awful wonder of the experience.

"Over here," said Pedlar, and led the way up the bluff to a small landslip on the right of the track. They pushed through a screen of frozen twigs and lowered themselves onto the snow at a spot where they could watch the track from an elevation of about twelve feet.

"Don't fire nor nothing!" said Pedlar firmly. "Just let 'em go by, Popey!"

265

"What do *you* think?" said Horace, and wished that his teeth would stop chattering.

He could hear an indistinct rattle now, coming out of the west. Then, as it grew louder, and his teeth began chattering so violently that he thought they would break loose in his mouth, he caught a glimpse of the first troop carrier, packed with rigid men and bristling with guns as it moved at about five miles an hour down the pass.

Fifty yards behind it came another troop carrier, then a tank and finally a large, bumping car with a fat man standing beside the driver holding a pair of binoculars to his eyes.

"It's Yanks!" said Horace, his voice rising to a squeak, as he tried to set limits to his jubilation. "It's Yanks! A whole flippin' army of 'em!"

He was on the point of leaping to his feet and shouting at the top of his voice but Pedlar anticipated this and grabbed him just in time.

"Take it easy, Popey!"

Horace remembered then how much caution it was necessary to use in greeting strange Americans with guns in their hands. At this range, and in broad daylight, the men in the truck could hardly miss with one of their slaphappy bursts.

"What'd we better do, Pedlar?" he asked very humbly, "just . . . just let 'em go by?"

It was strange that now, when glibness would have served him more readily than at any time in his life, he had nothing to say. No quip, no comment, no impudent or ironic greeting. He was silent, waiting upon Pedlar.

The gypsy did not fail him. Slowly and carefully he stood up, bracing his right leg against the cliff face so as to be ready to flatten himself instantly against the largest of the rocks that formed their ambush.

Out of the corner of his eye Horace saw a ripple of movement among the men on the far side of the truck and then he heard Pedlar's hoarse shout: *"Hiya!* Hi there! Okay! Okay Yanks! *Hiya!"*

The row of gun barrels flashed up but there was no volley.

266

As an introductory identification Pedlar's greeting had served its purpose.

The truck stopped at once and helmeted men poured over the sides, shouting and waving. Slowly, and, with infinite caution, Horace stood upright as Americans swarmed up the slope, their clamor launching echoes all the way down the pass.

The transport behind also stopped, disgorging a fresh stream of men who began to converge on the couple.

"What do you know?" roared a big sergeant, the first to reach them and begin pumping their hands. "It's Limeys! Two of 'em! Say brother, where's all the Krauts? They wiped out all your buddies? You got buddies around fellers?"

The end of the intolerable suspense was like a draft of raw spirit, flooding through Horace to the very tips of his numbed toes.

"There's a bunch of Jerries up the road," he said, with a rather pitiful attempt at nonchalance, "but they won't give you guys no trouble! Me an' Pedlar fixed 'em for you! 'Bout a baker's dozen of 'em I reckon, don't you Pedlar?"

"Arrr," said Pedlar, blushing and looking down at his boots. "About that I reckon, Popey!"

They clambered down to the track, Americans on all sides of them. The babel of voices stunned them. Men shouted orders. Vehicles crunched off down the pass. A car pulled up and the portly four-star general stepped out, beaming at them through rimless glasses. Combat Americans were not distinguished for deference shown to high-ranking officers, but they were delighted to encounter a general in an advance reconnaissance party and stepped back, grinning and saluting.

Darius approached the two airmen.

"You fellers better tell me what happened," he said kindly. "You better fix yourselves a drink first, then tell me exactly what happened!"

The sergeant came forward with a water bottle and gave Horace a drink that made him splutter.

"Lumme!" he said, forgetting the general for a moment. "What's that, Sarge? The real McCoy?"

"Yes, *sir!*" said the sergeant, hastily reclaiming his water bottle. "That's the real McCoy, I guess! It's Limey issue!"

"Aren't there none of our boys around?" asked Darius wistfully. He had come plunging through the snow to find Leonidas, and all that remained of his gallant three hundred, and was a little disappointed to find the Thermopylae of the Ardennes empty of yelling hordes and garrisoned by two British enlisted men. But when they had adjourned to his car, and had followed the troop carriers up the pass to the hut, when Horace had given him a brief account of their encounter with the Snowdrop, of the advance of the Germans masquerading as Americans, and of the battle at sunset and the long watch in the light of the burning lorry, all traces of disappointment fell away and his face glowed like Mr. Pickwick's. What did it matter if the Spartans were only British airmen? Here, before his eyes, an act of sheer heroism had been performed. Here, on this spot, two men had scorned to fly when the last of their allies had been slain. Two humble rankers (who were not even grounded fliers, but what a British officer would have dismissed as "Penguins"), had remained, holding the Hun offensive through a long, bitter night!

When he had inspected the shell of the truck, the hut, the body of Snowdrop, and finally the body of the man Pedlar had shot when running for cover, Darius put his hand on Horace's shoulder and regarded him with a respect that no general should demonstrate to anyone below the rank of President. "My boy," he said soberly, "Uncle Sam salutes you! Yes *sir!* Salutes you!" and what is more he actually did salute and Horace was so astonished that he forgot to salute back.

Darius did not appear to notice this omission. Slowly he lowered his hand and called to a captain who was standing close by, awaiting orders to deploy and advance through the woods.

"Take these two men back to Colonel Churt at once," he said. "Present my compliments and ask him to see that they are fed and rested! Then send a signal to—what was it my boy?" and he turned back to Horace.

"Number four-one-eight flying supply column, sir," said Horace, "but I don't know where you'll locate 'em, sir. We 'aven't seen nothing of 'em since we left Lille, nearly a week ago!"

"Young man," said Darius, with paternal irony, "just you leave all the admin. to us! We're used to it, eh Captain?"

"Yes, sir!" said the captain, saluting, and led the way across to the general's car, which the driver had turned in a clearing beyond the bend.

"I'm flipped if I know," muttered Horace to Pedlar, as they trudged in the wake of the captain, "I always told you I didn't want no bloody medals but I got a feelin' someone's gonner give us some whether we like it or not!"

They skirted the wreck of the burned-out truck and as they did so Horace gave the ruin a swift, sorrowful glance.

"Lumme!" he murmured. "They could stick all the medals if on'y we 'ad what was in that flippin' tool kit and that's for sure, that is!"

"You guys want to pick up any kit?" asked the captain pleasantly.

"No," said Horace glumly. "Wot we might've wanted to take 'ome went up in smoke, sir!"

"Ah," said the captain genially, for he was a very observant young man and had taken his cue from the general, "we'll soon replace anything you lost when we get back to Field H.Q."

"Beggin' your pardon, I don't reckon you will, sir!" said Horace. "What we lost ain't exactly issued in no Equipment Store!"

"Something of sentimental value?" asked the captain sympathetically.

"Very!" said Horace, and settled back into the car, folding his arms and closing his eyes.

There were, he reflected, so many, many things one could never hope to explain to anyone above the rank of temporary corporal.

3

Wing Commander Reggie Baldwin, D.S.O., D.F.C., the officer commanding the Allied transport pool of which Horace's flying column was a small, straying unit, ran his eye down the closely typed sheets of General Potford's detailed report and confessed himself completely baffled.

He had worked with Americans at SHAEF all through the previous summer and was stoically resigned to their unpredictability, their sudden, blush-making enthusiasm, and their sale of ideas that seemed, to a pipe-smoking Englishman, to come straight out of the comics he had read when at prep school.

This story of a feat of heroism in a pass of the Ardennes, for instance, involving as it did an allegedly heroic act by two men said to belong to one of his own units, appeared to him an insult to the readers of schoolboy fiction. It was almost indecently bizarre, conjuring up memories of Tarzan films and Garth, the currently popular cartoon strip. It simply did not belong in the records of a Service where modesty was far more important than the overthrow of the enemy.

Having read the report twice, and smoked two pipes in the process, he appealed to Fred Bascomb, his adjutant.

Fred was his wife's youngest brother and they had attended the same public school, where Fred had once been his fag, so that it was altogether fitting that here in Brussels, in the final year of the war against the unspeakable Hun, Fred should have reverted to his former role and hover about his fagmaster's desk giving respectful advice and pushing bells for lesser men to run errands.

"What do you make of it, old boy?" Baldwin asked, after giving Fred ten minutes to study the report. "Do these bods really belong to our outfit? 'Pope 303', 'Pascoe 305'? And if so, would you mind explaining what they were doing in the Ardennes? And how they got there? Or how a couple of Wingless Wonders got mixed up in that fearful Yank shambles?"

Flight Lieutenant Bascomb went slightly red, looking exactly as he used to look on the occasions when he had forgotten to oil "Bingo" Baldwin's cricket bat, or had burned his toast over the study fire. The wing commander was not an observant man but he had been closely associated with his adjutant since childhood and at once recognized embarrassment.

"Fact is, Bingo (they still used their Hearthover names whenever they were in private but outside the office, of course, "Bingo" and "Scruffy" became "Sir" and "Adj."), fact is, we seem to have put up rather a black, don't you know?"

"How come?" asked Bingo. He was to have serious trouble with his wife, Dorothy, after the war, on account of his absent-minded use of Americanisms. "This clod of a General Whatsis-name—Potbelly or Potbury—he seems quite gaga about two of our bods. He says they sent a whole bunch of Huns for a Burton! I don't believe that old man! Can't, can you? But where does the black come in, Scruffy?"

"Fact is, these bods got left behind when we moved up here from Lille," admitted Scruffy. "Fact is, we'd forgotten they existed, Bingo!"

The wing commander lit his pipe again and sucked it in silence for a few moments. He always did this when he was perturbed for he had discovered that it gave the impression of profound imperturbability and had even fooled men like Portal and Sholto-Douglas.

"They were attached to Heston-Roberts' mob if they were in the flying column," he said at length, "so they must have been his responsibility! Dammit man . . . !" his eye flashed, just as it used to flash when Scruffy Bascomb had been dishing out cocoa at a first-fifteen meeting, and someone had suggested that the Blundell's pack were too heavy to be brushed aside in the scrums, "Dammit, old boy, we can't be expected to keep tabs on every stray man in the Group, can we? What have you found out about these bods? What did the Wing warrant officer have to say about it when he got his finger out and checked up on them?"

"After all, that's the drill isn't it? You remember that Irish corporal we had, O'Duffy was it, or O'Duffell?"

"Hang it, Scruffy, O'Duffy was a semi-permanent drunk

and these two haven't a blot on their copybooks according to their one-two-ones! Dammit, they haven't *any* entries at all, good, bad or indifferent!"

"That's what made the W.O. so suspicious!" Scruffy told him. "He said it usually means that types like this had access to their documents all through their service. They probably replaced those crime sheets over and over again! Wherever they've been they've had the orderly room taped. The W.O. says this isn't uncommon. The real bad'uns always keep their one-two-ones tidy by one means or the other. He had these two types in and gave them a thorough going over. They're real frowsters, you see Bingo, the sort we used to catch reading the dirty bits in the Bible when they should have been practicing down at the nets!"

"I see," said Bingo, now in possession of a very accurate picture of Pope and Pascoe. "What else?"

"Well, the W.O. told me he'd only found out a fraction of what they'd been up to, but even that was enough to get 'em fifty-six days in the cooler. Good God, Bingo, do you suppose we've got many others like this skulling about? No wonder it's taken us six years to get the Hun on the run! Dam' bad show, don't you think? Shockin' bad show!"

Scruffy Bascomb swallowed and looked away. For some reason he was hangdog and ill at ease. "Well?"

"They'd already been posted A.W.O.L., Bingo," he said at length. "The W.O. says they're two of the scruffiest types in the outfit and he's had his eye on them for months, waiting to wheel 'em in for the chop! W.O. says they had no business to be in Yank territory at all, said they'd actually gone down there to flog cigarettes and soap to the French, said they've been making a business of this ever since they came to us, don't you see?"

He handed the C.O. four documents, two blue and two white. The blue ones, known as One-Two-Ones, were the Service Conduct Sheets and the white ones were the Service Records, known as Fifteen-Eighties.

Wing Commander Baldwin inspected the documents gravely, noting that the conduct sheets were quite blank, except for the initial entries of name, rank and number, whereas the fifteen-eighties were covered with scrawl showing the erratic movements of their owners up and down the country over nearly four years of active service.

"They do seem to have been around a bit," he commented, "but what does that prove, Scruffy?"

"Warrant officer says it means that every unit passed them on to somebody else," said Scruffy.

The wing commander digested Scruffy's information and this process saw him silently through the next two pipes. He was a hidebound man, and his mental processes had atrophied under years and years of merciless regimentation throughout childhood, boyhood and youth, but he was not completely stupid. He knew, for instance, when to come to terms with life and despite the tradition on which he had been reared—that of the Englishman never knowing when he is beaten—he had always known precisely when to stop struggling. That was why he was a wing commander and Scruffy was only an acting flight lieutenant.

"Get me SHAEF on the blower," he said at length. "Ask for Tubby Rawlins, in Personnel. Tell him it's Bingo Baldwin from Transport, and jump to it, Scruffy! Take your finger out, old man!"

"What are you going to do, Bingo?" asked the adjutant, his hand poised over the bell marked "Orderly Room Corporal."

The wing commander removed his pipe from his mouth and knitted his brows with irritation. Scruffy remembered that he had looked just like that when he had surprised a group of fifth-formers smoking in the latrines when they should have been out on the touchline watching a junior match.

"What *can* I do?" he asked flatly. "I'm recommending them both for a gong! The best gong I can get!"

"But hang it all . . ." protested Scruffy.

The wing commander waved his hand. "Ask yourself, old man, do we wash our dirty linen in Brussels with all those Fleet Street wallahs looking on?"

Scruffy Bascomb smiled and relaxed. Good old Bingo! No wonder he had been captain of rugger and captain of cricket for four years in succession! No wonder he had been head boy all the time he was trying to pass the Air Force Entrance Examination in the late twenties!

4

So it came about that on the last day of April, 1944, when the Third Reich that was to have lasted a thousand years was disappearing in twelve, and when the cities of Germany were shrouded in dust that rose from the scudding heels of millions of oppressed German democrats, the men who had struggled so manfully and unavailingly against the tyranny of Hitler since 1933, a special parade was convened on an airfield near Brussels. Its purpose was to do honor to two humble leading aircraftmen for displaying courage and initiative above and beyond the call of duty.

It was a very notable occasion and a good deal more newsworthy than a normal investiture.

Here were three Allied nations, all eager to pin medals on the breasts of a man who had once sold rubber toys from a stall in the Caledonian Market and his huge, stupid-looking comrade, who had once been an Exmoor gypsy and had sold rush mats at cottage doors. This was Democracy vindicated and the captain and kings of Democracy had come together to honor these men as a pair of typical (if unlikely-looking) bulldogs, inheritors of the Drake-Nelson-Wellingtonian tradition, men who had scorned to throw up their hands or fly when assailed by hordes of Germans but had held on, blocking a vital pass and saving the discomfiture of an army group!

For General Darius McClellan Leonidas Potford it was a particularly proud day, for he was the instigator of the ceremony. It was he who had come upon these men, still alert and still full of fight, and he who had urged recognition of their heroism, reasoning that not only was such recognition excellent propaganda, it also spotlighted his own presence at the very tip of the American counterattack!

When the band struck up "Stars and Stripes," and he

stepped forward with the American medals, he beamed down at Horace and up at Pedlar with the paternal pride of a true father to his men. At this moment he was not Napoleon, or Leonidas, or even Little Mac' of the Army of the Potomac. He was Ulysses Grant, at Appottomax.

"Mighty proud to do this on behalf of the American army!" he said. And then: "Mighty proud, fellers! *Mighty proud!*"

When the band played the "Marseillaise," and a lean French colonel stepped forward with the Liberation Medal, he said a great deal more than this, rattling away like Pedlar's tommy gun and bending forward from the hips to implant a resounding kiss on the pale cheeks of each hero. Luckily, he was a tall, spare man and once he had secured leverage on Pedlar's shoulders he could just manage to brush the lopsided jawline with his black moustache. Then, as he stepped back saluting, the band changed its tune again. To the measured strains of the "National Anthem" a pale but composed Wing Commander Baldwin stepped forward, clipped on the medals, crushed each of their hands, muttered "Jolly good show, chaps!" and stepped smartly back looking as though a spasm of colic had gripped his bowels.

The parade was over. Witnessing troops wheeled and marched away and Horace almost fainted with relief.

"Christ!" he murmured softly, but loud enough for Pedlar to hear him. "Wot a flippin' carry-on, eh? I'm that shook up I couldn't write 'bum' on the wall!"

As soon as it was over authority seemed to lose interest in them. Horace guided Pedlar toward the N.A.A.F.I. tent near the gate, but seeing a crowd of airmen inside they slipped quietly past and out onto the Brussels road.

"Popey," said Pedlar, as they headed for the nearest café, "d'you reckon we could flog these medals, soon as we get home?"

Horace gave him a sidelong glance and it was full of tolerant amusement. Pedlar had been, he reflected, a flippin' good buddy, but in spite of years of training by a virtuoso he had failed to absorb the rudiments of commercial enterprise.

"Sell 'em?" he exclaimed, "wot, *these? Gongs?* Lumme, o'

course we won't! By the time we get back in civvy street every-one'll 'ave 'em! Come on for Chrissake! I'm parched and if you ain't you flippin' well oughter be after a flippin' general 'as slobbered over you!"

CHAPTER THIRTEEN

The wind came whipping round the Wembly Stadium, lifting the brims of civilian trilbys worn by self-conscious airmen emerging from the demob sausage machine and stepping into a world made safe for bureaucrats.

They had been awaiting this moment for years but now that it was here it had the same, anti-climatical douche of VE and VJ Days. Instead of leaping and cheering they stood about in little groups, sniggering and cracking stale jokes, like wedding guests after the bridal couple has departed in a shower of confetti. There was an air of waiting at a station for a train that refused to start. The wind swept the litter along the gutters and the civvy outfits did not seem to resist it as valiantly as had service greatcoats.

Pedlar felt more desolate than any of them. Throughout each stage of the sausage-machine process he had clung to Horace, moving like a child following its mother through a Christmas shopping crowd. He tried hard not to think of the immediate future, of what now looked like an inevitable drift back to the hollow, leaderless, aimless, Popeless. For Pope had become a way of life with him, part of his blood, flesh and bone.

Pedlar could not recall a single day since their first encounter in 1941, when he had not awakened in tent, barn or billet and

277

glanced across at Popey's narrow face, listening to his measured, adenoidal snore. There had not been a single night for years when he had gone to sleep without first contemplating Popey's needs or Popey's schemes, and the prospect of life without his friend's guidance and impetus was drab and profitless.

They stood together outside the door marked "Exit Only," watching men shake hands and shout pleasantries at one another.

"'Struth, Chalkey! Who gave you that cheesecutter? You look like the bloke calling for the rent!" or "How about this raincoat, eh? Not that you'll catch me out in it, chum, not for a bit anyhow! I'm staying in bed for a month! Get up them stairs!"

At last Pedlar forced himself to speak and his voice seemed to Horace to emerge from his stiff, size-twelve brogues.

"What we gonner do, Popey? What's to become of us?"

The same problem had been tormenting Horace ever since their demobilization number had been announced several weeks ago. At first he had shrugged it off, confident that something would turn up. He would run into a market acquaintance with an idea, or half an idea, and perhaps Pedlar could be drawn into it, so that their exit from the Wembley machine would not write "finis" to their long association. For if Horace had become a habit of mind with Pedlar then the big gypsy was a kind of gangplank for Horace, a bridge between the real, innermost Pope and the big world outside, a world waiting to be wheedled, bluffed and exploited.

Ever since that crisp morning in the Ardennes, when Pedlar had understood his frantic request to be gone and they had set off together down the pass, Horace had lost the aggressive self-confidence that made him such a thrustful individualist. Until the adventure in the pass Pedlar's friendship had been a comfort but never a vital necessity. In a pinch, Horace felt, he could have managed well enough on his own, especially if he had the backing of the money and jewelry that had gone up in smoke. Now, without capital, if one discounted a miserly gratuity, he was adrift and the mere prospect of sailing on alone, of combating this endless queue of men without Pedlar at his elbow to receive the hard knocks, made him sweat with uncertainty. He licked his lips, glanced up and down the street, stroked himself from lapel to pocket, but derived no comfort at all from his new civilian clothes and their passport to independence.

If only they had had a plan, a ghost of a plan, they might manage with their pooled resources. In a world tormented by shortages, promising fiddles must exist by the thousand. He was aware of this but he was conscious also of his rawness in civilian fields, of the rustiness of his civilian techniques, and of the prospect of new fields of enterprise, where there were no easily gulled officers, free bed and board, or carelessly guarded sources of supply to meet sudden demands.

In civvy street things were so different. If you wanted a bus ride you usually had to pay for it. Even in prewar days it had not always been easy to stare hard at the conductor when he held out his hand for the fare, or persuade him that he had already issued you with a ticket. This kind of drawback had the widest implications. If one needed new clothes, for instance, there was no equipment basher to bribe or cajole. Nobody in Burton's or Marks & Spencers would part with a pullover or a pair of gauntlets in exchange for a promise of sausage and mash, a lift into town, or a leave pass bearing a facsimile of the C.O.'s signature. He was, in short, about to enter a world where this kind of currency was thoroughly debased, without the purchasing power of a ten-centimes piece. It was a solemn and sobering thought.

He turned to the waiting Pedlar, anxiety putting a sharp edge on his tone.

"Ain't you goin' 'ome? Ain't you got no place to go?"

"I got the hollow," said Pedlar slowly. "I dunno if my kin are still there but if they're not I reckon I could soon catch up with 'em somewhere. They won't be far off. We always got ways of finding one another, Popey!"

"Well?" The tone was still edgy and querulous.

Pedlar shifted his enormous weight from one foot to the other and stared hard at the ground.

"I grown out of wantin' 'em I reckon, Popey!"

"You mean you finished wi' that gypsy lark? You're done with it?"

"That's so." Pedlar brightened momentarily. "Unless o' course you'd come down there and shakedown with us. I reckon you'd soon get into our ways, Popey!"

Horace grinned. "Me! Live in a flippin' caravan? Flog flippin' baskets an' rush mats round the cottages! *Me?* You kiddin'?"

Pedlar recognized the utter improbability of the idea and dismissed it from his mind at once. Pope liked to sleep soft and eat regularly. The terrible uncertainties of an open-air life were not for him.

"No, I don't reckon it'd work," he admitted. "Not enough to it, Popey!"

"You bet your sweet life there ain't!" said Horace, with savage emphasis. "There's a lot better fiddles than that lyin' around, especially while rationing keeps on!"

"Sure there is," said Pedlar loyally, "but what, Popey? I mean, what could you an' me do, supposin' we didn't split up?"

Here it was then, a final testing of his ingenuity! Their gratuity would last them about a month, and after that how would they support themselves and each other? What was new? What was promising? What would supply the bare minimum for a roof, three meals a day, cigarettes and clothes when this civvy outfit had worn out or been flogged? And beyond that, beyond mere necessities? What, for instance, would provide the wherewithal for the modest pleasures of life, a visit to the cinema, an odd cup of coffee and a sandwich, an occasion jig with a Judy?

In mounting panic he told himself he did not know. If he took Pedlar home they could probably flannel their bed and board for a week, but certainly for no longer. Pope Senior, who had taken parental responsibilities very lightly indeed when Horace was still a baby in arms, would certainly jib at supporting both him and his friend, unless of course they brought good money into the house.

Besides—and here was the crux of the problem—Horace

realized that he did not want to go home. At home there was constant argy-bargy and, what was far worse, razor-keen competition in every field of speculation and commercial endeavor. He wanted to start fresh somewhere and if he was to do this then Pedlar's presence, as comforter, valet, hatchet-man and friend, was absolutely essential, as essential as the opportunity itself!

He kicked sullenly at an empty cigarette packet and avoided Pedlar's eye. The man was standing there like a sheep dog awaiting a decision, waiting with the faith and patience of a huge, half-witted child.

Suddenly, with a rush of feeling that made him shudder, he was aware of his responsibilities toward the gypsy and acutely conscious of a terrifying obligation to repay him for years of devotion, ministrations and blind loyalty. He thought of all the times that Pedlar had made up his bed in the billet, brought him supper from the cookhouse, shouldered a passage through angry, muttering queues on his behalf, silenced truculent opponents with that curious flat-handed swipe of his and generally eased his path through what might have been a lonely and merciless jungle. He thought too of their day and night in the pass and in his mind's eye he saw Pedlar roll from the back of the ditched lorry with an armful of tommy guns and dash across the track to give covering fire as Horace raced for the hut.

"I gotter think o' something!" he told himself bitterly, "I just gotter!"

An earnest-looking sergeant hurried out of the depot and stood on the steps, addressing the dozen or so men who were still there, smoking and gossiping.

"Anyone here called 'Pope'?" he demanded. " 'Pope 303' or . . ." he glanced quickly at a long envelope he was holding, " 'Pascoe 305'?"

"That's me," said Horace, mildly surprised, and reached out for the envelope.

The sergeant held it back. "Have you got docs to prove it?" he asked officiously. "I can't just accept your word for it, can I?"

Wearily Horace pulled out his wallet and satisfied the sergeant as to his identity. Pedlar also produced his papers and having studied them the sergeant handed over the letter.

"It came over by runner from your last unit," he said. "Must have arrived soon after you left!"

Horace looked at the envelope with some curiosity but rather more suspicion. It crossed his mind that it was a come-back. He had never known much good emerge from an envelope bearing an official-paid postage mark.

"Someone's caught up with us, I reckon," he said. "Do I open it or sling it away, Pedlar? After all, if you ain't 'eard about it they can't pin it on yer, can they?"

"We're civvies now," Pedlar reminded him, "they can't pin nothin' on us!"

"That's right," said Horace more cheerfully. "Flipped if I 'adn't clean forgotten!"

He thumbed open the envelope and ran his eye down the single typed sheet. Pedlar, watching him closely, saw his lips purse to begin whistling "Pasadena." Then his features wrinkled with amazement.

"Well, fer crying out loud!" he said softly. "If this ain't the answer to a maiden's prayer!"

He handed the crackling letter to Pedlar and waited, his face flushed and body tense.

Pedlar began to read aloud. He read slowly and carefully, as always, stumbling here and there over the longer words.

It was a longish letter, and according to the heading, originated from the American Embassy in Grosvenor Square, but Pedlar found its contents incomprehensible. It was couched in long, unwieldy paragraphs, and studded with unfamiliar words.

After the second paragraph he gave it up and looked hopefully at Horace. Horace said impatiently:

"Don't worry about all the bumff, just concentrate on the last bits, that bit about our old pal General Potford. You remember, that Yank brass, who fixed us up wi' medals, remember?"

Pedlar glanced down to the final paragraph and read:

In view of the above, enquiries were made at American Headquarters in the field, and on the recommendation of General Darius L. M. Potford, the officer who advanced your names for a decoration, this invitation is cordially extended to both of you. The newspaper concerned will, of course, be notified by cable immediately upon your acceptance.

There followed a signature executed with an immense flourish and underneath, in type, the name of the official that the flourish represented.

Pedlar was still very confused.

"What's it all mean?" he asked. "What's it got to do with us, Popey?"

Horace was now jigging about on the edge of the pavement and even in the jubilation of the moment he realized that his new shoes were going to pinch abominably.

"It's a flippin' free trip to the States, you clod! It's a ruddy welcome mat, don't you see? All on account o' you and me carvin' up them flippin' Jerries, back at Christmas!"

"Us? But why?"

Horace spread his hands. He was considerably taken aback by the invitation but the motives that had prompted it did not puzzle him. He was a man who could both enlarge his achievements or minimize his culpability as occasion required. He did this so naturally that hard facts were never able to steady his imagination or correct his memories.

Already he saw himself as a man who, with a little help from Pedlar, had converted an American debacle into a military triumph.

"Why *us*?" he said. "Well, why not? We stopped the rot, didn't we? It's one o' them newspaper stunts, like they 'ave over here sometimes. You know, a bloke answers all the questions in some soppy competition and then gets took up to town, an' given a slap-up dinner and a free ticket to the Cup Final! On'y this ain't just a come-and-go lark, it's a flippin' Cook's tour, with Army escorts, transport, and all the trimmings! Lumme, I've always wanted to go to the States, but I never reckoned to go for nixes *and* 'ave me picture took, like a flippin' film star steppin' off the boat!"

"You and me . . . we're going to America?" said Pedlar incredulously. "You mean it, Popey! We're gonner stay together after all?"

"Lumme, o' course we are! It says both of us, don't it? And once we're over there, once we got the feel of it, how can we miss in a place like that? Lumme, America's a fiddler's paradise, ain't it?"

He looked slightly worried for a moment. "You ain't gonner let me go on me lonesome, are you Pedlar? You wouldn't back down, would you, not if I went along?"

Pedlar relaxed, his huge hands swinging loose, his blunt fingers curling and uncurling, as though flexing themselves before coming to physical grips with a new and bewildering situation.

"Aw, I don't mind *where* we go, Popey," he said slowly, "not so long as we stick together!"

He had never thought about America in the geographical sense. It was simply a place far away, which had disgorged all those men in potlike helmets, who ranged about chewing their gum and shouting "Hiya!" and "Howdy!" at him. It was, he realized, so different for Popey. Popey was clever and Popey would know all about America, where it was, how big it was, how you got there and what happened to you when you did. With Popey in charge it would be just like moving out of one camp and across country to another. Then Popey would at once set about organizing their lives, fixing the cookhouse, getting soft jobs, finding a billet that was not subject to weekly inspections, and organizing a means of income to supplement their fortnightly pay.

With Popey around the names of countries were no more important than the names of camps in the official Air Force list. They were just places, where people could be fixed, so as to make their lives easy, uneventful, safe and reasonably predictable.

"Okay, Popey!" he said, "let's go! It's cold just standing here!"

Horace looked up at him and swallowed hard. It occurred to him that if they had received an invitation to Peking, or Batavia, or the most remote planet in the universe, Pedlar would have said "Okay, let's go!" providing he had been assured that he, Horace Pope, would lead the way. Then he looked down at the embossed address on the notepaper and thought hard for a moment. "Grosvenor Square from Wembley Stadium? Bus or tube?"

He shook himself and stuffed the letter in his pocket.

"For crying out loud!" he shouted, "we ain't just *any* civvies! We got a row o' flippin' medals, haven't we?"

He ran out into the road shouting *"Taxi! TAXI!"* at the top of his voice.